PRAISE FOR
BEN KANE

'Richard the Lionheart's name echoes down the centuries as one of history's greatest warriors, and **this book will immortalise him** even more. **A rip-roaring epic**, filled with arrows and spattered with blood. **Gird yourself with mail when you start**'

Paul Finch, author of *Strangers*

'Ben's **deeply authoritative depiction of the time** is delivered in a **deft manner**. I was **immersed in the detail of Rufus's life**, with its heat and cold, its odours, foods, clothing, beats, politics and all the other minutiae of the age'

Simon Scarrow, author of the Eagles of the Empire series

'Kane's virtues as a writer of historical adventures – **lively prose, thorough research, colourful action** – are again apparent'

Nick Rennison, *The Sunday Times*

'*Lionheart* has plenty of **betrayal, bloodshed and rich historical detail**'

Martin Chilton, *Independent*

'Plenty of **action, blood, scheming, hatred, stealth and politics** here, if that's what you want in your read – **and you know it is!**'

Sunday Sport

'To read one of Ben Kane's **astonishingly well-researched**, bestselling novels is to know that you are, historically speaking, in safe hands'

Elizabeth Buchan, *Daily Mail*

'This is a **stunningly visual and powerful** read: Kane's power of description is **second to none** . . . Perfect for anyone who is suffering from *Game of Thrones* withdrawal symptoms'

Helena Gumley-Mason, *The Lady*

'**Fans of battle-heavy historical fiction will, justly, adore *Clash of Empires*.** With its rounded historical characters and **fascinating** historical setting, it deserves a wider audience'

Antonia Senior, *The Times*

'**Grabs you from the start and never lets go**. Thrilling action combines with historical authenticity to summon up a whole world in a sweeping tale of politics and war. **A triumph!'**

Harry Sidebottom, author of the *The Last Hour*

'The word **epic** is overused to describe books, but with *Clash of Empires* it fits like a gladius in its scabbard. What Kane does, with such mastery, is place the big story – Rome vs Greece – in the background, while making this a story about ordinary men caught up in world-defining events. In short, **I haven't enjoyed a book this much for ages. There aren't many writers today who could take on this story and do it well. There might be none who could do it better than Ben Kane**'

Giles Kristian, author of *Lancelot*

'**Exceptional**. Kane's excelled once again in capturing the terror and the glory . . . of the ancient battlefield, and this story is one that's been begging for an expert hand for a long time'

Anthony Riches, author of the Empire series

'**Carried off with panache** and Kane's expansive, engaging, action-packed style. A complex, **fraught, moving and passionate** slice of history **from one of our generation's most ambitious and engaging writers**'

Manda Scott, author of the Boudica series

'It's a broad canvas Kane is painting on, but he does it with **vivid** colours and, like the Romans themselves, he can show great admiration for a Greek enemy and still kick them in the balls'
Robert Low, author of the Oathsworn series

'Ben Kane manages to marry broad narrative invention with detailed historical research . . . in taut, authoritative prose . . . **his passion for the past, and for the craft of story-telling, shines from every page**'
Toby Clements, author of the Kingmaker series

'This **thrilling** series opener delivers every cough, spit, curse and gush of blood to set up the mighty clash of the title. Can't really fault this one'
Jon Wise, *Weekend Sport*

'Ben Kane's new series **explores the bloody final clash between ancient Greece and upstart Rome**, focusing on soldiers and leaders from both worlds and **telling the story of a bloody war with style**'
Charlotte Heathcote, *Sunday Express S Magazine*

'**A thumping good read.** You can feel the earth tremble from the great battle scenes and feel the desperation of those caught up in the conflict. Kane's brilliant research weaves its way lightly throughout'
David Gilman, author of the Master of War series

BEN KANE is one of the most hard-working and successful historical writers in the industry. His third book, *The Road to Rome*, was a *Sunday Times* number four bestseller, and almost every title since has been a top ten bestseller. Born in Kenya, Kane moved to Ireland at the age of seven. After qualifying as a veterinarian, he worked in small animal practice and during the terrible Foot and Mouth Disease outbreak in 2001. Despite his veterinary career, he retained a deep love of history; this led him to begin writing.

His first novel, *The Forgotten Legion*, was published in 2008; since then he has written five series of Roman novels. Kane lives in Somerset with his two children.

SANDS OF THE ARENA AND OTHER STORIES

BEN KANE

ORION

First published in Great Britain in 2021 by Orion Fiction,
an imprint of The Orion Publishing Group Ltd.,
Carmelite House, 50 Victoria Embankment
London EC4Y 0DZ

An Hachette UK company

1 3 5 7 9 10 8 6 4 2

A CIP catalogue record for this book
is available from the British Library.

ISBN (Hardback) 978 1 3987 0598 2
ISBN (eBook) 978 1 3987 0599 9

Typeset by Input Data Services Ltd, Somerset

Printed and bound in Great Britain by Clays Ltd, Elcograf S.p.A.

www.orionbooks.co.uk

For Killian.
You know why.

CONTENTS

SANDS OF THE ARENA

PART I

The ludus at Capua, summer AD 39

I t was hot, cursedly hot. Even the flies were dozing. The air was fetid with the smell of oiled leather, unwashed bodies and bean-farts. Eyes closed, I slouched on my bunk, back sweat-stuck to the wall, feet on the dirt floor, in the only position that provided a modicum of cool in the stuffy cell. My roommates sprawled on their own bunks, silent or asleep, one above me, two opposite. It amazed me how they could lie on the rough woollen blankets and straw ticks in this heat, while I could not.

And yet it was not that surprising. I, fair-skinned and Hibernian, was used to cool, rainy weather, not this form of Hades, which is what the summer months in Capua felt like to me. You could say the other three had been born to it, Piye the Nubian most of all. Black as charcoal, he, I reckoned, could fall asleep in the midday sun. Big Dog, tall and long-limbed, was from the far south of Gaul, a place almost as hot as Italia. Dapyx – skin-inked on his chest and mad as a rabid wolf – was from north of Thrace. I had no real idea where that was, other than it was far to the east, and if he was to be believed, a place with scorching summers and winters cold enough to freeze a man's breath.

From the courtyard, a familiar sound started up, the *thwack, thwack* of wood hitting wood. It was not a time of day to be training, I thought. A man would soon get heat stroke. Curious, I leaned forward to peer through the bars. Our cell was like all the others, a ground floor, square room twelve paces by ten; it faced onto the centre of the ludus, where we exercised and trained. Opposite was another rank of cells, as well as the kitchens, dining area, hospital and the armoury. On the first floor there were offices, and living quarters for Crixus, our gloriously named lanista, and the trainers.

Thanks to the semicircle of wooden seating that occupied one half of the courtyard – used when private shows were staged – many cells had no view of the fighting area. Mine did, which meant that I could see the two unfortunates who had been set to fighting one another on the burning sand. I did not recognise either. Crixus was also there, lank-haired, pot-bellied, his whip dangling from his right hand as ever. His armed guards, whom he was never without, lounged nearby.

Tirones, I thought. Fresh from the slave block.

It was clear why Crixus had bought the pair. Both were young and well-built, and the one nearest me was a hand taller than Big Dog, which took some doing. It was impossible to assess a man's fighting ability in the market, however, where the vendors would swear blind that this man was Hercules reborn, and that one the killer of five legionaries before he was captured. Not until Crixus got them back here and placed wooden swords in their fists, and set them at each other would he know if the coin he had paid out had been wasted, or potentially well spent.

PART II

'*Mi-deer.*' Dapyx mangled whatever language he spoke, save his own, and my name was no exception.

I did not turn my head. 'What?' I spoke in Latin. None of us spoke it well, but it was the lingua franca that allowed we gladiators, dragged from every corner of the earth, to communicate.

'Who . . . out there?'

'What am I – your pissing slave? Look for yourself, you lazy bastard.' My cocky answer was designed to show I was not weak. In the ludus, strength was everything, and weakness a sure path to Charon's hammer. I had no idea if I could beat Dapyx in a fight, and I did not ever want to have to try.

There was a thump as Dapyx hopped down onto the floor and came to see. He grunted something foul-sounding at me in his own tongue. Wondering if, hoping I had not, gone too far, I ignored him. The unfolding duel soon grabbed my attention. I quickly decided that the two newcomers were strangers, because they were going at each other like there was a blood feud between them. I had been in the ludus only a few months, but that was long enough to spot friends who arrived together. It often took a thorough whipping before they were prepared to harm one another. This pair, however, were holding back not at all.

The taller one was slim, but he had a longer reach, and was using that advantage to belt the other every chance he got. His opponent, who by his skin colour and chlamys garment could have been Greek or Illyrian, already had red welts on both his muscular arms and on one side of his face. He was angry too, snarling and trying to close with the tall man, who, light on his feet as a Minoan bull rider, kept skipping back and out of the way. Then he got a punch in with his left fist, a solid blow to the midriff that made the tall man *oofff* with surprise and pain.

'He . . . strong,' said Dapyx. 'Another punch, and . . . over.'

'I think you are right,' I said.

'I . . . always right.'

I thought of a smart answer, and swallowed it down.

'You are talking out of your arse, Dapyx.' Piye had come to watch as well. 'The way you always do.'

Dapyx snorted. 'Piss off.'

I listened to the banter, jealous of it; the two were friends, mismatched, the complete opposite of each other, and yet close as brothers. I had no idea why.

Whack, whack. The tall man landed one blow on the Greek – as I had come to think of him – and then another. Throwing the second was risky, because it was still not a bout-ending strike, and it allowed the Greek to close on him. The punch he took as a result was so powerful that we heard his teeth snap shut. It lifted him up in the air, and, already unconscious, he flew backwards, landing in a heap before an impassive-faced Crixus.

Dapyx elbowed me hard. 'What . . . I say?'

Ribs stinging, losing control for an instant, I shoved at him. 'Anyone could see he was going to win.'

Dapyx bared his teeth at me, and my skin crawled. I stared at him to show that I was not afraid – I was, though – and he glared back at me.

To my relief, Big Dog had woken, and clambered down from his bunk over mine. He came ambling up to the bars. 'Tirones?' he asked, shoving between me and Dapyx.

'Yes. One good fighter, one show-off.' Dapyx's attention shifted, as it tended to do. Like the mad creature he was, he paid me no more heed.

I kept the thought to myself that the tall man was quite skilled. If he had used more force, his blows might have downed the Greek before the sucker punch.

Big Dog peered out into the blinding sunlight. Directed by Crixus, a slave was upturning a bucket of water over the tall fighter. Coughing and spluttering, he woke. The Greek watched, no doubt wondering what would happen next.

Crixus began the speech he gave to all rookies: blood and guts, dire threats and flicks of his whip to and fro across the sand. I had heard it so many times now that I knew it almost by heart.

Big Dog chuckled. 'Drunken sot Crixus may be, but he can deliver.'

'True enough.' I glanced sideways at him, who was as near to a friend as I had in the cell. We had shared a few jokes, and neither of us farted too much.

PART III

Big Dog and Dapyx had had one fight before, when Dapyx had arrived in our cell half a month earlier. Separated by a trainer, it had been a brutal affair – cuts and bruises had marked them for days after – and to all intents, a draw. An odd truce had sprung up between them since, which both seemed content to observe. It left me as the only potential enemy for Dapyx, a situation which I did not like. Trouble simmered between us, but not in any predictable way. He was not a one for throttling a man in his sleep – nor was I – but the harsh words we had just exchanged might have sent him into one of his killing rages.

There was no way of predicting his reaction to the most banal thing, which meant that I constantly had to be on my guard, and my nerves were the worse for it.

I had wondered about trying to earn his friendship, but nothing had presented itself.

Maybe I should just kill him in his sleep, and have done, I thought. An image of the last fighter to murder another sprang into my mind: crucified in the yard, he had taken three full days and nights to die. His moans had been our lullabies at night, and his cries for water the cockcrow at dawn. It had been a mercy when he finally succumbed.

I could not slay Dapyx, I decided.

Nor could I avoid him.

We had to become comrades, but quite how a man could befriend a dog as likely to bite him as wag its tail, I had no idea. It was either that or become a gladiator even better than Dapyx, something I was not sure was possible. Lean as a gazehound I am, you see, with the ribs to show it. 'All sinew, you are,' my mother had always said. 'Born to run.'

Scarcely ideal gladiator material.

I had only survived my own tiro bout by using the old ruse of

8

flinging sand into my opponent's eyes. Momentarily blinded, he had fallen before my determined assault. Crixus had sneered, and told me that I would need better tricks if I was to survive my second contest in the arena.

Which was how I became a retiarius, a fisherman.

'They aren't prisoners of war,' said Big Dog.

'Too well fed,' said Piye.

'Not auctorati,' Dapyx put in. 'Look like slaves.' Those who volunteered to become gladiators were citizens.

'*Damnati ad ludos* then,' I added. 'I wonder what they did.' Slaves who had displeased or angered their owners were often sold into the ludus.

'The Greek ploughed his master once too often, and got caught by his mistress,' said Big Dog.

Dapyx laughed. So did Piye.

I snorted. 'Not every Greek is a molles.' Molles meant 'soft', and was a derogatory term for those who preferred to lie with men.

'That *tiro* looks like one,' said Big Dog, waggling his eyebrows and pouting. 'Put a hand on his arse in the kitchen queue – that will tell you if I am right.'

I stared at the Greek, who seemed no different to any other man. 'Piss off!'

Big Dog laughed.

Crixus had finished his speech.

We stopped talking.

PART IV

The voices from other cells – plenty of men were watching – also fell silent. No one wanted to miss the spectacle. Now came the moment that we had all gone through, the taking of the gladiatorial vow. It was, according to Crixus and the trainers, more binding than any other oath in the Roman world. It bound us all, made a familia of us, a brotherhood linked by blood, sand and the sword.

'Miserable specimens you might be, but you are about to become gladiators,' said Crixus in a loud voice. 'Once taken, you will be comrades with every man inside these walls.'

We cheered. Spoons rattled off the bars. Feet were stamped.

The tall man and the Greek glanced at each other.

Like a master orator speaking at a public gathering in the forum, Crixus waited until it was quieter. 'Repeat after me . . .'

Total silence descended on the ludus. The whining creak of a dry-axled wagon from beyond the walls – not a sound that would normally carry within – was shockingly loud.

'We swear . . .'

'To be burned, flogged, beaten . . .'

I was watching the tirones' faces as they echoed Crixus. There was a trace of fear in the tall man's expression, but he mouthed the words without hesitation. The Greek looked most unhappy.

'And to be killed with cold steel – or whatever else is ordered.'

'And to be killed with cold steel,' said the tall man and the Greek. A moment's hesitation, and they added in unison, 'or whatever else is ordered.'

Crixus made a gesture, and slaves came forward from the direction of the forge, where our weapons, helmets and some armour were made. With thick lengths of wood as carrying arms, they were bearing a three-legged iron brazier. Its base was a dull red colour, a mark of the hot charcoal within.

Everyone watching knew what would happen next, but it only dawned on the tirones when they saw the iron pokers. They quailed, but there was nowhere to go. The trainers and guards had closed in around them, sticks at the ready, weapons on their belts if either turned stupid. Urged by Crixus, the two men lay down, and did not resist as their arms and legs were pinioned.

Into the brazier went the irons. Crixus turned them every so often. When the first was ready, he lifted it up appraisingly. I could not take my eyes off the dull-red glow. Its end, I knew, had been twisted into a neat arrangement of small letters. They read: LUD. CAP., which was cursive Latin for Ludus Capua, our gladiator school. Every man in the place had the same brand on the upper surface of his right forearm. Marked for life, even if you won the rudis and were freed.

'A denarius the tall one screams,' said Big Dog.

'Done,' I said. Before he could change his mind, I shook his hand.

Hiss. There is nothing quite like the sound of a branding iron being pushed against flesh. Nothing quite like the charred stench of it either.

The Greek wailed and sobbed like a newborn left half a day without milk.

A groan escaped the tall man, and no more.

Delighted, I needled Big Dog until he went back to his bunk for the coin.

PART V

That afternoon, as the sun disappeared behind the top storey of the ludus, and the gong rang for food, I made sure to join the queue behind the tall tiro. My confrontation with Dapyx had decided me to be on the lookout for an ally, and a newcomer was a good place to start. His face was drawn, and he kept looking at the salve-covered wound on his right forearm.

'It hurts like a bastard,' I said.

He glanced at me warily. 'Aye.'

'The first two or three days are the worst. I can get you some poppy juice if you want.' The ludus surgeon would sell anything to a man with the coin. He had a taste for whores and gambling, which meant his purse was always empty.

A suspicious look. 'Why would you do that?'

I shrugged. 'Just being friendly.'

He turned his back.

We moved a few steps nearer the kitchen. Big Dog joined me.

'My name is Midir. I'm a retiarius. This long streak of misery is Big Dog. He fights as a murmillo.'

The tall tiro glanced over his shoulder. 'Mattheus.'

'Unusual to meet another cloud-toucher,' said Big Dog. 'You a Gaul too?'

'No. I am half-Jewish, half-Roman.'

'Explains the name,' I said. 'You must be a slave then, rather than a prisoner of war like me. I am from Hibernia, which is a rain-misted isle—'

'I know where it is. North-west of Gaul and west of Britannia.'

Respect flared in Big Dog's eyes. 'That's more than I knew when this flea-bitten dog told where he was whelped.'

'That is because you are a brute with no education,' I retorted.

Big Dog snorted. 'Says the man who cannot read and write.'

I laughed, partly in relief that he had taken my insults and thrown at least one back. He *was* becoming a friend.

We shuffled another half dozen steps.

'I was a scribe to a merchant,' said Mattheus. 'He caught me stealing. The first couple of times, he beat me black and blue. The third, he sold me to the ludus.'

'Why did you keep thieving?' I asked curiously.

'You would laugh if I told you.'

'We are going to take the piss out of you anyway,' said Big Dog cheerily. 'That's the way life is here.'

'He's right,' I said.

Mattheus scowled. 'I was buying books.'

'Books?'

Big Dog looked as nonplussed as I.

'It is I who should be mocking you,' said Mattheus. 'But I will not.'

A wise choice, I thought. For all our jocularity, we would have turned on him like wild dogs if he, the unaccepted newcomer, had had the temerity to poke fun at us.

'Books are stories, set down on parchment,' said Mattheus. 'There can be more information in one book than in all the tales you have ever heard.'

'Stealing money to pay for drink or whores, that I can understand,' said Big Dog, shaking his head. 'But *books?*'

'All that learning isn't of much use here,' I said. 'In the ludus, life is about survival.'

'I thought that,' said Mattheus, looking again at his still-weeping brand.

PART VI

'Are you going to stand there gossiping all day?' growled a voice behind us. 'Get a move on, cocksuckers.'

I rolled my eyes. The gap between Mattheus and the next man along was no more than five paces. There was always an impatient one, however – someone whose belly thought his throat had been cut. It was not worth a fight, but to back down meekly was not wise either. I glowered at the man who had spoken, while nudging Mattheus forward.

'Don't get any ideas about jumping the line,' Big Dog warned over his shoulder, but he was also moving.

Our conversation ceased as we reached the doorway into the kitchen, where a table served as the counter. One of the cooks, a sour-faced German, stood with a ladle in hand. In front of him was a large steaming pot and a pile of loaves. Simple clay bowls were stacked to one side.

Mattheus pointed. 'What is it?'

The cook sneered. 'Surprise.'

'Take a bowl,' I said quietly. 'Hold it out. Move on.'

Mattheus bridled.

'Unless you want him to spit in it as well, do what I say,' I said.

Mattheus obeyed, but he was grumbling under his breath.

The cook gave him no bread.

I was next, and Mattheus realised he had been deprived. He made to go back, but I shoved him on. 'Did the wooden sword scramble your wits? Do not annoy the cook, or you will be eating weevils and maggots for the rest of your time here.'

'He's a slave like us,' protested Mattheus.

'Aye, but he serves the food, and you don't,' said Big Dog.

Each mealtime, the tables that usually stood up against one of the courtyard's side walls were moved out onto the sand. We found a table that was unoccupied – always the best policy – and sat down.

'Where's the Greek?' I asked. 'The one who knocked you out.'

Mattheus scowled. 'I have no idea. Not in my cell. And he is no Greek. He's from Asia Minor.'

I stared. He might as well have said the Garden of the Hesperides to me – that was a fantastical place at the end of the world, apparently.

'Have you heard of Troy?'

'No, I haven't,' I snarled.

'Nor me neither,' said Big Dog.

Mattheus sighed.

I had had enough. 'See here,' I said, flattening my hands on the table in order not to bunch them into fists, 'we might not be educated like you, but we know how to survive in the ludus.'

'So far,' said Big Dog in a droll voice.

'Aye, so far. You, on the other hand, seem to be a smart arse. Keep looking down your nose at us, and if we don't leave your brains leaking out on the floor of the latrines, someone a lot meaner than us will. And that's after he has raped you. Not noticed the looks you have been getting?'

Mattheus' eyes flickered around the tables. More than one man was staring in his direction. One licked his lips; another rubbed his groin. 'I hope you like biting the pillow,' called a third. Mattheus' gaze returned to me and Big Dog. 'I do not mean to insult,' he said. 'Forgive me. The world I have been used to is very different to this.'

'You don't say,' I said.

'For a soft-handed scribe, you fought all right, though,' said Big Dog. 'How come?'

'A few years ago, the master's premises were robbed several times in quick succession,' Mattheus replied. 'All his male slaves had to learn how to fight. It is not something I liked, but I was good at it.'

'Aye, well, fighting in the arena is different to anything you will have experienced. Best pay attention to the *doctores*, the instructors,' I said. 'A few other things also. Mouth shut. Ears and eyes open. Avoid eye contact if you can, but if someone gives you shit, give it back verbally.'

'It's a balancing act,' said Big Dog cheerily. 'You have to know how far you can push a man before it becomes dangerous.'

Mattheus looked less than happy, but he nodded. 'I will do what you say. Is there room in your cell for another?'

'No,' I replied, wishing that I could swap him with Dapyx.

15

'Who's that?' Big Dog was gazing at the entrance, which was always manned by two armed guards. They had unlocked the gate and admitted a self-important-looking type in a richly cut tunic and stylish sandals. He was escorted by one straight to Crixus' quarters.

'If that is one of the magistrates' lackeys, I've never seen him before,' said Big Dog, who had been in the ludus for a year and a half. 'He's from out of town.'

My interest pricked, I watched the dandy enter Crixus' reception room on the first floor, the entrance to which I could see from our table.

Little did any of us know it, but the visitor would change all of our lives.

PART VII

Peace fell on the courtyard. A hum of conversation filled the air, broken by occasional bursts of laughter. Everyone had eaten; soon we would be locked into our cells for the night, and so men were playing dice or latrunculus, and drinking wine if they had it. Two Thracians were arm wrestling, and being egged on by a dozen others. My bladder was full, and I was debating whether to risk using the facilities – a dangerous place on one's own – or to wait and piss in the pot that we shared. Imagining the abuse I would get from the others for using it so soon after lockdown, I decided to go now. Big Dog declared he would join me; Mattheus quickly said the same.

My worries eased. There was little chance of getting jumped in a group of three. We made for the latrine, which was close to the kitchen. A square room with seats on three sides, it was a fuggy, foul-smelling place in which one did not linger. As yet, the aqueduct did not supply the ludus, so there was no channel of running water to carry away the waste. Under the wooden seats was a deep trench; when it filled up, it had to be emptied, which was a task everyone hated.

'Be careful when you piss,' Big Dog said to me as we went in. 'The next man who needs a shit doesn't want to sit on your efforts.'

It was a standing joke. No one sat down unless they absolutely had to. I cheerfully told him where he could shove a blunt stick, and we chose our spots. Side by side, obviously – that was the safest. Mattheus, awkward, still unsure, moved as far from us as possible. I was about to warn him, but Big Dog muttered, 'Leave him. He has to learn.'

I held my tongue, and lifting my tunic, sighed as my overfull bladder began to empty.

Voices behind; my skin crawled. I looked around. In came the Greek who had knocked out Mattheus. His face was thunderous. My mouth opened to warn Mattheus, but then the arm-wrestling Thracians came in close behind him, and on their tails was another of their cronies.

'Trouble,' I said quietly to Big Dog, explaining what I had seen.

I do not wish to describe what the Thracians wanted. I suspect that it has always been the same in places where violent men are deprived of women's company. Whether the Greek had realised what they were about I do not know, but his strangled protest as they leaped on him made it clear that he did not want it.

I finished. 'Ready?' I asked Big Dog.

'Aye.' He had his fists bunched, in case we needed to fight our way out.

'Mattheus.' I stared over the knot of punching, grabbing bodies on the floor. 'Can you get around them?'

'I – we . . .' he said. 'Should we not help him?'

PART VIII

'Who?' I asked innocently.

'The G-Greek. From Asia Minor.' His eyes kept darting to the struggle. The Greek had landed a mighty punch, and knocked out one of the Thracians, but he had taken a kick to the balls, and his strength was fast ebbing.

'Unless you want what is about to befall him to happen to you also, I suggest you leave. Now. With us.'

His face tortured, Mattheus scuttled around the seats to where we stood. 'This is not right. It's vile. An abomination.'

'Aye,' I said. 'It is. Coming?'

Fists at the ready, eyes on the door, I led the way outside.

Perhaps five heartbeats later, a roar followed us, such as is made by a man at the limits of desperation.

Heads turned. Seeing us, Dapyx leered, as if to suggest we had been involved. I paid him no heed.

Two guards came running, cudgels in hand.

We sauntered back to our table, and watched.

In went the guards. *Crack, crack* came the sound of their staffs, indiscriminately, I had no doubt. Out sloped two of the Thracians, supporting the third between them. The Greek was last, weak-legged, a purple weal ringing his throat, but still able to walk. His undergarment was also in place, for which I was glad. The filthy Thracians had not succeeded.

Crixus came storming down from his office, sword in hand.

The guards prodded the Thracians and the Greek to stand before him.

'That shout would have woken Somnus himself!' snarled Crixus. 'Who made it?'

No one answered.

19

'I am in no mood to humour fools. Someone speak,' warned Crixus. 'Quickly.'

One of the guards said, 'These barbarians –' he indicated the Thracians – 'were attacking the Greek. I think it was he who cried out, *dominus*.'

Crixus' eyes, flintier than ever, bore down on the Greek. 'Well?'

'I slipped and fell. I was in a lot of pain.'

A snort. 'That's what they all say.' Crixus stared at the Thracians, and very slowly, as if speaking to small children, growled, 'What have you to say?'

A shared glance.

The biggest Thracian said, 'We . . . arguing . . . between us.'

The two others nodded like puppets bouncing on the end of strings.

Crixus clicked his fingers, and one of the guards tossed him his cudgel. Catching it in his left hand, the lanista laid into the big Thracian, toppling him to the ground with a flurry of vicious blows. His companions looked on in horror. One took a step forward, but Crixus anticipated it. His sword whipped up, and the Thracian froze, lucky not to impale himself on the tip.

Crixus paused to make sure we were all watching. There was a mad look in his eyes, which reminded me of Dapyx. A deathly silence hung over the ludus as Crixus resumed beating the biggest Thracian. He continued long after his victim had stopped moving.

Never had I seen a man beaten to death before. What lingered in my mind afterwards were the wet cracks, those of breaking bone.

Panting, his face spattered with red, Crixus pointed the cudgel at the remaining Thracians and the Greek. 'Cross me again, and the same will happen to you. Understand?'

Thoroughly cowed, they all nodded.

PART IX

Quietness still reigned over the courtyard. Hardened fighters, tirones, ordinary slaves, we were stunned by the savagery of what we had just witnessed. The Thracian had been killed for no apparent reason.

Except of course Crixus *had* had a reason; I realised this as someone began to clap.

My gaze shifted to the balustraded walkway that ran around the first floor in front of the offices and bedrooms. There stood the dandy who had come in during our meal, an unpleasant smile on his face.

'Past it, am I?' Crixus called up to him.

'It would seem not,' replied the dandy. 'Let us talk again.'

Crixus did not bother to wash off the gore before he went back up the stairs.

The guards had the Thracian's companions drag his corpse to the gate. It left a revolting trail of brain slime in the sand. The body was left sprawled by the entrance. If he had paid into the burial fund, he would have a grave; if not, he was bound for the town rubbish heap, where his eyeballs would be taken by the birds, and the soft bits – tongue, ears, prick – by the rats. Within a day, his belly would begin to blacken and bloat. I was grateful when Mattheus asked me a question, and took my mind from the disturbing images.

'Who in Hades is the dandy?'

'No idea.' I glanced about. The query, or versions of it, was falling from everyone's lips.

Big Dog shook his head. 'Never seen him before.'

I asked Dapyx and Piye, who had come walking over. They didn't know either.

'Did you see the guards he left on the street?' This from Sextus, a tough secutor with the little finger missing on his left hand.

'No.'

'I was by the gate when he came in.' Limping over, he said in a low voice, 'Those are a couple of Praetorians out there, or I'm an Egyptian dancing girl.'

'I've seen you do a good impression of one of those,' said Siccum, one of his cronies, who fought as a Samnite. Siccum, so named because of his dry humour, was averagely tall, and averagely built. He was also quiet, and balding at the temples. That caused men to underestimate him, which was foolish, because he was a dangerous bastard.

Sextus snorted. 'They were Praetorians, I'm telling you. Arrogant as you like, with big-city accents and ivory-handled swords. Who else carries weapons like that in Capua?'

'The emperor wants a show, maybe,' I said.

Sextus nodded. 'Why else would a perfumed arselover like him come in here?'

'Gaius Julius Caesar Augustus Germanicus,' said Mattheus, lingering over the words. 'Caligula.'

We sucked on the marrow of that troubling idea.

Siccum said in a quiet voice, 'Meant to be a right whoreson, he is.'

'He wasn't always like that,' said Big Dog. 'Everyone loved him at the start.'

I hadn't been a slave two years earlier, when Caligula had taken the purple, but I had heard tales of the extravagant games he had thrown on at Rome. Months they had lasted, apparently.

'He has been denouncing senators,' said Mattheus.

It was delivered with such a tone of certainty that no one questioned it.

'I don't give a shit about senators,' said Siccum. 'I wonder if the dandy is here to buy some of us so the emperor can auction us off?' This had happened in Rome.

'It's contests to the death I would be more concerned with,' I said. Caligula was also known for his bloodlust.

PART X

'Gather round!' Crixus' voice rang out across the courtyard.
We exchanged a glance. The dandy was still upstairs. Whatever announcement was about to be made had something to do with him.

As we gathered below the spot where Crixus was standing, I found myself not just with my cellmates, but with Mattheus and Sextus and Siccum as well. It did not mean that they were my friends yet, but the suggestion was there. It felt good.

'The ludus has been honoured today with the visit of a member of the imperial household.' Gruesome with his still blood-marked face, Crixus indicated the dandy, who was by his side. 'This is Lucius Villius Tappulus.'

We stared at him.

He was a short-arse. Any man of us could have torn him limb from limb, but he did not give the slightest impression of caring, which said a lot for his exalted position compared to we gladiators.

'The Divine One, our emperor, wishes to hold a munus,' Crixus went on. 'And this ludus has been given the honour of supplying the fighters. It is—'

'How many of us?' Siccum shouted.

Crixus glared at being interrupted, but in the bright sunlight, he could not see who had spoken.

Tappulus spoke for the first time. 'All of you.'

Surprise rippled through us. This was unheard of. There were seventy-odd of us, which meant thirty-five paired fights, and at the least, a lot of injuries.

'There will be fine prizes for the victors,' said Tappulus. 'Gold. Jewels. Women. The emperor may even ask to meet some of you, should you impress him.'

23

I liked the sound of that. So did others, but I could see Mattheus wasn't happy. Rookie, I thought. Sextus was frowning too, however, and listening to Siccum mutter in his ear. Unease tickled my spine.

Sextus cupped a hand to his mouth, and asked, 'And the losers?'

Tappulus' smile reminded me of Dapyx's, when he had killed his last opponent. 'They will receive iron.'

The term we used for being slain in the arena sounded odd coming from his lips, and seeing the expressions of the more experienced fighters change, my unhappiness grew.

'All of them?' yelled Big Dog.

'Yes.' Tappulus' expression was gloating.

I glanced at Big Dog. The same horrible realisation was in his eyes. If we were pitted against each other, only one of us would walk away.

Dapyx, Piye, Sextus and Siccum were eyeing each other up and down.

Mattheus was looking at the sand between his feet.

Dread filled me. I had fought only once in the arena since arriving in the ludus, whereas the majority had done so on multiple occasions. The betmakers who plied their trade in the arches that ran around the base of the amphitheatre would give me poor odds indeed.

'The contests shall take place in ten days,' Crixus announced. 'That will be all.'

I felt sick.

Ten days.

Ten days until my life was over.

PART XI

I lay on my bunk that night, unable to sleep, thinking about my home and family. This was not something I normally allowed myself to do, for it led me down a spiralling path of misery that culminated in me considering whether I should open my veins or pick a fight with Dapyx. Tonight, however, was different.

I had grown up in a small settlement on the east coast of Hibernia, the older of two boys. I had a younger sister also. My parents farmed, as did most of our neighbours. We had hens, and a thin-boned cow. Life was hard, or so I had thought it until I entered the ludus. Unceasing toil on the land, foraging in summer and autumn, and hunting for extra meat were all I knew. It was not entirely bad, of course. We bathed in the sea in sunny weather, and danced around the bonfires every midsummer. Wintertime was easier, confined as we were to the house, but those dark days were also when food ran short, and we went to bed hungry more often than not.

That existence would still have been mine – and I would probably have been married – but for the events of a fateful day about a year before. Our settlement was attacked by British tribesmen, come over the sea in small craft, in search of slaves. Although every man in our village possessed a spear, we were farmers, not warriors. We were easy prey.

It was a cloud-ridden, showery day when the raiders appeared, causing complete panic. Women shrieked, snatched up their babes and ran. Old crones and greybeards stared in confusion, or wailed and cried. Men cursed and picked up whatever was to hand as weapons. I had fought as well as I might, stabbing one Briton in the meaty part of his thigh and driving off another from the door of our one-room hut. I had not seen the warrior with a club coming at me from the side until it was too late. Knocked senseless, I woke, trussed like a pig for the slaughter, with blood in my eyes and my mother's screams filling my ears.

I tried to shove away the memories, but I could not. My sister had been lucky – she fought so hard that the Briton trying to rape her had in the end slit her throat. Her lithe-limbed corpse had lain beside my poor mother, who had suffered the most unimaginable horrors before she had died.

How cruel are the gods, I thought. Never would I revenge myself on the Britons who had murdered my family. Never would I marry the freckle-faced laughing girl from the farm near our settlement upon whom I had set my heart. Never would I return to Hibernia, the land of my birth.

Tears formed in the corners of my eyes; I could not fight them away.

I was going to die in the Capuan amphitheatre, with an emperor watching.

PART XII

I do not remember at what time my eyes closed, but roseate fingers of light were creeping down the walls on the other side of the courtyard. It seemed like I had had only a few moments of sleep when one of the doctores came to wake us. It was their habit to run a wooden sword across the cell bars, *rap, rap, rap*, and loudly tell us that another day had dawned. This morning, the doctor was using a real blade. Whatever chance I had of not waking up with the former, there was no possibility with this method. I was muzzily aware that the use of the sword was not a coincidence either.

'Up, up, you gelded grunters! Wake up, you ex-tenants of pigsties!' *Tong, tong, tong* went his sword.

I heard Big Dog mutter something under his breath.

'Out of your bunks!'

'We heard you,' growled Dapyx.

'Not asleep,' said Piye.

'Feet on the floor then!'

Dapyx and Piye made no reply, and the doctor ran the sword blade over the bars faster and faster, a metallic cacophony that reverberated inside my exhausted skull. I wanted to tell him to piss off, that we were awake, but I had the wits not to. Giving lip to the trainers was foolish. A beating might result, or shortened rations, or being pitted against a tougher fighter in the training bouts that would follow our morning meal.

It was better to say nothing, and to think the insult I wanted to shout. Donkey ears, I thought. The trainer outside our cell had long ears which waggled when he spoke or got excited. I prised my gummy eyelids open, and sat up. Big Dog's feet were already hanging down from the bunk above. The doctor leered at us. 'Rested? Ready for a hard day's training?'

No and no, I wanted to snarl at him. Instead I nodded.

Big Dog muttered something again, but quietly enough that it did not carry over the din from the courtyard – the other doctores were making sure that everyone had woken in the same way.

Out of nowhere, Dapyx leaped to the ground and swarmed forward from the depths of the cell. He came so fast, with his teeth bared, that the doctor took a step backwards, like a man would if a caged beast he has taunted snaps at him.

'I . . . ready. Want . . . fight me?' Dapyx asked. 'Real weapons . . . not wood.'

The doctor's lip curled, but fear sparked in his eyes. He stabbed the sword forward, through the bars. 'Back, filth!'

Dapyx did not move an inch.

If the doctor had used all his strength, he would have spitted Dapyx like a piece of meat on a cook's skewer. He realised too late that his victim was not moving, but had enough time – just – to weaken the thrust. Nonetheless, I winced as the V-shaped point struck.

Dapyx made not a sound.

I stared.

The doctor pulled back his right arm, his gaze fixed on the end of the blade, the very tip of which was crimson. It had gone into the top of Dapyx's abdomen, perhaps half a finger's breadth.

PART XIII

Dapyx did not look at the blood trickling down his belly. Instead he leered at the doctor, and asked, 'Is that . . . your best?'

The doctor's eyes travelled up to meet Dapyx's stone-cold ones, and went back down to the wet-lipped wound he had caused.

'If I die . . . Crixus . . . not happy.' Dapyx sounded delighted.

He was right, I thought. If the cut turned septic, Crixus would lose one of his best fighters. That would have been bad in ordinary circumstances, but with the imperial contests imminent, it bordered on catastrophic.

The doctor was not about to admit anything, but he unlocked the cell gate and jerked a thumb in the direction of the surgeon's quarters. 'Go and get that looked at.'

'The wine sponge will still be snoring,' I said.

'At least he will be sober, or some way towards being sober,' said Big Dog. 'Imagine if this had happened at midday.'

'Shut your mouths!' snarled the doctor, trying to regain control of a situation that had spiralled far beyond his intention. 'Move,' he said to Dapyx.

'I eat,' Dapyx replied, making to walk out into the courtyard.

Blustering, but unwilling to get himself into any more trouble than he already had, the doctor watched impotently as Dapyx strolled towards the kitchen.

Men noticed the blood. Voices called out, asking if he was all right.

Dapyx laughed. 'I . . . hungry. Bread first!'

'He's mad,' I said.

'Iron hard,' said Big Dog, shaking his head in awe, disbelief, or both.

'Why didn't you stop him?' I asked Piye.

A shrug. 'I am not his master.'

If I had the misfortune to be pitted against Dapyx when the time came, I hoped that his injury was still causing him problems.

'Outside!' the doctor shouted.

I went first, willing away the tiredness that stung my eyes and clouded my head. I buried my grief, and thoughts of home, and asked my gods to hear my prayers, as they had not appeared to do since my capture.

The first man out of the next cell was Atticus, a tall Briton with hazel eyes and a bleak sense of humour. He gave me a nod, which I returned. Atticus had been in the ludus for only a short time longer than I; he too had only fought in the arena once. We could soon end up facing each other, I thought, because he was a secutor, a 'chaser'. Thus far, no indications had come of how Caligula wanted the fights to proceed. Half of us were to die, but how? Would it be veteran against veteran, Dapyx against Piye, and rookie against rookie, me versus Atticus? Maybe the emperor would just want a slaughter. Place a veteran in with a novice, or a tiro, and the contest would quickly be over. Dapyx would slice up Atticus inside fifty heartbeats, I thought, trying to shove away the knowledge that he would probably do the same to me.

'What happened with Dapyx?' Atticus asked.

I told him. 'He does not care about anyone, or anything. Pray that you are not pitted against him in Caligula's munus.'

Atticus nodded. 'Any idea what will happen?'

'Your guess is as good as mine.' I hesitated, and then added what he would probably think, if he wasn't thinking it already, 'You might have to fight me.'

'We should make a bargain, in case it does,' said Atticus in a serious tone.

'What do you mean?'

'We give each other a death wound, so that both of us die. That will piss off the emperor.'

I cast a wary look at him, almost sure he was joking, but also wondering if he was as demented as Dapyx.

He gave me a shove. 'I was joking!'

'I knew that,' I lied, giving him a belt back.

PART XIV

Munching on a hot-from-the-oven loaf, Dapyx took himself off to see the surgeon. Curious glances were thrown after him aplenty, but the morning began to unfold in its usual fashion. Men emerged from their cells, yawning and stretching. A queue formed outside the kitchen, and another outside the toilets. Those who liked to keep clean were splashing water over themselves from buckets. There was no bathing complex like the one used by the townspeople just a few blocks away; we made do with what came in from the street via a leaden pipe.

That water could be brought from hills many miles away in sufficient quantity to supply an entire city was still something a little beyond my comprehension. I had seen the baths on my way here, and marvelled at the structure, a block in size. I still struggled to believe that inside were cold pools and warm ones, and sweltering rooms where clouds of moisture filled the air, but it was not unique. I had seen similar edifices in towns all the way from Gaul to Italia.

Big Dog came out of the cell. 'Daydreaming again?'

I snorted, annoyed, because he was right. 'I'm for a piss.'

'Me too.' He glanced about. 'There's Mattheus.'

Our new friend, who had emerged from his cell, hurried over.

'You made it through the first night?' I asked.

'I did. Atticus is all right. The others seem to be as well. You going to the latrine?'

I nodded.

'I take it it's safer to go together?'

'Aye,' I said, following Big Dog. 'After what Crixus did to the Thracian, it's unlikely that anyone would be boneheaded enough to start a fight in there, but you never know.'

'What about the Nubian?'

'Piye?' I chuckled. 'No one wants to tangle with him, believe me.'

'His shit also stinks like you would not believe,' Big Dog threw over his shoulder. 'That's why men stay away from him.'

Mattheus' lips twitched.

'Did you hear what happened with Dapyx?' I asked.

'Yes. The doctor had a face on him like a slapped arse.'

I laid out the tale. 'Dapyx is a law unto himself.'

'I suppose it's a good place to be, not caring whether you live or die,' said Mattheus.

'Hard to argue with that,' I replied.

'Another ten days from now, and only half of us will still be alive.'

'Enough,' I snarled, uncomfortable with the reminder that I would likely be one of those waiting for the ferryman.

'Why?'

I rounded on him, fist raised.

Mattheus made no attempt to protect himself. 'I am a dead man walking.'

I lowered my arm. 'You don't know that.'

'What are my chances?' His eyes moved over the nearest fighters, and mine followed.

'It isn't much different for me,' I admitted.

PART XV

We had reached the line of men waiting to enter the latrine. I appraised each one, trying to imagine a bout against them, with thousands of people roaring and cheering every move we made. The Thracians – I could not beat either of them, unless they fell or made a similar blunder. Sextus was too tough for me as well, and as for Siccum, well, at least I would have a quick death. Big Dog shuffled forward a couple of steps, and glanced back to see if we were following. Could I kill him? I wondered. Maybe, but not very likely. Dapyx and Piye would cut me into little pieces.

A fierce anger burst into flame inside me that Caligula – the soft-handed emperor, who had probably never handled a weapon in anger, who had slaves to wait hand and foot upon him night and day – should so easily determine my fate.

Standing there in the queue to empty my bladder, I made a vow to myself. I would not die in the upcoming munus.

I did not know how yet, but I would survive.

The morning meal was barley porridge, as always. Filling, nutritious, it helped to build our muscles, but by the gods, it was boring. Honey would have made it taste more palatable, but I had almost no coin. I did not bother annoying myself by looking at the tables of top fighters like the Thracians. They had their own bowl of honey, and fruit as well.

We were given a short time to digest our food, and to oil our muscles – something I had learned was useful to prevent injury – and then the doctores ordered us out into the centre of the courtyard. Tables had been set up behind them, and slaves were walking to and from the armoury, carrying bundles of weapons. My interest pricked. Normally, we trained with wooden swords and in my case, a crudely fashioned trident. Allowing us to use the real thing was rare, because of what had happened in this very ludus.

A century before, a slave rebellion had started here. Led by a charismatic Thracian called Spartacus, the uprising had seen him assemble an army of slaves, more than one hundred thousand strong. Over a two-year period, he had marched the length and breadth of Italia, defeating every Roman army in his path. After his defeat, gladiators' existence had changed forever. No longer were they allowed to come and go, to leave the ludus whenever they wished. Their weapons, once easily accessible, were kept under permanent lock and key, and they were confined to their cells much of the time.

A fantastical idea popped into my mind. I counted the doctores: one, two, three, four, five. They had whips and daggers. The guards at the main gate were armed with swords and shields, but there were only two of them. Swarm forward as a group, seize a weapon each, and we would be out of the ludus in no time.

Impulse seized me. 'We could escape,' I said to Big Dog.

He glanced at me in surprise. 'Eh?'

I whispered my plan.

'Kill them all?'

PART XVI

'Why not? They would slay us at need without even blinking.' His eyes narrowed, and he regarded the laden-down tables. 'It could work, I suppose.'

Somehow Atticus had heard. 'Are you mad? Don't you know what happened to Spartacus' men at the end?'

I had chosen not to think about that. I pictured the thousands of crucifixes that had lined the road all the way from Capua to the capital.

'One hundred and forty miles it is to Rome,' said Atticus, 'and there was a crucified man every two score paces. They put guards on them too, so no one could give the wretches water or food, or try to rescue them. The bodies were left until they rotted. Can you imagine the stench? It is said that the vultures grew so fat they could not fly.'

I shoved the horrific image from my mind. 'We could still get out of here. Rush the doctores, grab the weapons, kill the bastards, and out! Take a ship to Gaul or Hispania, and we would be free men.'

My voice had risen. Sextus, Siccum and Dapyx had joined Big Dog, Mattheus and Atticus, and formed a little circle around me.

I could see the interest growing in their eyes. Even with the huge risks, freedom appealed more than a one-in-two chance of death in the arena. Someone with no knowledge of a ludus might have wondered why we had not considered this measure before, but the answer was simple. Bouts with real weapons were strictly controlled, and only the swords or tridents needed for the individual contests were taken from the armoury. Never before had enough blades for all of us been laid out in plain view.

My eyes went round the others' faces. 'We need to move now. *Now.* Who's with me?'

'I am,' said Mattheus, his voice trembling.

I gave him a quick nod, but I needed better fighters. 'Big Dog?' Get someone like him to join, I thought, and others would follow.

Big Dog's gaze flickered to the table of weapons, and past it, to the gate. 'Aye,' he said. 'I will go.'

'Me too,' said Atticus.

'Aye,' Sextus added.

I almost charged then and there, but still I needed more accomplices. 'Siccum?'

He nodded.

Dapyx laughed. 'If you . . . stupid enough to try . . . I am in.'

'Come on then,' I muttered. 'With luck, others will come too.' I took a step forward.

Mattheus shot in front of me.

Until that moment, I had not realised quite how desperate he had felt.

He broke into a run, when we should have all gone together.

I tensed, about to spring after him.

PART XVII

A hand seized my upper arm. I wheeled, a curse on my lips.
    It was Siccum who had grabbed me. He put a finger to his lips,
and then, with a flicker of his eyes at the walkway above, indicated
danger.

My guts wrenched. 'Mattheus!'

He checked, but the fool kept running.

'Mattheus, stop!'

He paid no heed.

A bowstring twanged.

Mattheus jerked, as if someone had shoved him. Down he went,
face first, a feathered head sprouting between his shoulder blades.

Anguish tore at me. My eyes shot to the walkway. There stood
Crixus, watching like a hawk. Beside him were two guards with bows,
one of whom was nocking a second arrow to his string. The other was
ready to loose.

'Try it,' called Crixus, his lizard eyes on us. 'Go on!'

In my fury, I almost broke free of Siccum's grasp.

'Stay calm.' Sextus' voice was in my ear. 'Otherwise you'll be next.'

Reason seeped in through the red mist. However bad my chances
were in the arena, they were better than trying to dodge two archers
and get past the gate guards. 'Aye,' I said thickly. 'Our chance is gone.'

'We should have moved faster,' said Atticus. 'Crixus will not make
that mistake again.'

'No, he will not,' I said, casting a look at the malevolent lanista.
He reminded me of nothing so much as a spider, perched at one high
corner of his web, waiting for prey to land.

'Anyone else care to run?' Crixus called.

No one spoke.

'Good. In that case, it is time to train. Choose your weapons!'

We joined the queue. Glances aplenty were thrown at Mattheus' corpse, which still lay where it had fallen. I got looks too, and so did my companions, the men who had clearly been planning to do the same as Mattheus. No one said a word to us.

We reached the table. The best weapons had already gone, and the net I chose was full of holes. Not for the first time, I wished I had been chosen to fight in a class other than that of retiarius. It wasn't my weapon that I disliked; with its long reach, the trident was superior to a sword. I hefted the one I had picked up, and imagined having to plunge it deep into a man, or cutting the throat of a defeated enemy with my other weapon, a dagger. In my one fight, I had only ripped a few chunks out of my opponent's flesh. No, I thought, walking on to the piles of padding and shields, it was the lack of protection. True, I wore a manica, a thick-stuffed linen arm covering, like most fighters, but everyone else had leg coverings *and* a shield, while I had only a high bronze shoulder-guard called a galerus. It did not compare to a shield, and retiarii did not wear helmets either.

PART XVIII

Instead of Big Dog, I found myself beside Sextus. We helped one another to don our manicae; he settled the galerus to my satisfaction and buckled the leather strap that ran from it over my chest, under my right armpit and back around to my left shoulder. We had come out of our cells wearing the broad leather belts and undergarments worn by every fighter; all that remained was for Sextus to put on his helmet.

It was one of only two ways to tell between him and a murmillo in the arena. There was no broad brim or box crest, just a narrow ridge that ran front to back; instead of grillwork eyepieces, there was a pair of small round holes. It left him with a very narrow field of vision. The other way of knowing was to pick the helmet up and feel the weight. Thicker, heavier, affording more protection than those worn by other fighters, it was hellish to wear for more than a short time.

'Comfortable?' I asked Sextus.

'What?'

I had forgotten he could barely hear inside the close-fitting helm. 'Comfortable?' I repeated, louder.

He made a small adjustment, and nodded.

I fastened the clasp at the back that locked him inside it.

'You fight . . . Sextus?' asked Dapyx, materialising by my side. He was no Thracian, but that was how Crixus had ordered he should fight. He had a griffon-crested helmet, small square shield, and a vicious, short, curved blade called a sica.

'I hope not,' I answered, hating even the thought.

'Me too,' came Sextus' muffled voice. 'I would rather kill someone else than you, Midir.'

My laugh was a note higher than I wanted it to be. 'I would kill you, egghead,' I joked.

He aimed a slap at me, which I dodged. Slipping around behind

39

him, where he could not see me, I rapped on the back of his helmet. 'See how easy that was?' I taunted. 'If that was my trident, I would have skewered you through the back of the neck.'

Muffled laughter came from inside Sextus' helmet. 'As if that would happen.'

He turned, and we stared at each other, him through the tiny eye-holes, me trying not to let my fear show.

'The gods would be cruel to pit us against each other,' I said, sticking out my hand. 'We are brothers.'

Sextus stared at my hand.

My mouth was dry. He had been about to join my escape before Mattheus was slain. Don't be a fool, I told myself. It did not matter what he thought of me. If we were picked to fight each other in Caligula's munus, only one would walk out of the Gate of Life. The other's corpse would be hauled through the Gate of Death, and on the floor of the mortuary have his throat slit to make sure he wasn't playing dead.

And, like as not, it would be me.

Sextus accepted the grip, and shook. 'Let us pray we fight other men, eh?'

I nodded. The small gesture of friendship meant a lot.

PART XIX

'You two!'
   Crixus' voice turned our heads. He had seen us. His lip was curled in disapproval. 'Best of mates now, are you?'
   'I wouldn't say that,' said Sextus, but the lanista wasn't listening.
   'Train together. I'll be watching, so better impress!'
   We were to use protection on our weapons that morning – there was no sense in men being crippled or injured before the lucrative contest ordered by the emperor – and I was grateful. Sextus wrapped his sword blade in strips of leather, and I did the same with my dagger and the prongs of my trident.
   Into the centre of the courtyard we walked, the archers watching from above, arrows on their strings. Pairs of men were sparring, and the doctores pacing to and fro, barking orders, giving advice and encouragement. There was room for about twelve of us; any more than that and we would have been squeezed up against one another. Dapyx was pitted against Piye, and the pair of them were enjoying it, if the obscenities they were hurling was anything to go by. Atticus had been selected to fight Siccum. Big Dog was circling the new Greek, the one Mattheus had knocked out.
   'Ready?' asked Sextus, his voice seeming to come from the bottom of a well.
   I licked my lips, and tried to remember my training. 'Yes.'
   Without hesitation, he came at me, shield high, right elbow bent, his sword at the ready.
   Sand ground between my toes as I retreated, trident held over my right shoulder, net trailing by my left side.
   He advanced at speed, hoping to close.
   I jabbed my trident at his head, *one-two*, forcing him to duck behind his shield, but still he came forward, and I abandoned any pretence of

attack. Dancing on the balls of my feet, I darted to his left, trying to get around him. His helmet turned, he desperate to keep me in sight. I broke into a run, and he twisted. The leaden weights at the edges of my net flew about my head in a blur as I whirled it around. Keeping hold of one edge, I launched it at him.

It was not my best effort, but a decent section landed on his helmet. It did not catch, sliding instead onto his left shoulder. He cursed, and tried to shake the net off. It was enough. I came in, trident prod-prodding at his unprotected right foot. I landed a blow, and I shouted. 'Hit!'

It was almost my undoing. An angry rumble came from inside Sextus' helmet, and he barrelled forward, my net falling to the sand, his shield ready to smash me down and after it, his sword to finish the job.

I scrambled backwards, protesting. 'Hit – I hit you!'

Sextus paid no heed. His shield boss connected with my sternum, and I yelled in pain, even as I fell, landing hard on my back. I stared up at the eyeholes of his helmet and the tip of his blade, which was ready to thrust down into me.

'You are mine now,' he said in triumph. 'Yield!'

PART XX

I refused to make the gesture for mercy. 'I hit you,' I snarled. 'There is no way you could have attacked me like that in the arena. Your foot would be pumping blood. You'd still be limping about and roaring in pain.' Giving me a chance, I thought.

Sextus snorted. His sword came down, frightening despite its leather cover, until the point was only a handsbreadth from my throat. 'Yield.'

He wasn't going to let me up until I gave in, I decided. No doubt his pride was stinging because of my lucky strike; there was no point antagonising him further. My mouth opened.

Thwack. The impact of the blow rocked Sextus. 'Let him up!' roared Gaius, the oldest doctor, a snaggle-toothed veteran of more than thirty fights, twenty-four of them victories. He waved his stick in the air. 'Think you can get away with cheating?'

Sextus' head turned, and he glared at Gaius.

'The retiarius hit you in the foot. Not a mortal wound by any means, but there is no question that you could have attacked him at once. You should have backed up, and let him take his chance.'

Sextus muttered something inside his helmet.

I clambered to my feet.

Gaius told us to go at it again.

This time, Sextus made no mistake. I was subjected to a battering attack from close range, *one-two*s from his sword and shield that I had no answer to. Inside twenty heartbeats I was flat on the warm sand again, staring up at him and totally at his mercy. I am not proud. I raised the index finger of my right hand. 'Missio,' I said loudly.

In my head, I could hear the crowd roaring, 'Iugula! *Kill him!*' At Caligula's munus, there would be no cries of 'mitte', to indicate that I should walk free.

'The fight is over,' said Gaius.

43

Sextus laughed and stood aside so I could get up.

My cheeks hot with both the physical effort and my shame, I retrieved my net and trident. I had seen how my life would end, and there was little I could do about it. My eyes roved over the nearest fighters: Dapyx, the Thracians, Piye, Big Dog, Siccum and so many others. If it wasn't Sextus whom I faced, one of these men would send me to the underworld, the place the Romans called Hades.

Sextus laid down his blade, and stood his shield upright. He took hold of his left hand with his right, and with a little sigh, began rubbing vigorously at his palm, and the place where his little finger had been.

Hope flared in my breast, and I looked away in case he saw. His hand was hurting not just because the shield was cursedly heavy, but also from the lack of a digit. Wrench hard enough on the top rim of his shield, and maybe, just maybe, he would not have the strength to stop me ripping it from his grasp.

I changed my prayer to the gods at once.

Now I *wanted* to be pitted against Sextus.

PART XXI

The training session was not over. I had to fight Sextus again. Tempted though I was to try out my theory about his weaker hand, I refrained. If we were drawn against each other, and Sextus had the slightest inkling I knew, he would end the fight faster than fast – before I had a chance to grab at his shield. So I put on a good show, enough to convince both him and Gaius that I was not faking, and let him beat me for a second time. At this point, Crixus bawled out the command that after a short rest we were all to change opponents. My bout had ended before some of the others. Under normal circumstances, I would have sought out the shade and a dipper of cool water, but now I slaked my thirst in the sun, watching Dapyx and Piye.

The wound had slowed down Dapyx, but there was still a deadly grace in his movements. He reminded me of a lynx. Just once in my life had I caught sight of one of the secretive wildcats, on a hunting trip in the southern mountains with my father. Lithe, precise, wary, lethal, I would even have used the word beautiful to describe the creature. Dapyx was the same in human form, and whatever he was, so was Piye. Muscles rippling and coiling under his black skin, his movements reminded me of a dancer. An expert swordsman also, he was what my father would have called a natural warrior, whereas I was someone who fought only when he had to.

Piye won the bout, in the main I suspected because of Dapyx's injury. Dapyx made no complaint. He lost the second round as well, which confirmed my suspicion. I found myself guiltily hoping that his wound festered; if that happened, I wanted to be selected to fight him. My spirits rose a little. Although the number of men in the ludus meant that the odds were against either Dapyx or Sextus and I being thrown together, here were two contests that I had at least a chance of winning.

Then Gaius put me up against one of the Thracians, and he battered me to the sand even quicker than Sextus had the second time we fought. He ignored Gaius' shouts as well, and hammered me a couple of times with his iron shield boss, bruising my ribs as well as my dignity. Ignoring my cries for missio, he only backed off when Gaius beat him about the shoulders with his staff, and threatened worse.

The Thracian laughed, and threw back, 'What are you going to do, kill me?'

Gaius spluttered and mentioned a whipping, and the Thracian laughed again. 'Whip me. I do not care.'

Gaius poked him with the stick, and told him to watch his mouth, and to stop when he was told in future.

The Thracian swaggered away, turning his back not just on Gaius but on me. It was all I could do not to rip the guards off the prongs of my trident and plant the thing in his back. I restrained myself, because to do *that* would seal my fate in Caligula's munus even faster than was likely already.

PART XXII

Whether it was because he had effectively lost the confrontation with the Thracian, or because he felt sorry for me, Gaius did not make us fight again. Gruffly, he told me to get a drink. Atticus would be my next opponent, he said. Hoping that I could win at least one training session, I walked gingerly to the water barrel, which stood by the entrance to the kitchen. I threw back the contents of the dipper, uncaring that scores of men had used it before me. I could easily have downed another two or three, but I did not. A slopping belly full of water was the last thing I needed.

My gaze wandered over the courtyard. Atticus was fighting Siccum, and making heavy weather of it. Siccum, economical in his movements, and each one measured, looked as if he were playfighting with a child. For a moment, I pitied Atticus. He would die even quicker in the arena than I. Down he went, with Siccum darting forward to stand over his prone body, his sword tip resting on Atticus' throat. Atticus' left index finger went up in the signal for missio, and the doctor shouted for Siccum to step away.

I blinked, seeing myself in that situation, and I quenched my pity. Caligula's munus was about who would survive and who would not. I had to concentrate on myself and no one else.

When my turn came, I also made short work of Atticus. A third opponent I could face, I thought, and probably the most likely to offer me a chance of life.

And so our days passed.

Training, sweating, eating, exercising, and sleeping.

Caligula's official Tappulus came to visit several times, to watch our progress. Each time he did, Crixus would force us to heroic efforts. It was difficult to know if Tappulus was impressed or not – his face remained as impassive as a statue's – but he said nothing that had Crixus

47

storm down to beat a man to death, and for that, we were grateful.

The last day, the one before the munus, we did not have to train. It was better to allow tired muscles to recover, Crixus told us, leering, before their final exertions. Unctores were brought in, slaves trained in massage, and we were each given a session. Gods above and below, it was bliss. I could have lain on the table all day. So enjoyable was it that I fell asleep, and had to be prodded awake by the smiling unctor.

That evening, we were to feast in Capua. The cena libera was a grand affair, celebrating the gladiators; anyone could attend. I had been to one before, on the eve of my first fight, and the memories of it were still vivid in my mind. Better food than we were ever fed in the ludus; unlimited wine flowing; rapacious-eyed women enticing fighters off into the shadows.

I was in no mood for it, but there was no option of refusal. At sunset, our wrists were bound with light shackles, and we were marched under guard to Capua's forum, a grand rectangular space at the city's centre.

PART XXIII

Every single man stared at the amphitheatre as we passed by. Shrouded in darkness, it loomed out of the night, squat and brooding. I spied a couple of enterprising stallholders who had already set up their booths, taking the best spots for what would be a booming trade the following day. The normally tantalising aroma of frying sausages carried to me, but instead of rumbling, my belly gave a sickening roll. Seeing the building where we would soon fight hammered home my fate as never before.

Drool filled my mouth. I spat, and I was not alone. I heard a man retching further down the column. A barrage of jokes at his expense began. The loudest voices felt the same way, I decided. They were trying to take their minds off what awaited us. If I had been in better mood, I might have wagered with Big Dog over who would be first to vomit when the sumptuous dishes began to arrive. Instead I hoped not to be the one myself.

The only parts of Capua I had seen were the outskirts through which I had walked to the ludus, and the route to the amphitheatre. As we entered the forum, which was bright with torchlight, I forgot my nausea and had to stop myself from gaping like a fool. The scale and majesty on every side was staggering. Mighty-pillared temples, a colonnaded market, vast civic buildings. The open space was equally impressive, dotted with huge painted statues, the plinths they stood on stone islands in the sea of people. I recognised Jupiter and one of Caligula, but I had no idea about the rest.

We were noticed at once.

A man pointed. 'There they are!'

The shouts went up. 'The gladiators!' 'The hordearii, the barley men!'

Men whistled. Boys waved toy swords in the air. Some of the women made eyes at the better physical specimens among us. 'Show us your steel!' cried one, running the tip of her tongue around her lips. More lewd suggestions rang out. A matron – clearly the worse for wine – sidled up to Piye and ran her fingernails down his chest, stopping at his groin. He stopped and let her grope, giving her arse a squeeze at the same time. She moulded herself to him, and it seemed more might have happened if one of the guards had not intervened.

Piye reluctantly peeled away from the matron, who pulled him back for a kiss with tongues.

'Move,' said the guard, stepping closer. 'You can do more of that, and whatever else you like, when we get there.'

'Come and find me,' Piye said in his thick-accented Latin. 'I'll show you why they call me lord of the maidens.'

The matron pouted, which was no doubt meant to make her seem alluring. All it did was make me think, mutton dressed as lamb.

The fawning continued. The closer we got to the tables that had been arranged in the centre of the forum, the more women there were. Hands pawed at us, not at me, but at the Thracians, Dapyx and Piye, Big Dog, Sextus and Siccum. They seemed happy enough with the attention. I stared at the animated faces pressing in around us and read in them, lust, adulation, and fear.

I was reminded of what I had heard Crixus say once.

Ferrum est quod amant. They are in love with the steel.

PART XXIV

The tables had been arranged like three sides of a square. A trio of three-person reclining couches stood in the middle of that space, where they could be looked on by all. The best fighters were accompanied to these – Dapyx, Piye, the Thracians, and five others, among them Siccum – where they reclined to hoots and jeers from the rest of us. They made obscene gestures in reply; we did the same back. Sextus muscled his way to a place at the central table. Atticus made for the end of one of the 'arms', where the weakest fighters were congregating. I would have followed, but Big Dog took my arm.

'Don't sit with him.'

'Why? I want no trouble. Look at the squabbles already.' Men were arguing and shoving one another over who sat where. Everyone wanted to be on the central table, or the parts of the 'arms' that were closest to it.

'The she-wolves will not want men who perch at the edges.'

'You go,' I said wearily. 'I have no desire to make the beast with two backs tonight.'

Big Dog muttered something under his breath, but when I walked off, he came after me.

'Changed your mind about ploughing a Roman woman?' I asked.

'If the right one came along, I might be persuaded.'

'Why are you here then, with me?'

'Loyalty.'

Shocked, delighted – touched – I glanced at him. 'You are a good man, Big Dog.'

He punched me, hard.

I thumped him back. Like a moth drawn to a flame, I could not stop myself from saying, 'And if tomorrow—'

'Don't.'

Our eyes met.

'Gods willing, you and I will not face each other.'

'But if we do?'

'Both of us will do what is necessary.'

I nodded, grateful at least that he would make my end swift. There was no guarantee of that with the Thracians, say. They liked to play with their defeated opponents, slicing and dicing them, covering the sand in blood, and making the crowd bay and scream.

We parked ourselves beside a surprised-but-pleased-looking Atticus. Picking up the nearby jug, he poured us all a cup. 'Comradeship,' he said.

We drank.

I smacked my lips with approval. 'This is good – not like the piss they serve in the ludus.'

'Only the best for Caligula's chosen,' said Big Dog, downing his in one. He banged down the cup, making everything close by rattle, and said to Atticus, 'Fill her up.'

Although the vintage was good, and the wine watered down after the Roman fashion, I was still unused to it. In Hibernia, we drank beer; that would have been my first choice, but if it existed in Italia, I had yet to be offered any. I had no wish for the wine to go to my head either. In the amphitheatre, I would need every scatter of wit I had.

Only a fool would lessen his own chance of survival – or so you would have thought. Big Dog soon reined himself in, but I watched with amazement as others drank as if there was no munus in the morning. I began to wish that every murmillo and secutor – my most likely opponents – would drink until he slid off the benches.

It was a faint hope, of course.

PART XXV

Food began to arrive, great platters of roasted pork and beef. There was fish too, more types than I had ever seen, served whole, fried, grilled, and baked in the oven with herbs. One serving dish in particular is worthy of mention; each fish on it was chased and pursued by another. Mouths almost touched tails in an eternally doomed attempt to catch the prey. In the centre was set a mound of enormous oysters.

My appetite had returned somewhat, and I tucked into the shellfish with gusto, much to my companions' disgust. 'Try one,' I said to Big Dog, cutting it open with a swift jerk of my table knife, and proffering the glistening oyster on one half of the shell. I winked. 'It stiffens the rod, or so they say. You might need it before the night is over.'

He gave me a shove that slopped the oyster onto the table, and called me a savage. I laughed, and scooped up the oyster with my fingers, downing it in one swallow. I ate two more, but stopped then, lest they gave me diarrhoea, as sometimes happened.

I ate a couple of herb sausages, and a hunk of bread, and decided that would do me. The food kept coming, pigs' feet in mustard, shellfish with a cumin sauce, and fried balls of squid meat, and of chicken, and of a bird I had never heard of, peacock. There were faggots made from pork liver, wrapped in bay leaves and smoked – Atticus raved about these, although he could not persuade me to try them – and the womb of a sow, stuffed with a mixture of leek, dill, pine nuts and spices.

Nothing short of an exemption from the munus would have made me taste the last dish.

Piye ate a whole plate, however, and slapped his tight stomach afterwards, announcing that it was victor's food, and that we should all try it.

'I hope it rots in his guts and gives him the screaming shits,' said Atticus vehemently.

'Worried you will face him?' I asked.

Atticus' expression blackened. 'Aye.'

'I am too.' My fists tightened around my cup. As gladiators, I thought, we were supposed to accept the risk that we might one day die on the sand. We were supposed to spit in the eye of death, and to take the iron proudly when defeated. It was not right, not fair, that one in two of us should bleed out, should travel to the underworld, over the course of just one munus – and all because a spoiled cocksucker in a purple-edged toga commanded it be so.

'Caligula,' I muttered. 'What I would give to have him here now.'

'We would tear him limb from limb,' said Big Dog, as if he could think of nothing more pleasurable in life.

'And make him eat one of the bloody stumps,' said Atticus.

We drank to that.

PART XXVI

S weetmeats and pastries came out, but few had any interest. One of the guards, a paunchy type with bad teeth, ate half a platter on his own. I hoped he choked on them.

As if a silent summons had gone out to the crowds watching us at our meal, people began drifting towards the tables. Most were women, a mixture of all sorts, ordinary woman in plain stolas, matrons dripping with jewellery, girls barely old enough to marry. Not all were here to lie with a gladiator – I knew this from my first cena libera – most just wanted to get close to we dangerous beasts, we condemned men.

Gladiators were outcasts from society, Crixus had thundered on my introduction to the ludus. Each of us was infamis, a man without worth or dignity. But the citizenry are fascinated by us, he had gone on. 'They love and fear you in equal measure. Make the most of it!'

Although the majority of the spectators made for the reclining couches and the central table, there were so many that we too received our share of visitors. Big Dog was being asked questions by a generously bosomed woman with long black hair. Atticus and I exchanged a smile. If anything came of this, I whispered in his ear, we would never let Big Dog hear the end of it. And if any of us survived, added a spiteful voice in my head.

'What is your name?'

It took a moment to realise that the question was directed at me.

The woman who had asked it was short and slim with brown hair, and a pleasant face. She was old enough to be my grandmother. A younger woman, similar looking enough to be her daughter, was by her side.

'Ah, ah, Midir,' I stumbled.

'*Mi-deer?*' she said, mangling it.

I repeated my name, and this time, she almost got it right.

55

'I am from Hibernia,' I said.

'Where is that?' A loud cry from the central table made her head turn, and I saw that she had a small white scar on one side of her nose.

'It is an island, west of Britannia.'

'Everyone from there is supposed to be a savage, but you do not look like that.'

I smiled, thinking: and yet you are here. Nor did she have the look of someone would enjoy watching men bleed to death in the arena.

'You remind me of my son.'

I cast about, looking for a man who resembled her, but could see no one.

'You and he could have been twins.'

I bit back my question whether he was with her, and said gently, 'Could have.'

A spasm of grief twisted her face. 'He is gone. Plague, two years hence.'

Her daughter took her hand.

'I am sorry,' I said. 'What was his name?'

'Julius. He would have been forty this autumn. You are not that old.'

'Twenty-three.' Too young to die, I thought.

Her hazel eyes said the same thing to me.

PART XXVII

Not knowing what else to say, I asked, 'Are you enjoying the cena libera?'

'I would have stayed at home, but my husband insisted we come.' She waved a hand at the crowd surrounding the reclining couches. 'He is over there, trying to assess who will win the main bouts, if I know him. A lot of money is being wagered on the munus, and he intends to do well out of it.'

Rage welled up in inside me that men should gamble on our lives and deaths.

She saw it in my expression. 'I do not agree with that either. Nor does my daughter here. What the emperor is doing—' A sharp nudge from her daughter silenced her. She made a helpless gesture.

'It is good to know that not every Roman thirsts for the blood of innocent men,' I said dryly.

'Innocent?' said the daughter. 'You are criminals, most of you.'

'Is that what you think?' I shot back bitterly. 'In fact the majority of us are slaves, and no more than that. I was a free man in my own land until I was captured by raiders and sold. I ended up in the ludus having committed *no* crime, having wronged *no one*. And my reward? To die on the morrow for the amusement of Caligula.'

Even as shock filled their faces, Atticus, whose brief conversation with a crone seemed to have ended, gave me a sharp dig with his elbow. 'One of the guards is listening,' he hissed.

I shot a glance behind me, realising that, fuelled by my anger, my voice had grown louder. The guard was scowling, and seemed about to march over. 'Do not listen to me,' I declared to the women in a confident tone. 'I have had too much wine.' To my relief, the guard's suspicion eased; he stayed where he was. I turned back to the pair, and was pleased to find them still there. The interaction with them, even if unsettling in part, reminded me that there had once been a life outside the ludus. Sadly, it seemed to be ending.

'We must go,' said the woman. 'May Fortuna watch over you tomorrow.'

'I shall need her help,' I replied, nodding my thanks. As she walked away, I called out, 'What is your name?'

'Calpurnia,' came the reply.

'I shall look for you in the crowd.' That seemed to please her.

'We will cheer for you,' said the daughter unexpectedly.

'Gratitude.' I pulled a smile, thinking grimly: you will be the only two.

PART XXVIII

Crixus brought the dinner to an end not long after. Announcing to what remained of the crowd that his fighters needed to go to bed – that they, the audience, would have a much better show if the gladiators got enough rest – he gave oily thanks to the citizens of Capua for their attendance. While he did this, the guards paced up and down threateningly behind us, quietly repeating his command. I was glad to be leaving. So were most men. Our bellies were full, we had had enough wine, and our voices were hoarse from singing. Only the handful who had been coupling with Roman women were displeased, but Crixus' threat of a whipping soon saw them back into their clothes.

The convivial air which had hung over the gathering dissipated the instant we left the forum. Conversation died away, leaving our heavy tread the only sound. The cool night air, not noticed as we sat and talked and drank, brought up gooseflesh on my arms. As the amphitheatre loomed again out of the darkness, I was not alone in muttering a prayer. When a wild beast roared from somewhere deep inside its bowels, I almost jumped out of my skin.

'What in all the gods' names was that?' I asked Siccum, who happened to be beside me.

'Lion.'

'I have heard of them, but never seen one. Are they as big as men say?'

'A male can be three or four times the size of a large wolf. Their front teeth are this long.' Siccum held two fingers so far away from each other. 'The claws are the same. One lion can tear a man apart quicker than you can fry an egg. Two of them . . .'

I shuddered. Better to be a retiarius than a venator, a beast hunter, I decided, or a criminal designated to die in the circle of sand.

My black thoughts continued on the way to the ludus. It was a dark, eerie walk, dimly lit by a half moon, the only sounds those of feral cats yowling at one another. The streets were deserted, every window shuttered against the night. A couple of stray dogs nosed about in the waste left outside an eatery; I tried not to think about the bodies they might feast on after the munus tomorrow, one of which might be mine. Clouds of vultures hung over the town dump daily, making the location impossible to miss. Given the ugly, bald-headed birds' grisly vocation, I found it bizarre that the Romans regarded them as talismans of happiness.

After our contest, they would have full bellies for many days, I thought.

We trooped through the gate, its slam behind us yet another unpleasant reminder of our fate. Peace reigned in the courtyard; its sand was warm beneath my bare feet. The palus against which we trained stood alone, a sentinel watching over the ludus. Something took my gaze upward. Crixus was standing on the walkway watching, the old, patient spider on his web. A dull hate for him throbbed in my heart, but I gave no thought to a mad rush up the stairs. There was an archer by his side – even at this late hour, the bastard took no chances.

PART XXIX

The silence continued as we were locked into our cell. There were no lewd comments about Roman matrons, about who would snore loudest. Weary as if I had trained all day, I lay on my bunk; the others did the same. *Clang, clang,* went the other cell doors as they were pushed to. Dapyx farted. In normal circumstances, this would have brought down a barrage of abuse. Nothing. Big Dog shifted on his mattress above me, and the wooden slats creaked. It was a normal, comforting sound, one I was used to hearing, and to falling asleep to. Now it was disquieting. The pair of us were so close – perhaps a foot and a half the separation, no more. We were friends, but tomorrow we might have to try and kill one another.

No indication had been given about how the pairings for the individual fights would be made. Wary no doubt of stabbings in the toilets or throttling in cells, Crixus had delayed his announcement until the day itself. Were we to find out at our morning meal, I wondered, or would it be in the amphitheatre? I judged the latter.

I thought about killing Big Dog as he slept. Even I could manage that, I decided, as long as he didn't make enough noise to wake either of the others. Sharp-fanged guilt tore instantly at me for even giving birth to the idea. I had no basis for assuming that I would be pitted against him as opposed to another gladiator. Robbed of this, my fevered mind went in search of other possibilities. An even more brutal, shocking one soon came to me. I trembled to think it.

I soon decided it was utter madness. Even if I somehow managed to end the lives of *all three* of my cellmates, thereby removing them from the list of potential opponents, I would not escape a contest on the circle of sand. In revenge, Crixus would send me in to meet one of the Thracians, say, perhaps even both. He would want to see that I suffered in the most terrible ways possible before I was slain. In my head, I heard the lion's stomach-curdling roar again. It was even possible that he might ask imperial permission to have me thrown to the wild beasts rather than fight as a gladiator.

Despair swamped me; it washed over me in great waves.

The *only* way out was to end my own life before dawn came. I cursed myself for not having unwound the thong from a sword hilt after training. It would have been easily done, the leather to serve as a ligature. Wait long enough, until everyone had dropped off, I thought miserably, and I could have hung myself from the topmost cross bar on the cell door. With luck, no one would have heard until it was too late.

Inspiration struck. The laces on Roman sandals were incredibly long. If I tied mine and Big Dog's together, I would have enough length for a noose. The laces were not thick, but I did not weigh that much. To be sure, I decided, I would take Dapyx's laces as well. Doubled up, three sets of laces would do the job.

PART XXX

M ind made up – suicide tonight seemed worlds more preferable to being toyed with and slain before a screaming mob tomorrow – I settled myself down to wait until everyone was asleep.

Thoughts of home came, happier times. I remembered sitting by the fire after a successful boar hunt, my belly tight as a tick's. Wrestling and rough play with my friends; the beer we had shared after. Dancing around the bonfires of midsummer, kissing girls behind haystacks, and fishing in the rivers near our farm. My mother's smile when she saw me returning from a trading trip to the coast. The pride in my father's eyes when I had, unasked, chopped up a storm-downed oak tree, providing our family with enough firewood for an entire winter.

The tears came at last. I could no more hold them back than escape from my cell, but I palmed them away roughly. Snivelling and crying would get me nowhere. Grimly purposed, I listened. Dapyx was emitting little bubbling whistles: he was asleep. Piye's breathing was deep and regular. I stared at the wooden slats above me, wondering if Big Dog was still awake. He hadn't moved in some time, but he was not making any noise either. I decided to let more time go by. I would get only one chance. To be thwarted simply because I had not waited would be galling beyond belief.

An odd sound carried through the still night air.

I twisted on my mattress, trying to work out what in all the gods' names it was. I peered through the bars into the blackness. It seemed to be coming from a cell directly opposite ours. It was not a voice. I pricked my ears even harder. At last it came to me. Horrified, I realised that I was not the only one who had decided to commit suicide. Thirty paces away, a man was suffocating, like as not with a ligature around his neck as I had planned.

I almost got up and started making a racket, to wake the man's cellmates, or the guards – anybody who could stop him. I did not, however. This was his fate, I decided. It was not for me to intervene. And so I lay there and listened as the man choked, and rasped his way to oblivion. There was a little more noise when his heels drummed on the floor, but still no one in his cell stirred.

It was frightening how short a time it took for his struggling to end. It concluded with a last bubbling sound, one I could never forget, and the scrape of his feet along the ground. Silence descended, and I realised that I had been holding my breath. I sagged down on my mattress, exhausted and yet clear-minded. I imagined the poor wretch, purple-faced, tongue protruding, lying slumped in a pool of his own piss and shit.

That was not the end I wanted.

No, I decided, I would fight – to the bitter last.

Death in the arena was better than what I had just listened to.

PART XXXI

Despite the horrors of the night, and my racing mind, sleep took me in the end. If I dreamed, I did not remember them, which was a small mercy. I was woken as I had on so many 'normal' mornings by the rap of the doctor's staff on the bars. I lay there, eyes closed, as brutal reality sank in. Today was different to those that had gone before. Today, like as not, I would take my last journey – to the underworld.

My despair reignited, and threatened to take control.

I dragged together the remnants of the determination I had felt as I listened to the suicide, and told myself I would not meet my end easily. Where there was life, there was hope, my mother had always said. I rolled over and sat up, and licked some moisture onto my dry lips.

Piye was watching me. His teeth were very white in the blackness of his face as he grinned. 'Sleep well?'

I glared. 'No.'

'I sleep like . . . baby.'

A shout, and my gaze crossed the courtyard. A doctor was pointing, and demanding answers of the men in a cell opposite. Past him, hanging off the bars, I made out the slumped form of a body. Ask all the questions you like, I thought. Nobody will have heard or seen a thing.

Piye had not noticed, or did not care – or both. 'Today . . . the day,' he said conversationally.

'It is,' I muttered.

Dapyx jumped to the floor, and leaned in over Piye. 'Today . . . I kill you!'

Piye laughed. 'I kill you first, bastard.'

Dapyx snorted. 'We will see.' He glanced at me. 'Hungry?'

I could not believe my ears. Food was the last thing on my mind. 'No.'

'I . . . starving.'

I wanted to say he was crazy, but there was no point. All that mattered between me and Dapyx was that Crixus did not pit us against each other. The same with Piye. And Big Dog. And Sextus, and Siccum. And the Thracians. Stop it, I thought. What will be, will be. I was not without any hope. Dapyx was still not completely recovered from the wound he took, and Sextus' left hand was weak because of his missing finger. The Thracians were as stupid as they were big – insult them enough and they might drop their guard in some way.

'Did you hear him?' Big Dog had clambered down from his bunk. He jerked his chin at the corpse, which was being dragged out into the early morning sunshine. 'Last night.'

'Aye.'

'Me too. It sounded a bad way to go.'

'I was going to do the same thing.'

'What stopped you?'

'He did.' I flicked my eyes at the body.

The lanista, summoned from upstairs, had come down to look. He kicked it, a dull, meaty sound.

'Crixus is a cunt,' I said.

PART XXXII

A glance upward told me that the archers were not ready – neither had arrows on the string – which meant I could reach Crixus before either had a chance to loose. I was not sure if I could break his bull neck, however, so I decided to save my strength for later.

Big Dog continued to act his normal friendly self. Lost for a better approach, I did the same. Being antagonistic served no one. We greeted a wary Atticus as he emerged from his cell – he looked as if he had not had a wink of sleep – and invited him to join us at the breakfast table. As Big Dog said, I declared, a man had to line his stomach with something, even if it was only porridge. Atticus shrugged, and muttered something that might have been a yes. Sextus and Siccum ambled over too, and a short time later, when Dapyx and Piye sat down as well, we found ourselves sitting together as might have occurred on any other day.

Despite our solidarity, conversation was limited. Dapyx ate a whole bowl of honey-laced porridge; Piye did too. I managed a few spoonfuls; the others picked at theirs. Although Big Dog had talked of filling his belly, he did not finish his either.

Few men went up for seconds. The sense of expectation which had threatened could no longer be denied.

I think everyone was glad when Crixus hammered a sword on the railing to get our attention. All eyes swivelled up to the walkway.

'The first fights will not take place for some hours. As you know, the beast hunts and executions of criminals come first. Better it is, though, to be there nice and early. Oil your muscles, if that is what you like to do, and say your prayers. We leave soon.'

I almost brought up my porridge.

They chained us for the journey, no surprise. Every guard in the ludus was also to accompany us. As we passed through the front archway, I did not look back. Good riddance, I thought, and yet despite my loathing of the four-walled prison, I wanted to return to it later, because that meant I would be alive, not a hooked corpse dragged out of the Gate of Death as the audience cheered.

It was more than half a mile to the amphitheatre, and hours still before the spectacle began, but a goodly number of Capua's citizens had come to see us pass. A desultory cheer went up as Crixus saluted the crowd. I heard wolf-whistles, and the piping voices of small boys calling out the gladiators they recognised. Enterprising betmakers touted for business; I heard Dapyx's name, and some of the other favourites. No one mentioned me, for which I was glad. Fifty-to-one, or worse, the odds would have been. Evidence that I was doomed.

PART XXXIII

Soon we had left the people behind, apart from a few bolder urchins who ran alongside, waving toy wooden swords, and telling us that we would all die. That palled swiftly; it was inaccurate, but no one needed reminding about the poor chances of survival. Siccum told them to piss off, which only encouraged the little sewer rats. 'I heard the emperor is going to have anyone who displeases him crucified in the arena,' crowed one, the ringleader, a strapping lad of about thirteen. His pals hooted with amusement, and two of them stuck their arms out at right angles from the shoulder, mimicking the posture of a man nailed to the cross. 'Ahhhh,' they cried in a hideous chorus. I turned my face away.

Big Dog nudged me. 'Look!'

I turned back to see the ringleader sprawling in the dirt. One of the Thracians had caught him with a half-decent kick as he passed.

The urchins shouted in protest, but the guards did not intervene. We laughed. It felt like some kind of justice, and now we were left to walk in peace.

The sunshine was pleasant, although looking at the clear sky, I decided that would soon change. Inside the high walls of the amphi-theatre, the sands would already be growing hot. By the time we fought, they would be burning to the touch. The soles of our feet were like leather, but if a man fell down, by the gods it would hurt.

The ground close to the arena was already thronged. Stallholders were hawking food – sausages, bread, pastries, cheese, fried fish – and drink – fruit juices, wine from every part of the empire. There were flute players and jugglers, acrobats and soothsayers. A couple of cynical-faced whores were half-heartedly offering tricks in a nearby alley, and the betmakers were present in force.

'There he is!' cried one.

I paid no heed. I could see the gate through which we would enter. Once it clanged behind us, we had a stone staircase to negotiate. Under the building, the two levels of cells were arrayed in circles, following the layout of the seating above. Gladiators were locked into the lowest level, because it was easier to make us walk up to the circle of sand than animals.

'The new retiarius – see him? The scrawny one there, near the back. A hundred-to-one I will give on him! Any takers?'

To my horror, I realised the betmaker was talking about me.

Siccum, who was just in front, turned and winked. 'I might put some coin on you.'

'Put a few denarii on for me as well. I will pay you out of my winnings.' Despite my best effort, my retort sounded weak.

Siccum did not mock, however. 'Good enough,' he said. He was as good as his word, calling over a betmaker, and laying down thirty denarii on account. 'Five for you, Midir,' he said.

'Gratitude,' I replied, wondering how much five hundred Roman silver coins – my winnings, should I survive – was worth.

PART XXXIV

Never having coin in the ludus, or the need to buy anything even if I had some, I still knew little about the cost of life in Italia. Spotting more prostitutes, these ones lurking under the arches of the amphitheatre, I thought, I know how much they cost. Women like them were frequent visitors to the gladiator school; although I had not sampled their wares, the prices they charged were common knowledge. Five hundred denarii would see me rut myself to death, if I wanted.

When I said as much to Big Dog, he laughed and told me that if my cock hadn't fallen off by the time I had spent it, the pox would have got me. 'It sends you mad in the end, that disease,' he said. 'A surgeon told me once.'

'Dying from too much screwing?' said Sextus. 'Sounds all right to me.'

'Aye.' Siccum snorted with laughter. 'Better than receiving iron, that is for certain.'

A general rumble of agreement followed, and I took comfort that even these strong fighters, the ones of the first grade as they were known, were scared.

Closer to the gladiators' entrance we came. Advertisements announcing the contest had been painted on either side. I could not read the cursive Latin, but Atticus was literate. The munus was in honour of our beloved emperor Gaius Julius Caesar Augustus Germanicus, he declared. 'No mention of Caligula?' demanded Sextus. Thirty-five pairs of gladiators, Atticus continued. We jeered. Awnings would be provided.

'And taken away again when it's hottest,' cried Siccum. This was Caligula's habit, apparently.

Rosewater would also be used, Atticus muttered. None of us liked that. It was sprayed liberally in amphitheatres to conceal the rank odour of shit and piss, and was not that effective. Today, also, the rosewater would be needed because of our blood.

A crowd of diehards stood around the entrance, ordinary citizens with calloused hands and work-stained tunics. Scattered between them were a few better-off men, marked by a gold finger ring here or a manicured hair cut there. A lone togatus, one of the nobility, stood a little apart, studying a piece of parchment. How it had ever come about that the high and mighty of Rome should wear a massively thick woollen garment in summer weather, I had no idea. It looked ridiculous.

'The togatus has the list, the libellus munerarius,' said Atticus suddenly.

His words caught everyone's attention. We still had no idea who would fight who, but the toga-clad nose-in-the-air type did. I wanted to march over and rip it from his hands. Big Dog muttered something about doing just that himself. Sextus even took a step towards the toff, but one of the guards shoved him back into line.

In we filed. A single oil light guttered every twenty paces along the passageway; in between, a dank gloom reigned. Down the stairs we went, men cursing as they stubbed toes, or smacked foreheads on the low stonework. I could smell animals, and their ordure, could hear movement, growls and angry bellows. Despite my fear about what would happen to me, I was glad not to be one of the noxii, the criminals destined to be torn limb from limb by the caged beasts nearby.

PART XXXV

There was more light at the foot of the stairs, and space. A wide passageway ran off to either side, curving out of sight as it followed the amphitheatre's circular shape. There were cells here, all around the back wall, and their doors gaped open, like the entrances to so many tombs.

'Four at a time. In you go!' ordered a leering worker.

Habit made me, Big Dog, Dapyx and Piye enter the same cell. Clang went the gate; the key turned in the lock. With a final leer, the worker moved on. The square space was a dozen paces wide by ten deep. It was comfortless: no bunks, or seats of any description. We could stand, or sit on the stone floor. I paced to and fro. Graffiti marked the plaster here and there, tiny stick figures with swords and helmets, and names and numbers scratched below. How many of the men who had left these mementoes were still alive? I wondered. Not many. Perhaps two or three in every ten fighters lived long enough to win the rudis, the wooden sword that symbolised freedom. I turned away from the etchings, thinking that they were lucky bastards. Half of the men in the cells around me would see the sun set.

Cries and shouts broke out above us. Something was happening in the arena. Eager not to dwell on my own fate, I moved to the bars, and tried to peer along the passageway. All I could see was brickwork, but I could discern the voices of workers, and perhaps our guards. One came strolling along a moment later, swinging his club. He was friendlier than the rest, so I called out, 'What is going on?'

'Beast hunt,' he said. 'Nothing interesting. Deer and a couple of venatores.'

There was little applause for the spectacle, which did not last long. As the guard commented acidly, there was probably a bigger, more enthusiastic crowd waiting outside the Gate of Death, hoping that a deer carcass might be thrown out. Free meat was of more interest to the poorest than second-rate entertainment.

More beast hunts followed. Informed by the amphitheatre staff, the guard relayed to us their content. Two bears, hidden in an artificial forest, and one man, a criminal, set to hunt them both. Loud cheering signalled his death. A pack of wolves, not fed for days, and three venatores with spears. There was much applause as each died, less as they killed wolves. Strange, long-necked and long-legged birds from Africa, the size of men and bigger, were hunted down one by one. Another act involved a bull and a bear, chained together, and a criminal wearing almost nothing, who was sent in with a hooked stick, his task to separate them. It sounded insane, and unbelievably cruel.

I could not keep silent. 'What happens if he refuses to try?'

A withering look from the guard. 'The archers will shoot him.'

Of course, I thought. Stationed around the perimeter of the sand, their task to protect the audience from animals that might leap out of the arena, the bowmen also acted as lethal encouragement to those who did not play their part.

I did not need to ask what would happen to the unarmed criminal if he succeeded in freeing the bull from the bear.

PART XXXVI

Time dragged past. The temperature climbed; it was still pleasant on our level, but in the circle of sand it would be burning hot. Our misfortune was added to by the emperor's whim that we should fight at the height of summer, not a usual time of the year for a munus.

The most exotic animals were saved until the last, much as the best gladiator contests came towards the day's end. Compared to Rome, Capua's stock of animals tended to the mundane. The guard, who seemed to enjoy talking down to me – the ignorant savage who knew so little about munera – reported that ten lions, a brace of elephants, and other outlandish creatures had been especially transported from Rome. One went by the name of a Hyrcanian tiger. Seeing my confusion – Big Dog and the others didn't know what it was either – the guard waxed lyrical.

'Went to take a look at it, I did. It's a monster – twice as large as the biggest lion you have ever seen. From nose to tail it must be as long as two men lying head to toe.'

My stomach roiled, and for once, I was glad to be behind bars.

'Orange it is all over, save its underside, and striped in black. Big teeth the length of your middle finger, claws even longer than that.' The guard shivered with fear and not a little delight. 'Never seen the like, I haven't.'

'It will tear men apart, surely,' I said.

'Oh aye, and the emperor will be in raptures. To make the contest a little less one-sided, the tiger is to be chained by the back legs.' The guard chuckled. 'That's not to say it won't still reap a fine harvest.'

It was revolting even to think of, but a tiny bit of me would have watched the display, had I been allowed.

'With all that talking, you must be thirsty,' said Big Dog.

The guard cast him a suspicious look.

Silver glinted in Big Dog's hand. 'There's enough here for three jugs of wine. Two for you and your mates, one for us. What do you say?'

'I could come in and take it all,' said the guard, fingers tightening on his club.

'Aye, you could. You would probably beat the shit out of us too, but my offer is easier, no?' said Big Dog mildly.

Of course the truth of it was that we could easily overpower one guard, club or no. Big Dog was giving him an easy way out.

The guard nodded, and stuck a hand through the bars.

Clink went the coins.

The guard vanished along the passageway, returning a short while later gripping three jugs in his fists. He called to his friends, who stood ready in case we tried anything as he opened the gate and handed over the wine.

'Gratitude,' said Big Dog.

The wine was watered down as the Romans liked it, and not the best quality either – he had probably spent more on his two jugs, I decided, and less on ours – but it went down smooth as a drink from the gods themselves. We shared it equally, smacking our lips and making loud noises of appreciation.

PART XXXVII

'Another jug would be good,' said Big Dog, 'but I want a clear head to fight.'

I felt the same way, and for once, Dapyx agreed. Piye did not say anything, but he had never drunk much anyway.

A fierce bugling told us that the elephants had been sent into the arena. They too were chained, the guard said, being so big. I would not have wanted to be one of the wretches facing them just the same. From the shouts of delight, cries of shock, and trumpeting by the elephants, I judged a great deal of blood to have been shed and horrific injuries caused ere the end.

The killing of the elephants was the final beast hunt. Peace fell for a time, and I imagined mules hauling the immense carcasses out of the arena, and the bloody drag marks they would leave in the glinting mica-rich sand. Crixus had told us how it had been shipped in just for the emperor, just like the Hyrcanian tiger. No expense spared, boys, he had crowed. It did not quite make sense to me. Dapyx, Piye, and the Thracians were tough men and good fighters, but they were not in the same class as gladiators from the ludi in Rome. I said as much to the others, but they just looked at me as if I had gone sun-mad, so I gave up.

Laughter broke out, hoots and jeers, and catcalls. I thought I heard the distant *clack, clack* of wood against wood, and I glanced at Big Dog. 'Paegniarii – is that what you call them – clowns?'

'That's right. Could be one or more, dressed in tight-fitting costumes, and armed with wooden swords and whips; they will be up against dwarfs or the like.'

I could scarcely believe my ears. The Romans' appetite for weird savagery seemed to have no limits. My opinion was reinforced soon by the guard's revelation. Even he was shocked. The paegniarius in the arena was not fighting dwarfs, but respectable citizens selected by the emperor's officials because of their physical infirmity. A humpback, a man with a crookedly healed leg, another who was missing an arm, a leper missing all his fingers and half his face. From the deafening noise, the audience seemed to love it.

'Caligula is a sick bastard,' I said quietly to Big Dog.

'Aye. Seems his reputation is true.'

'It makes me think again,' I said, 'that just having us fight in pairs to the death will not be all that happens out there.'

This time, he paid me more attention. 'What do you mean?'

'I'm not sure, but I have a nasty feeling in my belly.'

Hearing my last words, Dapyx said, 'Why, little man? Because . . . you die . . . soon?'

'That's right,' I said, telling him in my head to go and hump his mother.

Trumpet blasts, loud and long, brought the conversation to an end. More cheering. More fanfares. The stamping of thousands of feet.

'The emperor must be here,' I said to the cell in general.

'Aren't you the clever one?' sneered the guard. He went off to look, nonetheless.

PART XXXVIII

I was right. The din was for Caligula, and a short time later, we were allowed to leave our cells for the pompa, the procession around the arena that marked the beginning of every munus. Along the corridor we went, towards the narrow staircase that led up to ground level. A wait followed as those who began the pompa emerged from the Gate of Life and began walking around the edge of the sand. There would be lictores first, Atticus told me, officials who symbolised the emperor's position and power.

I knew who came next, thanks to my first munus. Trumpeters, blasting the air for all they were worth, and then slaves bearing the ferculum, a platform laden with images of the gods being honoured today. According to our friendly guard, those were Caligula himself, and Jupiter Optimus Maximus, Greatest and Best. Behind the ferculum came slaves carrying biers upon which were displayed our weapons and armour.

Those at the front of the file began to ascend the stairs, which told us that the procession was moving smoothly. I could picture it. After the weapons came the prizes that Caligula would bestow on the winners, and perhaps on fighters he liked.

Next were more musicians, and then the gladiators.

Big Dog, who was in front of me, entered the narrow doorway and put his foot on the first step. I was behind him. We climbed, slowly. Stone enclosed us, amplifying the cheering and applause that carried down from above. The crescendo was deafening. Terrifying.

Up we went, past the doorway that marked the entrance to the beasts' level, and on. The noise grew even louder, a wall of sound that drowned out everything else. My stomach had tied itself in knots. I was not alone. A moment later the acrid smell of vomit hit me. Then I stood in it, barefooted. Revulsed, I could do nothing but keep following Big Dog.

I reached ground level and entered the arched passageway that led into the arena: the Gate of Life. I gave no heed to the massive locked doors behind us, which gave onto the area outside the amphitheatre. No escape was possible there. It had been a mistake to think the arena would not be hot, I thought, as a great blast of heat hit me. The circle in which we would fight was now a furnace. The light was blinding too, the sun's rays reflecting off the white sand into our poor, gloom-adjusted eyes.

'Don't just stand there – move!' Guards with spears prodded at us, and we walked forward, following those in front.

I could smell blood and shit and rosewater, all mixed, the true smells of the arena. My feet touched the sand, and I forgot about the vomit between my toes. Hard though my soles were, they could not hold out the heat for long. Soon, I thought, we would each be shifting about, and then capering like drunks at a religious festival. I said it to Big Dog as we turned left, and he replied that if I was correct about things being odd, perhaps holding the munus at midsummer was also part of Caligula's twisted purpose.

PART XXXIX

The trumpets' blare continued, and the audience's appreciation of the pompa showed no sign of abating either. I glanced at the first levels of seating, only a few feet above my head. A sea of men's faces was watching us. These were the richest of Capuan citizens, the ones with the power and influence in the city. That did not stop their fingers from pointing, or comments being made in their neighbours' ears, or encouragements and insults shouted at us. Thanks to the noise, I could not make out what was being said, which I deemed a good thing. I had caught a couple of men staring at me and sneering. Briefly, I lifted my gaze to the levels above, all the way up to the top of the amphi-theatre, where the poor and the women stood underneath the awnings. I thought of Calpurnia and her daughter, and wondered if they were in the audience, and if they would cheer for me as promised.

The tiniest of lulls in the crescendo of sound allowed the shouted words 'new retiarius' and a mocking laugh to reach my ears. Hunching my shoulders and staring at my poor, burning feet, I put Calpurnia from my mind. Whether she was here and what she shouted for would make no difference to my fate.

Around the circle of the arena we paced. The spectators cheered themselves hoarse, the trumpets sang. The front of the procession had almost reached the Gate of Life, but we still had a long way to go. Not wanting to look at the bloodthirsty faces on my left, I glanced occasionally across the blinding expanse of the sand. Something drew my attention. I squinted, trying to focus through the glare. Then, being sure, I nudged Siccum, who had been walking beside me for a time.

'See over there.' I jerked my head to the right. 'The men behind the prizes.'

'Eh?' He sounded hot and irritated. He did not look.

'The fighters behind the slaves with the prizes. They're wearing cloaks. None of our lot have cloaks.'

He raised a hand to his eyes against the glare. Peered. Cursed. 'Who are they?'

'They are not from our ludus, that is certain,' I said, thinking, there *is* trickery afoot, and Caligula is at the bottom of it.

'Maybe they are to put on extra bouts,' said Siccum, but he did not sound certain.

'Aye, or maybe they are fighters of the first class, brought from Rome to show Capua what real gladiators are like.'

Siccum sucked on the marrow of that; it did not look as if he enjoyed the taste. He twisted around and told Sextus. I did the same with Big Dog; he informed Atticus. Each of them looked; none seemed happy. Like me, however, they were helpless to do anything but rage inside, and worry about the strange fighters' role.

We drew nearer to the pulvinar, the imperial box, where numerous guards stood on the brickwork lip of the arena, or just inside it, spears and bows at the ready. A little further on, Caligula and his cronies lounged on couches. I could not stop myself from staring; everyone was the same. My eyes roved the box, studying the reclining figures, behind each of whom stood slaves holding umbrellas and massive fans. The one nearest the lip of the arena had to be Caligula, I thought, the man wearing a magnificent toga bordered with purple. He seemed tall, and had very pale skin. With deep-set hollow eyes and a broad forehead, he was balding, which made his hairy arms look all the odder.

'Ugly bastard, eh?' I muttered to Big Dog.

'Aye. Don't stare, though!'

PART XL

'He hates being looked at, especially from above,' Atticus revealed. 'Anyone caught doing it is executed.'

'The same if you mention a goat in his presence,' said Siccum, chuckling. 'Stupid whoreson.'

How bizarre it was, I thought, that our fates and those of innumerable people all over the empire rested in the hands of a balding, ugly man with a horror of being looked on from above and an aversion to goats. Better proof of the gods' fickleness I could not imagine.

I kept my gaze fixed on the mica-glinting sand as we passed the pulvinar. Thankfully, no shout came from Caligula to stop the pompa and haul me or one of my comrades out for some public degradation. The rest of the procession passed without event. Groans of relief went up as we filed back through the Gate of Life. Some lay down at once on the cool stone floor. Others grabbed water skins from the arena workers, and drank and drank. Wary of having an overfull belly for my fight, I supped only a few mouthfuls.

We watched the summa rudis, the referee, testing the weapons that would be used for sharpness. Although I knew just what a sharp edge could do to flesh, it was sobering to see the ease with which the blades cut the lengths of fabric held out at arm's length by the referee's second-in-command, the seconda rudis. Our respite was not that long; summoned back out onto the sand then by the trumpets, we loosened our muscles and practised our moves – or some of them, at least – on each other. Our weapons were wooden still – even now we were not to be trusted. Knowing there would be no blood, thirsty from sitting in the heat, few of the audience paid us any heed. They sought shade in the cool of the passageways under the seats, gossiped with their neighbours, or sought out the drink-sellers and betmakers.

I was glad when the session was over. I had held my own against

Atticus, but been soundly beaten by Dapyx, twice. I had a fat lip, still swelling with blood, and my head yet rang from the *thwack* he had given it at the end, after the summa rudis had shouted at him to stop. Bastard, I had mouthed at him. Dapyx had laughed.

Crixus was waiting for us under the archway; he had the list of contests in his hand. Not a word would he say about it, however, until we filed downstairs to the cells. Lagging behind, in a foul mood, I got there when most of the fighters had already been locked up. Our weapons – the real, sharp ones – were being neatly laid out on the stone floor by arena staff, ready to be picked up by each pair of men as they were released for their bout. I glanced at them and at the guards, deciding that I *could* reach one and kill Crixus before they reacted. I would die, of course. Was it a price worth paying?

Even as I tossed the mad notion to and fro, Crixus cleared his throat, and prepared to read out the list. Instantly nervous, I was also surprised. As I have said, not all of us were behind bars. The lanista had either decided that those yet free were not dangerous – one only had to look at Big Dog to know that that was untrue – or the arrogant arse could no longer contain himself. I decided the latter to be more likely. Grateful that the guard at our backs had stopped to beg a drink of wine from a comrade, I slowed my pace to that of a snail. I kept my eyes on the sharp weapons, wondering if I should die now, taking Crixus with me, or die in the arena, as the crowd laughed at my inexperience and lack of skill.

The lanista spoke, loud and clear. 'The first fight will be between Dapyx and Piye.'

PART XLI

B are feet pounded the cell floors. There were cries of 'Dapyx!' and 'Piye!' I saw that the pair had been separated, which would have given them an inkling of what was to happen before Crixus' announcement. Two of the best fighters in the ludus would begin the entertainment. It was a solid choice, guaranteed to please the audience, and with luck, Caligula. I silently thanked my gods; Dapyx and Piye were at the top of the list of men I did not want to face.

'The second contest will pit the Thracian –' Crixus mangled the unpronounceable name – 'against Atticus.'

I felt a mixture of relief that I would not have to fight the Thracian, another unbeatable opponent, and sympathy for Atticus, still only a tiro like me.

Sudden movement. A figure, breaking from the open gate to a cell, running at full tilt towards the weapons.

'It's Atticus!' hissed Big Dog.

I stared, riveted by the insanity of Atticus' actions. I willed him on, however. Let out a little cry of delight when he snatched up a gladius, and groaned when the proximity of a guard prevented him from picking up a shield. I joined in the huge cheer that went up as he charged at Crixus.

The distance he had to cover was too far. The lanista, with an agility belying his girth and advancing years, retreated behind a couple of guards. In a voice taut with fear, he screeched that they should kill Atticus.

Spears lunged. Incredibly, Atticus dodged them both, and stooping low, slashed open the leg of a guard. He went down screaming. Blood gushed from the awful wound: an artery had been cut. Atticus went on the offensive once more, managing to get inside the second guard's reach again. He hammered a blow onto the rim of the man's shield, but the guard braced himself and cleverly shoved Atticus backwards with it. Atticus shouted something incoherent, and pointed his sword at Crixus. The lanista's face was a picture, a mixture of disbelief and unadulterated fear. It was a beautiful thing to see.

'A-tti-cus!' I roared, deeply moved. 'A-tti-cus!'

I think every gladiator took up my cry.

'A-TTI-CUS!' we shouted. 'IUGULA! *KILL HIM!*'

Sad to say, he did not. Guards now came swarming in from every angle. Atticus twisted and turned, but he could not avoid the hungry spears seeking a home in his flesh. Pierced through in four or five places, roaring with pain, he strained and bucked to no avail. Somehow his sword still waved at Crixus.

'Kill him!' the lanista ordered.

Another guard rammed his spear so hard into Atticus' mouth that the tip burst free, spraying crimson from the back of his neck.

PART XLII

'They are all distracted. We could grab a weapon and shield each,' I said to Big Dog. I was talking horseshit, and I knew it.

'You go. I will take my chances in the arena,' he said. Meek as a lamb, he stepped into the nearest empty cell.

Raging that he would not help, and aware that he was right not to do so, I stormed in after him. We did not speak, nor even look at each other.

It took a short while before order had been restored, every fighter locked up, and for Crixus to regain his composure. Standing over Atticus' bloodied corpse, he kicked it a few times, grunting with satisfaction.

I stared out from between the bars, hating the lanista with every fibre of my being, and hating myself more for not joining Atticus, even though I too would have been lying there, a target for his military-style hobnailed sandals.

'This piece of shit –' Crixus kicked Atticus again – 'elected to go to Hades early, which means his place will be taken by . . .'

I closed my eyes. Not me, please, I prayed.

Crixus dragged out the silence for a few more heartbeats.

'Tell us, and have done, you cocksucker!' shouted a voice.

The comment freed our voices the way a pebble can start a rockslide. We rained down abuse on Crixus, our curses and profanities acting as the weapons we did not have. The weapons which lay so tantalisingly close, and yet so impossibly far away.

Irate yet impotent, he could only order the guards to jab their spears through the bars of our cells, which made us shout louder.

The confrontation was brought to an end by the arrival of an arena official, who glanced, shocked, at Atticus' body and then spoke with Crixus. From the pointing and gesticulating, and the fawning manner of the lanista in return, I judged him to be on the receiving end of a dressing down. The first bout was due to begin at any moment, and instead of finding two fighters ready to climb up to the arena level, the official had walked into a charnel house where an almost-riot was going on.

I caught one sentence, and exulted: 'If Caligula gets wind of this, it will be you out there on the sand!'

Crixus' placating seemed to work in the end. The official jabbed a forefinger at him, snarled something, and departed whence he had come. The lanista rolled up the libellus munerarius, and ordered the door to the cell containing Dapyx and Piye opened. 'Out!' he cried.

The pair sauntered out, bold as fighting cocks, ignoring the guards' levelled spears. Their courage made my heart sing. Crixus barked that they were to prepare with all haste. The emperor was waiting, he said. Dapyx spat on the floor, and Piye laughed. The circle of spears closed in, and they looked at each other, as if wondering whether to choose Atticus' end. The power of their invisible connection was incredible – goose skin formed on my arms – and tangible even to the guards, who did not move any nearer.

PART XLIII

Then Dapyx laughed and, bending, picked up a magnificent helmet with a white feather standing proud on either side of a griffon crest. 'This . . . mine,' he said.

Piye nodded, and selected a bronze helm. Its box crest, broad brim and grillwork eye-pieces were distinctive to a murmillo.

We all watched intently as they got ready. Each helped the other to secure his manica, the protection for the right arm. The thickly padded linen was held in place by leather thongs and a strap that ran across to the opposite armpit. Dapyx had similar coverings on both his legs, right up to the groin, and over these, greaves that reached to mid-thigh, but Piye had wrappings on his left leg only, up to the knee, and one smaller greave.

They were each handed a shield: for Piye, a large scutum, very similar to a legionary's, and for Dapyx a small rectangular one, the parma. Finally, the pair were allowed to arm themselves. Piye had a gladius, Dapyx a short, curved sica, such as his people used. I saw another look pass between the pair, as if they were considering an attack on Crixus, even though eight guards had spears aimed at them.

'Up!' shouted the lanista. 'Up! Caligula is waiting!'

Dapyx spat again, but the moment was gone. With guards walking in front, he swaggered to the doorway and the staircase beyond, and Piye followed. More guards took up the rear, with Crixus, wary to the last, at the very back.

We cheered our comrades until long after they had vanished from sight.

An uneasy silence fell as reality sank in again. We were not all friends to Dapyx and Piye, but one of the twain would die in the contest that followed, even if he fought well. In his haste, Crixus had not announced the Thracian's opponent, or any of the bouts that would come after. Those of us who were not fighters of the first class – men like me – still had no idea who we would face. And then there were the strange gladiators I had seen, rumour of which was spreading from cell to cell.

All our fates hung in the balance, I thought, twisting gently while the Fates' shears hovered nearby.

Silence fell in the amphitheatre. All conversation ceased. The wail of double reed-pipes carried down the staircase, and I shivered. The musicians playing these announced each combat. Dapyx and Piye were about to walk out of the Gate of Life.

Cheering and roaring broke out above.

'In they go,' said Big Dog, looking at the ceiling, wishing no doubt as I was, that he could see what was happening.

From this point, the noise made by the audience came in waves. Whistles and shouts, cries and applause were interspersed with short silences. Now and again, the noise of metal on metal reached us as sword met sword, or iron shield rim. Try as I might, it was impossible to judge how the fight was proceeding, or have any idea who was winning. The guard who had relayed information to us about the Hyrcanian tiger and the elephants had gone upstairs with the rest. For the moment, we were alone in the bowels of the building. I rattled the gate speculatively, but it was locked fast.

Hating the not-knowing whether Dapyx or Piye would die, but more important, who would be my opponent, I gave in again to despair. Knowing my luck, I thought, it would be me against the Thracian next. Sliding down the cell wall, I parked my arse on the floor and stuck my legs out in front of me. I shut my eyes, and tried in vain to rest.

Cries of shock, repeated all around the amphitheatre.

My eyes jerked open.

PART XLIV

'Something unexpected has happened.' Siccum's voice came from the cell beside me.

The air filled with noise as opinions were bandied about. Dapyx had overreached and caused his newly healed injury to flare up. Piye had been too slow to retreat from an attack, and taken a bad cut. Caligula, unhappy with the contest, had ordered the fight stopped and both men executed.

Cheering made us all look up again, wondering.

Then, the unmistakeable, 'Iugula! Iugula!' Louder and louder the chant rose, until the very stones of the amphitheatre seemed to resound with it. If anyone was shouting, 'Mitte! Let him go!' I thought grimly, they were in a tiny minority.

My eyes went to Big Dog. 'Dapyx?' I mouthed. 'Piye?'

He shrugged.

Another mighty roar, even louder than the ones before. 'Habet!'

Who had 'got it'? I wondered. I hoped it was not Piye. In the unlikely event that I survived, he would be a better cellmate than the wildly unpredictable Dapyx.

Loud speculation continued, with no majority for either fighter, until Crixus came clattering down the stairs in a rush. We fell silent, and I noted the thunderous expression on his face. Six guards were with the lanista, two having been left behind, I judged, to watch over the winner of the contest.

Our attention transferred to him. Questions rained down. 'Who is winning?' 'Who's hurt?' 'Is the emperor angry?'

Crixus, impatient, ignored us and directed the Thracian with the unpronounceable name to be released. My stomach did a neat, vomit-making roll as he came pacing along the row of cells for the second fighter. As he drew alongside me, my courage failed me, and I looked away. To my amazement, his sandaled feet walked past, stopping out-side Siccum's cell. He ordered out a German who fought as a murmillo, a pigtailed beast of a man who liked fighting, whoring and beer.

'He's going for another crowd-pleaser,' I said to Big Dog.

The Thracian and German, having eyeballed each other, began to dress and arm themselves. Satisfied that they were not going to act like Atticus, Crixus asked us if we wanted to know who had emerged victorious in the contest between Dapyx and Piye. We shouted and stamped our feet, and rattled the bars of our cells in response.

Cheering from above – I assumed it was the crowd, acknowledging whoever the winner had been.

'Piye almost won,' Crixus revealed. 'He knew that Dapyx's wound was his weak spot, so he shoulder-charged him a few times, and man-aged to wind him. After that it should only have been a matter of time. Piye got cocky, however, and stopped concentrating. He let Dapyx back into the fight. Realising that he had to end it or risk losing himself, he attacked again, fast and furious. Dapyx was waiting. He reached up and over as Piye got close, and snick, cut the muscle between Piye's left shoulder and his neck.'

Exclamations of surprise went up, and Crixus continued, 'Now Piye could not hold up his shield, and Dapyx was on him like a starving wolf bringing down a deer.'

PART XLV

Shouts and jeers carried down the staircase, even booing. I cocked my head, confused, but I seemed to be alone in noticing. Crixus had everyone else in the palm of his hand.

'Piye fell to the sand a long way from the pulvinar, however,' the lanista continued. 'Caligula was not going to be able to see the death blow, so he ordered Dapyx to march Piye closer. Dapyx pretended not to understand the message he was given by the summa rudis, and killed Piye where he was. The crowd, oblivious to the emperor's command, loved it, but Caligula was not happy.'

He fell silent as shocked, excited yells and cries carried down from the arena.

After a short delay, to everyone's surprise, we heard, 'Habet! Hoc habet!'

I had never seen Crixus so shocked, or dismayed.

Siccum had an idea. 'That crazy bastard Dapyx got summoned to stand before the pulvinar, I wager, and he didn't like what he saw. Fifty denarii says he spat at Caligula, or made an obscene gesture at him.'

He got no takers, for we were all thinking similar thoughts.

There was a delay before we found out the exact details, for Crixus and the guards had escorted the Thracian and the German upstairs. Then a couple of arena staff appeared, sent down to count how many of us were left. They were only too happy to relate the tale. Dapyx *was* also dead. Stamping over to the imperial box from Piye's corpse with the summa rudis, he had refused to kneel before Caligula. The emperor, furious, ordered the nearby archers to level their bows at him. Again Dapyx refused to obey. To the astonishment of all, he had undone the waistband of his undergarment, and whipping around, bared his arse. A volley of arrows had followed.

Despite the grim ending, I swear the laughter that followed this revelation carried up to the audience.

'Dapyx was lucky that Little Boots lost his temper,' said Siccum as the clamour died down. 'If the emperor had kept calm, he would have been tortured for days.'

Reed-pipes wailed again. Silence fell above us, and in the cells as well, as the Thracian and the German entered the arena. Again we listened to the cries and shouts, the yells and jeers, and tried to predict what was happening. In the midst of the fight, Crixus' senior guard, a lantern-jawed man with a jaundiced view of life, appeared in his master's stead to fetch the next pair of fighters. Five of his comrades were with him. There were to be no more Atticus-like disasters.

He opened my cell door. My stomach heaved. Let it be Big Dog he chooses, I prayed.

'You. Hibernian. Out,' he said.

I cast a look at Big Dog. He said nothing. Nor did I. Out I walked, with dragging feet, stopping only when a guard's spear tip brushed against my chest. It pricked me, but I did not care. I turned, that I might see who my opponent would be.

'Sextus,' said the guard, turning the key in the lock of a cell two down from mine. 'You're on next as well.'

PART XLVI

From the depths of Stygian darkness, a ray of hope. Sextus was a far better fighter than I, but I had 'wounded' him in a training session; I had also noted the weakness in his left hand. Perhaps, just perhaps, I could beat him. Certainly, I had a better chance than against any of the other first-ranked gladiators from our ludus. Rather than despair, as I had for most of the day, I resolved to make the most of it. I would act with confidence, as best I could.

Sextus was a decent man. 'This was not what I wanted, Midir,' he said as we prepared.

'Nor I,' I replied, half lying and half telling the truth. I ran my thumb across the blade of a plain, wood-handled dagger, and wondered if I could cut his throat with it. I decided that I could. If I was victorious, I would not throw away my life as Dapyx had done.

Cheers and applause from above. A pause.

I began to wonder if the contest between the Thracian and the German was over already.

No 'iugula' demands came, however, and bouts of fresh shouting proved that the fight continued.

We armed ourselves. I picked the best trident I could find, and made sure that its prongs were razor sharp. I went over the net I had chosen, checking that none of the lead weights – so vital in ensnaring my opponent – would come loose. I saw Sextus tugging on the thong that ran from the hilt of his sword, looping around his wrist. Small details that could mean the difference between life and death. So the doctores had always said, and I had no reason to disbelieve them.

Ordered up the stairs by the jaundiced-opinion guard, I threw a last look at the cells. I caught Big Dog's eye. His muttered 'Fortuna be with you' warmed my heart. I nodded, and spent the climb to the arena praying to the fickle goddess of luck. Perhaps she was watching, for I did not step in the little puddles of piss and vomit that caked many a step.

In the shaded area that led to the Gate of Life, we found Crixus observing the fight in progress. The guards were as eager as we to watch it; surrounded by them, close as brothers, Sextus and I inched right up to the limit of the shadows cast by the arch overhead. Waves of sweltering heat battered us; I hated to imagine how hot it was out on the sand.

'Look,' said one of the guards, sniggering, 'Little Boots has ordered the awnings taken down.'

Crixus, hearing, said, 'Likes his bit of fun, doesn't he?'

My eyes moved upwards, dragged away from the little figures of the Thracian and the German, dancing about one another on the far side of the white-glinting circle. High above, the cloth coverings that shaded large parts of the audience from the worst of the sun were being hauled back by slaves. It was blackly amusing, I decided, that the citizens who were watching and cheering as men fought, bled and died for their entertainment should now bake in the same heat.

'Good enough for the bastards,' I growled. I felt a trace of sympathy for Calpurnia and her daughter.

PART XLVII

Crixus turned. Rather than castigation, I saw in his expression what might have been a trace of respect. 'The tiro has some spine, it seems,' he said.

'Maybe he has a chance after all,' threw in one of the guards. 'Three denarii says he gives iron to the secutor.'

'He hasn't a chance in Hades!' cried the jaundiced-opinion guard.

Uncaring that I was standing there between them, a loud discussion began. The consensus was that I would die within moments of entering the arena, that I would only last if Sextus played with me, cat with mouse, that I would spend the entire contest running away from Sextus, hoping against hope to tire him out. The last tactic could not work, because Caligula, already angered by Dapyx's contempt, would order me shot down in the same way.

Doggedly, the guard who had offered the wager stuck his ground. He made bets with two of his fellows, and then, clapping me on the back, declared I had better not fail him. I ignored him, because I could sense Sextus' eyes on me. I had been a fool to say anything, I thought. I did not want him to think anything but I was a weakling with no experience, who knew he would lose, and end up as a skull-battered corpse being hauled through the Gate of Death opposite.

Our attention returned to the Thracian and the German, whose struggle had brought them much closer. Now we could see that both were hurt. The Thracian had a shallow cut across the top of his chest, and the German a through-and-through wound in the meat of his right calf. The Thracian's belly was decorated in runnels of crimson, and the German left a red trail behind his right foot with each step. Neither injury was immediately fight-ending, but they were serious. The Thracian appeared to have lost a decent quantity of blood, and the

97

German was limping heavily. I doubted he could move faster than his current shuffle.

Nonetheless, the pair continued to fight well. The Thracian was adept with his sica, shorter though it was than the German's gladius. Using his greater speed and mobility, he leaped around his opponent, his blade ever seeking flesh. The German, solid and determined, relied on his massive shield to protect him, every so often using his greater weight to drive forward.

One-two, one-two went his gladius and shield in the classic legionary training move. *Stab-punch, stab-punch.* One good connection in the Thracian's torso was all he needed. Should the gladius slide in two-to-three-fingers' depth, or the iron shield boss land with enough force, the fight would be over.

The Thracian knew it too. Up and down went his griffon crest as he bobbed about, keeping out of the German's reach yet still managing to threaten with his sica. The German gave back as good as he got, time and again almost landing a blow on the Thracian. The crowd loved it, roaring with a passion I had not yet heard that day.

Into a gap in the noise came a shout. 'Crixus!'

PART XLVIII

The voice was behind us.

The lanista twisted and peered. Like me, his sun-blasted eyes were unable to make out who had spoken in the virtual darkness deep under the arch. 'Who calls?' he yelled back.

It was an arena official. Muttering under his breath, 'What in the gods' names do they want now?' Crixus shoved past.

Curious, I turned my head and let my eyes adjust to the gloom. I spied a thin, officious-looking type talking to the lanista. He gestured and his hands weaved a shape in the air. Crixus didn't seem best pleased, but he nodded his acceptance. The official disappeared; a moment later, the lanista went to confer with another figure who was standing by the entrance to the stairwell. I did not recognise the man, a cadaverously thin figure with thinning hair. His bony face was all angles, as if the skin had been drawn taut as a drum cover. He had armed men with him.

The realisation hit me as the man nodded at whatever Crixus was saying, turned and slipped through the doorway that led downstairs.

'Crixus has talked to the other lanista,' I hissed to Sextus.

He looked at me sidelong. 'What?'

I explained my theory, that the official had told Crixus something that had him talk to the lanista of the other gladiators we had seen during the pompa. 'Another fighter is coming up,' I said.

'Three of us in the arena together? That almost never happens,' Sextus said, frowning.

He was right, and I told myself that my mind was running wild.

Riotous applause brought our attention back to the contest in the arena.

The Thracian had managed to slice the German's injured calf again. Whether he had cut the Achilles tendon or not, I could not be sure, but the German seemed no longer able to bear weight on his right foot. Knee buckling every time he tried to straighten the leg, he stood facing the Thracian. A rapidly expanding circle of red marked the sand at his feet.

The Thracian began to circle the German with increasing speed, forcing his opponent to turn, and no doubt cause agonising pain to his injured leg. In and out the Thracian danced, his sica thrusting and lunging. Desperate, the German advanced a step, his gladius and shield at the ready. The Thracian simply retreated a few steps, and then raced to the left and around behind the German, who, twisting, almost fell over.

The first cries of 'Iugula!' went up.

Working the crowd, the Thracian began to play with the German even more.

I wanted to keep watching the uneven but gripping fight, but could not stop wondering what was about to happen to me and Sextus. I kept glancing behind me, peering at the doorway, and when the skeletally thin man appeared with his guards, I was horrified but unsurprised to see a man dressed as a secutor with them.

My heart thumped painfully, and I elbowed Sextus. 'Look!'

PART XLIX

He cursed. 'They are going to build a pons.'

I had no idea what he meant, but cold fear uncoiled in my belly just the same. 'A pons?'

'A bridge.' Quickly, he explained. A framework would be set up in the middle of the arena, with a flat area of planking at the top. 'There will be a ramp on either side,' he said, not quite able to meet my eye.

'Let me guess,' I snarled. 'I stand at the top, and the two secutores are at the bottom, one on either side.'

He nodded.

My mouth was bone dry, my forehead coated in sweat. I'm a dead man, I thought. Atticus was right. I should have tried to kill Crixus with him. Together we might have succeeded, and that would have been a better death.

The guard who had wagered on me said something to one of his fellows, and I wanted to tell him that he had wasted his money. Miserable, however, I said not a word, and pulled my gaze back to the struggle on the sand.

The German was still fighting, but he had lost a lot of blood, and was no longer trying to chase the Thracian. The guards and arena staff around me were rapt; Crixus had a look of pure concentration on his face. The roars of 'Iugula!' were now constant. It was a deep, rhythmic sound laden with horror, but it drew me in too.

The German made one last, desperate attack, lunging half a dozen shambling steps after the Thracian. It was a wasted effort. His nimble opponent did not run – even now, that might alienate the audience or worse, the emperor – but swiftly retreated a little before whipping around the German, graceful as an acrobat. Sunlight bounced off his sica as it flicked in, cut the back of the German's right shoulder open, and away, out of reach. The din made by the spectators drowned out the German's cry of pain – he must have let one out, so deep was the Thracian's cut – but no one could miss his stagger. His gladius dropped to the sand.

The crowd went crazy. I closed my eyes briefly. Poor bastard, I thought.

When I looked back, the German was kneeling, and using his left arm to hold up his now-powerless right one. The index finger of his right hand was pointed at the sky. Ad digitum, it was called – the appeal for mercy.

'A waste of time today,' said one of the guards callously.

His fellows laughed.

I did not concern myself with the German's fate, which was sealed. I glanced again at the strange secutor. Crixus was close by him; he had gone to confer with the bony-faced man, the other lanista, for a second time. I did not like it, but that was not what had my guts churning. The waiting was almost more than I could bear. I wanted my fight to begin, to have done with it.

Outside, Caligula must have denied the German's appeal for clemency. Only one sound could be heard now, overpowering, filling the circle of sand, deafening in its bloodlust.

'IUGULA!'

I did not watch the death blow, but knew by the cheering that erupted a moment later that it had fallen.

PART L

'You're up next,' said one of the guards to me and Sextus, cheerful as if he were discussing the weather. 'It will be hard to improve on that contest.' He winked in the direction of his comrade who had gambled on me. 'Got the coin ready?'

The betting guard scowled.

I felt no sympathy for him. All I could think of was the pons, and the other secutor in the darkness behind.

The guard received no mercy from his fellows, however. When they noticed the new secutor, they rained down jeers and insults on the better's head. He might as well have pissed his money against the wall, one crowed. Another demanded his winnings on the spot. I felt the tiniest amount of satisfaction that he refused to pay up. 'The fight's not over until it's over,' he said stubbornly.

Out came the libitinarii. They loaded the dead German onto the stretcher, and carried him to the Gate of Death. There they laid him down so Charon could smack him with his hammer. Few of the audience noticed, and none cared, I thought, fighting bleak despair. They were more interested in buying fruit juices or wine from the mobile vendors, or gossiping with their neighbours, or seeking a brief moment of shade beneath the seating.

'Caligula likes the Thracian,' said Crixus, sounding pleased.

Again dragged from my misery, I stared out into the circle of sand.

Head garlanded with a palm wreath, his left hand gripping several bulging purses, the Thracian was parading to and fro, weaving a slow path towards us, and lapping up the recognition from the nearest sections of the audience.

Slaves appeared behind us from the doorway opposite that which we had used. They bore lengths of timber. Others followed, carrying tools: hammers, saws, bags of nails.

I glanced at Sextus. 'The bridge?'

Crixus heard me somehow. He leered. 'Aye, Hibernian. It's a special treat – Caligula asked for it just now. Bad luck, really – it's nothing against you in particular.' He sounded as caring as if talking about a biting insect about to be flattened by a stamping foot.

I hated him so much in that moment. 'I almost acted with Atticus,' I snarled. 'I wish I had!'

'A pity you didn't,' Crixus said, chuckling. 'Instead you will face Sextus here, and our friend from the ludus in Rome. Twelve fights he's won, if the honey-tongued snake who owns him can be believed.'

We stared at each other, eye-to-eye, like two stiff-backed, bristling-haired dogs about to set upon each other. If it had not been for the guards between us, I might have thrown myself at him, unarmed as I was.

Sextus' touch was light on my arm. Quietly, he said, 'Midir. Try anything, and he'll substitute you for one of the others, and then crucify you later – or worse.'

I set my jaw, and looked away from Crixus' lizard gaze.

Out on the sand, the slaves and their overseer were working fast. The bridge was already more than half finished.

'Time for them to go out,' said an official to Crixus. 'They should walk around the perimeter together. Get the crowd excited.'

'You heard him!' said Crixus, his voice mocking.

PART LI

Sextus had delayed putting on his helmet because of the heat. Wearing it, he had told me before, was torture in the hot sun. Now, however, the moment had come. On went his sheepskin arming cap, and then the polished iron dome. A guard locked him into it. Ready, Sextus stared at me from the tiny eyeholes. In no way did this fearsome, helmeted gladiator resemble my friend. He seemed like a pure killer, who would happily end my life. I turned my gaze away. The other secutor – from the ludus in Rome – had donned his helm also. He looked as outlandish as Sextus, and as unhuman. I would tell them apart by their build, and the motifs on their shields.

'OUT!' Crixus was growing impatient.

The guards were no longer paying as much attention, so I jabbed my trident at him, and laughed as he scrambled back. 'Come out and fight too, you cunt,' I said.

Crixus spat, and ordered the guards to force me outside with their spears. Proudly, I walked out before they could. Sextus was a step behind, and after him, the secutor from Rome.

The heat struck with an almost physical blow. It came from everywhere – the burning sand, the stone wall on my left, but most of all from the scorching white orb that was the sun. Even breathing was unpleasant. Walking was worse. Fighting would be brutal beyond belief. I cursed the fact that I came from cold, wet Hibernia, where the brightest summer day never came close to what I was experiencing now. Sextus, on the other hand, was from the warm climes of Iberia, and the swarthy skin of my other opponent suggested he too was from a hotter place than I.

We began the walk around the arena's perimeter, our ears ringing with the cheers and shouts, the encouragements and insults of the crowd. My gaze moved to the now-completed pons. It was just over a man's height from the sand. Acutely aware that from the start, both secutores would try to climb their ramps and attack me at the same time, worried that the extreme heat would rapidly sap my strength, I racked my mind for anything I could do. Anything.

No tactic presented itself. No answer came to me.

We reached the pulvinar, and as I had during the pompa, I kept my gaze firmly directed at the ground.

The din from the audience died away.

I sensed Sextus glance upward, but I kept walking.

'Halt!'

I did not know who had spoken, but the order had come from above, and the emperor – a living god to the Romans, some said – was close. I obeyed.

'Raise your head,' commanded the voice.

My bowels threatened to loosen. I dragged my eyes up to the imperial box. To my horror, it was Caligula who had spoken, and he who was staring into my face.

PART LII

This time, I noticed his thinning hair far more than I had the first time, and the hairiness of his arms.

'Do not stare at the emperor!' The roar came from an official by Caligula's left hand.

I bowed deeply and dropped my gaze. I wondered, guts churning, if the most powerful man in the world was going to address me. Or order me beaten or killed.

He spoke. 'You are to fight these secutores?'

'Yes, imperator,' I said.

He snorted, whether at my bad Latin, the unevenness of the contest, or both, I could not be sure. 'How many fights have you had in the arena?'

'One, imperator.'

'A win or a loss?'

'A win, imperator.'

'You.' Caligula addressed Sextus. 'How many fights?'

'Ten, imperator.'

'Wins?'

'Seven, imperator. One draw, and two losses.'

The emperor next addressed the secutor from Rome, who revealed that he had won twelve bouts and lost just one. The stark figures rammed home my fate even harder. I thought about baring my arse at Caligula, as Dapyx had done. Half a dozen arrows would be a swifter death than the slicing-up I would receive from my opponents. Then I remembered Siccum's words. I did not want to be tortured for days. And so I stared at the bits of mica glinting up at me from between my toes, and tried not to think about the man above.

'I wanted a real contest, not the farce this will be.' Caligula was talking to someone.

'A thousand apologies, imperator. I will summon the lanistae, have the retiarius replaced with a fighter of better quality.'

In the silence that followed, I imagined the jeers that would greet me when I was returned to the cells while Sextus was not. Crixus, humiliated and possibly punished for entering me in this bout, would be in a vile humour. Like as not, he would leave me to fester until midway through the munus, close to an interval perhaps, and have me fight the second Thracian – who would gut me like a fish. Better it was, I decided, to end it now. Dragging what remained of my courage together, I said loudly, 'Let me fight the secutores, imperator.'

Sounds of shock – gasps from above, Sextus shifting his feet, the eyes of the second secutor heavy on me. I paid them no heed.

Then, a chuckle. 'The little retiarius has balls,' said Caligula. 'Why do you wish to fight these two men, who are so much better than you?'

I dared to glance at him, although only for a moment. 'Because, imperator, you have not seen my agility, nor my skill. Those are the reasons Crixus pitted me against a secutor with more experience. He could have changed me for another retiarius when your fantastic idea of the pons was revealed, but he did not. He can see my potential, imperator.'

I shut my mouth, praying that I had not said too much, and that he did not see my simple trap. I was lying through my teeth, of course – Crixus did not rate me at all – but I *had* sounded plausible. Caligula, moreover, had just recognised my spirit.

'Can he, I wonder?' said Caligula with a disbelieving snort. 'We shall see. Let the contest remain as it is.'

Our time in the imperial presence was over. The official ordered us to continue our march around the arena, 'as fast as possible, because the emperor is growing impatient.'

My gamble had worked.

At least my suffering would be short, I decided. That was a better fate.

PART LIII

I practically danced up the steep ramp to the top of the pons, delighting in the relative cool of the timber it was constructed from. I had overtaken Sextus and the other secutor, and had a moment to glance at the pulvinar. I could make out the emperor through the shimmering waves of heat. After the taking down of the awnings, it was hard not to conclude that our forced walk on the scorching sand had been part of Caligula's malign plan.

It had also granted me the tiniest of advantages. I could stand on the pons all day without burning my feet, while my opponents, already shifting about more than was normal, were in a considerable amount of discomfort. Inspired, I let my left hand, the net hand, trail down by my side. Judging that the audience facing me would not be paying close attention, and that my net would conceal what my fingertips were doing, I was able to tug loose the thong holding the top of my greave in place.

I straightened. Sextus had taken up position at the foot of the ramp to my right. The secutor from Rome was moving towards the one on my left, encouraged by the summa rudis. 'Get a move on,' I heard him say. 'The emperor wants the fight to start.'

The secutor's muttered retort was irritated. I noted he had a large rust spot on the top of his helmet. He said, louder, 'The sooner it starts, the sooner I finish the runt and get off the cursed sand.'

My anger pricked. I was no runt. I held my peace, however. Give away nothing, I thought. I glanced at Sextus, who was rolling his shoulders, and came to a decision. Between the possibility of his still not wanting to kill me and Rust Spot being eager to do so, it was probable that he would reach the top of the pons second. *That* meant I had to defend against Rust Spot first.

The summa rudis called out to the seconda rudis, who was standing behind Sextus. 'Ready?'

'Ready!' came the answer.

The crowd bayed their enthusiasm. The rolling animal sound, laden with bloodlust, would have turned my bowels to water had I not been concentrating so hard on my ploy.

The summa rudis raised high his staff of office.

Sextus and Rust Spot tensed, ready to charge up the ramp.

'Wait!' I roared.

Scowling, the summa rudis looked at me. 'What?'

'I have a loose tie on my greave.'

He peered, saw that I was not lying, and scowled again. 'Can you fasten it without coming down?' To do that would only delay the contest further.

'I think so,' I said, making no effort to lay down my trident and net.

'Well, get on with it, fool!'

PART LIV

U nhappy noises came from the crowd – demands that the fight start, names and insults being hurled at the summa rudis, and at we gladiators – but still I did not hurry. Every passing moment increased the pain in Sextus' and Rust Spot's feet. Leisurely as a man lacing his sandal on the street while talking to an old friend, I set down my trident and undid the strap that attached the net to my wrist. Only then did I begin to tie the thong at the top of my greave.

'Faster!' ordered the summa rudis, spurred on by the audience's growing unhappiness, and, no doubt, by images of a furious Caligula.

I paid no heed. I did not look at Sextus either. To my left, however, at the edge of my vision, Rust Spot was bobbing about from foot to foot. Irritation and fury oozed from him. Good, I thought. The angrier you are, the better.

'There,' I said, completing the knot. Lifting my net and trident, *but without retying my wrist strap*, I beamed at the summa rudis. 'Ready!'

His staff went up for a second time, and without hesitation, dropped. His lips moved, but so loud was the roar from the spectators that no one heard his command, 'Begin!'

This was the moment when everything hinged on my assessment of Sextus and more importantly, Rust Spot. If I was wrong, the contest would be over before it had begun. I spun and with all my speed, ran to the top of Rust Spot's ramp.

He was already halfway up, legs pumping, shield held out in front. I shot the fastest of glances over my shoulder. There was no sign of Sextus at the far end of the pons. Back to Rust Spot I looked. I twirled my net once, getting the feel of its weight. I would have liked another arm swing, but Rust Spot was closing fast. The eyeholes of his enclosed helmet were visible over the top rim of his shield; his gladius tip glinted from halfway down its side.

I threw the net. It snagged his shield, as good an effort as I had ever made.

He came on another two paces.

I wrenched my net arm down and to the right.

I had not the power to rip the shield from his grasp, but that was not my intention. Unbalanced by the tug of the weighted net, Rust Spot staggered and then, as I heaved even harder, he tumbled from the ramp. He took the net with him, but not me – because I had not retied the wrist strap.

Without hesitation, I leaped down after him.

Rust Spot landed heavily, still gripping his shield, and because of that, twisted his left wrist. A muted cry of pain came from within his iron domed helmet. With its narrow field of vision, he didn't see me coming either. He heard the thump of my feet on the sand, however, and desperate, struggled to get up. His sword flailed about in the air, like a toy brandished by a small boy.

I jabbed my trident into the hollow at the base of his neck, and he froze. I was sorely tempted to stick it in, end his life fast, but I restrained myself. I must not anger Caligula.

'Yield!' I shouted.

PART LV

I n his eyes, just visible behind the eyeholes, I saw fear, rage and a flash of devilry. I pricked his throat. He jerked back, and three fat drops of blood welled in the wounds the prongs had made.

'Drop the sword!' I shouted, acutely aware – terrified – that Sextus might fall on me from on high. Until Rust Spot surrendered, he could attack me with no consequences. Again I roared, 'YIELD!'

His fingers tightened on the sword hilt, and I thought I was going to have to give him iron. Then the last of his spirit crumpled, and he let go. *Thump* went the blade on the sand. Up went his index finger. 'Missio!' he cried.

The din – cheering, laughter, whistles and catcalls – was so loud no one heard.

I yelled for the summa rudis. 'Missio! He asks for missio!'

Thankfully, the referee reached my side before Sextus, on the planking above and behind, had the chance to leap down and end me. Staff raised so that the emperor and audience knew the bout was paused, the summa rudis waited for a modicum of calm.

So excited – and disbelieving – was the crowd's reaction that we just had to stand there and wait.

They were glorious moments, I admit, and I drank them in. Beyond all hope, I had beaten the more skilled of my two opponents. The battle was only half over, however. Do not lose the run of yourself, I told myself, something my mother had often said. My trident firm on Rust Spot's throat, I kept my gaze directed at the pulvinar, and Caligula.

At last the noise diminished enough for the summa rudis to call to the emperor that Rust Spot had been beaten, and was requesting missio.

A veritable barrage of abuse filled the air – the spectators wanted no mercy today.

Caligula wasted no time. Out went his right arm, straight, stiff-elbowed, and then without ceremony, he jerked his thumb back towards his throat.

'IUGULA!' The mob – there was no other word for the baying crowd – screamed with joy. 'IUGULA!'

The emperor's command was no surprise, and yet my heart gave a painful thump off my ribs. The Romans were savages, I thought. Brutes. My determination did not waver, though, not even a fraction. The mountain-heavy door that had been closing on my fate remained – just – ajar. Fail to execute Rust Spot, and its inexorable inward momentum would continue.

'You are sentenced to death,' said the summa rudis to Rust Spot.

He nodded, the gesture so resigned that I felt a trace of pity.

'Kneel,' I said, my dry mouth bringing the word out as a croak.

Sprained left wrist cradled in his right hand, Rust Spot obeyed.

I placed my trident on the sand and tugged out the wood-handled dagger I had selected what seemed years before, under the arena. Worried that it might have grown blunt, even though I had not used it, I ran a thumb across its edge. It was reassuringly, horribly sharp.

PART LVI

When I lifted my gaze, Rust Spot was removing his helmet. This I had not expected; in the ludus, there was an agreement that defeated fighters would leave their helms on for the death blow, thus allowing their comrades not to look them in the eye. A stranger, hating me for having won, Rust Spot wanted my task to be as grisly and difficult as possible.

Seeing me flinch, he sneered. 'Not got the stomach for it, little man?'

I said not a word, but stepped adroitly behind him. Seizing his chin, I drew the dagger across his throat. Hot blood gouted over my fingers. Practised at butchering sheep since my youth, I sawed the blade to and fro, deeper, until I felt it grate off his neck bones. Skin, blood vessels, tendons, muscles, windpipe. It sliced them all, easy as a scythe cuts wheat at harvest time. More blood sprayed, patterning the ground in front of us. Rust Spot's head lolled in my grip, slack, lifeless. Disgusted now, I let him go. He flopped down onto the crimson-soaked sand, more resembling a limp puppet than a formidable gladiator.

'IUGULA!' The audience was ecstatic. 'IUGULA! IUGULA!'

Sucking my cheeks together, I drew together enough moisture to spit my contempt. Bastard Romans, I thought. They were all bad, save Calpurnia and her daughter, perhaps. The goat-hating, hairy-armed Caligula was the worst of the lot.

A pair of libitinarii, who had been waiting close by, approached with their stretcher. Another followed, his purpose to gather up Rust Spot's helmet, shield and weapon.

The summa rudis pointed his staff at me, and then at Sextus. 'Ready?'

'No,' I said, with a show of cockiness. Wiping the dagger clean on Rust Spot's undergarment, I reattached the strap on the net to my wrist. Trident in my right fist, net dangling from my left, I paced to the bottom of the ramp where Rust Spot had begun the fight. Sextus was standing at the top, waiting. Outlined by the sun's blinding light, he was an ominous black figure with a shield and sword.

My stomach flip-flopped. Parched with thirst, now my mouth filled with unwelcome bile. I swallowed, hating the acid pain as it went down. My decision to jump from the pons had allowed me to beat Rust Spot, but had given Sextus the advantage of height. The bridge was his, and it was I who would have to charge up at him.

'Begin!' shouted the summa rudis.

Sextus did not move – he had no need.

Lost for an immediate idea, I did nothing.

'Come on!' shouted a man in the front row nearby. 'Get up there, scrawny legs!'

Laughter burst forth from those around him, and encouraged, he began to squawk like a farmyard hen. 'Flap those bony arms, retiarius! Fly up there, why don't you?'

PART LVII

F eet burning, I moved a step to my left and then another. Sextus moved, following me. Amused, I trotted the length of the pons, forcing him to keep pace lest I reached the far end first. At the bottom of the second ramp, I smiled up at him. 'Hot, isn't it?' I asked.

Inside his helmet, Sextus' eyebrows must have gone up. Muffled, his surprised voice replied, 'What?'

Without answer, I loped back whence I had come, again obliging him to chase after. From any other fighter, this cowardly behaviour would have brought down the crowd's rage, but gladiatorial custom dictated that retiarii were allowed to run about the arena, and especially when it made their opponent look stupid. Already I could hear hoots of laughter. I stopped midway along the pons. Sextus did the same, his chest heaving.

I danced a few steps to the left. He mimicked me. I ran ten steps to the right. So did he. Back and forth I went, and soon the audience was roaring their amusement at the foolish spectacle that Sextus made – pounding up and down the pons like some kind of great, heavily armed paegniarius.

I tried a sprint, to see how fast he could move. Unarmoured, far lighter than he, I reached the ramp bottom well before he had come to its top. I had no intention of pressing home a proper attack yet, but I scampered up as if that *were* my intention. Still with enough time to get a footing on the pons, I stopped dead a step before. Expecting a trick of some kind, Sextus checked. I took another pace forward, and turning my head towards the nearest members of the crowd, I pulled a terrified face. Then, swift as a running cat, I turned tail and retreated to the sand.

Sextus, furious, stamped to the top of the ramp and glared down at me.

I saluted him with my trident.

Sextus waved his sword angrily.

Cheering and clapping broke out. I heard voices shouting, 'Bring back the paegniarii!'

Again I made for the far end of the pons. Sextus followed. This time, however, I twisted suddenly and whipped my net up, aiming for his feet. I caught him off guard, but misjudged my throw. Instead of curling around both his ankles – a move that would have seen me pull him off the pons – it caught only one. He staggered, cursing, but did not fall. I tugged at the net, desperate that he did not slice it to ribbons with his sword, which even now was sweeping around from his right.

Lucky for me, Sextus could not resist taking a swipe at my unprotected head. I ducked low, tucking in my left arm as I did. The movement freed the net, and almost took him tumbling after it. I made a show of flicking my net at him again. Wary, he retreated a step or two.

Again the crowd applauded, but I detected less enthusiasm than before. I decided that my antics were starting to bore, and I dared not risk Caligula's opprobrium. A cold realisation bore down on me.

I could not win the fight by staying on the sand.

PART LVIII

An idea came to mind, and I berated myself for the missed chance. If I had stolen Rust Spot's sword and shield before the libitinarii had carried them away, I – armed just as Sextus was – might have gained the top of the pons with more ease. The move was illegal, but if it had amused the crowd, I might have got away with it.

I twisted my head, searching for the libitinarii, but they were long gone. My gaze lingered next on the Gate of Death, and the fateful shapes that were Mercury and Charon. As if he had seen, Charon hefted his hammer. My skin crawled, and I looked away.

The sun beat down on me. Both feet hurt as badly as if someone was holding a torch to them. My thick, dry tongue was stuck to the roof of my mouth. The trident felt as if it were made of lead, and the strands of the net were biting into my palm, so tight was I holding them.

'Get up here, Midir.'

Glancing at Sextus, I wondered if I had imagined the weariness in his voice. All along, the purpose of my antics had been to tire him out against the moment when I would have to climb the ramp. Maybe it had worked.

I decided to test the theory by running almost to the end of the far ramp, and, with a couple of sidelong glances, judging his speed. He was slower, I was almost sure of it.

Enough to gamble your life? asked a little devil in my head.

I had no answer, and no other idea of what to do next, so I placed a foot on the ramp, as if about to ascend. I waited until Sextus came to the top. His posture seemed wary, so I put my other foot onto the planking. He squared his shoulders, and shook his shield, as if preparing to smash its boss into my face. I took a step upward, making sure the hook of my ruse was lodging in his mouth. He shifted a little, and the tip of his sword went back and forth as he prepared to thrust.

Instead of climbing, however, I sprinted with all my might for the far end. This time, I did not look up to see how close he was behind me. I knew I was faster, and less tired. Sand arced into the air as I skidded to a halt. I threw myself onto the ramp, and went up it with all speed. When I reached the top, Sextus was only halfway along the pons. I had done it.

Done it? asked the devil in my head, laughing. You have to fight him now.

I had to move fast too, to keep what little advantage I had. I slid my feet forward, left and right, right and left. I extended my right arm, so my trident threatened Sextus. Jab, jab, I went. I lifted the net, and flicked it back and forth experimentally, looking for the chance to throw it at him.

PART LIX

He was up for the fight too. Head so low behind his shield I could barely see his eyeholes, he came at me. Punch. He tried to hit me with the iron shield boss. About to try and net-catch the crest of his helmet, but forced to retreat unless I wanted ribs broken, my poor effort landed the weighted strands on the front of his shield. The lumps of lead clattered off the wood, and the net dropped.

Sextus, wily as a fox, stamped on it, with one foot and then the other. Terrified that I would lose it to him, being unable to rip it free from under his entire body weight, I went on the attack again.

With a loud cry, I raised my trident high.

Sextus' eyes rose, following it.

Instead of aiming at his head, I changed my grip a little and rammed the trident steeply downward, at his leading foot.

The prongs missed by less than an inch.

Wary of a second strike, he shuffled back a step, and I was able – just – to whip free the net again.

Again I flung it, and this time my aim was better. Right over his helmet the net landed, the weights pulling it down on either side of him behind his shield. I wrenched as hard as I could. Catching the fish crest as I had intended, the net pulled his head towards me, and he staggered. Elated, starting to believe that I could topple him from the pons, I tugged again.

I had badly misjudged Sextus' strength and determination. Hunching his shoulders, disregarding the net draped over him, he came at me like a charging bull. It mattered not that his sword was tangled in the mesh, or that his head was trapped. Hit me hard enough with the shield, or better still, its boss, and I would go tumbling down on my arse, maybe even to the sand below. Either way, I would lose control of the net, and possibly the trident as well.

I had one choice.

Fingers tightly gripping my trident – without that, I was lost – I stepped to my right, *off* the pons.

I landed standing, the impact jarring my heels. My left arm was wrenched hard, and then snap, the thong attaching my wrist to the net parted.

Sextus, who had been pulled off balance by my fall, was now released by the breaking of the thong. He swayed towards me, and then away, towards me and then away, but then to my dismay, regained his balance.

Panic bubbled up in my chest. The trick I had used to reach the top of the pons might work again, but it was unlikely that the audience would approve. Rather than laugh and applaud as I ran up and down, forcing Sextus to follow, they would shout and jeer. Even if I then managed to win, they would not be happy about the way I had gone about it, exhausting my opponent rather than beating him with skill.

How Caligula might react to my continued clowning I did not want to imagine.

PART LX

Of more immediate concern – a real threat to my life – was the fact that I no longer had the net. Still wrapped up in it, but out of my reach and therefore able to extricate himself, Sextus was already half-way towards getting it off. I had to act, and fast. Once he succeeded, and either sliced the net to ribbons, or just kept it from my reach, I was done. I could never take him off the pons with only a trident.

I reached up and stabbed at one of his feet, too fast. I missed, and the prongs drove deep into timber. Cursing myself for a fool, I pulled and heaved, and in no time at all had freed it. Sextus had not been idle, however. He was doing a quick backwards shuffle, sliding each foot one after the other along the wood. His sword was jammed into an armpit so that he had a hand to lift off the still-encumbering net.

I chased after, aware that now, if ever, was my chance.

Stab. I had another go at spiking him. I missed, but I did not care, for I saw how scared he was of being hurt. Faster went his shuffle, and his attempt to remove the net stalled. I increased my speed and taking greater care, thrust again. Only one of the prongs sank home, and not deeply, but the barb at its end caught hold. Savagely, I pulled backwards, ripping it out of Sextus' flesh.

He tried not to scream, but there was no missing the agony in the groan that came from under his helmet. Eager to finish him, I stabbed again and missed.

Heave. Sextus pulled the net up and over the fish crest, and the weight of it came into play, dragging it down and over the front of his shield. It fell, folds draping over both sides of the planking – within my reach. He did not try to pick it up, for that would have allowed me another attempt to stick him in the foot again, but instead beat a hasty retreat along the pons.

Seeing the trail of blood spots he left, the crowd roared.

'The retiarius will win now!' I heard a voice cry.

My spirits lifted a fraction.

'Are you mad?' came a loud retort. 'That runt will never beat the murmillo.'

Grabbing at the net, which fell neatly into my grasp, I loped after Sextus. This time as I drew near, however, he was ready. Fierce thrusts of his sword kept me from drawing close. It did not matter, for my trident's reach was greater. Slow, precise, I reached forward and stuck him. All three prongs went in, nice and deep.

Into his uninjured foot.

With gut-fierce pleasure, I wrenched my arm back, and let the barbs do their work.

Blood misted the air. It coated the sand before me.

This time, Sextus could not stop himself from roaring with pain.

The audience cheered. I dared to hope of victory.

PART LXI

Slap. A stinging pain across my shoulders; I turned, to be confronted by the furious summa rudis.

He waved his staff in my face. 'It is forbidden to attack your opponent from underneath!'

'No one told me.'

'I am telling you now,' he snarled.

I bridled. 'Why did the crowd not jeer or boo when I first attacked him?'

'They are fickle.' He pointed up at the pons. 'Get up there, lest Caligula, who is also fickle, need I remind you, send in his archers.'

I cursed under my breath. There was no point resisting, or I would pay. Sextus was wounded, I told myself. I still had a chance of beating him.

'Go on.' The point of the staff poked me in the chest, and not lightly.

There were approving shouts, and I realised that the spectators had been on the cusp of turning on me. The fact that I had not known I was breaking the rules did not matter. The bloodthirsty Romans did not particularly care who won. They did not want me to win because I was the underdog. All they cared about was being entertained, in as bloody and dramatic a fashion as possible.

I called the referee something unspeakable in Hibernian – really, I was cursing the audience as well – and secured the net thong to my wrist as best I could. Then I trotted to the ramp behind Sextus.

He had been watching. Moving heavily, limping, he turned around on the pons as fast as he could.

Heart thumping off my ribs, I climbed the ramp.

Sextus came to meet me, his steps slow and laboured. There was nothing wrong with his arms, regretfully. His gladius was ready, and his shield protected his entire body. His eyeholes stared at me, alien, implacable.

I had no doubt he would kill me if he could.

'Are your feet hurting?' I asked.

He made no reply, but closed several more steps.

'Looks like it,' I said. 'If they get infected, you could lose one. Happens easily, you know.'

'Screw you, Midir!' He sounded angry, which was my intent.

I flicked the net, gauging the moment to throw, and raised my trident overarm, as a fisherman would.

Sextus kept advancing. Although I could not see the pain that must be creasing his face, it was evident that each step cost him dearly.

Do not let him close with you, I thought. If he forced me backwards, and down off the ramp, I felt sure that the crowd would turn on me. I could imagine Caligula ordering his archers into the arena as the summa rudis had said, or perhaps sending another gladiator in against us, to replace Rust Spot. Anything was possible on this mad day.

Sextus moved another pace closer.

I danced forward, staying on the balls of my feet, and hurled the net at his fish crest. In the same moment, I stabbed down with the trident, at his leading left foot.

PART LXII

He ducked, trying to avoid the net, and pulled back his leg.
Awkward, because both arms were held out in front of me,
I powered forward, straight at him. Terrified in case he reached up
and slid his blade into my side, I half turned, and managed to batter
my left shoulder into his shield. The twisting movement dragged on
my net, which had fallen over his helmet. That pulled Sextus' head
forward a fraction, so his eyeholes were directed below the rim of his
shield.

Off balance, momentarily unable to see, he staggered back a step.
His right arm came up, flailing. Air moved close to my left hip as he
swept his blade up and down, blind, desperate to find my flesh.

I dropped my trident and let go of the net – it was time to gamble
all – and grabbed the top of his shield with both hands. Wrench. I
tugged down as hard as I could.

Sweet agony blossomed in my left side. He had cut me. My knees
almost buckled, so intense was the pain, and it would only get worse.
Frantic, I stamped up and down, trying to find one of his feet. I landed
a good strike on one, because he cried out. Knowing I could not let
up my assault for even a heartbeat, I pulled on his shield again. Then,
remembering his missing finger, I pulled it sideways, then heaved it
back the other way.

He groaned, and suddenly, the full weight of the shield was in my
grasp. He had let go.

Holding in a scream of my own – the pain in my side was fast
becoming unbearable, and he still had his sword – I pushed the shield
at Sextus, hard as I could.

Up came his helm, wrapped still in the net. Even with the tiny eyeholes, our gazes met. And then he was falling backwards. He slammed
down on his back, the shield on top. Incredibly, he did not let go of

his sword. Before he could lunge at me with it, I took a step back and stamped with all my strength on his worst-injured foot.

He mewled like a babe ripped from the tit. His blade dropped from nerveless fingers, and he sagged back on the timber of the pons, making no further attempt to fight.

Mistrustful – he might yet have a last ruse planned – I drew my dagger and stabbed one of the prong holes in his foot. He screamed, louder.

'Off the bridge,' I shouted. 'Now!'

He reached up to the shield, and sent it tumbling to the ground.

Pitiless, I shoved the dagger a little further into the wound. 'You too!'

He half-rolled, awkward, and dropped, landing close to his sword.

I was taking no chances. Leaping down as gently as I could, hissing at the pain from my side, oblivious now to the burning sand, I retrieved my trident. I paced back to Sextus, unsurprised that he had picked up his sword. As I knew myself, nothing fired a man's determination more than the desire to live. His effort came to nought, however, as I pricked at his wounded feet. He flung the blade away. I kicked it beyond his reach.

PART LXIII

Only then did I look down, and probe at my wound with the fingers of my left hand. I was somewhat relieved to feel a neat, lipped wound just above the hip. It was a 'through-and-through', to use the surgeons' term, and if I was lucky, none of my guts had been sliced.

From far away, I heard roars of 'IUGULA! IUGULA!'

I came back to the arena. To Sextus, lying a few paces away, his eyeholes fixed on me.

'IUGULA! IUGULA!'

Heartless whoresons, I thought. Despite my anger, the spectators would get what they wanted. If I hesitated at all, it would be me who received iron, not Sextus.

I walked over and placed the trident prongs at his throat.

His index finger went up in the familiar gesture. 'Missio,' he said, and then laughed. 'Caligula is a cocksucking goat-humper,' he added. 'He's not going to grant mercy.'

'He is not.' At last, sure of victory, I allowed myself to feel the sorrow I had denied until now. Sextus was my friend. My brother-in-arms. My fellow gladiator.

None of that mattered.

To have any chance of survival, I would have to kill him.

The shouts of the audience continued, relentless, as the summa rudis and his second-in-command came to stand by us. They glanced at the pulvinar, and the second-in-command said to me quietly, 'That was some fight.'

I ignored him.

Caligula was ready. He jerked his thumb at his throat.

The crowd went even wilder. Objects were being thrown into the arena. Coins, mostly, but also lucky amulets, and even a homemade wreath.

'Ready, brother?' I asked Sextus.

He nodded. 'Shall I take off my helmet?'

My heart wrenched. He was not doing it so I had to stare him in the eyes, but to make my task simpler. 'It's all right,' I said. 'The blade will not slip.'

I dropped the trident and stuck out a hand. He took my grip, coming up into a kneeling position.

'You're a tough one, Midir,' he said, and let his arm fall to his side, a final gesture of submission.

I clasped his shoulder as I moved around behind him. My dagger was still in my right hand. 'So are you,' I said, cupping his chin. 'If you weren't missing that finger . . .'

'I—'

I cut his throat. Hot, bubbling blood covered my fingers.

'Habet! Hoc habet!' The spectators yelled and shouted.

Forgive me, I said in my head. It was you or me, Sextus.

He did not answer. He would never answer anyone again. The last of his life gouted and sprayed from his throat, misting the sand before us.

Sick to my stomach, I let him down gently, rolling him so that he lay gaze to the sky, not into the dirt, like a criminal. I averted my eyes from the gaping slash that had sent him to the next life, and looked to the summa rudis. Now would come the emperor's acknowledgement of my double victory. There would be a wreath, purses of coin and more adulation from the crowd, which was still cheering what I had done.

I felt no joy.

PART LXIV

The applause continued for what seemed an age.

'What should I do?' I eventually asked the summa rudis. The pain in my side was so bad that my breath came and went in short, staccato gasps. 'Leave, or stay here?'

'Wait. The emperor might summon you to the pulvinar.'

Gods, do not let him do that, I prayed. I did not wish to test his capriciousness for a second time.

Already the libitinarii were close, stretcher with legs at the ready. They would un-helmet Sextus and carry him to the Gate of Death, for the ceremonial strike on the head from Charon's mallet. Then he would be borne to the spolarium. Black amusement took me. The method used in the mortuary to make sure a man wasn't playing dead was to slit his throat. There was no need of that with poor Sextus.

Still no summons came from Caligula. He was watching as a score of arena staff, high up in the stands, threw gifts to the poorer members of the audience. Cheers went up as a man leaped high to catch a purse. I saw pieces of meat being thrown too – probably carved from some of the animals slain earlier – and items that glittered as they flew through the air. Jewellery, I decided, caring for none of it. All I wanted was to lie down on the cool stone under the seating and have my wound stitched. Then I wanted to sleep for a seven night.

I swayed, and went down on one knee. My head swam. Black dots floated to and fro across my vision. If it had not been for the summa rudis' strong grip, I would have fallen to the sand.

'It doesn't seem as if the emperor is interested in you,' said the referee, in a not unkind tone. 'Come on, let's get you to the surgeon.' He signalled, and two libitinarii came to stand, one either side of me. 'These lads will help you out of the arena.'

I was about to accept when something made me look at the pulvinar.

Caligula, curse him, was staring in my direction. 'I am all right,' I said. 'I will use my trident as a staff, walk out on my own two legs.'

He peered at me, as if to assess the threat I posed with a weapon now that my contest was over, and then nodded. 'Ain't breaking the rules to go to the Gate of Life with your trident, far as I know.' He turned his head. 'Fetch it, one of you.'

I nodded my thanks as it was handed over. Gripping the wooden shaft tight as a drowning man holds a spar in the open sea, I began hobbling towards the opening through which I had come what felt like a lifetime before.

PART LXV

Each step was sweet agony. The sand, even hotter than before, was burning my feet. Every movement of my left leg sent knives of agony outward from the wound. I could feel ooze, liquid, running down from it into my undergarment. My vision was blurring again, and but for my iron grip on the trident, I would have toppled. Somehow I kept my legs moving, left, right, left, right. I knew in my gut that if I fell, Caligula might give the order to leave me where I was. Walk, I told myself. Walk. The emperor is watching. Walk. Count your steps. One, two, three, four. Focus on the Gate of Life – a blurred black opening some distance in front of me.

Slow as a cripple – one of those who sit outside temples, hands outstretched for a coin from a kind-hearted devotee – I picked a tortuous path, forty, then fifty paces. From far off, I could hear echoing, mocking laughter. I felt sure it was directed at me. The fickle bastards, I thought. Truly my life meant nothing.

Ignore them, I told myself. Reach the Gate of Life, and you can collapse. The surgeon will stitch you up. Crixus might even offer some praise. There would be wine, and better, fruit juice. I could rest. Bolstered by these thoughts, I shuffled another dozen steps. If I squinted, I could now see the Gate of Life clearly. Could see a crowd watching from inside the archway, guards, arena staff, an official in a toga, and two gladiators. One was Big Dog, smiling and beckoning. My heart warmed at the sight of him, and some strength returned to me.

Next I made out the guard who had gambled on my winning the bout. He was beaming, exposing rows of brown, peg-like teeth, and elbowing his comrades. 'See,' I heard him say, 'I told you the little retiarius would do it. You had best pay up before the day is out!'

He got curses by way of reply.

'Come on, Midir,' called Big Dog, although he did not step beyond the shadow cast by the archway over the gate. 'You can make it. What a champion you are!'

I tried to give him a smartarsed answer, but my mouth and throat were so dry, only a croak came out.

Big Dog gestured again, encouraging me. Perhaps fifteen paces separated us.

I have to reach it, I thought, pushing my right, stronger leg forward. I paused, sucked in a breath, and heaved my left leg in front of the right. Sheer, unadulterated pain radiated out from the wound. I gasped, but made myself repeat the movements. Right. Thirteen paces. Left. Twelve. Right. Eleven.

Big Dog took a step into the sunlight. 'That's it, Midir.'

One of the guards, a brute with lank, unwashed hair, laid a rough hand on his shoulder. 'Get back inside.'

Big Dog paid no heed. He beckoned. 'Almost there, brother.'

My lips peeled up in a cracked semblance of a smile. Ten steps, I thought.

'Halt!'

There was no mistaking the tone of command, or the fact that it had come from the pulvinar.

With sinking heart, I recognised the voice too – it was that of Caligula.

PART LXVI

Big Dog gave me a look of real dismay, and let the guard manhandle him back under the archway. I gave him a 'What can I do?' shrug, and tried not to think the worst of what was about to happen to me.

'Come here, retiarius.'

Weak as a newborn lamb though I was, I could no more refuse the emperor's command than stop the sun from rising in the east. I raised my free hand to show I had heard. 'Yes, imperator,' I croaked, loud as I could. Hissing with pain, lightheaded, I turned and began to shuffle towards the pulvinar.

It would take me a while, and as I suspected – hoped, even – Caligula was too impatient to wait. Two libitinarii soon appeared with a stretcher with legs, perhaps the very same sandapila that had taken away poor Sextus. They set it down beside me.

'Climb aboard,' one said.

I stared with fascinated distaste at the fresh, wet blood staining the leather. It *was* the same stretcher that had carried away Sextus, and Rust Spot, maybe Dapyx and Piye as well.

'Get a move on!' said the libitinarius. 'Little Boots is waiting!'

Jerked back to horrible reality, I eased my back end down onto the stretcher. Unsure whether to lie or to try and stay sitting up, the decision was made for me as the pair grabbed the handles and lifted. Unable to prevent myself from falling backwards, I cried out as I landed, and the impact sent out fresh waves of agony from my wound. Full lucidity returned to me by the intense pain, I stared up at the blue sky, the burning sun, and the wisps of white cloud I had not noticed until now. It was bizarre, and all the more so considering the manner of my carriage.

'You're the first living man as ever been on this,' said the libitinarius cheerily. 'Enjoy the ride!'

I said nothing, dreading our imminent arrival below the pulvinar. I had no idea what would happen, but presumed it would be bad. I still had my trident – it was lying alongside me – although I should have been disarmed. Pressured to bear me to Caligula as fast as possible, the libitinarii had overlooked this detail. I trembled at the realisation.

To stand within killing distance of the emperor was something I had never dreamed possible. If he pronounced sentence of death on me because I had displeased him – this was one fate tumbling around my frantic mind – I could hurl it at him. Whether I would succeed, weakened as I was, with him guarded by spearmen and archers, I had no idea, but it felt good to know that I had the option.

I would not go to my death without a fight.

Thump. The sandapila was placed on the ground.

I saw from the corner of my eye the libitinarii bowing. 'Get up!' one hissed.

Biting my tongue to stop from crying out, I half rolled over, onto my right side. Awkwardly planting the trident in the sand as a support, I pulled myself into a sitting position, and got my feet over the side. A groan escaped me as I managed to stand. I faced the pulvinar.

Caligula was looking down at me with an odd expression.

PART LXVII

'Imperator,' I said, and trying to bow, I fell to one knee.

Laughter rose from those nearby.

'Silence!' cried the emperor. 'Taking a knee shows even greater respect than bowing.'

Quiet descended, punctuated by the nervous titters of those unsure if he was serious or not.

I was beyond caring. Slowly, panting, I dragged myself up to a standing position. I wrapped my fingers around the trident shaft, and decided I could make a good attempt of spearing him with it if I had to. 'Imperator,' I said again.

'Your lanista was right.'

Confused, faint – I could not remember the details of my lie earlier – I said, stupidly, 'Imperator?'

'You said he saw your potential.'

'Ah, yes, imperator, of course.' Terrified that I might have annoyed him, I added, 'My apologies, imperator.'

His lips twitched. 'There is no denying you have balls. I have rarely seen such a dramatic fight.'

I bobbed my head, feeling a tiny spark of hope. 'Gratitude, imperator. I am honoured to have pleased you.' The last was nothing more than brown-nosing, as my father called it, but I gambled that the pompous prick was so used to fawning and sycophancy that he would not notice.

'For you to kill the first secutor was remarkable, not least because of his experience. You cost his lanista a tidy sum by giving him iron.' Caligula chuckled. 'He looked as if he was sucking a lemon when you cut the secutor's throat.'

'Imperator.' I could not say what I thought, which was: I do not give a shit for the other lanista, or for Rust Spot, who would have opened *my* throat.

'That you also killed the second secutor . . .' Caligula glanced at the nearest official. 'Have you ever seen a contest like it?'

'I have not, imperator,' came the honeysweet fawning answer.

Heads shook around the emperor.

'A man could not be blamed for thinking that the contest had been rigged.'

Panic swept through me with the force of a spring tide. Somehow I kept my face blank. Show my concern, and Caligula would attack, like a vicious dog that sees the lone child's fear. 'Rigged, imperator? Forgive me, my Latin is not good. I have not long been in Italia.'

He made a little gesture of annoyance. 'Fixed. The result agreed beforehand.'

Scared that he believed this nonsense, I loosed my emotions. 'No, imperator, it was not! I fought because I wanted to live, because you, you –' here I had to quell my rage, my burning desire to hurl my trident at his flabby white imperial throat – 'had ordered that one gladiator in every fight had to die. I had no chance – none, imperator, but I wanted to live!'

Spent, worried that I had gone too far – the shocked faces of those around Caligula seemed to indicate this – I dropped my gaze. Dully, I noticed the crimson pooling in the sand around my left foot. It was trickling from my hip all the way down my leg. I looked at the wound, and wished I hadn't. Perhaps set off by my fall onto the sandapila, it was bleeding quite badly. It did not matter, I thought, so weary that I had to lock my knees not to drop where I stood. The emperor was about to pronounce some dreadful fate upon me for daring to speak the truth.

PART LXVIII

'R etiarius.'

I looked up. 'Yes, imperator?'

'What do they call you?'

'Midir, imperator.' Seeing his face cloud, I added, 'It is a name from Hibernia, imperator.'

'Hibernia – is that not a wild isle near Britannia?'

'It is, imperator. To the west.'

'Are your people warlike?'

'After their own fashion, imperator.'

'Would they all fight like you?'

I thought of the big men in our tribe, those who took the lead in a cattle raid, or defending the settlement from pirates. They had always been figures I looked up to. 'Yes, imperator, or better,' I said truthfully.

He smiled, and it was not pleasant. 'How would they stand up Rome's legions, I wonder?' The question was not aimed at me, but more said in a musing tone.

'They would run, imperator, and hide in the hillth and bogth,' said a heavy-browed man near Caligula. Dressed in the ornate armour of a high-ranking Praetorian, strongly built, heavily muscled, he had an oddly high, lisping voice, at odds with his physical bulk. 'The way all thavageth do.'

The emperor nodded. 'They could not beat the legions anyway, Lassie – no one can.'

My pride was stung; so was that of the heavy-browed Praetorian, for all that he tried to hide it. To hide my emotion, I stared at the sand, while he continued to talk, asking the emperor, 'Are you thinking to take Hibernia after Britannia, imperator?'

'Maybe, Lassie. Maybe.' Caligula looked down at me again. 'Is there gold in Hibernia? Silver?'

'A very little gold, imperator,' I replied, horrified to think of thousands of legionaries landing on the shores of my home.

'Tin? Lead?'

'No, imperator. Not that I know of.' I was grateful for the truth ringing from my voice.

His lip curled. 'Is there aught of use there?'

I thought with longing of the green rolling landscape, and the rain, misting and cool, and the simple life I had once had. The arrival of Rome would change that forever. 'My Latin, imperator,' I said beseechingly. 'It is not good.'

I swear, he rolled his eyes. 'Are there cities, and riches?'

I shook my head, and put from my mind the heavy gold torcs worn by tribal kings. Few men were affluent as that where I came from. 'No cities, imperator, and little in the way of wealth.'

'They thay the hunting dogth from Hibernia are thome of the betht to be found, imperator,' lisped the heavy-browed Praetorian.

Caligula waved a hand in irritation. 'Hounds are scarcely a reason to invade somewhere, Lassie.'

'It rains almost every day, imperator,' I ventured. 'A month can go by without seeing the sun.'

Caligula's lips thinned. 'Weather does not stop the legions.'

'No, imperator.' Wary of his fluctuating mood, I bent my head again. How long was he going to toy with me? I wondered. How long would it be before I lost consciousness? The black dots had returned, bobbing up and down before my eyes, and I felt as if I were not really within my own body, but outside it.

'We shall see. Once Britannia is conquered, and I have visited, I shall consider whether Hibernia is worth attacking.'

PART LXIX

'O f courthe, imperator. Whatever your dethire, it thall be fulfilled.'
The voice of the heavy-browed Praetorian.

I prayed that the emperor's invasion of Britannia came to nothing, and that he forgot all about Hibernia.

'Waging war is an expensive business.' Again, Caligula seemed to be speaking to himself. 'And the treasury's coffers are in a poor state.'

No one said a word.

But even I, a lowly gladiator, knew why this was. A month before, the area had witnessed the most extravagant bringing to life of the emperor's whims and desires. A marvel of engineering, a two-mile-long bridge from Baiae to Puteoli in the nearby Bay of Neapolis, it had been built from requisitioned merchant vessels and ships constructed on the spot. A road was built on top, and resting places and lodges erected at various points along its length. Crixus had gone to see it with his own eyes; I had heard him talking in marvelling tones that evening of how the emperor had ridden across it wearing the breastplate of someone called Alexander. The day after, he had driven back the other way in a four-horse chariot.

'This retiarius has shown himself to be a good fighter,' said Caligula.

Loud voices of agreement in the pulvinar.

'Perhaps I shall buy him from the lanista.'

He does not mean to kill me, I thought with a rush of relief. Uncertainty swept in at once, for I had no idea what it would mean to be the personal property of the emperor. My left knee buckled. With an effort, I straightened it, but my strength was almost gone.

'You would purchase him from me afterwards, eh, Lassie?'

I looked up to see the heavy-browed Praetorian's face register surprise. It was masked fast. He smiled broadly. 'It would be an honour, if that wath your command, imperator.'

'I would not mark up the price too much, Lassie. Ten times what I paid the lanista, perhaps. No more than fifteen.'

The heavy-browed Praetorian's smile grew even more fixed. 'The thum would be yourth to name, imperator.'

'I know.' This was said with a petulant, self-satisfied viciousness.

Caligula would probably force Crixus to sell at rock bottom price, I decided, and pretend to the Praetorian that he had paid a fortune, thereby increasing his profit even more.

It was the last thought I had, for blackness took me, and I fell.

PART LXX

I woke with a pulling, stinging sensation in my left side. I reached a hand down to my hip.

'Hold him!' said a voice.

My wrist was seized, not ungently, and guided down to my side. 'Easy,' said a second voice.

Someone was touching my wound, probing, pushing. Hissing with pain, I opened my eyes, came back to the world of the living. I was lying on a wooden table. The pleasantly cool air and patterned brick-work of the wall told me I was still within the amphitheatre. My gaze moved upward, taking in the upside-down face – very close – of a man bent over me. His arms went down either side of my chest: it was he who was holding my wrists.

A head, grey-haired, was bent over my lower half. A surgeon, I thought.

'Where am I?' My words came out as a croak.

'The hospital. Don't struggle.' The upside-down-faced man leered, and visited me with a whiff of bad breath and cheap wine. 'He's more likely to slip with the needle.'

'Demetrios does not slip.' The surgeon's voice was droll.

The upside-down-faced man winked, which looked very strange. 'So he says.'

The tugging came again, and I could not stop from crying out.

'Give him some poppy juice,' said Demetrios. Like so many of his kind, he was Greek.

'Do not touch the wound,' said the upside-down-faced man. When I nodded my agreement, he let my wrists go and walked away. He returned with a clay beaker, which he brought to my lips. 'Drink. It will dull the pain.'

The liquid had a curious, bitter taste. Eager to escape the throbbing

143

agony which was fast returning to the whole area around my hip, I would have downed it all had he not stopped me after a few swallows.

They left me for a time, to allow the drug to take effect. As I lay there, enjoying the pain's easing and the soporific feeling creeping over me, I heard from far above the roars and shouts of the crowd. Big Dog, I thought muzzily. Was he still fighting, or had I been unconscious for so long that his contest was already over? For all I knew, he could be lying with Sextus in the spolarium. No, please, I thought. Perhaps he had won, and was enjoying the acclaim of the audience and the favour of the emperor.

Memories of *my* last moments in the arena returned. I might not belong to Crixus anymore, but Caligula, or even the heavy-browed Praetorian. I did not know what to think of that, so I did not think at all. It mattered not who owned me, I decided. The edges of my awareness blurred even further. I was falling, falling. I closed my eyes, and let myself go.

When I came to for the second time, the pattern of the brickwork in the wall was not the same. I was in a different room – still flat on a table, but my probing fingers told me that I now had a thick bandage around my waist. The pain in my hip was still there, but it was a dull throbbing rather than the naked blades it had been before. My mouth was dry as a month-finished jug of wine. 'Water,' I said. 'Water.'

'Ah, he is back with us. Welcome, Midir.' The voice was familiar, and not that of the surgeon or the upside-down-faced man.

My head twisted. There on another table, sitting rather than lying, was Big Dog. Heavy strapping covered his left thigh, but otherwise he seemed whole.

'You're alive!' I said, delighted.

A wry smile. 'It appears so. You are here too, although quite how, I do not know. One tough bastard, you are, Midir, and no mistake.'

'I don't know about that,' I said, awkward, but thrilled with the real respect on his face.

PART LXXI

He eased down to the floor, and gingerly lifted a jug and cup from the floor beside his table. Filling one from the other, he limped over to me and held the cup for me as I drank thirstily. 'Do not sell yourself short. You slew two secutores. I did not see the first one, but I was under the arch for your fight with Sextus. It was an incredible display.'

Laying my head back down, I said nothing. Cutting Rust Spot's throat I could live with, but I did not like to think of Sextus.

'You had to kill him. It was that or your own life.'

'Aye.' The realisation did not ease my guilt.

'Dis manibus,' said Big Dog, the familiar invocation.

I echoed it, and sent after it a prayer to my own gods, that Sextus and even Rust Spot would reach the underworld safely. 'Who did you face?' I asked, hoping it had not been Siccum. I had just remembered the wagers he had made, including the one on my behalf. I stood to win a huge sum of money – but only as long as Siccum was there to collect it. The betmakers would laugh in my face if I attempted to claim his winnings.

'The Greek – the one from Asia Minor who came in with Mattheus.'

'He's dead?'

'Aye.'

'I guess that would have been an easy contest for you.'

His lips worked. 'I tried to drag it out a little, so it didn't end too fast, and displease the crowd – or Caligula. But the prick stuck me when I let down my guard too obviously.' He indicated the bandage on his thigh. 'I decided to finish him quickly then, before my strength left me. I battered him good and proper, so much so that there was a little booing by the time I knocked the sword from his hand. I thought I had overdone it, and worried that the emperor might turn on me, but most of the audience pointed their thumbs in the right direction. I marched the Greek over to the pulvinar – they loved that – and gave him iron right in front of Caligula.'

'I am glad you won.' The Greek had not been my enemy, but Big Dog was my friend.

A chuckle. 'I am too.'

PART LXXII

Above us, the crowd erupted. Feet pounded in their tens of thousands. 'IUGULA!'

Sudden concern tugged at me. 'Siccum?'

'I don't know,' said Big Dog.

'How long have I been here? How long have you?'

'You were already on the table when I came down. Another retiarius had just gone out, facing one of our secutores. That ended a little while ago, and another fight started. Siccum could be in the arena, or he might still be in the cells.'

'For all we know, the current bout is between two of the gladiators from Rome.'

'Aye. Let's hope they are to fight one another, not like it was for you.'

'That is a faint hope. Caligula will not have brought them all the way to Capua to go up against men they know.'

Big Dog gave me an unhappy look. 'A slick lot, they will be, if that secutor you killed is anything to go by.'

He was right, I thought grimly. The day could come to an end with most of our fighters dead, the majority of the winners coming from the ludus in the capital.

A key in the lock. Big Dog's head turned; his lips turned down. 'Crixus,' he whispered.

I tensed. Helpless on the table, unable to see the lanista, I waited with churning stomach to find out why he was here.

'Dominus,' said Big Dog, his tone neutral but respectful.

Crixus grunted. 'How bad?'

I guessed he was pointing at Big Dog's bandage.

'The wound is clean, dominus, according to the surgeon. It went into the muscle, rather than across it, which is good. It did not need too many stitches either.'

'How soon until you can train?'

'A month for light training, dominus. Two months, he said, before I can fight again.'

Crixus' grunt was not happy, but he did not argue. Only a fool would rush a gladiator back into the arena, and he knew it.

The tread of his feet came nearer, and I moved my head around. 'Dominus,' I muttered, hating that I had to say it.

'Here he is, the killer of killers.' The words dripped sarcasm.

'Dominus.' I met Crixus' stony gaze with confusion. I thought he would have been pleased with my success.

'I did not bet a single as on you.'

Understanding his anger in part, I struggled for any response that would not rile him further. 'Dominus,' I managed.

'A hundred-to-one, the betmakers were giving – some were even offering a hundred-and-fifty-to-one!' Little drops of spit showered down.

I exulted inside. If Siccum lived to see the sun go down, I would make a fortune, while Crixus would make nothing at all. The irony of it was beautiful. 'I did not think I would survive, dominus,' I said in an effort to calm him.

'It would have been far better if you had died. Not only did I win nothing from your victory – I am no longer your owner.' His fist thumped the table, close to my injured hip.

Trying not to wince at the threat – quite deliberate, I was sure – I feigned ignorance. 'Why, dominus?'

'The emperor, in his wisdom –' his voice was full of false deference – 'saw fit to buy you.'

PART LXXIII

'I hope he paid a good price, dominus,' I said.

'Did he, Hades!' A fresh shower of spittle rained down from Crixus' lips. 'You are worth a tidy sum after your bout, but I am to receive only the amount I paid for you in the slave market.'

Amused even more, I decided prudence was the best policy, and said nothing.

'As if that wasn't bad enough,' Crixus ranted, 'I understand that he sold you straight away to a Praetorian tribune by the name of Cassius Chaerea, an ugly bastard with a brow you could rest a cup of wine on.'

The lisping officer who had been talking with Caligula. Clear-headed enough to reflect on my fate, I decided it was a better one than remaining in the ludus at Capua. It was not just because I was to escape Crixus; I was now prized property. Chaerea would not be happy with the inflated price extracted from him by the emperor, but its size would probably mean I was treated well henceforth. There would be contests in the arena, but the chance of them being to the death would be relatively small from this point onward. A fierce spark kindled in my breast. It was not impossible that in a few years, I could earn the rudis and gain my freedom. Do not be hasty, I told myself. I would have to earn plenty of contests first, so Gaius recouped his outlay on me.

'Well?'

I realised that Crixus had asked me a question. 'Your pardon, dominus. I am still lightheaded.'

'It is an outrage, I said!'

'Yes, dominus,' I agreed, meek as a little child, while inside, I thought: screw you, you old bastard.

Behind Crixus, Big Dog was grinning from ear to ear, happy for me.

'That is, if you can fight again,' said Crixus, his expression growing calculating. 'How bad is your wound? What did the surgeon say?'

'I wasn't conscious, when he treated me, dominus,' I said truthfully. I went on, genuinely scared that he was about to do me injury. 'The pain is terrible, dominus.' It was not, but I did not know how else to convince him.

Crixus ran a finger under the edge of my bandage and lifted. 'Did the blade slice any guts, I wonder?'

'Dominus, please . . .'

Ignoring me, he bent his head to sniff. 'Smells clean,' he said in a disappointed voice. He jabbed the cut, hard, and I cried out.

'Dominus,' said Big Dog.

Crixus poked me again, and I yelped louder. I lifted a hand, but his free one grabbed it and would not let go. I raised my other hand, and his eyes bored into mine. 'Touch me and I will wring your filthy little neck.'

I laid my arm down on the table again.

He bent to his purpose now, rummaging at the bandage so he could reach the cut better.

If he opened the wound and shoved his fingers in, I thought with terror, he would introduce infection, from which I could easily die.

Lying against my side – the one he could not see – my right fist bunched. I was as weak as a kitten, and lying down with him standing over me, but if I did not fight back, I was a dead man.

PART LXXIV

'Big Dog,' I said.

I sensed him take a step towards us.

'Move another muscle, and I will see *you* on a cross,' snarled Crixus. 'Get in here,' he ordered. One of his men, who had been outside, waited as the door was opened for him, then padded in. 'Watch that fool,' said Crixus.

Big Dog did not come any closer.

With a little exclamation of satisfaction, Crixus pulled back the bandage entirely.

Footsteps in the corridor outside. 'Ah, lanista,' said a loud voice. 'Come to check on your men?'

Crixus tugged the bandage back into place as best he could while meeting the gaze of the newcomer. 'Aye. One of them only is mine. The retiarius here –' his finger, marked with my blood, pointed at me – 'now belongs to a Praetorian sitting by Caligula in the pulvinar.'

'Ah, one of the emperor's little get-rich-quick schemes. I have heard of them.'

'I had not, until just now,' grumbled Crixus.

Again the door creaked open and shut, and was locked again.

'They are common in Rome, I believe.' A pleased note entered the voice. 'Ah, the retiarius has come to.'

I realised that the man who had entered was probably the surgeon. Even more grateful that it was he who had interrupted Crixus, I managed to lever myself up onto my right elbow.

'The dead arise.' The surgeon came over to the table. He was short with close-cut grey hair – the same person I remembered bent over me. 'How are you feeling?'

Crixus did not move, but stood protectively by – trying to hide the clearly-interfered-with bandage.

'I have been better.'

The surgeon gestured with his hands at Crixus. 'Excuse me, could you—' His gaze fell on the linen wrap around my middle. 'Hades, what has happened here?'

Even as he stepped back, Crixus' eyes were heavy on me.

I could have revealed what he had done, but he would deny all knowledge. It would be my word, that of a slave gladiator, against his, a Roman citizen. The surgeon had no power over him either. 'That must have been me, when I was still unconscious,' I said.

Tutting, but making no further comment, the surgeon asked, 'Can you sit up?'

Taking his outstretched hand, I eased up, wincing.

He untied the bandage and worked around my middle, rolling it back onto itself. All the while, Crixus watched, his gaze full of malevolence. I glanced at Big Dog, who was in turn staring at the lanista with pure hatred.

The last of the wrapping came away, and the surgeon examined the cut Sextus had given me. 'The stitches are still in place. That is something, but it looks as if you got your fingers under the bandage. Hand me that bowl and sponge, will you?' The question was directed at Crixus.

With poor grace, he obeyed.

'This will sting,' said the surgeon. 'It is acetum, to clean the wound again.'

As the pain began, I tried to feel glad that Crixus had done me no serious harm, but I was not out of danger yet. He might try again when the surgeon left, and if my new owner Chaerea did not take possession of me by the day's end, I would be returned to the ludus. There I would be entirely at Crixus' mercy.

PART LXXV

Cleaning finished, the surgeon rebandaged my middle and gently helped me to lie back down.

'Gratitude,' I said, thinking, and not just for seeing to my injury again.

'Try to keep from touching it,' he replied.

'Are you done?' asked Crixus.

'No. I have to clean my instruments. There'll be another patient along soon too, I have no doubt,' said the surgeon.

Thwarted – I had no doubt that he wished to attack me again – Crixus paced to and fro, glowered at me and Big Dog, and then departed with his guard.

Barely had the noise of their sandals died away when the surgeon asked, 'It was him who was at the bandage, wasn't it?'

'Aye,' I muttered.

'Why, because the emperor had forced him to sell you?'

'That, and because he didn't lay a bet on me for the fight.'

'The odds must have been long indeed, but to try and hurt you so maliciously . . . your friend, did he try to stop him?'

'He threatened me with crucifixion,' said Big Dog.

The surgeon shook his head. 'There are some right evil people in this world. You will be glad to see the back of him.'

'I will, if he doesn't return when you are gone and try again,' I said.

'That I can do something about,' said the surgeon.

He was as good as his word, staying until one of his orderlies turned up, and instructing him to remain with us until the end of the day. I clasped his hand, and told him he was a good man. Smiling, he took his leave.

The orderly brought word that Siccum had been victorious, delighting me in particular – I had high hopes now of receiving my winnings

– but also Big Dog. Siccum himself was unhurt, which was more good news. The next fight had already started, a contest between one of our Thracians and a highly fancied Gaul from the ludus in Rome. By the frequent shouts and thumping of feet from above, it was a dramatic spectacle.

Weakened further by the second treatment of my wound, secure for the moment from Crixus, I closed my eyes. The orderly was rolling fresh strips of bandage, and whistling to himself. Big Dog seemed content not to talk; the rest would do him good too, I thought, already drowsy. Sucked downward by the still-effective poppy juice, I slept. Mercifully, I did not dream.

I was woken by screams. It was a harsh wake-up call. My eyes opened, focusing on the roof of the treatment room. The smell of blood and acetum filled my nostrils.

'It hurts, it hurts!' wailed a voice I recognised. 'Hades, make it stop!'

'Hold him!' The surgeon's voice. 'Get the poppy juice!'

I rolled over. Several men stood with their backs to me, restraining another on a table. One leg freed itself, and kicked up and down. His torso lifted and fell on the planking; I heard his head bang on it too. 'It *hurrrrrrrtttttts*!' he screamed.

PART LXXVI

'Hold him, or the bleeding will start again. The bandage can only do so much,' said the surgeon, who was standing at one end of the table, looking down at his patient. 'Where is that cursed poppy juice?'

An orderly hurried over, cup in hand. 'Here, dominus.'

The surgeon bent to speak in the yelling man's ear. 'You have to drink this. It will take away the pain.'

The maimed man's reason was not all gone. He let the orderly place the cup to his lips; he took a mouthful, and another.

'That is enough – you have already had more than you should,' said the surgeon, gesturing at the orderly to take away the cup. He went on, 'Any more, and you risk never waking up.'

'What matter if that happened?' The voice – which belonged to the Thracian class fighter from the most recent bout – was bitter. 'A gladiator with one arm is like a bull with no balls. Crixus will have no use for me any longer. Nor will any auctioneer at the market. Cut my throat now, why don't you, and end my misery?'

'I am sworn to help the sick, not to murder them,' said the surgeon wearily.

'Well, you needn't have bothered with me,' snarled the fighter. 'I am better off dead.'

The surgeon did not reply, instead making sure the orderlies kept a good hold until the extra dose of poppy juice took effect.

When the man slipped into unconsciousness and the orderlies stepped away, I peered with horrified fascination at the crimson-stained wrappings that covered the stump of his left arm. It had been amputated above the elbow, by the surgeon presumably, in the room where I had been stitched up.

'Poor bastard,' said Big Dog. 'He's right about Crixus having no use for him.'

'Will he have one of the guards give him iron?' I had not seen a gladiator in the ludus with such a severe, but non-life-threatening, injury.

'Perhaps. But it will piss Crixus off to get back none of the money he laid out. My guess is he will sell him to the beast trainers. Training a lion to kill humans isn't always easy, I have heard. They are naturally afraid of us. Starving them helps, of course, but there is more to it than that. Throw in a man who can't defend himself, maybe one with a fresh, bloody wound, and . . .' Big Dog paused. 'You can imagine the rest.'

It was brutal enough, I thought, to execute criminals by throwing them in with wild beasts, but to treat a wounded gladiator so . . . my stomach turned. I did not let myself dwell on the amputee's fate, for my own yet hung in the balance. Brooding on that was unsettling also, so when Big Dog borrowed some dice from one of the orderlies and asked me if I wanted to play, I accepted with alacrity.

We played incessantly through the afternoon, our games accompanied by the familiar chorus of sound from the amphitheatre above. Cheers, howls of abuse, feet pounding the floor, cries of 'Iugula!' and 'Hoc habet!' and much less often, 'Mitte!' A succession of wounded men were carried in on stretchers, some of whom we knew, and others we did not. Their injuries varied from minor to much worse than that. Two died as I was watching, rattling out their last breaths with no one there to hold their hands or provide reassurance as they slipped into the underworld.

PART LXXVII

Relayed to us by the orderlies and stretcher-bearers, the death toll from the fights was grim. Our gladiators were losing far more than they were winning. Matters were not helped when Caligula, in an effort to please the crowd, or as Big Dog opined, just because he was a sick animal, had an expanded version of the pons contest put on. Two of our retiarii were pitted against four secutores from Rome. Both died, and fast.

The emperor's next perverted ploy was to accelerate the fights. The water organ would start to play, and first blood had to be drawn by the end of the wheezing tune. If one man had not emerged victorious by the close of the third piece of music, he had both executed. After it had happened once, we were told, new pairs of fighters went at each other with the fury of enemies settling an old feud.

More of our men died. I forgot when I had last heard one of our own beating one of the gladiators from Rome. There was no sign of Crixus, because as I said scornfully to Big Dog, he was probably having an apoplectic fit somewhere. It had been one thing to contemplate losing half his fighters in the day's contest: the original arrangement. It would be quite another to see the vast majority slain in one day. No amount of coin – he was to be paid for every life lost, as was the norm – could compensate him for the loss of his entire troupe. It took years to build up the stock of a ludus. Crixus might well be ruined by the day's end, said Big Dog.

Although I held no ill will against those of Crixus' gladiators who yet lived, I prayed that it was so.

The surprises in the arena continued as Caligula's malice grew. A special interlude was announced for a slave who had been caught stealing a purse in one of the covered passages beneath the banked seating. The unfortunate individual was dragged out onto the sand and had both

157

his hands chopped off. After the bleeding had been stemmed with hot irons, the laughing emperor ordered the severed hands tied together with a length of cord. The grisliest of trophies, it was hung around the slave's neck, along with a placard that read, SO ARE PUNISHED ALL THIEVES. He was then forced to walk around the perimeter of the arena, a never-ending circle of agony and degradation that would probably end, the orderly who told us the tale said, when the last fight was over.

'I have heard the officials say he will instruct his archers to use him as a living target,' said the orderly ghoulishly.

'Fortuna be thanked we won, eh, Midir?' said Big Dog.

I nodded and took a long swallow of the watered-down wine that the surgeon had given us on his most recent visit. Big Dog held out a hand, and I passed over the jug. There wasn't enough to get us both blind, fall-asleep drunk, sadly, so I tried to put from my mind the image of the handless, eyes-mad-with-pain slave, stumbling around the outer edge of the circle of sand as the crowd hooted its derision.

By the time we had been in the infirmary for some hours, the contests were coming to an end. We told ourselves that soon it would all be over, that my new owner Chaerea would send one of his servants or slaves to fetch me, that Big Dog and Siccum would return to the ludus, and a magnificent feast.

Neither of us had reckoned on Caligula's depravity.

PART LXXVIII

Our first inkling that something unusual was going on came at the end of what most thought would be the final bout, between the best of our Thracians and a crupellarius, a fully armoured fighter rarely seen in the arena. The contest ended with a win for the invulnerable crupellarius, unsurprisingly, and the cries of 'Hoc habet!' were still rolling around the amphitheatre when the trumpets blared, strident and commanding.

'What's that for?' I asked Big Dog. This had not happened the day I had first fought on the sand.

'No idea,' he said, frowning. 'But I do not like it.'

We were still talking about what the fanfare meant when armed guards came clattering down the stairs. The door was opened, and in they came, swaggering like dogs with two cocks.

'On your feet!' ordered their leader, a stubble-jawed brute with an irregular, purple cicatrice on his neck. 'All of you!'

I looked at him in disbelief, and glanced at Big Dog. He seemed as amazed as I.

'Do you know what is happening, friend?' Big Dog asked.

'No questions! Up, I say, up!' The leader prodded the man who had lost an arm with his spear.

He yelped with pain, and snarled, 'Are you blind, cocksucker? I have one arm!'

'One arm, one leg, blind, it matters not! The emperor has ordered you all into the arena. Now, I do not care if a few of you die here first – Caligula doesn't know how many of you vermin are still breathing – it is your choice. So I say, *once more*, get on your stinking feet!'

He jabbed at the one-armed man again, who quickly stood up. The leader chuckled. 'See, that was easy!'

Big Dog came over and threw an arm around my shoulders. I slipped

159

my right hand around his back and gripped the top of his right arm. Supported like that, I was able to stand. The one-armed man could do so, and so could many others, but there were a handful of fighters who were too badly hurt to get up. To my horror, they were stabbed harder and harder by the guards. One managed to get on his feet, bleeding from multiple wounds, but two others merely cried and moaned. The braver ones among the orderlies protested in vain as, at a gesture from the leader, they were slain.

In a file of misery, we shuffled up the stairwell that led to the upper levels. So narrow was it that we were forced to go single file – Big Dog could not help, but I was able to use my hands on the walls to keep me upright.

'What in all the gods' names is going on?' I whispered to Big Dog.

'I have no idea,' came his answer.

There was no reason he should have known, but the doom in his voice, and the still-blaring trumpets, sent my spirits spiralling down into the dark.

The devil in my head had a theory. Caligula is going to execute you all, it jeered.

You are probably right, I thought, too weary and in too much pain to think about anything beyond the next step.

PART LXXIX

We passed the level with the gladiator cells. Curious, I peered through the narrow doorway. Every door lay open. Not a soul was to be seen. My unease deepening, I realised that the remaining whole-bodied fighters, mostly the winners, had also been summoned to the arena. I said as much to Big Dog, who merely grunted in reply. His limp was more pronounced now, and I judged the steep stairs were no good for the wound in his thigh.

On the ground level, the guards urged us towards the Gate of Life, which I had hoped not to have to pass under for quite some time. There were men standing at the sides of the passageway, Crixus, a figure I thought might be the other lanista, imperial officials. Crixus looked angrier than ever, and twice as impotent.

'What is happening, dominus?' Big Dog asked him as we passed.

'You have as much clue as I, but something tells me that more of you are about to die,' he retorted. He let out a sarcastic laugh. 'I shall be ruined. Ruined!'

Even now, the piece of shit only thinks of himself, I thought, my hatred for him so strong that if I could have grabbed a weapon, I would have happily died trying to take him with me.

We were ordered to walk the last few steps out of the Gate of Life. Waves of baking heat carried in from the sand. Squinting against the blinding light, I could see figures already waiting, a band of some thirty-odd figures. The winners, I thought. They were armed, which was odd. I said as much to Big Dog.

'There are more fights coming, I know it,' he answered.

Helping each other, hobbling, limping and even staggering, the group of us – about a dozen – made our slow entrance into the arena. A strange silence fell as we were noticed. There was none of the usual cheering, or the opposite, hurled insults. I looked up into the audience, and the faces I saw were shocked, even sympathetic. Here we were, the walking wounded, the sliced-up, stabbed and maimed, some as near to death as they had ever been – the living evidence of what their bloodlust had caused, and they did not like it.

Just outside, tables had been arrayed with weapons and armour. Shields were stacked up against the wall. I did not count them, but judged there were enough for each of us to arm himself. When the guards urged us towards the equipment, I glanced at Big Dog, sick to my stomach.

'He means to make us fight again.'

'Doubtless you are right,' said Big Dog, sounding more tired than I had ever heard him.

I felt the same way. Even if my opponent was the one-armed man, I did not think I could fight another bout, less still survive one.

After we wounded had made our way across the burning sand to the winners, the trumpets sounded again. An expectant hush fell over the audience.

A loud announcement was made. The entertainment was not over. In his wisdom, the emperor had decided that new pairings would be made. All the remaining gladiators would have to fight again, to the death.

All for the glory of Rome, the announcer crowed, and the spectators cheered their reawakened bloodlust.

PART LXXX

As the noise died down, the air of expectation resurfaced. Caligula stood up in the pulvinar. Silence fell. My mouth was horribly dry; my nerves were in tatters. I had emerged victorious from a contest I should never have won. Now I was to be butchered along with the rest of the wounded, just to satiate the already gorged-with-blood-and-death audience. Never had the futility of gladiator fights been more evident. Spying my new master Chaerea in the pulvinar, I felt a tickle of black humour. Would he still have to pay the emperor after I was dead?

Caligula pointed. 'Him and him.'

The guards separated out a murmillo and a secutor, neither of whom I recognised, which meant they were from the ludus in Rome. Caring nothing for them, I paid them no more heed.

Next the emperor selected the one-armed man to fight a retiarius whose face had been slashed. Heavy bandaging all around his head held his face together – half of it had been hanging off in a bloody lump of flesh before.

As Caligula was deciding the third pairing, I heard shouting from the top of a section of the seating, under where the velarium would be attached to the wall. It was a woman's voice, no, two or even three.

I strained my ears. 'Mitte,' I said urgently to Big Dog. 'They're asking for mercy.'

My hope that hearing their call the crowd would swing behind them, failed. A few people joined in the demand, but as the women's shouts grew louder, far more boos and jeers were hurled back. Fingers were pointed, lumps of bread thrown. People on the other side of the arena began noticing the commotion.

Undeterred, the two women stood and cupped their hands to their mouths. 'Mitte!' they shouted again and again.

'They're wasting their breath,' said a guard.

A second added, 'If they piss off Little Boots—'

He was still speaking when Caligula, hearing the clamour, turned and looked back into the crowd. He said something; one of his officials barked an order at a guard, and an instant later, half a dozen Praetorians were pounding up the steps that separated one section of seating from another. Seeing them come, the women fell silent and sat down. No doubt they were hoping to escape notice, but a barked threat from the Praetorians' officer saw their neighbours denounce them at once. Those few who had also been shouting 'Mitte!' stopped.

The women were dragged by the hair, screaming, down to the level of the pulvinar. A short interaction with the emperor followed, and then an imperial gesture saw both of them pitched over the parapet. They landed in a tangle of limbs, on top of each other, and Caligula laughed.

Large sections of the audience cheered.

'It could have been any of them,' I said, utterly disgusted.

'That's why they react with such enthusiasm,' said Siccum, who was not far from me. 'The greater the terror, the greater the ecstasy. Vile, eh?'

The wretched women got to their feet. Sobbing, clinging to one another, they were forced to walk towards us by guards with outstretched spears.

'I think they are related,' said Siccum.

I stared. 'No. *No!*'

It was Calpurnia and her daughter.

PART LXXXI

B oth women were wailing and crying. 'We have done nothing
wrong,' Calpurnia said. 'Nothing.'

The guards ignored her, instead urging them closer to us.

Your 'crime' was to show human decency, a quality lacking in the
emperor, I thought bitterly.

The terrified pair came to a halt ten paces from the line of gladiators.
None of us moved.

'See those women,' I shouted. 'They spoke to me at the cena libera.
They disagree with the fights today. They are good people, not like the
rest of the scum in this amphitheatre.'

Pride filled me, because not a fighter moved a muscle.

Calpurnia's face, meanwhile, filled with surprise as she recognised
me.

I smiled at her, raging that I could not do more. Their fate, like ours,
was sealed.

The lead guard, his face a mixture of fear and resentment, twisted
around to regard the pulvinar.

An official angrily flicked his hand in a forward-moving gesture.

The guard muttered something under his breath, and turned back
around. 'Kill these women,' he shouted at us.

No one stirred.

He shoved Calpurnia, who tripped forward a step. With a cry, her
daughter caught her arm and prevented her from falling to the burning
sand.

'Kill them, I say!' repeated the guard.

'Do it yourself,' I snarled.

'Gladiators do not butcher unarmed women,' said Siccum proudly.

The guard pushed Calpurnia again. Half his weight, elderly, she could
not stop herself from taking another pace towards us. Her anguished

daughter stayed with her, even as she pleaded with the guard. 'You do not have to do this. Please. Please.'

'If I don't do it, it will be me who is next,' he growled. Eyeing Siccum, who was straight in front of the women, he said, 'Finish these bitches, you sewer rat.'

'I will not.'

Individual guards began to issue dire threats, and thrust their spears toward us, but still none of us moved.

Much of the crowd was silent, shocked no doubt by this latest horror, but sections of it were growing impatient. They yelled and whistled. Stamped their feet. Their mood was turning petulant, ugly, like a small child denied the pastry right in front of its eyes.

'Iugula!' shouted someone.

'IUGULA!' came the answering roar.

The lead guard looked nervously over his shoulder. Caligula had a face sour enough to curdle an egg, and the apoplectic official began to scream threats.

'I am going to count to three,' said the lead guard, turning back, 'and then you are going to give these women iron. If you do not, my spear goes into the nearest gladiator.' He issued an order, and the rest of the guards spread out along the line. 'Each of my men will do the same. It is your choice. One.'

None of the guards were facing me, but there was one opposite Big Dog, and another in front of Siccum.

'I'm going to fight,' I muttered, preparing to lift my trident. With luck, I could stick the one who came for Big Dog.

'And I,' said Big Dog.

My heart squeezed.

Siccum had heard too; he also had had enough, it seemed. 'Come any nearer, and you will regret it,' he cried.

Never had I felt such comradeship.

'Two,' said the lead guard.

His men drew back their spears.

PART LXXXII

A crupellarius – maybe the same one who had slain our Thracian – stepped forward and with a matter-of-fact, in-out movement, stuck Calpurnia in the chest. She was dead before he even tugged the blade out and the crimson flowed.

I would have run forward, but Big Dog's arm blocked my path. He could not have stopped me if I had shoved past, but it was enough to restore my senses. My ears full of Calpurnia's daughter's screams, I stayed where I was.

Precise, ruthless, the crupellarius next thrust at Calpurnia's daughter. Distracted perhaps by her banshee-like ululating, he cut open one of her arms instead of delivering a death blow. Blood sprayed everywhere. The daughter shrieked. He did better the second time. Deep went the iron, sideways into her throat, cutting skin, muscle, vessels. She dropped lifeless on top of her mother.

A long, satisfied *aaahhhh* sound went up from thousands of throats.

I stared at the two of them, a pathetic, bloodied, conjoined heap on the white-gold sand. Tears ran unchecked down my cheeks. A killing rage filled me. I could have murdered every last person in the audience in that moment, and not even blinked, but weak from my injury, my head swimming, I prayed instead that my soon-to-arrive end was swift and painless.

Caligula's selection resumed, two fighters at a time. He was mostly choosing the uninjured men, pitting them against each other pair by pair. I looked out for our gladiators in this group; they were the only ones I cared anything for. Most important of all was Siccum, who, standing near me, was one of the last whole-bodied individuals.

I had not counted on there being an odd number of uninjured fighters. Caligula selected a final pair, a Thracian against a Gaul, leaving only Siccum.

I glanced at him; he met my gaze.

We both suspected what would happen next. The emperor would not let Siccum return to the cells; he would just make him fight one of the wounded and maimed.

A moment later, he pointed at Siccum, who stepped forward.

I could taste sick at the back of my mouth. Against Siccum, I had less than no chance.

The emperor's finger stabbed forward again.

Not at me.

At Big Dog.

Oh gods, I thought, with a sickening slide of dread. He – Caligula – cannot do this. I will not let him.

'Let me go,' I said. 'I will volunteer.'

'This is not your fate, Midir,' said Big Dog, leaving the line. Over his shoulder, he said, 'With luck, you will get that Greek with the really bad belly wound. Fortuna be with you.'

I did not reply, for reason had left me. Using my trident as a crutch, I took a big step after Big Dog. If I could catch him up, and gain Caligula's attention, I would make the grandiose claim that I was a better opponent to take on Siccum than Big Dog. I, the killer of two gladiators in a single bout, was ready to show my skill to the emperor again. This time, my efforts would dazzle even more.

It was nonsense, of course, and more likely to result in a spear in the guts than imperial permission to fight Siccum, but it was all I had.

I shuffled faster. Big Dog was only five or six steps ahead.

Caligula was already picking the next pair of men.

I caught up, clutched at Big Dog's arm. 'Wait. Let me.'

He stopped. Turned. 'No.'

'Yes,' I said, my determination growing.

I never saw his fist, but it smacked into the middle of my wound.

An explosion of pain. My knees buckled. Vision dimmed to a long tunnel, sound entering my ears as if I were deep underwater, I felt myself falling.

Falling.

Hot sand against my cheek, my chest, my legs.

Then, nothing.

PART LXXXIII

The first sensation was pain. Waves of it, rolling over me like the incoming tide approaching a shore. I sank in its deepness, went under again. The last spark of me that was left did not care. I wanted to drown, avoid all memory. To never wake again.

After a time – I have no idea how long – the surface drew near once more. The pain had eased, although it pulsed from the area above my left hip with a beat as regular as my heart, as well as from other areas. I could feel my arms, hands, fingers. My legs were still there. Voices rose and fell near me, but I could not understand what they were saying.

I prised my gummy eyelids apart, seeing a familiar brick ceiling above.

I tried to speak, but all that came out was a strangled croak.

Footsteps approached.

'He is awake,' said a voice I recognised as the surgeon's. 'Praise the gods.'

I tried to lift my head from the table, and failed.

An instant later, he was standing right over me, eyes full of concern. 'Water?'

I gave him a weak nod.

He went and came back. Gentle as a shepherd with a newborn lamb, he lifted my head so that my lips touched the clay cup in his hand. 'Sip,' he ordered. 'Carefully.'

The water was finer than any wine or beer I had ever drunk.

After three or four mouthfuls, my throat was wet enough to speak. 'What happened?'

'After your friend's punch? You dropped like a stone, I am told, and nothing could revive you – Caligula had the guards prick you with their spears to no avail. You were halfway to Hades, and that is where you would be had I not happened to arrive as they bore you out of the

Gate of Death. To the spolarium you were bound, for an opened throat and a criminal's end on the rubbish heap.'

'They carried me out of the arena?' I asked, still confused, not understanding.

'Aye, so the fights could start.'

Big Dog. Siccum, I thought, grief tearing at me. I closed my eyes.

The surgeon took my silence as an indication to continue. 'Stop, I told the libitinarius in charge. Stay your hand with that blade. The emperor has given no direct order for his death! That confounded him, the wretch, for I was right. In his haste to start the new contests, Caligula had not given instructions about your fate. One success often follows another, as they say, so hoping that my authority continued to prevail, I ordered the libitinarii to carry you here, and here you have been these many hours.'

My eyes opened again. *That* was why I could hear no cheering, no trumpets. 'What time of day is it?'

'Sunset was several hours ago. The moon climbs high in the sky, and Capua sleeps.'

'All the contests are over then.'

'A long time ago.'

My heart ached. 'My friend – the murmillo with the leg wound?'

He shook his head.

'And the other, the Samnite who fought him?'

'I am sorry.'

Not you too, Siccum, I wanted to scream.

PART LXXXIV

I glared at the surgeon, and said, 'But if he beat the wounded murmillo, he should be alive!'

'So he should.' The surgeon's voice was sad. With his eyes, he indicated that we were not alone, then whispered in my ear, 'Caligula was in an evil mood. Most of the victors in the final contests were slain afterwards – executed. This one had not fought well enough. That one's bow towards the pulvinar was too shallow. Another turned his back on the emperor when he had been summoned – the poor wretch had not seen Caligula beckon him, but that did not matter. Your friend the Samnite, I recall one of the guards saying, seemed reluctant to give iron to the murmillo.'

'That is because they were friends,' I spat.

'There is seldom mercy on the sands of the arena,' said the doctor, sighing. 'And certainly not today. The emperor's archers killed both your friends.'

I hoped their end had been quick at least. Guiltily, furiously, I thought also of the wager Siccum had placed for me, and how hard it would be to claim my winnings. Impossible, I decided. 'Did *any* fighters from my ludus survive?'

'Not a single one, aside from you, of course.' He gave me a sympathetic smile.

I could not smile back. A sense of desolation bathed me. They were all gone – every last man of them. I had hated some, disliked others, not known many, and been friends to a few. All, however, had been my comrades, my brothers-in-arms. I thought of Crixus then, and consumed by black amusement, I chuckled. Noticing the surgeon's confusion, I explained, 'I am not laughing at the deaths of my fellows, but rather the lanista.'

'Crixus.'

'Aye. A vicious bastard, he is. Now, thanks to the gods, and,' I added, 'in no small part, the emperor, he is ruined. I am right glad. My new owner cannot be any worse than he.' I pictured Chaerea, who had been forced to buy me for an extortionate sum, and in the same moment, I thought of freedom. If the crowds had left the amphitheatre, and only the surgeon was down here in the bowels of the building . . . a better opportunity of escape might never come my way. The surgeon would have a key to the door, and he seemed the type who might, *just*, be persuaded to let me go. I hoped so. Old as he was, I had not the strength to overpower him.

The very thought, however, of rising from the table and trying to stand, let alone walk out of the treatment room, filled me with trepidation. My hip ached dreadfully, and stabbing pains emanated from various points on my chest, arms and legs – no doubt the stab wounds inflicted when the guards had tried to rouse me after Big Dog's punch.

I had to try. I thought of the green landscape of Hibernia, and imagined clambering out of an anchored ship, wading through the shallows onto the shingly beach near my home. I could smell fresh-cut grass, wilting in the sun to make hay, and hear the crackle of flame as the midsummer fires were lit. Music, and song, and dance, the whole night through – and the girls, all fluttering eyelashes and sidelong looks – the lusty, joyful memories gave me strength, and purpose.

PART LXXXV

I prepared myself, and with an effort, rolled onto my good side. I was facing two other tables, both of which were bare, and a side wall of the room. The surgeon was behind me, I thought.

The movement had caused fresh pain to thrust at me from everywhere, but I breathed into it and thought of home. After a few moments, I was able to ease up onto my elbow. I *could* get to my feet, I told myself. I *could* climb the stairs to the ground level, and walk into Capua. Where I would go then, I had no idea, but there would be time to worry about that once I was out of the amphitheatre, the cursed place that had claimed so many lives today.

'You should be resting.' The surgeon came around to my side, fussing like a mother hen. 'There is no need to move, unless . . . do you need to empty your bladder?'

Now that he mentioned it, I did. 'Aye,' I said.

'You can do that lying on your side. Wait.' Off he hurried, to get a receptacle, I assumed.

I twisted my head to look at the gate to the room, hoping that perhaps it lay ajar.

It was shut.

Worse, far worse than that, was the Praetorian perched on a stool on the other side of the bars. Back to the wall, drawn sword laid across his knees, he appeared to be asleep.

The surgeon saw me staring, and gave me an apologetic glance. 'There by the order of your new owner, Chaerea,' he said in a quiet tone. 'He came down to look at you when the contests were over. His "new investment", he called you. Told me to make sure you recovered.'

'Of course he did. And the prick did not want to risk my making a run for it,' I muttered, sinking into utter despair.

'Ah,' said the surgeon, his gaze sliding to the gate, and back to me.

173

Quietly, he said, 'You do not really need a piss, do you? Escape was more on your mind.'

I twitched my lips. 'You see through me, but I do actually need that.' I reached out for the wide-necked clay vessel in his hand. He hovered, but I waved him away. Doubtless I had been stripped naked when he was first treating me, but the small dignity of urinating without help seemed important. It was, I realised as the vessel began to fill slowly, almost the only power, the only freedom I possessed.

When I was done, though, I still had to ask him to take it away.

He made me drink some poppy juice after, to help the pain, he said. Really, I think he knew how seeing the guard at the gate had dragged my spirits to a new low.

I closed my eyes, weary to the bone, to the very marrow.

Tomorrow was a new day, I decided. Tomorrow I would find out whether my new master Chaerea truly was more humane than Crixus. I hoped so. Unless he was sick in the head, he would want to recoup his outlay. I would still have to fight in the circle of sand, therefore, but I would mostly be pitted against men of similar quality. Death would be a risk, but after my success today, I had a reasonable chance of building a career, and earning significant amounts of coin. Of winning the rudis, and after the compulsory period that followed, achieving the status of libertus, freedman.

There was another thing, I realised with a stab of hope.

Remaining as a gladiator, winning my freedom, meant that I had the tiniest of chances of revenging myself on Caligula for what he had done today.

I wanted to kill him far more than Crixus. Far more. And so that infinitesimal chance would have to do.

Holding that thought tight as a lover, I let the poppy juice carry me away.

To merciful sleep.

PART LXXXVI

The ludus at Rome, January AD 41

I lay on my bunk, mouth-breathing in a vain attempt to avoid the smelly farts of my sleeping cellmate, which came wafting across the room with monotonous regularity. Almost a year and a half had passed, and I was still in a gladiator school. Nonetheless, my life was immeasurably better than it had been. I was in rude health. My master, the Praetorian tribune Cassius Chaerea, was humane and his fingers light-handed on the strings of my fate. I was a champion fighter now, a well-known retiarius, not a tiro with no hope of survival on the sands of the arena. I shared with one man – albeit a monstrous producer of wind – instead of three, and our cell was large and spacious. I ate the finest produce from Rome's shops and stalls. My tunics and sandals were of good quality; I slept on a comfortable mattress; bathed and had a massage whenever I wished. And satisfyingly, my account in the ludus savings club was deep in the black.

Crowning all, I had completed half of the mandatory three years before I could claim the rudis, the wooden sword that symbolised a gladiator's freedom. Eighteen months, I told myself, that's all that is left. It was not quite true. Another two years' service had to be completed after that before I could walk out of the ludus gate, genuinely a freedman.

One weeping sore festered in my soul. I had accepted that it would be there for the rest of my days. Caligula, who had so callously overseen the slaughter of my friends and comrades, remained unpunished. As untouchable as the sun in the sky, he continued to reign supreme over the empire. I had railed silently against this for long months, fantasised that he was my opponent in every training bout, during every contest in the arena. I had sought divine intercession, making extravagant offerings at every temple in Rome. Nothing made a jot of difference, of course. I had eventually come to the answer that had been staring me in the face from the outset. I could never touch him, never make him pay for what he had done. So I buried my hatred of Caligula, and my desire for revenge, and focused on earning the rudis, an achievable goal. Once I returned to Hibernia, I told myself, I could purge his name from my mind forever.

Another loud fart shredded the air, and I rolled my eyes. Maximus Iulianus and I had been sharing for a long time, and got on well. It helped that our styles of fighting meant we would never face each other. An essedarius, a new class of gladiator who fought from a chariot, the stylish Iulianus was fast becoming one of the darlings of Rome. His popularity had not gone to his head, as it did with so many, which made him all the more likeable.

Driven from my bunk by the smell, I wandered outside. Our cell was on the first floor, another privilege of rank. I went a little way along the walkway, beyond the reach of Iulianus' farts, and leaned on the wooden rail. It was late afternoon; the light was fading from the sky and the day's scant heat was fast vanishing, yet that did not halt training. Many of our fighters, myself among them, would be taking part in the soon-to-be-held games in honour of the emperor. I had finished my practice perhaps an hour before, but a dozen or more were still sparring, watched over by three doctores.

'Ho, Midir, why are you not hard at it?' a familiar, lisping voice called.

PART LXXXVII

Peering into the lengthening shade below me, I was startled to recognise Chaerea, my owner. With him were two other Praetorian prefects I knew also, Sextus Papinius and Cornelius Sabinus. None of the three were in uniform, nor even in togas, something I found odd. Never before had I seen those of such rank in plain, working men's garb. They could have passed for ordinary citizens.

'Dominus,' I cried, smiling. 'I will come down to you and explain.'

Running a hand over my hair, straightening my tunic – it was odd, I thought, how I acted like a pupil about to see his tutor – I hurried to the stairway, where I was surprised for a second time. Chaerea was already on his way up, his companions a step or two behind. At their back, an ingratiating expression on his face, came the lanista, Fulvius Plautianus (known to one and all as Gnasher, thanks to his terrible teeth).

I waited until they reached the top of the stairs, then I bowed deeply. Chaerea liked me, and treated me well, but I was still his property, his slave, and until the manumission document was in my very grasp, I would show him every respect. 'Dominus,' I said. 'This is most un-expected.' Chaerea tended to send word of his coming; on those days, I delayed my training so he might watch.

It was as if he had not heard. 'I had thought to show Papiniuth and Thabinuth your thkills with the net.' His high, lisping voice was at odds with his bulky, masculine presence, but his companions, as used to it as I, made no comment.

'It would be my pleasure, dominus,' I cried, thinking that despite his words, his companions did not seem remotely interested. If anything, their expressions were tense, even nervous. That was none of my concern, however, and I added, 'I shall fetch my gear from the armoury at once! I will find a partner easily enough in the yard.'

Gnasher bobbed his head in agreement. 'Quicker than cooking asparagus, he'll be, dominus.'

Chaerea made a dismissive gesture. 'Another time. Ath I thaid, lanithta, I require the uthe of your offithe.'

'What is mine is yours, dominus.' Bowing and scraping, Gnasher worked his way round us and with a sweep of his arm, said, 'This way, if you will.'

Confused, intrigued, I too bowed as the three Praetorians followed the lanista past the sick ward and the strongroom to his office. In they went. Gnasher soon re-emerged, backing out. 'Some wine, dominus?'

Chaerea's voice answered, short, succinct.

'No, dominus, I understand. No one will disturb you. Take as long as you wish.' Gnasher shut the door and padded along the walkway towards me. Seeing my naked curiosity, he said brusquely, 'Back to your cell, Midir. Leave them to it.'

'Yes, dominus.' This was no time to challenge his authority.

PART LXXXVIII

Iulianus stirred as I came in. He rubbed a hand across his face, and peered drowsily past me. 'It's getting dark. How long have I been asleep?'

'Long enough to make the room smell like a sewer. Drove me out, you did.' I scowled at him, half serious.

'I'm not finished yet.' Chuckling, he let another fart rip.

'You filthy dog.' My retort was without heat; I was already peering round the jamb of the entrance to see if Gnasher had gone down the stairs, and across, at the cells opposite, to make sure no one was looking at me. I soon roused Iulianus' interest.

'What are you doing?' His tone, as ever, was loud.

I ducked back in, shot him a glare. There were also men in the cells to either side of ours. 'Shhhh.'

He was on his feet, fully awake, an instant later, and joining me. He made to stick his head around the jamb, but I pulled him back. 'What is it?' he demanded, this time in a whisper.

Beckoning, I led him to the back wall, the furthest point from the walkway, and under my breath, explained what had happened.

''Tis strange,' he admitted, 'but to me it seems only that Chaerea seeks a quiet, private meeting. Imagine trying to hold such a thing in the palace. The whole bloody place must be overrun with slaves and court officials, every one of them ready to tittle-tattle on what they have heard.'

'Why didn't they meet in the Praetorian barracks then?' I challenged.

'Maybe they can't trust their own men.'

I jabbed him in the chest with a forefinger. 'And if you are right about that, what in Hades are they needing to talk about?'

'I don't know.' His brow wrinkled, then cleared. 'Nor do I care. Of far more interest is what the cook can offer me in the way of sustenance. I'm starving.'

I rolled my eyes. Iulianus was a simple type, and not given much to thinking. As long as he was well fed and had ample wine, and was rubbed down after every fight, he was a happy man. Throw in a whore whenever he needed it, and he was pretty much like the proverbial pig in shit.

'Do you want anything from the kitchen?' This, over his shoulder as he strolled outside.

'I'm fine.' My gaze went past his ambling shape and the stairs, to Gnasher's office. Frustratingly, the *clack* of wooden weapons and the grunts from below prevented me from hearing anything – not that I would have been able to hear much at that distance beyond the murmur of voices.

There was more to this clandestine meeting than Iulianus' simple explanation, I felt sure. Sure enough, that when he came back munching bread and cheese, with a brimming jug of wine in one hand, to tell him not to say a word as I stole onto the walkway. He told me, frowning, not to go poking my nose where it didn't belong, and when I didn't pause, that I was a fool. I warred with myself briefly, but my curiosity got the better of me. On I went, light-footed as an alleyway cutpurse.

PART LXXXIX

By now the gloom had emptied the courtyard; voices carried from the kitchen, sweaty, hungry men asking for food and drink. Again I glanced at the cells opposite, and was gratified that their occupants were either lying on their bunks, or not looking outside.

Nearing the top of the stairs, I hesitated. For all I knew, the surgeon might decide to come up, or send one of his helpers. Gnasher might appear, or one of the fighters from the few cells in this section. I would be undone, found out – and if Chaerea realised, only the gods knew what would happen to me. Spying a guard at the bottom of the stairway, I halted, deep enough in shadow to remain unseen.

My suspicions were soon fuelled; one of the surgeon's orderlies, a hirsute, guttural-voiced Dacian, hove into sight, and the guard quickly barred his way. 'No one allowed past for the moment. Gnasher's orders.' A question, and then, 'No, I don't know when you can go up. Now piss off, before I get annoyed.'

The Dacian's response sounded suspiciously like an oath, but he walked away.

Gnasher's command made my mind up – I would risk trying to eavesdrop on Chaerea and his colleagues – and the guard's presence meant no one would disturb me, from behind at least. That did not stop my heart from pumping harder as I tiptoed along the walkway, halting by the entrance to the sick bay. Mercifully, it had a timber door rather than the bars of a cell, and there was, to my knowledge, only one current patient within. His broken leg had been set the day before, so he wasn't going to be clambering out of bed and coming to disturb me.

The strongroom was locked, as always, and after it, just a few steps, was Gnasher's office. Sliding my bare feet with utmost caution across the planking, wary of splinters and creaks, I eased into a position whereby I could place an ear against the door.

'. . . he wath never the thame after that bout of illneth, thix monthth after hith accthethion –' Chaerea mangled this last word almost beyond recognition before finishing – 'to the purple.'

'Gods, do you remember the bridge from Baiae to Neapolis?' This, contemptuous, was Sabinus.

An angry snort from Chaerea. 'How can I forget? I had to ride behind him, remember, with him calling me "Lathie" all the way.'

'It is shameful how he has treated you,' said Papinius. 'Not to mention . . .' His voice died away.

'Thay it,' grated Chaerea. 'We were all there.'

'The obscene gesture he made at the soldiers when you kissed his hand recently,' Papinius finished.

'To be called effeminate, inthulted by a yellow-liver who hath never drawn a blade in anger!' Chaerea's voice was outraged. 'If it had been any other man, I would have thruck him down on the thpot.'

Their conversation about the emperor had taken an ominous turn; I had no doubt as to the fate of anyone caught listening in. Utterly gripped, however, and confident that the Praetorians would not hear me – I was being quieter than a mouse with a cat outside its hole – I stayed put.

PART XC

'It is his love of murder – even of those loyal to him – that has brought me here,' said Sabinus. 'If the imperial governor of Germany and the emperor's brother-in-law can be executed on a whim, what chance have we – his closest protectors – should suspicion fall on us?'

'Even tho. Plenty of otherth have met the thame fate thince Gaetuliculth and Lepiduth. Ath he ith tho fond of thaying, "Remember that I have the right to do anything to anybody." In my opinion, it ith only a matter of time before hith attention fallth on one, or all of uth,' said Chaerea. 'Rumour hath it that there are other conthpiratorth, but we do not know how determined they are. *We* mutht act, therefore, and thoon.'

In the yawning silence that followed, I guessed that the three were staring at each other, waiting to see who would commit himself to the bloody-handed act that was in all their minds.

Papinius was first to speak. 'I am with you, Chaerea.'

'And I,' said Sabinus quickly.

'Even unto murder?' my master asked.

I did not wait for his companions' assent. I had heard too much already. Even more conscious of the need for silence, I twisted around and took a pace towards my cell.

A dreadful yowl split the air. A skinny cat leaped up straight in front of me, its fur standing on end. I had trodden on the tail of one of the ludus strays, which must have come slinking in behind me, eager for attention. It landed running, and took off like a streak of black lightning.

Panicking, I followed, breaking into a run.

Behind me the door opened. A heavy tread came out onto the walkway.

Ball-clenchingly terrified, I did not stop.

183

'Midir?' Chaerea's voice was strident with surprise. *'MIDIR!'*

Undone – I had nowhere to go, other than my cell – I stopped. 'Dominus,' I muttered.

'Come here.' Two words, laden with icy threat.

I considered my options. Retreat to my bunk. Attempt to get past the guard, who was already halfway up the stairs, his out-thrust spear at the ready. Leap over the rail and down into the courtyard, and try to get past the two sentries at the front gate.

All were choices which implied guilt. To obey Chaerea felt only marginally better, but beggars cannot be choosers.

I turned and with dragging feet, walked past the bemused-looking guard – and behind him, an outraged Gnasher – to stand before Chaerea. I bowed deeply. 'Dominus.'

'Inthide.' He gestured with the dagger I had not known he was carrying. Over my shoulder, he said to Gnasher and the guard, 'No, I do not need you. Jutht make thertain that no one elthe eavethdropth, d'you hear?' There was no mistaking the threat or the venom in his voice.

Papinius and Sabinus gave me death stares as I entered. Both of them also had daggers at the ready. 'On your knees, sewer rat,' Sabinus ordered.

I obeyed, my bowels threatening to turn to water, wondering which of the three would be my executioner.

The door closed. Chaerea joined his colleagues. His usually pleasant face could have been carved from granite, so unyielding was it.

'How long were you there?' he demanded. 'What did you hear? I would know the truth ere I have you nailed to a croth.'

PART XCI

Barely managing to keep myself from babbling like a small child caught with a hand in the sweetmeats, I revealed what I had heard.

As I finished, a significant look passed between the three. Chaerea nodded, and Sabinus moved to stand behind me. Intuiting what was about to happen, panicking, I squawked, 'Dominus, do not kill me!'

He made no reply. I sensed Sabinus at my back. A meaty hand – his left – seized my chin and hauled it back, exposing my throat. From the corner of my eye, I saw the dagger in his right fist. I almost pissed myself. Nothing I did would make any difference. Nothing I said.

I gave up.

Almost.

Down came the blade.

'I also hate Caligula, dominus!' The words burst free, coming from I knew not where. Knowing my fate was sealed anyway, I closed my eyes.

My heart beat half a dozen, a dozen times off my ribs.

There was no rush of agony as the dagger opened my flesh. No stars bursting across my vision, no spatter of hot blood on the floor.

The cruel bastards are playing with me, I thought, but the tattered remnants of my pride meant I would not beg for my life.

'Why do you hate him?' Chaerea's voice.

Startled to be addressed, to be alive, I risked opening one eye, and then the other. My master was regarding me with a quizzical expression.

'Becauthe of what he did in Capua?' he asked.

'Yes, dominus.' All the old rage and hate came pouring back, fresh as it had been that burning-hot summer's day. I saw my friends' faces: Big Dog, Siccum, Sextus, Mattheus and Atticus. The others I had known. Dapyx, Piye, Calpurnia and her daughter, the wounded and maimed gladiators forced to fight one another.

'So many people died that day, dominus, for nothing more than the amusement of that –' I drew a breath, deciding I had nothing to lose, and said – 'that goat-hating, hairy-armed, scared-of-being-looked-down-on-from-above *cunt*! I would leave this life a happy man even to witness his death. To play a part in it, gods, that would be the best reward of all. Better than the rudis.' I was surprised myself by that last revelation, but it had come from my soul.

No one said anything, and my guts lurched. I was a fool, I told myself, even to hope that these high-and-mighty types would give the smallest shit what I, a lowlife gladiator, thought. Weary beyond belief, I lifted my chin high for Sabinus' blade. 'Make it quick,' I said.

Again the blow did not fall.

The faintest spark of hope lit in my breast. I did not dare to blow on it, so faint was it, but my gaze moved to Chaerea.

He was staring at me, and I swear, the corners of his mouth were twitching.

I did not know what to think. I looked back at him, dumb as an ox.

'I think, my friendth,' said Chaerea, 'that we have found thomeone who dethpitheth Caligula even more than we do.'

Behind me, Sabinus chuckled. 'And calling the emperor a cunt takes some balls.'

'Thtand up, Midir,' said Chaerea. 'We need to talk.'

My hope burst into flame.

PART XCII

A little after midday on the twenty-fourth of the month, I was standing with a knot of Praetorian guardsmen outside the temporary auditorium that stood close to the imperial palace. We had been there for hours; it was the last day of the Palatine Games and Caligula was within, presumably enjoying the mimed play *Laureolus* and after, the tragedy *Cinyras*. Both were being performed by the great actor Mnester, a man I had never heard of, but of whom Chaerea spoke highly. For my own part, with murder in my heart, I preferred to wait outside, rather than have to pretend to enjoy plays I would struggle to understand. (My Latin remained strictly functional; I had no head for poetry or theatre.) Dressed in a belted workman's tunic, I wore a dirty, brown-coloured hooded cloak. I stamped about, trying to keep warm, no different in appearance to the crowds of urban poor and slaves thronging the area – excepting, of course, the razor-sharp gladius hidden by my cloak.

Today was the day that Caligula would die, or so Chaerea and his co-conspirators planned. Their original intent had been to act on the first day of the games, but arguments and indecision had seen the plan postponed until today. The risks of discovery had been mounting – the city was alive with gossip of plots to assassinate the emperor – but as Chaerea's slave and a minor player in the plot, I had been able only to wait until my master was ready.

And thank all the gods, I thought fervently, he was ready at last.

'Hades, my guts are in knots,' I heard one of the officers say to another. 'I wish he would just come out, so we can be done with it.' *He* was the emperor.

'You're not the only one,' said his companion with feeling. 'I must have pissed a dozen times since this morning.'

'We could be here a long while yet,' said the first. 'Last I heard, he was staying put instead of heading to the palace for lunch and a bath.'

His companion groaned. 'Why?'

'A bad stomach, apparently. He overindulged last night.'

This was news to me; I cursed inwardly, but I stayed put. I would wait here, night and day, until the far-off summer if I had to. I had no thought beyond the assassination. If I were slain in the attack on the emperor – some of his bodyguards would remain loyal, as might the troops positioned along the route back to the palace – it mattered not.

I watched a small boy pulling a carved horse on wheels along the cobbles. His tongue stuck out as he guided it over gaps between the stones, and I smiled at his fierce concentration. Summoned in no uncertain terms by his mother, a stallholder selling hot sausages nearby, he picked it up and walked back to her, his bottom lip jutting with temper.

Amused by the narrow constraints of his world, part of me wishing that my life were so simple, I let my gaze wander over his mother. Close to my own age, light-brown-skinned with black hair, she was very attractive. From the shouted comments with her vendor neighbours, I knew her husband was dead. If I survive today, I thought, and live to receive my rudis, I might wed a woman like that.

'He's coming!' cried a voice.

PART XCIII

My lustful thoughts vanished; my gaze shot to the officers whose conversation I had been listening to. A guardsman stood before them, chest heaving. 'Some of the senators persuaded him that a bath and a rest would help him to feel better.'

The Praetorians nodded at each other. One of them cast a look at me. 'Ready, fisherman?'

'I am.'

Chaerea had given me a dangerous but vital job. I was to obstruct Caligula's path somehow, to slow his progress and divert his attention so he and his co-conspirators could attack.

Dry-mouthed, nervous, my gaze on the exit from which the guardsman had come, I felt under my cloak for my sword hilt. Its solidity was reassuring. The gladius was not my usual weapon, but I knew how to use it well enough. I would not go far wrong with the common training refrain, 'Stick 'em with the pointy end', I decided wryly.

An excited crowd began emerging, ordinary citizens eager to catch a sight of the emperor – he was still popular with the public – hangers-on and officials. I went on tiptoe, spying the first Praetorians, the men who surrounded the emperor wherever he went. They posed the biggest risk to me when I knelt to lace my sandal – my intended ruse – heaving me out of the way with a curse was their most probable reaction.

There he was – Caligula – easy to spot because of his height. Hollow-eyed and bald on top, he really was unattractive. He was in a good mood, however, despite his upset stomach, talking animatedly with a pair of toga-clad men, two of the many senators and nobles with him.

'Claudius and Valerius Asiaticus,' said one of the Praetorian officers, telling me what I did not know. 'Cowards, both of them. They won't cause us any problem.'

'The rank and file guardsmen could – a good number still love him,' said his companion warily.

'True enough. But some will obey their senior officers.' Chaerea, Sabinus and Papinius were tribunes; they had also recruited their commander, the prefect Marcus Arrecinus Clemens. The plan was to attack Caligula, simultaneously ordering the guardsmen not to draw their weapons.

'And some won't.' The officers' eyes moved to me, and my skin crawled. There was a good chance I would die, once the loyal guardsmen realised I was part of the ambush, and they knew it. I shoved away my fear, and concentrated on the image of Caligula lying in his own blood.

I spied Chaerea, Sabinus and Papinius a few steps behind Caligula. Clemens was with them; the four were talking and laughing as if on a stroll in the palace gardens.

There were so many people with the emperor – more than twenty, I guessed, and that excluded the screen of guardsmen – that my ploy of lacing my sandal began to seem foolish. I might halt the imperial party, but getting close to Caligula with my blade? It will be enough if he dies, I told myself.

That prospect was still not definite. I glanced down the avenue that led to the palace, Caligula's usual route. Praetorian guardsmen stood on either side of the road, every twenty to thirty paces as far as the eye could see. A pitched battle was not impossible. The contest would be massively skewed in favour of the guardsmen, armed and armoured as they were.

You can do nothing about that, I thought. Concentrate on the task at hand. Stay in front of the emperor. Block his path. Trust that Chaerea and his colleagues do the rest.

PART XCIV

Blank-faced, meeting no one's gaze, I ambled in front of the throng that accompanied the imperial party, as if joining them. Ten paces I went towards the palace. Twenty. I swallowed. There was no reason to delay. I lifted a foot as if to free a pebble from inside my sandal, and unobtrusively tugged one end of the lace free. I walked on, angled my path a little so it was directly in front of the emperor, and prepared to kneel down.

'Wait!' Caligula's voice was petulant.

I turned, as did many in the crowd.

'I am tired. It is too far to the palace that way.' He pointed to the right, into a narrow alleyway. 'We shall go that way.'

'A shortcut, imperator, patht Tiberiuth' house,' said Chaerea. 'A fine idea.'

Clemens, Sabinus and Papinius echoed him.

The crowd began to disperse. There would be no imperial largesse in the alley, no pause to watch acrobats or jugglers.

My delight grew as, irritated with his hangers-on, Caligula dismissed most of those with him. Claudius and Asiaticus remained with him; so did Chaerea and his co-conspirators.

I had lost my place in front of the emperor, however. Reasoning that I could work my way ahead of him, I ducked into a laneway that ran roughly parallel with the path Caligula had chosen. Once inside it, I retied my lace and then broke into a run. Pottery and other refuse crunched beneath my feet. An old woman perched on a stool in the doorway of a house, her rheumy eyes beady as a crow's. I went a couple of hundred paces and turned right. That proved to be a dead end; I retraced my steps, and tension gnawing at my belly in case Caligula got ahead of me, continued down the lane. I took another wrong turn, and then offered a coin to a rag-wearing girl of perhaps seven. I thanked the gods that Chaerea had mentioned Tiberius' house. Mention of that was enough. Expertly, the girl led me straight and true to a T-shaped junction.

'This is it,' she said, her hand out.

Distrustful of street urchins, I kept a firm grip on her payment. Stepping out into the alley, I looked to my right. Relief flooded through me. A group of men was approaching, and among them I could see brightly coloured feathered helmet crests, such as Chaerea and his colleagues wore. I tossed the coin at the girl.

She examined it closely, before nodding her satisfaction. 'Wanting to see the emperor?' she asked.

Surprised that she knew who was approaching, I muttered, 'Aye.'

'I've never seen him up close.'

I ignored her.

She remained where she was.

'Go on,' I said, eager that she should leave, and not know me as one of the assassins. 'Go.'

She did not move. 'You're not my father.'

Exasperated, unwilling to risk playing my role – Caligula was now perhaps thirty paces away – I ignored her and, once again, undid my lace. Taking a deep breath, I walked out into the alley and made my way towards the imperial party.

'What are you doing?' Her childish voice was pipingly high.

PART XCV

Praying that no one heard, I went perhaps half a dozen paces. Then one of the lead guardsmen saw me.

'Out of the way!' he cried. 'Make way for the emperor!'

I gaped, attempting to look like a surprised, none-too-intelligent citizen. 'Eh?'

He repeated his command, louder. Laid a hand to his sword.

Still I did not move. My gaze moved past the guardsman and the emperor, to Chaerea. Our eyes met. He gave me a tiny nod. It was all I needed.

'Are you deaf, fool?' shouted the guardsman.

'S-sorry, sir,' I said. I took a step backward, then stood on my undone lace, tripping myself. Down I went. A shooting pain radiated from my left knee as it connected with something sharp. Hissing with real pain, watching the guardsman from the corner of my eye, willing him not to draw his blade but to kick me instead, I fumbled with my lace. 'A thousand apologies, sir,' I said loudly. 'I tripped on my lace. I am a clumsy fool.'

'That you are,' he snarled, but the edge had gone out of his voice. 'Out of the way! Caligula waits for no gutter sweepings.'

I flashed him a nervous and not-entirely-acted look, but I did not move. 'One moment,' I said, fingers tying the knot. 'Nearly there.'

The guardsman halted, thereby forcing those behind him to do so. He scowled, and drew back his sole-studded boot for a kick. 'I told you!'

I tensed, hoping he would not break too many ribs.

'Now!' roared Chaerea.

Time seemed to stop.

The confused guardsman twisted around.

I stood up. Saw Caligula staring at Chaerea. At the dagger in his upraised fist.

'Hoc age! Take that!' screamed Chaerea. There was a soft impact, one I knew intimately, of a blade entering flesh.

Caligula let out a cry of pain. Put a hand to the back of his neck, and regarded his blood-covered fingers with incredulity.

'Repete!' yelled Chaerea. 'And again!'

Caligula moaned. Staggered.

Sabinus had his back to me, but I saw his right arm lunge forward, burying a dagger in Caligula's chest. 'Accipe ratum!' he said. 'So be it!'

The guardsman in front of me finally reacted. 'To the emperor!' Out came his blade.

I stabbed him in the back. Slew his comrade even as he half turned in horror. Cut and thrust with a third guardsman, finishing the contest with a savage slice of my blade that opened his thigh to the bone. Then I was through the ring of guardsmen. The petrified toga-wearing toffs in my path scrambled to get beyond my reach. I reached Sabinus, who stood, his crimson-tipped dagger dangling by his side, regarding a prone Caligula. Chaerea was facing us, Papinius by his side. Clemens was shouting at the guardsmen, ordering them to stay where they were. 'It is over,' he shouted.

I barely registered his cry. All my attention was on the emperor.

Caligula's face was pale as a shroud, and his toga was marked with multiple expanding circles of red. Blood was pooling on the ground beneath his head. One of his hands came up, the fingers reaching out to Sabinus in entreaty. His lips moved, trying to speak, but no words came out.

'Tho dieth the tyrant,' intoned Chaerea.

Not yet, I prayed, dropping to my knees by Caligula. I leaned over him, staring into his eyes. To my intense relief, sense yet remained in them.

'Like as not, you do not recognise me,' I snarled. 'But I know you. I am the retiarius who defeated two opponents on a pons in Capua a year and a half ago.'

To my joy, his eyes widened. He remembered.

'I was the only man to survive the slaughter.' There were tears in my eyes, remembering my friends, but my arm was rock steady as I drew back my gladius. I thrust it deep into Caligula's groin. Right through him it went, out the other side, and into the dirt of the alleyway.

A mewl of agony rose. The emperor's hands reached down to my blade, but had no power to shift it.

I felt not a shred of pity. 'That is for Big Dog, and all the rest,' I told him.

As Caligula choked and gasped his way to the underworld, I stood, leaving the blade where it was, and met Chaerea's approving gaze.

'Dominus,' I said.

Despite the clamour and the cheers, he heard. He smiled.

My heart soared. I could almost see the rudis in my hand.

AUTHOR'S NOTE

I n case you were wondering, gelded grunters, ex-tenants of pigsties, donkey ears and egghead are all attested Roman insults. The quote about loving the steel is from Juvenal, and 'lord of the maidens' comes from a graffito in Pompeii written by a gladiator. My descriptions of the amphitheatre, the crowds, the unfolding of the day's contests – from the pompa to the blade-sharpening, practice for the gladiators and so on – are all accurate.

The two-mile bridge built in the Bay of Naples in the summer of AD 39 was the most decadent of Caligula's spectacles. He was an ugly man, and scared of goats. He also hated being looked on from above. To replenish the gaping hole left in his treasury thanks to his profligate lifestyle, he introduced measures such as selling gladiators to senators at grossly inflated prices. It was my invention to have Midir sold instead to a senior Praetorian. Chaerea was a tribune in the Praetorians, and mocked by Caligula as I described. His co-conspirators included his fellow tribunes Sabinus and Papinius, and their commander Clemens. The events on the day of Caligula's assassination all come straight from Suetonius, right down to the cries of the assassins.

2020 will forever be known as the year COVID-19 hit the world. Each and every one of you will have your own memories of this time – weird, awful, tragic, with some rare but truly uplifting moments. I'm sure a million books will be written about it. Keen to help readers caught in lockdown, in late March 2020 I started Authors Without Borders, an online initiative providing new historical fiction content five to seven days a week. I roped in as many of my author friends and colleagues as I could – thank you all! – and we each began writing separate short stories, first on Facebook and then on a dedicated website. It's still there: authorswithoutborders.org). Big thanks to Rob McClellan for setting that up FOC.

'Sands of the Arena' had its origins in my long-held desire to write another story set in the amphitheatre after *The Forgotten Legion*. Raising money for charity via online raffles, I picked six readers who feature. They are: Big Dog – John Weiland; Mattheus – Matthew Dean; Siccum – Wim DC; Sextus – Andy Fairbairn; Atticus – Iain Callaway, and Calpurnia – Sarah Dimmock. I hope you enjoyed your brief time in the sun! Thanks also to everyone who donated but failed to win.

I am proud to say that I continued the story for the full period of UK lockdown, over almost three months and eighty-something episodes, and that countless people contacted me and the other authors to thank us for our efforts. It helped a little, I hope.

I deliberately did not finish Midir's tale, because I wanted to publish the story in book format if possible. Happily, that has now happened, and so you can read the full story here, as well as many other stories that have previously only been published in digital format, or in the case of 'Hannibal: Good Omens', only in a few hundred self-published paperbacks – extra material for Jenny Dolfen's marvellous *Darkness Over Cannae*.

Enjoy!

HANNIBAL:
GOOD OMENS

SOUTHERN IBERIA,
LATE SPRING 218 BC

It was a crisp morning, and to the east of the city, the sky was turning red-pink. Dawn was coming to Gades. Large, prosperous and well situated, it had been the pride and joy of Carthaginian colonies since its founding more than five centuries before. Like its mother city, Tyre, Gades was located at the end of a long peninsula that protruded into the sea at an acute angle. Surrounded on three sides by water, its defences were close to impregnable. The natural harbour to its north, formed by the peninsula's proximity to the mainland, was ideal for shipping. Protected from the weather, it also contained the mouth of a large river that was used for much trade.

The absence of the usual sea breezes had caused temperatures to fall lower than was usual over the previous few days. Inside people's houses, fires had been lit to drive away the early morning chill, and to cook the morning meal. Smoke trickled upward from a thousand roofs. Sounds carried in the still air. Babies cried, mothers soothed. Sheep and cattle complained from the livestock market. The *ting, ting, ting* of a coppersmith's hammer competed with the ill-mannered screeching of gulls overhead and the far-off shouts of ships' captains from the dockside.

Tradesmen were already passing through the streets – the need to make a living didn't stop because it was cold – but they were cloaked, one and all. The figure that slipped out of the side gate of the central palace was garbed in similar attire, so it attracted little attention. This suited the individual – Hannibal Barca – well. Anonymity gave a man options, and never more so when the person concerned was the de facto ruler of the Iberian Peninsula. It was a relief to escape, if only for a time, the entourage of scribes, staff officers, servants and bodyguards that accompanied him everywhere. It was, he thought, none of their business if he chose to pay a private visit to the shrine of Melqart, his family's favoured god.

Hannibal was of average build, but years of military training and campaigning had given him an athletic, well-muscled frame. Like most Carthaginians, he was brown-skinned and black-haired. His close-trimmed beard was unusual; so too was his unflinching gaze, which men tended to avoid. Like as not, it would give him away, so within a few paces he had pulled forward the cowl of his cloak to shadow his face.

Blending in, Hannibal made his way east, towards the edge of the city. He passed the streets lined with cloth merchants and vendors of Tyrian purple, the priceless dye extracted from murex shellfish, and the stinking alleyways in which the fullers practised their trade. Many of the thoroughfares were paved, but plenty were not. The uneven surface outside half a dozen contiguous butchers' shops ran with blood, and skinny mongrels fought over lengths of still-steaming intestines. It had been an oversight by the city's rulers, thought Hannibal as he picked his way around the gore, not to invest in paving stones throughout the commercial districts.

A wry smile twisted his lips. They wouldn't get the chance to do it for the foreseeable future. After a gap of twenty-two years, the fight against Rome had begun again. Any spare monies – and more besides – would be levied in tax by his officials, to fund what would be a bottomless war chest. Yet Hannibal felt no remorse for Gades' inhabitants, rich or poor. The hardships they might endure in the coming seasons would be as nothing compared to those faced by his soldiers. Plenty of men had died already, during the recent siege of Saguntum, a coastal city allied to Rome, and these losses would pale into insignificance beside those his army would suffer once they reached Italia, and faced the might of its legions.

The soft-handed jeweller giving him a suspicious look from the doorway of his fine shop wouldn't last a day in the forthcoming campaign. Nor would the paunchy baker, bawling about his fresh pastries from behind his open counter, or the haughty-looking perfume merchant over there with his plucked eyebrows and manicured fingernails. Hannibal put them all from his mind. Not everyone was a soldier. As long as they paid their taxes, he would be content.

It wasn't impossible that the war would come to Gades, of course, but that was unlikely. If things came to that, thought Hannibal, the Romans would have overrun all the Carthaginian territory in Iberia, and defeated every army in their path. To prevent that eventuality, he was leaving behind able generals, and decent numbers of troops. The local tribes, courageous and warlike, were also a deep reservoir for more recruits. It would take much to threaten this great city, and if he got his way, his enemies would never be granted the opportunity. Victory in battle over the legions, something Hannibal had been preparing for his entire life, would allow him to march through Italy, offering freedom to the peoples subjugated by Rome. Shattering the Italian confederation in this manner would destroy the Republic as an earthquake brings down the mightiest of buildings.

The Romans had humiliated Carthage after the first war between their peoples, and Hannibal's desire to avenge this injustice formed the bedrock of his existence. The first clash – Saguntum – was over, but a mountainous task remained. To see the thing through to its end, he had to remain calm, composed and most of all, ready for anything. Being able to adapt, to overcome the obstacles thrown in one's path, had been a skill taught to him by his father, Hamilcar.

Hamilcar had been an expert on Roman battlefield tactics. 'Their generals win time and again because of their men's discipline,' he'd told Hannibal a hundred times. 'What opponents fail to identify is that Rome's strength in battle is also one of its weaknesses. They use three combat lines, in identical order, with the cavalry on the wings; they attack using the same methods almost every time. Despite their record of successes, they tend not to use enough horsemen, or to vary their infantry formations. They won't fight at night, or from ambush, and so on. An inventive leader who attacks where the Romans are not expecting – with the right troops, of course – could cause havoc. *Would* cause havoc!'

Catching sight of a party of Libyan spearmen, recognisable by the massive shields slung from their backs, Hannibal thought, I *have* the right soldiers. The army's core, tens of thousands veterans strong, would provide both hammer and anvil to crush the Romans. Taking a deep breath, he squared his shoulders. I also have the ability. Rome will learn that in time.

Remembering his destination, he assumed a humbler air. It was rare for the gods to offer proof of their blessing. Regardless of that, it was imperative for the success of Hannibal's venture that he made generous enough offerings to ensure they did not grow angry with him. To this end, he would present himself formally at the temple later in the day, and gift Melqart's priests with a score of fine bulls, and three times that number of sheep. There was no doubt that *that* visit would go well – in the face of such bounty, the priests wouldn't be stupid enough to give him bad omens – but he wished to attend the shrine on his own first. Favourable portents granted to an anonymous stranger who mentioned an intended 'trade war' against an 'old enemy' would ease his privately held concerns about the forthcoming war.

Hannibal spent the remainder of his journey deep in thought, running over the preparations that were still needed before his army could begin its great march north-east, towards Gaul, and Italia.

A piping voice broke his reverie. 'Need something to sacrifice?' A desperate-eyed hen was dangled under his nose from the fist of a snot-nosed boy. 'A finer bird you'll never see. A drachm, and it's yours.'

'That wretched thing isn't worth a quarter of that amount.' Hannibal hadn't noticed that the temple to Melqart – his destination – was drawing near. He cast a look down the street, which was empty of the merchants, soothsayers, and peddlers of trinkets who congregated around temples. The shrine still lay three or four blocks away, and he waved the urchin away with an impatient hand. 'Enterprising of you to harass me here. Fewer competitors equals more business, eh?'

A sly grin. 'Something like that. Give me half a drachm.'

'Forget it!'

'You're beggaring me,' said the urchin, letting out a heavy if unconvincing sigh. 'I'll take a quarter drachm.'

Hannibal chuckled at the boy's spirit, only then taking in his pinched, world-weary face and stick-like limbs. Life on the streets was hard, he thought, in particular when you were six or seven summers old. Feeling more sympathetic, he reached for the purse at his belt.

From the corner of his eye, he caught the urchin's posture change. A heartbeat later, there was a rush of feet from behind. Instinct made Hannibal duck, and the blow meant for the back of his head struck him a hard but glancing blow on the left shoulder. Hissing with pain, Hannibal spun to face his assailant. Rather than one, however, he faced five ill-dressed men; all were armed with clubs or knives. The urchin, who had been the bait, danced from foot to foot behind them. 'Get him,' he cried. 'He's got a heavy purse!'

Cursing to have been easily duped, Hannibal tugged out his falcata sword, which had been concealed by his cloak. He laughed as the rob-bers' expressions changed. 'Didn't expect to rob a soldier, eh?'

'Give us your coin,' demanded the largest of the five, a thick-chested man with a bushy beard. He hefted his club. 'Do that, and we'll let you live.'

Hannibal wasn't sure that he could best his opponents, but a quick look up and down the street told him that there was no chance of help. Fearful for their own skins, the few people nearby were pretending to see nothing. Pride wouldn't let him call for help, and the rough brick wall at his back provided nowhere to go.

He was reminded of the time, soon after his arrival in Iberia at the age of nine, when he'd been set upon by a group of local youths. Hannibal had fought hard, but he had been much younger and smaller than his opponents. Bruised everywhere, and with two cracked ribs, he had lain in the dirt until his father had emerged from their house and picked him up. There had been little sympathy.

'Courage isn't enough in a fight. Next time, use your brain,' Hamilcar had said. 'Work out which of your enemies is strongest, and which weakest. If they're armed, decide who has the best weapon. Use your surroundings to your advantage if you can. Attack before they do. Getting in the first blow can win a fight. Sometimes it's best to kill the weakest man; at others it is the biggest you must go for.'

'Your purse,' ordered Bushy Beard, raising his club.

'If I hand it over, you'll murder me anyway,' replied Hannibal, slip-ping off his cloak and whipping it around his left forearm as best he could.

'That's not true,' protested Bushy Beard, but the flickering glance he gave his companions said otherwise.

Hannibal wasted no more time with talk. He darted forward at the nearest attacker, an emaciated youth with a rusty knife. A feint with his cloak-covered arm made the youth recoil. He never saw the falcata, which slid into his belly and back out again in the space of two heart-beats. Hannibal leaped backwards to the wall as the screaming youth collapsed, bleeding everywhere.

'You whoreson,' screamed one of the robbers, a bald pate who Hannibal judged to be the boy's father. Dropping to one knee, Bald Pate placed an ineffectual hand on the crimson-soaked stomach. The youth groaned, and Bald Pate cried out in distress.

'Three against one,' said Hannibal, giving Bushy Beard and his companions a hard stare. One of the two was a tousle-headed man carrying a smith's hammer, the other a wiry stripling with terrible teeth. 'I'm ready to meet the ferryman. Are you?'

'He can't take all of us,' growled Bushy Beard. 'Rush him, and it'll be over.'

'Mebbe so, but *one* of us will likely be dead.' The stripling spat towards Hannibal and began to back away. 'I prefer easier game.' Bushy Beard's protests were in vain. He vanished down an alley.

The two men left were the biggest, and the most dangerous, but Tousle Head was staring at the youth with the belly wound. Hannibal seized his chance. Three steps forward, an arcing slash with his falcata, and Tousle Head was down, clutching a gaping wound in his right calf. Hannibal retreated again to the wall.

'Up, get up,' shouted Bushy Beard at Tousle Head. 'He's a dead man if we charge him.'

'Kill him yourself.' Tousle Head was trying to stem the blood pouring from his leg. 'I'm done.'

Keeping an eye on the two injured men, Hannibal advanced towards Bushy Beard. 'Clear off, before I decorate the street with your guts.'

Bushy Beard let out a string of curses, but he retreated. Hannibal followed him until he too entered an alleyway.

Thunk. Fresh agony exploded in Hannibal's brain, eclipsing the discomfort from his shoulder. The boy, he thought. I forgot about him. He spun, sword at the ready. *Whizz!* Hannibal bent his knees just in time, and a second stone shot over his head. He ran at the urchin, who was stooping to pick up another missile. 'Run, you little bastard!'

The urchin moved, but not fast enough to avoid the point of Hannibal's leather boot, which connected at speed with his bony arse. Wailing, he was flung to land in a heap beside Bald Pate. Hauling himself up, he threw Hannibal a malevolent glance, but made no attempt to throw any more stones.

'You're clever,' said Hannibal. 'Cleverer than the rest of these fools. Get shot of them, or better still, pick a different trade. Otherwise you'll end up like him.' He gestured at the unconscious youth, who would be dead within the day.

There was no reply.

Hannibal did not linger. Without sheathing his sword, he headed for the temple. Every so often, he looked behind to make sure he was not being followed. At a hundred paces, he decided it was safe to clean his falcata on the hem of his cloak and slip it into the scabbard. His heart rate began to slow, and he wiped away the stinging sweat from his eyes.

The omens at the temple *would* be good, he decided. Melqart had just shown that he favoured him. Yet there had also been a salutary lesson to learn from the attack. Hannibal had been correct in his assessment of the five robbers, but he had misjudged the boy. If the stone had hit him but a trifle harder, it could have dazed him, with disastrous consequences. Bald Pate might have been encouraged to charge . . . Tousle Head could have helped him . . .

But he hadn't been stunned, and the injured men had been too scared to fight on. Spotting the grand entrance to Melqart's temple, Hannibal laid the matter to rest. He had overcome a seemingly insurmountable obstacle, with the god's help.

He would do the same against Rome.

THE MARCH

A Forgotten Legion short story

This story is dedicated with respect and kind regards to one of life's true gentlemen – Bruce Phillips – and with the same good wishes to his children, Seth and Layla.

PART I

Western bank of the River Hydaspes, autumn 43 BC

Immense peaks filled the northern and western horizons, snow-capped giants that almost seemed to reach the heavens. Glaciers covered their upper slopes; from the depths of the ice, fast-flowing rivers cut paths down the mountainsides. A distance lower, the treeline on each was a green girdle that ran all the way to the flat, fertile terrain below. Waterways criss-crossed this ground, farms and fields spreading out in a rich, uneven patchwork. Dense clouds lowered over the landscape; the air was thick and humid. Rain wasn't far away.

Two men stood by the broad expanse of the Hydaspes, which roiled past, laden with meltwater. One was tall and broad-shouldered, and in the prime of life. He had bright blue eyes and a short beard. Prominent on his right thigh was a thick scar; a tattoo of Mithras sacrificing the bull marked his upper right arm. The other was older, and had a slight stoop. A gold earring shone from one ear; his hair was grey. Close up, if a man stared, it was possible to make out a blade-shaped cicatrice on his caved-in left cheek. Their only companion was a tethered, laden-down donkey that grazed the lush grass nearby.

'Nine years,' said Romulus. 'It seems like yesterday that we stood here, with Brennus.' He closed his eyes, hearing again shouted orders, the ring of weapons, and the piteous screams of the wounded and dying. It was by this river that the Forgotten Legion – the name given to their unit by the survivors of Crassus' army – had fought to defend the Parthian empire's borders from a massive Indian host. Artillery, ditches and flood channels had wreaked havoc on the enemy, but in the end, numbers had told. Defeat had seemed inevitable when Tarquinius had led him and Brennus out of the fighting, to the water's edge.

Spotted by Vahram, their malevolent Parthian commander, they had been forced to fight. Maiming him, they had again been about to jump into the river when a raging war elephant had burst out of the chaos. Death had stared them all in the face. Romulus blinked, feeling Brennus push him to one side, out of the elephant's path. He could hear his calm voice. 'This is my quarrel, brother. A time for Brennus to stand and fight.' Romulus could see the love and acceptance in the Gaul's eyes clear as day. 'Return to Rome,' he ordered. 'Find your family.'

Grief flayed Romulus. 'I would have stayed,' he muttered. 'I would have fought the elephant too.'

'He knew that.' Tarquinius' voice was gentle. 'But it was his destiny to stay behind, not yours.'

'That doesn't make it any easier.' Eager to bury his gnawing guilt, Romulus put his back to the river and studied the ground around them. Swathes of green sward and crops rolled away into the distance; birds swooped and dived overhead; in the distance, cattle were lowing. The place could not have looked more peaceful, or more different to how he remembered it.

He had hoped to see some evidence of the battle, but the chance of that appeared slim. If a month of high temperatures and daily torrential rain could half rot away his leather sandals, thought Romulus, glancing at his tattered footwear, nine years would have seen the corpses of men and beasts disappear long since. He cast a hopeful look at Tarquinius. 'Do you know where we stood that day?'

'I do not.' The haruspex's dark eyes met his. 'My memory is not what it was, and the visions have not come to me these many months, as you know.'

'No matter. We can walk the ground.' Romulus smiled, and hid his worry. Their journey from Rome had taken a year and a half. The first part had been easy: ships sailed frequently from Ostia to Alexandria through the spring and summer. Reaching one of the trading ports on the narrow waterway between Egypt and Arabia had been more difficult than he had thought thanks to a tribal uprising in the area. Delayed several months, they had arrived too late to catch the south-west wind that helped ships sail to India. Faced with a year in a shithole port before the prevailing winds changed in their favour again, Romulus had almost despaired. Ever the one to spring surprises, Tarquinius had suggested a journey into the interior: they might even find King Solomon's treasure, he'd said, winking.

They hadn't found the legendary monarch's gold and silver; instead they had nearly died several times over. Between near drownings in fast-flowing rivers, ambushes from hostile tribes, dangerous wildlife and encounters with slave traders, it was a wonder that they were here at all. Their suffering had seen Tarquinius age five years in one. It was as well, thought Romulus, that they had continued the rest of their journey by ship rather than follow the haruspex's next suggestion. To cross the vast deserts of the Parthian empire, as they had done after the disaster of Carrhae would have tempted Fortuna too much, even if they'd had a guide. 'You stay here.'

'I may be old, but I'm not dead yet,' said Tarquinius, joining him. 'Have you forgotten those bandits two nights hence?'

'How could I? You remind me at every opportunity.' Despite the tart response, he was grateful. Tarquinius had been on sentry duty, when he'd heard movement in the darkness, and silently woken Romulus. Screaming at the tops of their voices, they had released a flurry of arrows into the trees, driving off the would-be thieves. Daylight had revealed a dozen sets of footprints, more enemies than they could have hoped to fight off. To their relief, there had been no sign of the bandits since. 'You did well,' said Romulus.

Tarquinius winked. 'There's life in this old dog yet.'

They wandered away from the river, pushing aside the crops, scuffing in vain at mounds of earth with their sandals, and peering into the drainage ditches that channelled lifegiving water from the Hydaspes to the fields.

'We'll never find it this way,' said Romulus, slapping at a biting fly.

'Even if we find a rusted spear head, say, it proves nothing more than we already know – the battle took place somewhere on this plain – and if we happen upon a few bones, only the gods will know who they belonged to.' Tarquinius' meaning was plain. It was beyond them to discover if Brennus had died here.

'I drove off an elephant at Thapsus,' said Romulus, voicing the hope that rolled around his head a dozen times a day. 'A warrior such as he would be able to do the same, surely?'

'I can think of no better man to achieve such a feat.' Tarquinius hesitated, then added sadly, 'But my visions never showed me Brennus anywhere other than here.'

'That doesn't mean he's dead,' Romulus shot back. 'You can't be sure, and you haven't seen anything reliable for months.'

'You speak true,' said Tarquinius, quickly continuing, 'I also wish to find the big Gaul alive, Romulus.'

'I know you do,' said Romulus with a sigh. 'But to find nothing after all these years is a hard burden to shoulder.'

'Did you think it would be easy? That we'd find Brennus sitting in the shade of yon tree, supping whatever the locals drink in place of wine?'

'Part of me did,' said Romulus with a laugh.

'The men of the Forgotten Legion were crack soldiers. I doubt they were all wiped out. Which means they returned to Margiana. Find a village nearby, and we may be able to confirm that.'

There was a flicker of movement at the edge of Romulus' vision, and he turned his head, nice and slow. 'Don't look, but we've got company,' he said quietly. 'Close to the donkey.'

'Bandits?'

'A boy looking to thieve what he can, more like. Pretend that I'm looking down there.' Romulus indicated the drainage ditch a few paces to their right. 'Call out questions and so on. I'll work my way back to the river and try to catch him unawares.'

Tarquinius nodded.

Handing the haruspex his sword and baldric, Romulus clambered down the muddy slope and into the waist-deep water. Taking back his blade, he made for the Hydaspes. Behind him, Tarquinius began a shouted conversation. Romulus waded as fast as he could. The skulking figure he'd seen wasn't big – the physical danger was minimal, he judged – but if the urchin made off with their donkey, life would become difficult and unpleasant. In addition to their tent and food, the beast was carrying their bows, arrows, and the trading goods bought to ease their passage through the Indian countryside. It had been foolish to leave the donkey unattended, he decided, hoping his mistake would not cost them dear.

A sharp stinging in his groin was an unpleasant reminder that leeches liked these waterways. Scowling, for he could not tarry to deal with the bloodsuckers, Romulus drove against the current, gauging his distance from the river – fifty paces – and glancing up at the ditch's lip. He didn't know exactly where the donkey was, and peering over the edge of the channel risked being seen. It was almost as if the beast sensed his need, for a moment later, there was a soft bray of complaint at whatever the urchin was doing. He was close – no more than twenty paces, Romulus judged. That would have to do, for the water was growing deeper, and the mud more glutinous.

Again the donkey came to his aid, its protests concealing the noise as he left the water and scrambled up the bank. For the first time since buying the troublesome creature, Romulus was grateful for its irritable nature.

As fortune would have it, the urchin had his back to the drainage ditch, and Romulus had him by the ear before he knew what was happening. The boy, for boy it was, squawked in dismay and twisted to see who had beset him. A notched bronze knife appeared in his right hand. He made a clumsy lunge at Romulus, who dealt him a mighty slap to the cheek. The blade dropped; the urchin howled. Romulus kicked it away, and studied his catch. The boy wore only a loincloth; he was as light as a feather. Stick-thin limbs and a head that was too big for his body gave him an almost comical appearance. Every bone of his ribcage and spine was sharply delineated beneath his dark brown skin, which was marked with a patchwork of scars, old and new. From under a mop of spiky black hair, a pair of dark eyes studied Romulus with deep suspicion.

Spotting the contents of at least one bundle of their possessions spread on the ground, Romulus said, 'Looking for the most valuable items, were you?'

His answer was a swinging kick, which missed, and an unintelligible stream of what Romulus assumed were insults.

'Got any friends with you?' Keeping a firm grip on the boy's ear, Romulus studied the undergrowth and nearest trees. He could see no one; it seemed the urchin operated on his own. 'Tarquinius!'

By the time the haruspex arrived, Romulus had tied the boy's hands and fitted a rope hobble round his ankles, preventing him moving faster than a slow shuffle. These actions had reduced his captive to a terrified silence; he quailed further at the sight of Tarquinius' bearded, scarred face.

Tarquinius eyed the jumble of blankets, pots and trinkets. 'He was thieving?'

'Aye. He's spirited too. Tried to gut me with that knife.' Romulus jerked a thumb.

'Would you have been any different at his age?'

215

'Perhaps not,' said Romulus, grinning. 'Can you speak his tongue?' Tarquinius was adept at picking up new languages; on the merchant ship from Egypt, the polyglot crew had offered the chance to learn several.

Tarquinius said something. The boy gazed blankly back. He tried again, with the same response. A third attempt failed too, but his fourth was more fruitful. The boy looked momentarily surprised to be addressed in his own language, then gabbled something lengthy to Tarquinius, who smiled.

'He says that his three brothers are huge, and that they are armed with bows. When they get closer, we will be riddled with arrows. Let him go, however, and he will ensure we are unharmed – as long as he takes your sword.' One of Tarquinius' eyebrows rose.

Chuckling, for the story was as tall as one of the far-off peaks, Romulus rummaged in a bag and produced a flat bread that he'd baked by the fire the night before. 'Here.' He proffered it to the urchin, whose eyes flickered from it to his face and back again. Shuffle forward. Snatch. Chewing furiously on the bread, the boy's gaze shot now from Romulus to Tarquinius, as if he were trying to gauge who was more dangerous.

'Where does he live?' said Romulus to the haruspex.

'In a village not far from here,' came the reply after a short exchange.

'Has he family?'

Another back-and-forth. 'His father died when he was a babe; his mother when he was six. He lives in the village forge, where he works for the smith – a bad man who drinks and often beats him,' said Tarquinius. 'The boy wants to know if we will eat him after we've murdered him.' In Latin, he added, 'It's not every day that two pale-skins like us appear, eh?' Even with their deep tans, they were still clearly of a different race to the Indians.

'Tell him we'll only cook him if he doesn't do what we say,' said Romulus, straight-faced.

The boy's eyes went as round as dishes when Tarquinius relayed those words.

'We won't eat you,' said Romulus gently. He held out a strip of cooked meat.

Snatch. The morsel vanished down the boy's gullet.

'If he can take us to the village, we'll let him go,' Romulus suggested. 'We might find out something there, eh?'

'Aye.' Tarquinius spoke again, his tone reassuring. The boy seemed placated. When Romulus undid his leg tethers and placed him on the donkey's back, delight replaced his suspicion. A happy babble of words followed. 'He's never been allowed to ride anything. It's so high up, he says,' revealed Tarquinius in amusement. 'Can the donkey not go faster?'

'Has he heard of a big battle here?' asked Romulus. He needed no translation for the boy's vigorous nod in reply.

'It is famous in the village. He was only a baby, but everyone had to flee to the hills. When the fighting was over, and it was safe to return, the fields were filled with dead. The smell travelled for miles. There was little food for months afterwards, as the armies had taken it before the battle. People starved. It was a bad time.'

'So the Bactrians treat their subjects no better than the Parthians,' said Romulus. The Forgotten Legion had had its own supplies.

'Great powers are little different,' said Tarquinius. 'Generals care nothing for the farmers who stand and watch their armies pass by. Ever it has been so.'

Romulus didn't hear. Rich imaginings filled his mind: that someone in the village would remember how the battle was turned by a mighty warrior slaying an elephant, or how the Parthian troops had paraded this warrior in honour at the front of their column as they had marched away.

He knew his hopes for wild fantasy, but they were more appealing than reality. In all likelihood, thought Romulus, Brennus had been stamped into oblivion by the elephant, and his bones had long since mouldered into the fertile ground on which they walked.

After a time, the three joined a muddy track that led towards the Hydaspes and the main road south in one direction, and towards the village in the other. Perhaps a mile further on, they came to a straggling collection of poor mudbrick huts roofed with straw. Their arrival brought life to a standstill. Small children screamed and ran away; older ones stood with open mouths, amazed by the two foreigners. Women scurried inside their huts, peeking around the door frames with wide eyes. The men were a little less wary, stopping their work and staring without a word. Only the livestock cared nothing for the new-comers. Hens pecked at the dirt, searching for grubs and insects; pigs snouted in dungheaps, and ribby dogs skulked close to the donkey, sniffing the air.

The boy was delighted with himself. Seeming to forget his bound wrists, he launched into a loud account of how he had met two wanderers, men who asked questions about the big battle from years before. Corrected by Tarquinius, he announced that the pair were also traders, who had come from the south, from the great city of Barbaricum.

'He loves this,' said Romulus, amused.

'I'd wager the wretch gets little but kicks and curses most of the time,' said Tarquinius.

That had been Romulus' thought too, and so when a burly, grimy-skinned man emerged from a forge and began berating the boy, he wasn't surprised to see their captive's face twist in fear. 'Tell him the smith won't hurt him,' he said to Tarquinius.

'Are you sure? They could turn against us.'

'Let them try,' said Romulus, feeling protective of the starveling. He cast a scornful eye at the gathering peasants.

Tarquinius spoke to the boy, who grinned, and then, in the precocious way children will do, thumbed his nose at his tormentor. Lumbering forward, muttering curses, the smith came to an abrupt halt as Romulus blocked his path. He shouted something. 'Get out of his way,' Tarquinius translated. 'The boy is his labourer.'

'He's not to harm him,' said Romulus, mind full of the beatings he'd endured at the hands of his master Gemellus.

Tarquinius' words made the smith snarl and bunch his fists.

A heartbeat later, he was lying in the dirt, his mouth an open 'O' of pain and surprise. Romulus' punch had driven deep into his solar plexus.

'Anyone else?' asked Romulus, his question echoed in the local language by Tarquinius.

No one moved. Even the boy fell silent.

'I think,' said Tarquinius, 'that we'd best ask our questions and move on.'

'Aye.' He'd take on a dozen of the farmers in daylight, thought Romulus, maybe even more, but darkness would lend them courage, and he and Tarquinius were but two. Best not to give them more reason to give chase when the pair left the village. With an obvious hand on his sword, he watched the ring of faces as Tarquinius' questions began.

'They seem happy to help,' said Romulus as answers flooded in.

'I've promised a piece of pottery to every man who gave a good answer to my questions.'

Romulus went to their bags and unpacked a bowl and a plate. Although it had been difficult to carry, the pair had endeavoured to bring from Italia plain red pottery, remembering from their previous visit to Barbaricum the high prices it had carried. Approving *ooh*s and *aah*s went up as he held them out.

Tarquinius' enquiries didn't last long. 'The battle is well remembered. Used to battles, the villagers abandoned their homes and made for the hills before the Indian army arrived. Most saw nothing of what happened – they were too far away. The noise of fighting was audible, but little else. Most agreed that the Indians had won, although they paid a heavy price. The Parthians retreated north, whence they had come. The villagers didn't dare to return for two days; they found the place destroyed, presumably by one side or another, searching for food. It fell to them and those from other villages to bury the dead in large pits. I asked if there were any wounded – they said no.' Tarquinius lowered his voice. 'You can imagine what happened to any that were found alive.'

'Aye,' said Romulus. Mithras, he prayed, let Brennus not have been among them, or any of my comrades. Let him have marched away with the survivors.

He gave each of the men who had been most helpful a plate or a bowl. They sold several more pieces but cut short any plans for further business. The smith had got to his feet, and was whispering in his fellows' ears. Romulus didn't like it; nor did Tarquinius.

Romulus slit the urchin's bonds with his dagger. 'You're free,' he said.

To his surprise, the boy's confidence vanished like early morning mist. He muttered something to Tarquinius, and gave Romulus a beseeching look.

'He wants to stay with us. The smith will beat him twice as badly because you knocked *him* down. The boy says he can look after the donkey, and clean our weapons, and if we show him, he will cook.' Tarquinius' lips twitched. 'He could prove useful. It's not as if he will

219

eat much. Yes, we'll be in danger, but his existence here rests on a knife edge.'

Romulus caught the smith giving the boy a filthy glare; that made up his mind. 'All right.' He stuck out his hand to the boy, Roman fashion. Hesitant, the boy took the grip. 'We are comrades now,' said Romulus. 'You look after us. We look after you.'

Tarquinius translated, and the boy beamed from ear to ear, pumping Romulus' hand with all his might.

The smith didn't like this clear display of friendship, and when Romulus turned the donkey's head and walked away with Tarquinius, he shouted at the boy to come back. Ready this time, Romulus prevented their new companion from thumbing his nose for a second time. 'Don't kick a wasp's nest more than once,' he said, receiving a blank look by way of reply.

The inability to communicate had to be dealt with at once, thought Romulus. He held up his sword, and spoke the word for it in Latin. Tarquinius explained. The boy's attempt to repeat it was an abject failure. Romulus tried again. Another spectacular mispronunciation followed.

Romulus groaned. 'Just as well it's a long way to Margiana.'

PART II

The mountains of southern Margiana

Wind whistled around the rocks, and Romulus pulled his cloak tighter. This high up, the towering banks of grey cloud were almost close enough to touch. Snow blanketed the slopes to either side; not a tree or bush was to be seen. A little way to his left, massive horns marked the resting place of a mountain goat. According to Tarquinius, the Greeks called the beast ixalos. There was no sign of whatever had killed it, but it must have been large, thought Romulus: perhaps an elusive snow leopard. If the opportunity ever presented itself to hunting one of *those*, he would seize it with both hands.

He was hunched behind a large boulder, squinting down at the plain far below. No one would see him on the rock-strewn slope unless they were very close, yet old habits died hard. A point would come when they had to leave the cover of the mountains, but until then he would use the terrain to his advantage and remain hidden when possible. Twenty days had gone by since their encounter with Vyas, the impudent urchin, by the Hydaspes. Apart from a botched ambush by the villagers the same night they had left Vyas' village, and a narrow escape from a landslide, their journey had been uneventful. The higher they had climbed, the fewer people they came across, which suited Romulus and Tarquinius. They had enough supplies to see them over the mountains, where they would eventually encounter Parthian patrols.

'Can you see anything?' Tarquinius was a short distance down the slope from Romulus with Vyas and the donkey.

'There's a fort, but it looks abandoned. No sign of movement anywhere.' He scrambled down to join the others. 'If enough men died fighting the Indians, and they weren't replaced, whoever replaced Vahram might not have enough troops to man every outpost.'

'Our journey towards the main camp will be easier for it, but we lose any chance of meeting former comrades in easy-to-talk situations.'

Romulus sucked on his lip. They had talked about setting up shop outside smaller forts, hawking their pottery while trying to discover if Brennus was alive. Doing the same outside a large fort, with a greater number of Parthians likely to be present, would be a good deal more dangerous. 'True enough, but I see no option other than to carry on.'

Tarquinius' dark eyes glittered. 'Nor I.'

'I not go back!' piped Vyas, who listened in to every conversation.

Romulus ruffled the boy's hair. 'We're of the same mind then.'

Vyas didn't know the friends' reasons for journeying into the Parthian empire, nor did he appear to care. As Tarquinius observed, his new life was worlds better than his miserable existence in the village. He was good company too, and able to help Tarquinius when his attempts to speak the local language faltered, and to teach Romulus some of his own tongue. Once he'd been shown how, Vyas happily tended to the donkey's every need. His cooking skills tended to result in charred, almost inedible disasters, but he could gather firewood, seek out camp sites, and oil, and sharpen their weapons. Romulus was already fond of the boy; even Tarquinius seemed to enjoy his company.

Romulus' spirits rose as they descended from the pass down a winding track. He had no more reason now to think that Brennus was alive, but seeing clear evidence of the Parthians – including a fort that he had marched past nine years before – had brought alive his memories of the big Gaul. He could see Brennus, laughing, training hard, drinking enough wine to fell a giant – and fighting like a hero.

'Look!' Tarquinius' voice was sharp with tension.

Romulus' gaze followed the haruspex's outstretched arm, and he cursed himself for not paying constant attention. Perhaps two miles off, along the road that led to the Forgotten Legion's camp, was a dust cloud. At its base, he could make out the figures of marching men, and riders. 'A Parthian patrol. They'll have seen us.'

'Unless they're blind,' said Tarquinius dryly. They were lower now, but few plants yet grew on the stony slopes; men's eyes would be drawn to the notch and the track bisecting it, where they were in plain sight. 'Do you want to turn around?'

Romulus considered their options. To go back would look suspicious, and might even cause pursuit. Continuing meant an encounter with Parthians. There might well be Romans in the patrol too, but the danger didn't lie with them. He set his jaw. 'It won't be much different to what might have happened outside a fortlet.'

'Not really.'

Romulus shrugged. 'On we go then.'

'Who are they?' asked Vyas, his eyes darting from Romulus' and Tarquinius' faces to the plain and back.

'Parthians,' said Romulus. 'And like as not, Romans – my people. The same soldiers who fought by the river near your village years ago. We will pretend that we are not Roman, however. It's *very* important the men down there do not know.'

Vyas looked at him as if he were mad. 'You not Indian,' he said, pointing to his own dark skin.

Romulus grinned. 'No. But there are lands over the sea other than Rome. We will say we are Phoenicians.'

'Phoenicians?' Vyas mangled the word.

'Aye. A trading people who travel further than most could ever dream of.'

'Like you,' said Vyas, who lived for the tales Romulus would tell him each night.

'I suppose,' admitted Romulus. With the ease of long practice, he and Tarquinius set about turning themselves into traders. Into the blankets on the donkey's back went his sword and the haruspex's double-headed axe, and their bows. Romulus' mail shirt was already hidden; he'd replaced his mildewed studded sandals with a pair of local leather ankle boots. Clad in nondescript tunics, deeply tanned and bearded, and armed with spears, they could pass for the Phoenician traders Romulus had met. That didn't mean the Parthians wouldn't recognise them – it was possible that some officers who'd been in the Forgotten Legion during their time would still be in place. The scar on Tarquinius' cheek was covered by his beard, but it remained the biggest chance of their being unmasked, as it were.

Romulus glanced at Tarquinius, whose expression was as blithe as if he were strolling by the Tiber. Vyas looked scared, and Romulus squeezed his shoulder. 'We're merchants, remember? No harm will come to us.' It was heartening how, despite the boy's fear, he nodded firmly.

'Speak no Latin in front of them,' Romulus warned.

'No Latin,' repeated Vyas, his face serious.

The ruined fort was perhaps half a mile from the bottom of the incline, but the three had come nowhere near it before a pair of riders came galloping towards them, sent no doubt by their commander to investigate the strangers.

'They're Parthian,' said Romulus, recognising their conical hats, four-cornered saddles, and most of all, the deep curve of their bows, and the arrow cases that sat on both men's hips. It was horse archers like these who had butchered Crassus' legion at Carrhae a decade before. One night, Romulus decided, Vyas would hear how he, Tarquinius, Brennus and their comrades had lived through the arrow storms and survived one of the bloodiest defeats ever suffered by Rome.

Romulus held up a hand, palm out, in the universal gesture of friendship. Tarquinius did the same. Nervous, Vyas held tight to the donkey's lead rope.

There were arrows fitted to the riders' bowstrings, but their bows were laid across their thighs, not levelled at the travellers. At fifty paces, the pair reined in. One shouted in Parthian, 'Who are you? Whither are you bound?'

'We are merchants,' shouted Romulus in Vyas' tongue. He still spoke some Parthian, but to reveal that would endanger them all.

The riders conferred. The second shouted in Indian, 'Merchants?'

'Aye. From over the sea,' said Romulus. 'From Phoenicia.'

The Parthians wheeled their mounts and returned to their comrades.

'We go back now?' ventured Vyas, his face markedly pale.

'No,' said Romulus. 'We go to the fort. Speak with the Parthians. See who is with them.' It wasn't impossible, he thought with a thrill, that Brennus was on the patrol.

The fort was in a bad state of repair; it clearly hadn't been in regular use for years. The crumbling ramparts were bare of sentries. Shattered by an unknown enemy, the remnants of the gates lay ajar; inside, roofless barracks lay open to the skies. The patrol was perhaps a quarter of a mile off; Romulus and Tarquinius decided to enter would be presumptive and riskier than simply waiting outside.

With mounting excitement and a little nervousness, he watched the column approach. Perhaps a century strong, the men in it were dressed as legionaries. A dozen Parthian riders led the way; at the front was a man with a finer horse than the rest, and was, to Romulus' relief, someone he'd never set eyes on before. Perhaps thirty-five, the officer was dark-skinned like all his kind, and wore a thick beard. His armour and weapons had a well-looked-after sheen, and he rode with an easy grace. A capable officer then, Romulus decided, and an experienced one. A man to be wary of.

'Well met,' the Parthian called at fifty paces. His Indian was heavily accented but intelligible. 'Travellers from the south are rare.'

'We met no one travelling in the same direction, sir,' said Romulus truthfully.

'What brings you to Parthia?'

'We are poor traders from Phoenicia.' Romulus adopted the wheedling tone used so often by merchants. 'We found many of our kind in the markets of Barbaricum this year; prices were not what they might have been. Venture inland, I told my partner, and we'll do better.'

'You are hardy souls.' The officer stopped in front of the gate. 'How do they call you?'

'My name is Hamilcar, sir. My companion is Muttumbaal.'

The officer gave Tarquinius a second, casual look, before glancing at Vyas with mild curiosity. 'The boy is no Phoenician.'

'No, sir. He fell in with us in a village on the southern side of the mountains.'

The Parthian had already turned away. 'You may camp inside the fort,' he threw over his shoulder.

'A thousand thanks, sir,' Romulus cried.

They stood and watched as the patrol marched through the arched gateway. Nine years was an age – his former comrades might have died in the battle by the Hydaspes, or since, or simply be back with the rest of the Forgotten Legion – but Romulus' heart raced as he watched the soldiers tramp by. It was hard not to feel disappointed as the last men passed. Brennus wasn't among their number; Romulus had recognised a few faces, but they weren't men he had known well.

Like the friends, the legionaries had beasts of burden – mules – to carry their heavy gear. After these had entered, Romulus led the way inside the fort. He was careful to set up their tent a good distance from the legionaries. As much as anything, he didn't want to be overheard speaking Latin to Tarquinius.

Discipline was good; with barely a word from the Parthian officer, the legionaries mounted guard on the four walls, erected their tents and dug a latrine trench outside the fort. Fires were lit, and soon the familiar smell of baking bread wafted across the courtyard. Romulus closed his eyes, remembering his years in the legions. He caught Tarquinius looking at him; the old haruspex smiled. 'Miss it?' he asked in a quiet voice.

'A little,' said Romulus. 'There were some good times, and many good comrades.'

'Did you spot Hadrianus?'

'You saw him?' Hadrianus had served in another cohort to Romulus, but he'd been known throughout the Forgotten Legion for having been struck by a slingshot bullet when he wasn't wearing his helmet, and surviving. He'd hovered between life and death for days, kept alive in part by the medicines and water that Tarquinius had trickled into his mouth. When Hadrianus had woken, he'd had no memory of what had happened. 'He's a good man,' said Romulus.

'He's generous too. For months after, he brought me a share of whatever he'd hunted outside the camp.'

'You saved his life.'

'Perhaps.'

'We can speak to him first,' said Romulus.

'Fire lit,' announced Vyas proudly. 'I prepare food?'

'See if there's a well,' said Romulus, eager for the boy's disastrous attempts not to be repeated until he'd been taught how to cook. 'The donkey needs water.'

Looking a little deflated, Vyas wandered off.

Romulus propped the iron tripod over the flames, and set about making a simple stew. Tarquinius vanished into the tent, like as not for a nap. It was his tendency to do this whenever the opportunity arose – another sign of his ageing.

'A merchant, eh?' The language was Indian, but the accent was unmistakeably Greek.

Romulus looked up to find a tall legionary with blond hair and blue eyes standing over him. A dent in his forehead gave him a distinctive look; he had a friendly air, however. 'Aye,' said Romulus. 'You Greek?'

The legionary twisted, presenting his left ear to Romulus. 'I'm deaf in the other side,' he explained. 'Got kicked in the head when I was a boy. What did you say again?'

Romulus repeated his question.

'I'm Bactrian. Parmenion is my name,' said the legionary, smiling. 'My people speak Greek thanks to Alexander.'

'I heard the stories,' said Romulus, switching to Greek – a language taught to him by Tarquinius on their long journey from Rome. 'They call me Hamilcar.'

'What have you got to sell?' Parmenion's face was keen. 'Traders are few and far between in this shithole part of the world.'

'I've got pottery. Some glassware, spices. A few medicines.' Romulus placed his right hand in the crook of his left elbow and raised his left forearm, fist bunched. 'I've also got something that will make you rock hard – every time.'

'I have no need of that,' retorted Parmenion. He smirked. 'I can think of a comrade who might need it, though. You'll lay out your goods later?'

'Aye. Once you have all eaten.'

Nodding a friendly farewell, Parmenion strolled off across the courtyard.

Three more curious legionaries came to investigate before the stew was cooked. Romulus heard them calling each other Marcus, Timotheus and Philippos. Short, slim and with a friendly smile, Marcus had unusual grey-blue eyes with green flecks around the pupils. Timotheus was stocky, had a scar right between his eyes, and spoke with a nicer accent than was normal among legionaries. Romulus vaguely recognised these two, but not Philippos, an amiable, burly soldier with a shiny burn scar on the inside of his left forearm. Romulus judged by his Greek name that he was another Bactrian. The trio also promised to return later.

Temperatures dropped fast as the sun fell below the western wall. Romulus was glad of the fire, and of the ready supply of wood from the dilapidated barracks. Wolves howled in the distance, making him grateful to be inside the fort. It was rare for such beasts to attack humans, but the donkey was a different matter. Tarquinius emerged soon after, drawn, he said, by the wonderful smell of the stew. Vyas trudged to and fro with a leather bucket, first filling their water carriers and then setting it down by the thirsty donkey. After, he watched Romulus cook. When the food was ready, they sat on their blankets. A comradely silence fell as they ate.

Vyas wiped his plate with a finger and licked it clean. 'Is tasty.'

Romulus inclined his head.

'Is more?' Vyas peered into the pot.

'Bottomless pit, you are,' said Romulus. 'Take what's left.' He watched with amusement as Vyas devoured the remnants of the stew.

'He has an appetite like Brennus,' said Tarquinius.

'Not quite. One day, if he grows to ten times his size.' Romulus leaned close to Tarquinius, and told him about the legionaries he'd met.

'A couple of Bactrians, eh? It's to be expected, I suppose. Dead men need replacing.'

'They won't want to join us.' Romulus and Tarquinius had talked about freeing Brennus if they found him. Their hope was that many former comrades would join in the escape. What they would do after remained a mystery. The majority might want to return to Italia, but Tarquinius' tales of the strange lands even further east had fired Romulus' imagination. With Brennus and Tarquinius by his side, gods willing, he would travel with his face towards the rising sun, until— he wasn't sure. While some of the Romans might join them, Bactrians, like as not, would simply want to return home.

'You don't know that. They won't have joined the Forgotten Legion willingly, remember.'

'True. But we approach the Romans first – they should judge who of their comrades can be trusted.'

By the light of small oil lamps, they laid out their goods on blankets. Soon off-duty legionaries wandered over to stare, to pick up and to haggle. By mutual agreement, Tarquinius stayed in the background, letting Romulus deal with their customers. Most transactions were short, but some men lingered, eager for any news from Italia. They listened agog to the story of Julius Caesar's military campaigns, his accession to power and recent murder, and the unrest that had followed. Romulus' hopes of winning men over soon rose. It was plain that years spent at the edges of the Parthian empire had not diminished ties to home and family. Legionaries left his 'stall' muttering among themselves and urging each other not to let the Parthians hear a word.

A short time passed; Romulus began to think his trade was over for the evening. He added a chunk of wood to the fire, and held out his hands to the warmth.

'What have we here?' A stocky legionary with thinning brown hair and a dimpled right cheek was studying his goods. A small bald spot behind his right ear brought memories flooding back, and Romulus had to bite his lip in order not to say, 'Well met, Hadrianus.'

Affecting his best Phoenician manner, he described in colourful terms each of his wares. In true merchant fashion, he made no mention of prices.

Hadrianus toyed with some coriander and black pepper. 'How much for these?'

'To you, nothing,' said Tarquinius, moving to Romulus' side.

Hadrianus raised an eyebrow. 'I've never known a Phoenician to give anything away for free.'

'I am no Phoenician,' said Tarquinius.

Hadrianus' hand dropped to his dagger.

'Do you still suffer from headaches?' This time, Tarquinius spoke in Latin.

'How could you know that?' demanded Hadrianus, his voice rising. 'Who are you?'

Romulus' heart leaped to his mouth; heads were turning in their direction.

'Many years ago,' said Tarquinius quickly, 'I nursed you after the slingshot bullet cracked your skull.'

Hadrianus blanched. 'T-Tarquinius?'

'None other.'

Hadrianus' eyes swivelled to Romulus. 'And you? Are you also Roman?'

'Aye. My name is Romulus. I too served in the Forgotten Legion.'

'You are ghosts,' muttered Hadrianus.

'We are flesh and blood, as you are,' said Tarquinius.

'Where have you been these past nine years?'

'It's a long story,' said Romulus. 'We came back for –' his voice caught – 'Brennus, if he yet lives.'

'That rogue?' Hadrianus grinned. 'He's alive and well.'

A little gasp escaped Romulus' lips. 'Mithras be thanked.'

'Aye. They keep trying to make him an officer, but he refuses, or does something to earn punishment duty so they can't.'

Romulus didn't know whether to laugh or cry with joy. In the event, he did a little of both. At once Hadrianus cleverly called him and Tarquinius 'Phoenician thieves' in a loud voice. Realising his ploy,

Romulus said he could offer a far better price. Those who'd looked over soon turned back to their fires.

'You're not here to rejoin the Forgotten Legion, that's plain.' Hadrianus' eyes were calculating.

'No. Anyone who wants to come with Brennus will be welcome to join our number,' said Romulus. 'Have many men escaped these past few years?'

'Perhaps fifty. Most were soon caught, but a few were never seen again. That's not to say they escaped. The fort is in the middle of nowhere, as you'll remember. Only the gods know how far they got, on foot, with limited supplies and water.' Hadrianus sighed. 'It's been an easier fate to stay where we are. The Parthian officers no longer treat us the way they did – soon after the Hydaspes, men like Brennus and the best of the optiones let them know there'd be mutiny if the situation continued. Their warning was heeded. Truth be told, most Parthians don't want to be in the arsehole of the empire either – oftentimes they're posted here as punishment. So these days, we follow orders from Ctesiphon, mount the necessary patrols, and keep our heads down. Many soldiers have taken local wives – mad to say it, but they've grown roots in this godsforsaken place. That's not to say that plenty wouldn't leave if the right men were to lead them. Brennus would be one. You, Tarquinius, would be another.'

Romulus slopped some of their precious wine into three cups and handed them out. 'This is worth a toast,' he whispered. 'To freedom!'

Hadrianus quietly echoed his words, and threw back his wine in a single mouthful. 'Gods, but that tastes good,' he said. 'I hate these patrols, but I'm fucking glad to have been chosen this time.'

Romulus caught the Parthian officer looking in their direction. They cut short their conversation to avoid suspicion, and Hadrianus returned to his comrades, promising to think about who might be trusted with the news of Romulus' and Tarquinius' return. They would talk further in the morning, and with luck, on the return journey to the main fort. Romulus and Tarquinius decided to stay until the patrol had completed its purpose, which was to scout to the top of the mountain pass and back. It wouldn't look out of place for traders to remain with the soldiers for reasons of safety.

It was many hours before sleep took Romulus that night.

Brennus was alive!

PART III

Things went well for several days. Patrols up to the pass and a little way beyond revealed nothing out of the ordinary. Tarquinius was able to rest. Romulus taught Vyas to cook; he sold some spices to the Parthians, who didn't seem suspicious of him or Tarquinius. The commanding officer didn't deign to approach them, which suited Romulus – he was the most likely to think their accents or appearance weren't quite right. Hadrianus spread the word to the comrades of his contubernium, who included Timotheus, Marcus, Parmenion and Philippos, and a joker with dark brown, almost black hair called Janus. The two Bactrians turned out to be dependable types, who would jump at the chance of escape.

For reasons of security, no one else was yet told. One slip of the tongue, one overheard remark, and their plan might be discovered. As Tarquinius said, it would be a grand shame to have travelled half the world twice over only to be betrayed by a fool who couldn't keep his lips from flapping. The plan was to return to the main camp with the patrol, there to engineer a meeting with Brennus. He would recruit leaders, and assess how many men might take part in what had become, in theory at least, a mutiny.

Everything seemed to be falling into place; the gods were smiling on them, Romulus decided.

Late on the fourth night, he was rolled up in his blankets in their tent. Tarquinius lay alongside. Between them, like a heated clay bottle to warm a winter bed, sprawled Vyas. On the morrow, the patrol was to set out on the march back to the Forgotten Legion's main camp. Seeing Brennus again seemed certain at last; an unquenchable joy filled Romulus at the thought of their reunion. It would have to be carefully done – any Parthian who witnessed it might see that the two knew each other.

'Gods, but it will be good to see him again,' he muttered to Tarquinius.

'It will,' came the reply.

'I never thought it would happen.'

'I hoped it might, but could never see if it would come to pass.'

'The big bastard will get the shock of his life. I can't wait to see his face.'

Dirt scuffed close by, and Tarquinius gripped Romulus' arm. 'Quiet.'

Romulus' stomach knotted. They'd been speaking in Latin, and in his excitement, his voice had risen above his usual whisper. There was no further noise from outside, but his unease remained. Mice made less noise, and continued to scurry about. There could be someone out there, listening.

'I need a piss,' he said in bad Carthaginian – Tarquinius had taught him a few words. Lips against the haruspex's ear, he whispered, 'I'll see if anyone's out there.' He fumbled for his dagger.

Tent flap unlaced, Romulus let his eyes grow accustomed to the dim light for a few moments, before emerging, yawning and stretching in the manner of a man woken by a full bladder. He kept his dagger down low, by his side.

'Phoenicians who speak Latin,' said a voice in Indian. The commanding officer loomed out of the darkness, hand on his sword. 'Raise the alarm!' he shouted.

Romulus could think of no plausible explanation, no way out other than to act. Pretending to stumble, he lurched forward and collided with the Parthian, who instinctively reached out to grab him. He didn't see Romulus' dagger until it was too late. He spoke no more. Eyes wide, he staggered back, emitting a soft, choking sound, while gouts of blood welled from the wound in his neck. Romulus' next thrust was more precise. He slid his blade in high up on the left side of the man's ribcage. The second time he did it, any remaining strength left the Parthian. Romulus grabbed hold, letting him down gently.

Feet pounded on the walkway – sentries were running for the stairs, shouting for their comrades. Confused cries rose from the tentlines. Romulus cried to Tarquinius for help, and then he sprinted for the Parthians' tents, four leather structures to one side of the legionaries'.

'Rise up, legionaries of Rome,' he bellowed in Latin. 'Time to free yourselves from the Parthian yoke! Tarquinius is here. I, Romulus, friend of Brennus the Gaul, am here. Rise up!'

The flap of the first tent opened, and a Parthian shoved his way outside. Romulus thrust with his dagger and heaved the dying man into the arms of a comrade, who was close behind. Even as the second Parthian tried to react, Romulus opened his throat with a vicious side swipe. The Parthian fell back inside. Urgent whispers inside followed as the other occupants conferred. He only had moments, thought Romulus, before they cut their way out of the tent's back. That wasn't taking into account the dozen Parthians in the other tents. He managed to stick the first man out of the next tent along, but then there were warriors everywhere. Retreating, his heart sank. After all he'd been through, to be undone because of his own carelessness seemed the worst of fates.

He ducked backward, avoiding a sword that would have taken off his leg, and wished he'd taken his own blade from the tent. He had three Parthians on him now, closing in with bared teeth and deadly intent.

'Roma!' came a cry from the darkness. 'Roma!'

The Parthians paid little heed. Two went left, the last right. They began to count out loud. 'One.'

They would rush him, thought Romulus, and he would die. He bent, still facing his enemies and scooped up a handful of dirt. With luck, he might blind one temporarily, and get inside the guard of another, where his dagger would be of some use. The third would kill him.

A little gasp left one of his attackers' lips. The Parthian's knees folded, and he fell onto his face. Romulus stared. Janus stood behind the Parthian, bloody sword in hand. Even as the man's companions turned, more legionaries swarmed out of the darkness. A flurry of blows rained in, and the Parthians died.

The fight was short and brutal. By its end, every Parthian had been accounted for. Eleven legionaries would never leave the fort. Two more had life-threatening wounds, and another five were injured less seriously. Sadly, some of the slain had been cut down by their comrades in the confusion – a couple had even fought with the Parthians against their fellow Romans. The fort was in Romulus' and Tarquinius' hands, however. Most of the legionaries still had no idea why the fighting had erupted, and so, after the injured had been tended to, Romulus ordered

233

a great fire lit. Every man was poured a draught of the sour beer served by the Parthians to their soldiers, and he began his and Tarquinius' story.

'I would not have left you by the Hydaspes that day,' he said, 'but the haruspex said it was my destiny, as it was for Brennus to fight the elephant.'

'He killed the brute,' said Janus, his voice full of awe. 'Saw it with my own eyes.'

Men's heads nodded. A mixture of pride and relief gripped Romulus: they didn't appear to be judging him for having essentially run away. He continued, giving the legionaries a truthful but abridged account of all that had befallen him and Tarquinius on their journey to Barbaricum and beyond. They listened, fascinated, to his tales of battles with Caesar's legions in Egypt, Asia Minor and North Africa. He did not speak of how he'd been sentenced to die in the arena and somehow killed a rhinoceros, or how his sister had helped Caesar's assassins. Fabiola had died, he told them, in a clash with a gang of street thieves. 'She took the blade meant for me,' Romulus said, emotion making his voice tremble. 'Her death left me with no reason to remain in Rome. I had long burned to know Brennus' fate, and yours, my brothers. It took us well over a year, but here we are. It was not my intent for this carnage –' he indicated the nearest Parthian bodies – 'but to take the main camp with as little bloodshed as possible.'

'That hope is well and truly gone,' snarled a legionary with a hideous scar that split his face from right eye to left jaw. With every breath he took, a little cloud of vapour escaped from the hole in his mangled nose. 'What the fuck are we supposed to do now?'

Romulus' gaze travelled around the faces. Perhaps half a dozen men appeared to agree with this troublemaker. 'It's not ideal, I know—'

'Ideal?' The man with the ruined nose glanced at his fellows. 'Life under the Parthians isn't that bad these days. This place isn't Italia, that's certain, but we aren't treated any worse than we were by our bastarding centurions. Thanks to this cocksucker, we're now mutineers. If the Parthians get hold of us, we'll be crucified, or my name's not Asinius.'

'What do you suggest?' demanded Romulus. 'Even if you murder me and the haruspex, the Parthians in the main fort will still be suspicious. Two men can't overcome fifteen warriors. Say there were more of us, and you've got the problem of no tracks leading away from here. You have committed yourself, Asinius, and so have your comrades. Let's make the best of it.'

Asinius glowered, but he stitched his lip and listened while Romulus laid out his idea. Off-duty legionaries were allowed out of the main fort to hunt – he'd confirmed this with Hadrianus – so they would make contact with one of these groups. Get word to Brennus, in order for him to get permission for a patrol. Reunited, they would come up with a plan to wrest control of the fort from the Parthians. Romulus was pleased to see fierce nods of agreement from Hadrianus, Timotheus and their comrades: it seemed that the years of captivity hadn't broken men's spirits.

Asinius wasn't won over yet. 'Even if you're successful, what then?'

'You'll be free to go wherever you wish,' declared Romulus. 'South to Barbaricum, and a ship to Egypt, and after, Italia. You can take service with Indian kings – they always need soldiers. Or you can come with me and Tarquinius. We plan to travel east with Brennus, towards the land of the Seres, there to seek our fortune.'

The mention of Italia had men muttering with excitement. Asinius didn't look convinced, but his support had vanished for the moment. Grumbling, he looked away.

Romulus put the troublesome legionary from his mind. 'Let us take stock of the supplies. We must bury the Parthians – even they do not deserve to be left for the vultures.' He glanced around the ring of faces. 'What are the chances of meeting another patrol?'

'Low,' said Marcus. His comrades voiced their agreement. 'I've never known it happen. Things have been quiet these past few years, see.'

'Good. If my memory serves, there are few places to hide should we encounter one.'

'Too true,' said Timotheus. 'There's barely a bush or tree between here and the fort.'

'We must use scouts therefore. Can you ride, Timotheus?' asked Romulus.

'I can't stand horses,' came the reply.

'Anyone else?' Romulus looked around.

The Bactrians and Asinius were among the five men to lift their hands.

Parmenion and Philippos would have to watch Asinius, Romulus decided, for he could not refuse a Roman a duty also taken by Bactrians, and he wouldn't put it past the surly legionary to make a run for the fort once he was astride a horse, there to alert the Parthians.

Three days passed. The diminished patrol marched to within a few miles of the Forgotten Legion's main camp without meeting a soul. To Romulus' relief, Asinius did not attempt to escape. Before the fort came into sight, Romulus led the legionaries east, to the mountains. Only these heights offered any cover, yet they were no place to linger. He would soon be forced to move on if they didn't quickly make contact with some legionaries. Mountain goats might supplement their dwindling food, but the wily creatures were hard to track. Shelter and fuel would be a problem too, if their wait was to be more than a few days. The barren landscape offered little in the way of fuel for fires, and the caves in the vicinity were not suitable for withstanding the savage weather to come.

If the gods didn't help them at once, the patience of men like Asinius would wear thin. He would gather support fast, thought Romulus, for the legionaries' dull but stable existence had been turned on its head. They were now homeless fugitives, and what they had done would not long remain secret. When the legion's commander grew concerned for his patrol, he would send men south to the abandoned fort, where the graves would be discovered. With every Parthian dead, and most of the legionaries vanished, it would be easy to deduce what had happened. Inside the next ten to fifteen days, a punitive force would be sent to seek out the killers – and every man knew it. Mayhap the Parthian commander would delay further action until reinforcements arrived – he might not trust his Roman troops to seek out and kill their fellows – but an attack would come before winter.

They had to act, Romulus decided, and fast.

His hopes of encountering legionaries on a hunt proved futile. He set a watch on the fort, but for whatever reason, only patrols emerged. His concerns were fuelled by the arrival three days later of a force of Parthian horsemen, perhaps five hundred strong. Romulus and Tarquinius decided it had to be coincidental, because the legion's commander still didn't know what had happened at the abandoned fortlet, and the great size of the Parthian empire meant that the new troops would have been travelling for at least half a month. The reinforcements would have come upon the scene anyway: it was his bad fortune that it happened to be now. Romulus' intention changed not a fraction. As he said to Tarquinius, it didn't matter how many Parthians there were, or how dangerous freeing Brennus might prove: he had to try.

The day after that, a patrol came haring up the road from the south – their urgency telling Romulus all he needed to know. Before word spread, and men like Asinius began whispering in others' ears, he called a meeting. All bar the sentries gathered round the fire by the main cave's entrance. Grimy-faced, cheeks drawn a little with hunger, their faces were expectant. Worried. Romulus could see fear too, and in some, resentment. He did not panic. The legionaries had murdered Parthians. Even if they refused to follow him and Tarquinius, they could not return to the fort. Their best hope, therefore, lay with what he could offer. He had spoken enough with Marcus, Timotheus, Hadrianus, Janus and the two Bactrians, Philippos and Parmenion, to know that most men in the Forgotten Legion were discontented. They lived with the status quo because there was nothing else on offer. Offer them the chance of freedom, however, and a leader, and they might well listen.

'I thank you for coming,' said Romulus.

Vyas grinned as if he'd been the only one to be asked.

'As if there's anything else to do in this hole,' replied Janus.

Plenty of men laughed, and Janus warmed to his task. 'I don't want to miss the chariot race that's on later, mind, so keep it brief.'

'I'm going to the bath-house, so I can't linger either,' Marcus chipped in.

'Bath-house?' cried Parmenion. 'The latrines are calling me – and that, let me tell you, cannot wait.' He leered into the chorus of farting noises and worse that followed.

Smiling his gratitude at the joke-makers – for the mood was now degrees more convivial than it had been – Romulus waited for the clamour to die down. 'It's good to laugh, but our situation *is* more serious than our friends imply. We cannot remain here forever. Even if we are not discovered by Parthian patrols, winter is coming. I need not tell you that these mountains are no place to be when the snow-laden winds howl down from the north. We *must* act. As I see it, there are several choices before us. We could march south at once, over the pass and into Bactria, to offer our services to the rulers there, or indeed to the kings whose lands live over the Hydaspes in India. Marching to the east is also an option, although more uncertain, thanks to the terrain and lack of supplies.'

His eyes roved over his audience, trying to gauge their thoughts. Some men, he saw, would be happy enough to save their own skins, and journey south, abandoning their comrades in the fort. Most, he was relieved to see, seemed to want him to lay out his every plan.

'It is possible to journey by river to the coast in the far south,' Romulus continued. 'The mighty city of Barbaricum is home to traders from everywhere under the sun. Once a year, ships sail from Barbaricum to Egypt. It is a perilous voyage, but Tarquinius and I did it, and the rewards of doing so are plain. Alexandria is but a short voyage from Italia.' There was naked hunger in men's eyes now, a longing that twisted at Romulus' heart. Most legionaries had been older than he at Carrhae; the majority had left wives and families behind. Until his almost magical reappearance with Tarquinius, the notion of seeing their loved ones again in this lifetime had been an absolute impossibility. He was offering them hope.

'My wife has married another man, like as not, but by all the gods, I would give anything to see my sons again ere I die.' Timotheus' voice shook with emotion.

'My daughters will be grown women by now, married with families of their own,' said Janus, his joking mien absent. 'Meeting them is my heart's greatest desire.'

'I just want to hold a cup of decent wine in my fist. If I could do it with the Italian sun on my face, I'd go to Hades a happy man,' declared Hadrianus, and men chuckled.

Heads were nodding everywhere Romulus looked, and he thought with a dark flash of humour, it will just be me and Tarquinius and Brennus, if we can free him, who travel eastward.

'There's another choice,' said Marcus, breaking the spell. 'You haven't mentioned that yet.'

'It's the riskiest,' said Romulus, 'but one we have to consider. If we leave, whether it's to the south or east, our comrades will remain captives of the Parthians. Yet every man in the Forgotten Legion deserves the chance to be free, to decide his own fate. I intend to scale the fort walls at night, and find Brennus.'

Asinius pursed his lips. 'What if you're caught?'

'I'll end my days on a cross,' said Romulus with a shrug. 'Which is why I ask no man to go in my place. Would you rather try?'

Asinius glowered by way of reply.

'And if the Parthians rouse before you have enough men to stand with you?' asked Philippos. 'There would be a bloodbath.'

'There would,' said Romulus into the rumble of worried mutters. 'Fortuna was in an evil mood when she sent those reinforcements. But a man has to play the game with the pieces he has. It may be that Brennus will say rising against the Parthians isn't a good idea, that we should just escape. He shall be the one to decide. But I'm going into the fort. I haven't come thousands of miles to find my friend to walk away from a final challenge. If I die, I'll die knowing I tried. That's all I have ever asked of a comrade.'

'And you, haruspex?' asked Parmenion.

All eyes turned to Tarquinius, who had said nothing throughout the entire discussion.

'I shall go with Romulus. Old I may be, with creaking bones, but this is not a fight to avoid. You fine men are comrades from my time in the Forgotten Legion, but so are many hundreds of others in the fort. It is my destiny to see them free, or die in the trying. My brothers should have their chance of returning home, of finding their wives and families – as you do.'

Romulus was about to speak, but Tarquinius' warning look silenced him.

Wind whistled around the cave's entrance, an eerie, unsettling noise.

'I go with you,' piped Vyas. 'I fight.'

Romulus' throat tightened. He squeezed the boy's bony shoulder. 'It's too dangerous.'

'I not care! I fight!' protested Vyas.

Romulus shook his head, no. Too many people he cared for had died; he could not bear to think of the impish Vyas joining their number.

'The haruspex has rarely been wrong, and the boy shames us,' said Janus. 'I'm with you.'

'And I,' said Hadrianus, Marcus and Timotheus in unison.

'Clever men think alike,' said Marcus.

'Fools seldom differ,' retorted Timotheus.

The three looked at each other and laughed.

'I have no wish to go to Italia. Bactria is my home,' said Philippos, 'but the gods would curse me if I didn't try to help my friends first. Parmenion here feels the same. We are with you.'

Their voices were like the first drops from a rain-laden cloud – soon every man was offering his support.

Even as delight filled Romulus, fresh sweat slid down his back. Sneaking into a camp full of Parthians was one of the more stupid things he had ever considered, yet he could think of nothing else.

If Brennus could not come to him, he would go to Brennus.

PART IV

I t was the night after the decision to enter the fort had been taken; Romulus and Tarquinius were lying on their bellies two hundred paces from the north wall. Ten volunteers were with them: Hadrianus, Timotheus, Marcus, Janus and the Bactrians, and four others. Vyas had again demanded to go with them, but of course had been left at the cave. Welcome clouds blanketed the moon – it was as dark as pitch. The hour was late; several hours remained until dawn. On the walkway, the sentries paced to and fro, but not often. If there was a good time to make their attempt, it was now.

Romulus placed his lips against Tarquinius' ear and whispered, 'Is it really your destiny to do this?'

Tarquinius twisted to regard him. 'I have no idea,' he muttered.

'Wily old dog. You said it to sway the men!'

'Your silver tongue would have won them over, but I wanted to make sure.' Tarquinius' teeth shone in the darkness.

Grinning, Romulus resumed his study of the ramparts. They had been in place for hours, a little file of men in dark tunics and mud-smeared faces with two rough-hewn ladders. No one wore armour or helmets for fear of drawing the sentries' attention. Swords were too cumbersome for the climb, so they carried daggers. According to Hadrianus and the rest, each corner tower of the fort had two sentries, and another pair were stationed along the length of each wall. At least one in every four was Parthian – these were the men who had to be identified and slain first, if possible. No one wanted to kill any of their own kind, but no risks could be taken. It had been agreed that one chance could be given to a Roman sentry. Nod assent to the suggestion he join them, and he would be allowed to live. Refusal meant a swift blade across the throat. The decision added to the risk, but the alternative – killing every single sentry – was too ruthless to contemplate.

Romulus hadn't seen any movement on the walkway for a good length of time. Judging by this, and the late hour, that the sentries' energy was at low ebb, he nudged Tarquinius. 'Ready?'

'As I will ever be.'

Romulus signalled to the others. He took his time approaching the wall; if they were heard at any stage, their attempt would be an utter failure. Unknowing that those in the darkness were their own comrades, the Roman sentries would raise the alarm as loud as if Sogdian raiders were attacking. They *had* to reach the walkway undetected.

A hundred paces out, Romulus had torn a knee open on a projecting stone, and his hands and lower legs were coated in mud. He stopped to study the sentries. None had moved, so he resumed his crawl to the ditch. Another pause at fifty paces gave him no cause for alarm. Twenty paces out, the same. Romulus reached the ditch's lip soon after; Tarquinius and the rest were dark shapes right behind him. Romulus peered up at the rampart. He had selected a position midway between the two sentries. Perhaps a hundred paces separated him from each.

Although Romulus would have preferred Tarquinius to follow him up the first ladder, he had decided to take Marcus. Possessed of a prodigious memory and practical nature – no one argued with this – he claimed to know every Roman in the Forgotten Legion by his face, and almost everyone by name. It would be his decision whether the sentries' nods could be trusted or not.

Romulus motioned for Marcus to join him. 'Ready?' he mouthed.

Marcus nodded.

Romulus inched his way down into the ditch. Probing with the point of a foot, he nudged a caltrop out of the way. A few moments of feeling about, and he had gathered a score of the deadly four-pronged pieces of iron. He made a neat pile of them to one side, and pointed them out to the rest. Next he took the ladder end from Marcus, and eased it into a standing position. Marcus and Tarquinius joined him, and together they lowered it inch by nail-biting inch towards the timbered wall. A faint *thunk* marked its connection. They all froze.

After thirty rapid beats of Romulus' heart, he had heard no reaction from above. He and Tarquinius exchanged an emotion-laden look – if things went awry, this might be the last time they saw each other – and then, gripping his dagger in his teeth, Romulus began to climb. He would remember the ascent to his dying day. Tiny creaks from the brand-new ladder. His shallow breaths. The pale blobs that were Tarquinius' and Marcus' faces watching from below. The shock that lanced through him as a man coughed in the distance, and the relief he felt at the realisation it was a sentry on another wall.

As agreed, Marcus started his climb when Romulus was two-thirds of the way up the ladder. They both reached the walkway without the sentries noticing. Kneeling, they glanced left and right. 'Which one?' whispered Romulus.

'Brennus' barracks are that way,' Marcus replied, pointing to their left.

Like that, it was settled.

If the ladder had been nerve-wracking, approaching the sentry was twice as bad. The gods were smiling on Romulus, however. He padded to within a dozen paces of the soldier, a legionary, without being seen. The man had to be dozing, Romulus decided – despite every effort, their approach had not been silent. Now it was time for speed. Glancing at Marcus, who nodded his readiness, Romulus darted forward.

The sentry woke with Romulus' hand over his mouth and the cold prick of iron at his throat. Facing out over the wall, he could see neither of his assailants.

'Be still. I am Roman,' hissed Romulus. 'Marcus?'

Marcus leaned in to peer at the terrified man's face. 'Fear not, Caius,' he whispered after a moment. 'It is I, Marcus, the carpenter. I was in the party that re-roofed your barracks in the spring, remember?'

The sentry's wide eyes flicked to Marcus. After a moment, his chin dipped in assent. Marcus explained quickly what had happened; that Romulus and the haruspex had returned. 'We're going to take the fort,' he whispered. 'Free the entire fucking legion. You with us?'

Caius' nod was so emphatic that Romulus released his grip at once.

Their good luck continued to hold. Caius' companion on the walkway was another Roman; he joined them without a murmur. Soon Tarquinius and the rest had clambered up to the rampart. Leaving the sentries in place in case a Parthian officer appeared, they made their way to the nearest set of stairs. Romulus' excitement grew with each step. Brennus' barracks was little more than a hundred paces away. After nine years, and countless battles, after thousands of miles of travel, and numerous brushes with death, he was about to see the big Gaul again. The man who had looked out for him almost from the first time they'd met. Who had been like a father to him. Who had stepped into the path of a raging bull elephant in order that he might escape.

Dirt crunched beneath their sandals. They stole across the wide space separating the walls from the neat lines of barracks, and into the shadow cast by one building. 'Six barracks over,' whispered Marcus.

Romulus grinned. I'm coming, brother, he thought. You'll never have had a wakening like it. Staying in the shadows, they crossed from the end of one barrack to another. And from a second to a third. Romulus couldn't have known that in the next gap were two Parthians. Too lazy to walk to the latrine trench, they were emptying their bladders against the barrack wall. They gaped at Romulus. One barked something in Parthian, then with a curse, repeated his demand in appalling Latin. 'What are you doing, skulking about at this hour?' Even as he spoke, the Parthian took in Romulus' blackened face, and the dagger in his fist.

'Quick!' hissed Romulus to his comrades, and sprinted forward.

He managed to kill the nearest Parthian, but fear gave the other one speed, and he tore off towards the other end of the gap, roaring at the top of his voice.

Panic flared in Romulus' belly, but Tarquinius' voice calmed him. 'Forget him. Parmenion, Philippos, find your comrades. Wake as many men as you can. Explain what's happening and get them armed. Meet us here. You lot do the same,' he said to four of the others. 'The rest of you, run. Run for Brennus' barracks!'

Marcus took off like an Olympic sprinter, with Romulus on his heels, and Tarquinius with four others trailing after. By the time they were nearing the right barracks, the alarm was sounding all over the fort. Fear that they would fail battered Romulus, but he shoved it away.

Marcus didn't know exactly which contubernium Brennus was in, so more time was lost as Romulus ripped open door after door, demanding of sleep-fuddled legionaries if the big Gaul was there, and telling them that the haruspex was back, and if they wanted to return home, they should get dressed and armed. By the fourth set of rooms, Romulus was wondering if Marcus had been wrong. There was fighting, and not far off. If they weren't all to die, he would have to forget Brennus for the moment, and gather men together.

'The Gaul?' croaked a legionary from the darkness of the room Romulus was staring into. 'He's not here.'

'Where in Hades is he then?' shouted Romulus.

'He went to play dice with one of his mates in the next barracks over,' came the reply.

Romulus was already running.

He didn't expect to meet a formed line of legionaries around the corner. Not all had helmets or mail on, but the shield wall was solid, and their swords looked ready. Someone had had the wit to light torches, which illuminated the scene enough to recognise friend from enemy. Romulus screeched to a stop. 'I'm looking for Brennus,' he bellowed. 'Where is the big bastard?'

Surprise marked the face of the nearest men.

'He's not here,' said one. 'Who are you?'

Romulus cursed. He could hear voices speaking Parthian approaching – his search was becoming too perilous. 'Romulus is my name. I was a comrade of yours at Carrhae. I escaped at the Hydaspes, but I have returned. The haruspex Tarquinius is with me.'

Tarquinius stood forward, so that men could see him. The shield wall wavered.

'These others are comrades of yours,' said Romulus, gesturing at Marcus and the rest. 'Are you going to stare at us all fucking night, or let us into the ranks?'

Awkward grins. Men shuffled apart, and they shoved in among the legionaries. Romulus made sure to stand at the front. Tarquinius was behind him; he could hear men muttering in awed voices. 'The haruspex – it *is* him.'

Further conversation was prevented by the arrival of two score Parthians. They made no attempt to close with the legionaries, instead relying on their powerful bows. If it hadn't been for the silk and cotton covering their shields, every man standing with Romulus would have died in the arrow storm that followed. Even with the protection, two men were slain and a handful more injured. Memories of Carrhae flooded Romulus' mind. Here, though, the Parthians were on foot. 'With me!' he roared. 'Charge the bastards, and we'll break them.'

He took off, trusting that the legionaries would follow. They did. The Parthians took to their heels, unwilling to stand and fight. Baying like hunting dogs, the legionaries hacked down the slowest. Their optio, a solid-looking type, prevented them from chasing the Parthians; they already looked to be rallying. He had his men form up again. Fresh arrows thumped into the shields of those at the front.

They charged, further this time, until the Parthians retreated beyond effective bow range.

'What's your plan?' the optio demanded of Romulus and Tarquinius.

'We were looking for Brennus,' said Romulus.

'Aye, well, he's not here, and the cursed Parthians won't be long coming back. What should we do?'

It was odd to be addressed so by an officer, but, thought Romulus, by appearing out of nowhere, he and Tarquinius had thrown the fates of every legionary into the hands of that most capricious of deities, Fortuna. Men wanted leaders.

'Let's move between the wall and the barracks and gather as many men as we can,' he said, glancing at Tarquinius for confirmation. 'Once we have a few hundred legionaries, we can move onto one of the avenues to look for more. We should be able to contain the Parthians once there are enough of us.'

'That's if men know that you're here. I'd bet a year's wages that the Parthians are telling everyone in barracks further away that Sogdians have got into the fort,' said the optio.

'Aye, well, that can't be helped,' said Tarquinius. 'Each group we meet, I'll talk to. Everyone remembers me.'

This seemed to satisfy the optio; Romulus quickly relayed their plan to the legionaries, who nodded grim assent.

They worked their way along the ends of the barracks, picking up motley bands of soldiers ranging in size from two to more than twenty. Most men were only part-dressed and armed, but all had shields and swords, which was enough. Clever heads among the Parthians soon sent men onto the walkway, from where arrows began raining down, but thanks to their silk-covered shields, casualties were light. Their progress was slowed by the inevitable demands about what was going on, and the legionaries' disbelief – until he stood forward – that the haruspex could have returned.

By the time they had reached a corner of the fort's wall, and the end of the barracks, they numbered perhaps four hundred. It was time, said Romulus to Tarquinius, to risk one of the larger avenues. The Parthians were growing more daring, shooting down heavy volleys from the walkway. Men were dying, and they had no way of retaliating other than suicidal charges up ladders. The danger was growing too; linger in the fort, and the Parthians would band together. Concentrated showers of arrows in the fort's confined space would wreak fearful casualties, silk covers on the shields or no, and his chance of finding Brennus in the mayhem would vanish. He shoved the depressing thought away.

A sweep down the avenue towards the headquarters added hundreds of legionaries to their number. Brennus was not among them, but Romulus began to take heart. By the time the central triple junction drew near, he had more than twelve hundred men behind him, including Parmenion, Philippos and the rest from the patrol. Men were calling out to comrades in the alleys between the barracks that the haruspex was come again, that they were seizing their freedom at last. Tarquinius continued to stand forward, holding aloft a torch so he could be seen. His presence was magnetic; legionaries hurried to join them.

Inevitably, Tarquinius was targeted by the Parthians. Unable perhaps to hear his words, they could see he was a rallying point. Romulus called for men to protect him; his heart warmed as Janus and Philippos took a position on either side of the haruspex. They pressed on. Upwards of a cohort joined them from the sets of barracks to their right. Several hundred more men appeared soon after, pursued by a large group of Parthians. These retreated at the sight of the massed legionaries, and a great cheer went up.

According to Parmenion, Hadrianus and the rest, the Forgotten Legion now numbered a shade over six thousand. A third of it was at Romulus' back, give or take. The rest had to be among the barracks on the far side of the headquarters – and so did the main body of Parthians. Romulus conferred quickly with Tarquinius and the optio he'd first met, and decided to stay on the main avenue. Protected on either side by the barracks, they offered fewer targets to the enemy. The wide area that ran around the inside of the walls would offer a better chance to form up, but the Parthians on the walkways would see it came at a heavy cost.

Concentrating on reaching the headquarters, Romulus' attention lapsed. As Tarquinius left the formation to speak with another group of legionaries, half a dozen Parthians sprang an ambush from a barrack roof. Arrows hissed in. Parmenion and Philippos went down, groaning. A shaft dinked off Tarquinius' helmet; another plucked at the arm of his tunic. Shouting to distract the archers, Romulus threw himself forward, shield upraised. He urged the haruspex in behind his shield. To his disbelief, Tarquinius had only a flesh wound to one leg. Retrieving Parmenion's shield so they both had one, they edged back to the rest, arrows *thunk*ing into their shields. They left the corpses of the friendly Bactrian and Philippos behind.

They were no Romans, thought Romulus sadly, but they were true comrades. 'You need to stay in the ranks from now on,' he said to Tarquinius.

At the next alleyway, the nervous and suspicious legionaries wouldn't believe that Tarquinius had returned until once again, he showed himself. Romulus had to give in. Again he called for volunteers to shield the haruspex; this time, Hadrianus, Janus, Marcus and Timotheus formed a square around him. 'Someone has to do it, and it might as well be us,' said Timotheus, winking. 'Every man in the legion will have to stand us drinks for the next year for keeping the haruspex from harm.'

'It's you who will get the best out of that,' said Marcus to Timotheus. 'You're always the last to leave a party.'

Timotheus shrugged, grinning, and they took their places around Tarquinius.

The danger did not abate; it seemed word of the haruspex's reappearance had spread among the enemy. By the time they had reached the headquarters, their numbers exceeded three thousand, but Janus and Timotheus were dead, and Marcus had taken an arrow through his sword arm. More legionaries had pressed forward to guard Tarquinius, but eventually, Romulus summoned them all back to the relative safety of the ranks.

'We have enough with us now – men will join us regardless. Half the legion isn't going to follow a ghost,' he said when Tarquinius protested.

The situation grew even more dangerous as they reached the front of the headquarters. Burning torches had been strewn everywhere, lighting the scene well for archers. More than fifty Parthians were waiting in each of the two other roads at the intersection. The instant that Romulus and his comrades came into sight, the air turned black with their arrows. The volleys' speed saw plenty of legionaries struck down before they had a chance to lift their shields in front of their faces. Romulus' good fortune was another's ill: the shaft that streaked past a fingers' breadth from his cheek drove deep into the eyesocket of a man behind him.

To hesitate now was to die; retreat would only offer the Parthians more chances to ambush them. Ordering a charge, Romulus led the way towards the main gate. The archers facing them loosed two more volleys before they broke and ran. Safer again between the rows of barracks, Romulus slowed his pace. Stinging attacks began at once from both sides; this was where the Parthian commander had marshalled his forces. There was nothing for it but to drive onward. Gods, let us meet Brennus, Romulus prayed as the arrows showered in, and men screamed. The whole cursed exercise would have been for nothing, not to say cost hundreds of men their lives, if they didn't find the big Gaul.

'Where is he?' he demanded of Tarquinius.

'Somewhere in the fort.'

Romulus bit back a savage retort. 'Can you not see?' This in an undertone.

'I've been a little busy,' came the acerbic reply. A moment's silence and then, 'The stars tell me nothing.'

Romulus' shield juddered beneath the impact of another arrow, and he swore. The instant he had a chance, he took the shield from a man behind, passing back his own. In the safety of the ranks, there was a chance of breaking off the arrow shafts to make the shield usable again.

Step by dogged step, they pushed their way to the main gate. Romulus had no way of knowing how many were being injured and slain in the main body of legionaries; he hoped it wasn't too many. Break out through the gate, and they could march for the mountains. Except, he realised with horror, they would be pursued at dawn. Why hadn't he thought of the cursed Parthians' horses before? Safely beyond javelin range on their mounts, the enemy would shoot their deadly arrows at leisure. While the silk-covered shields offered good protection, the Parthians would probe away at them, allowing no respite. The Forgotten Legion would haemorrhage men. They might make it to wherever they decided was best, but with no cavalry of their own, the losses would be catastrophic. And there was still no sign of Brennus.

A black mood took Romulus. When they reached the final set of barracks before the open ground and the gate – a scene lit by yet more burning torches – to be greeted with a massed force of Parthians, most on foot, but some already mounted, he laughed. His mood wasn't helped by the cohort of legionaries to the left of the gate. Shouts to join them were ignored. Like as not, they were Bactrians like Philippos and Parmenion, whose ties to their Roman comrades were thin. Atop the gate itself, scores of archers stood ready.

'Just as well the sight has left you,' Romulus muttered to Tarquinius. 'We travelled half the world to get back to Margiana, to die in this fort.'

'Do not lose hope,' came the quiet reply. 'Pull back. Talk to the optiones. Send some men between the barracks to come around to the enemy's rear and we may yet break them.'

The same thought had been in Romulus' mind. He ordered a steady retreat, and was grateful for the discipline that still prevailed. In good order, the legionaries pulled back between the barracks. Romulus shoved his way back ten ranks, and called for officers to join him. Quick as he laid out his plans to the optiones and other junior officers who presented themselves, the Parthians were quicker. The groups who had harried them before the headquarters, or maybe others, crept up the alleys between the barracks and along the roofs, and rained down hundreds more arrows on the legionaries.

Their attempt to flank the enemy was doomed to fail before it even began, Romulus decided, and the grim faces of the officers around him told him they were of the same mind. 'Any ideas?' he asked Tarquinius.

A rare emotion – regret – marked the haruspex's lined face. 'I am sorry, Romulus. I should never have encouraged you to come east. This is my fault.'

'Don't be a fool,' said Romulus. 'After Fabiola's death, Rome held nothing for me. What kind of a friend would I be if I hadn't come back to find Brennus?'

'Maybe he's already broken out,' said Hadrianus. 'I wouldn't put it past the big bastard.'

'Maybe that's why the Parthians are organised. They shut the door after the Gaul has bolted,' said Marcus, chuckling despite his pain.

A few men laughed, but the mood remained grim.

'As far as I see it,' said Romulus, 'our best chance is to drive straight at the gate. Two groups of men should make for the stairs either side, to clear the walkway of Parthians – being higher than us, they're the ones who will cause the most casualties. Open the gates, and we get out. They won't follow us until it's light. The mountains are what, fifteen miles away? If Fortuna is kind to us, we'll make it before the whoresons catch up.' He was lying, and everyone knew it, but it seemed the least bad of their options.

A loud voice – Tarquinius – cut across the worried talk. 'We will escape, brothers – I have seen it in the pattern of the stars.'

A reverential *aah* went up from those who heard. Romulus cast a look at the haruspex – this ran contrary to everything Tarquinius had advised – but he had the wit to say nothing.

Repeating what he'd said, Tarquinius worked his way through the legionaries. 'Escape!' he cried. 'The Forgotten Legion will escape!'

Romulus let the haruspex move towards the rear for as long as he dared – the Parthian volleys from either side continued raining in – and then, with a few encouraging words to the officers and to the legionaries he passed, he returned to the front rank. Hadrianus was there. Marcus stood behind him, shield in his good left hand, and somehow gripping a dagger in his right. They gave him fierce nods, and he thought: gods, but it felt good to be among comrades again.

'Ready, legionaries of the Forgotten Legion?' he roared.

'AYE!' It was an animal roar.

'Stay close. Keep those shields up, in particular at the sides and in the middle. Pass it on,' bellowed Romulus. 'Forward march.' Every part of him wanted to run, to break out of the fort as fast as possible, but a slow pace that allowed them to keep their shields together was vital.

The Parthians didn't start to loose until a good twenty ranks had emerged from the protection offered by the barracks. A shouted command, and then the bowstrings twanged. Romulus peered up for a heartbeat, and wished he hadn't. The sheer number of arrows was making the stars flicker like fireflies. He looked down again, and told himself that the man behind would keep his shield in place over them both. They tramped closer to the gate. The archers in front waited until the legionaries were perhaps four score paces away before they began to shoot. At the same time, the Bactrian legionaries to their left began to move.

Disaster beckoned, thought Romulus, if they were forced to turn and fight their own comrades. The volleys of arrows would become even deadlier. 'Faster,' he shouted, breaking into a run.

The Parthians redoubled their efforts. Arrows shot in, most hitting the shields, but inevitably, some finding the gaps between. Men screamed. Men fell. Men died. Men were trampled underfoot. Busy trying to stay alive, Romulus didn't see Hadrianus fall. Nor Marcus. Yet by the time he was fifty paces from the gate, neither man was with him. He had no time to grieve. No time to think about Brennus.

The man to his left dropped, an arrow buried in his skull just below the rim of his helmet. 'Keep those shields up!' shouted Romulus, now advancing without even looking. It seemed as if the Parthians heard; they began aiming at men's feet. Legionaries fell to their knees, cursing and sobbing with pain. Many wrenched the arrows out and hobbled on regardless. Their pace had dropped to a walk, however, and of course that let the Parthians rain down an even heavier storm of arrows.

Hooves pounded the dirt, and Romulus' heart sank. Any moment, and the horsemen would hit one flank, while the Bactrian legionaries attacked the other. Even seasoned soldiers could not stand before such a savage assault. Their attempt would end here, in front of the gate. Mithras, he thought. Help me.

Close up, the Parthians melted away from the entrance, running towards their fellows on either side, and swarming up the stairs, which, thanks to the efforts of the archers on the walkway, remained in their hands.

The gate lay in front of Romulus. Escape beckoned, but it could have been a world away. To his left, the Bactrians closed in. On his right, the horse archers were already loosing. He and the first however many ranks might get out, but the majority of the legionaries would be butchered. I left Brennus, thought Romulus. I cannot abandon these men too, when I have just found them again. An honourable death was preferable to saving his skin.

Jaw set, Romulus advanced to the gate. Once it was open, he would stay behind, fighting until every man escaped. If he died, so be it. With the help of several others, he lifted the locking bar and pulled the creaking doors wide. The black night beyond offered scant welcome; a night bird screeched, mocking his efforts. At least they'll have a chance, thought Romulus, urging the legionaries to march out of the fort.

Heartened by the refusal of many to leave their comrades, he kept half a century with him and sent the rest out into the darkness. 'We'll be right behind you,' he cried.

Romulus expected chaos already to be reigning within the walls.

To his surprise, the sounds of combat were less than they had been. The mounted Parthians had split up and were riding off into the gaps between the barracks, followed by their comrades on foot. Corpses of men and horses lay everywhere. The ground the riders had occupied was now filled with at least a double cohort of advancing legionaries. On the other side, the Bactrians were exchanging friendly greetings with the Roman legionaries. Atop the walkway, scores of soldiers were finishing off the archers.

Romulus set down his shield and studied the newcomers. There was a huge legionary in the front rank; he appeared to be shouting orders. Hope flared in Romulus' heart. He took a step forward, and then another. 'Is that you, Brennus?'

The massive legionary raised his sword in greeting.

Romulus was running, heedless of the occasional arrow humming down from the rampart. 'Brennus?'

The big legionary shoved free of his fellows, threw down his own shield, and took off his helmet. The pigtails were still there, albeit streaked with a little grey, the broad friendly face had more lines than before, but it *was* Brennus.

Romulus came to a halt several paces away. Emotion tightened his throat; tears pricked his eyes. The words struggled to come. In the end, he gave up trying and threw himself at the Gaul. They wrapped arms around each other, laughing and crying at the same time. Neither said anything for long moments.

'You came back,' muttered Brennus, squeezing Romulus until he thought his ribs would crack.

'Of course I did. You're still alive.'

'It takes more than an elephant to kill me.'

Romulus took a step back. '*Where* in Hades did you come from?'

A great belly laugh escaped Brennus. 'Someone had to let the horses out of their stables. We didn't get to all of them, but nine in every ten is wandering the plain beyond the fort – we let them out the western gate. Then I gathered as many men as I could, and headed here. It was clear where the fighting was. Best to come at the enemy from an angle they don't expect, I thought. They didn't even hear us coming.'

'And the Bactrians? Was it you who spoke to them?'

Brennus frowned. 'I didn't have time.'

Romulus gave silent thanks to Philippos and Parmenion. It could only have been them who had persuaded their fellows not to fight with the Parthians.

Romulus swore. 'I came back here to repay my debt to you, and here I find myself owing you my life again.'

Brennus shoved him, a buffet that sent him back a step. 'You travelled to Rome?'

'Aye.'

'Thousands of miles you went, and then came back – to find me. I call that a debt repaid.'

'Look who it is,' said a familiar voice.

Brennus looked over Romulus' shoulder, and swore. 'You're still alive, you rogue!'

'I could say the same about you.' Never one for physical affection, Tarquinius did not pull away from Brennus' bear hug.

Romulus threw an arm around both of them. 'Gods, but this is a good day.'

In fact, he thought, it was the best day of his life.

AUTHOR'S NOTE

I f I had a pound for every time I've been asked would I write another Forgotten Legion novel, I would have at least £10,000 – probably more. My answer had always been a firm but friendly 'No'. My reasons were simple: I felt the ending of *The Road to Rome* to be as realistic as one could be about a period that we know (comparatively) so little about. However, times change, as they say. Book sales dropped across this historical fiction genre, and so in late 2017, I decided to have a go on Kickstarter for a short story, with the topic to be chosen by my readers. The campaign was a runaway success, thanks to my amazing readers, and 'The March' – actually novella length – is the result. And no, I will not be writing any more books about Romulus and his friends.

I must mention a few names, those of people who appear in this story: Bruce Phillips (Philippos), to whom this short story is dedicated – thank you, Bruce. I think it's fair to say that we are now friends as well as author and reader. You're a star man. Adrian Tyte (Hadrianus): you have been a huge standout figure when it comes to supporting all my charitable endeavours. Thank you, sir – the first few pints are mine to buy when eventually we meet. Robin Carter (Parmenion): where to start? You're generous beyond measure, Robin, always offering to help with hundreds of pounds worth of books, help with stamps, advice and so on. Thank you! Timotheus (Tim Mileson), Janus (Joan Morgenstern), Marcus (Mark Downing): thank you for your support with the story, and for reading my books – you're fabulous, all of you. And to the more than one hundred others who donated and supported this short story – THANK YOU TOO! – without your backing, this project would never have got off the ground.

Some of you are, in non-alphabetical order: Stuart Lonie, Ollie Drake, Paul Brierton, Ben Pickersgill, Stephen McIntyre, Sean Head,

Josh Catlin, Alex Thornhill, Taff James, John O'Callaghan, Micheal Polanski, Dominic Bronk, Nick Born, Marcin Truskawa, Cliff Moon, Carl Chapman, Martins Berzins, Paul Harrison, Tony Baker, Noah Borch, Gary Toakley, Milca Gabb (as you were then!), Andy Wilson, Jonathan Lowe, and Troy Saville. Big apologies to the rest of you worthies – I neglected to note everyone down at the time, and Kickstarter doesn't store the info past a few years.

Rotted sandals – this was recorded among Alexander the Great's soldiers as they marched through India in the monsoon.

Ixalos – the ancient Greek word for ibex – possibly!

Vyas – an ancient Indian name, provided to me by Abhinav Ashish – thank you, sir, for your help.

THE SHRINE

A prelude to *Eagles at War*

MOGONTIACUM, GALLIA BELGICA, SPRING 6 BC

It was a fine day in the Roman province of Gallia Belgica. The scud-ding clouds overhead held little threat of rain, and regular intervals of warm sunshine were enough proof that winter had gone for another year. Outside the town of Mogontiacum, the road was packed with hundreds of legionaries and civilians, come to watch the annual foot race that formed part of the celebrations commemorating the tragic death three years previously of Drusus, beloved general of the local legions and stepson of the emperor Augustus.

The contest would end at Drusus' tall, marble-faced memorial. A cluster of high-ranking officers and civic officials watched there, from the comfort of a wooden stand that had been erected for the occasion. Lucius Cominius Tullus, a solid soldier with close-cut brown hair and a long jaw, had done well to secure a spot which afforded views right up to the monument. He had been passing through Mogontiacum the day before, and it had seemed a fine plan to stay for the race, which was famous far and wide.

Tullus was happy to linger because he was in no particular rush to finish his journey to Vetera, some two hundred miles down the River Rhenus. He needed a little time to think. His recent promotion from optio to centurion had meant leaving the 'Rapax' Twenty-First Legion, the unit which he'd joined as a stripling youth more than ten years before. It was a massive step – a positive one, to be sure, but one that needed to sink in. His future now lay with the Eighteenth Legion, in Vetera. If he kept his nose clean, led his men well and continued to distinguish himself in battle, he stood a decent chance of becoming a senior centurion, commanding a cohort, before the end of his career. A grin split his face. It was even possible that he could ascend to the dizzying heights of primus pilus, the highest-ranking centurion of the legion.

The loud conversations of those around him brought Tullus back to the present, and the race, which would end soon. Soldiers from every legion stationed on the Rhenus and Danuvius rivers were taking part. It didn't feel right to support men from the Eighteenth yet; until his journey ended, he hadn't actually joined his new legion. His loyalties remained in Castra Regina, with the Rapax.

It had been the most natural thing in the world, therefore, to place his bets on soldiers from the Rapax. Tullus didn't know Fusco and Justus, the two finest athletes in his old legion, but he knew *of* them. The twelve-to-one odds offered by local betmakers for either man to win the race had only added to the appeal of backing them. A sense of duty had made Tullus also place twenty denarii on the best of the Eighteenth's runners, although the long odds made it unlikely that he would ever see a return.

Tullus let out a loud, luxurious belch, then another. The soldier in front of him turned with a truculent expression, but seeing the optio's helmet tucked under Tullus' arm, decided to keep his peace. In a jovial mood thanks to the wine he had consumed, Tullus affected not to have noticed the legionary's aborted challenge, concentrating instead on the road before them. Narrow, paved, winding, and lined with tombs, it led right towards the large military camp and the town of Mogontia-cum, and left to the settlement of Borbetomagus. At his back, adjacent to the River Rhenus, was the local amphitheatre, and on the other side of the road, some three hundred paces distant, was the grand monument that honoured Drusus.

'The race is about five miles long, eh?' asked Tullus of the legionary who had wheeled around.

'That's right, sir,' came the penitent reply. 'They start at the gates of the main camp, head south on this road to the small encampment, and back again, to Drusus' monument. The first man to touch the inscription is the victor.'

'Who won the first two races?'

The legionary's chest puffed out. 'The same man, sir. Liberalis, of the Germanica. With Fortuna's help, he'll be victorious again this year.'

'Not if Helvius has anything to do with it,' yelled a soldier on the other side of the road. 'A-laudae! A-laudae! A-laudae!'

At once the pair and their companions exchanged a barrage of abuse.

Men from the local garrison – the First Germanica and the Fifth Alaudae legions – would have a big advantage over those from units further afield, thought Tullus. They would be familiar with the course, having trained on it as often as they wished. Entrants from the Rapax, his old unit, were only permitted to arrive at Mogontiacum a few days before the contest, and Tullus doubted that entrants from the other Rhenus legions were allowed to act any different.

'Here they come,' called a voice.

Cheering broke out among the spectators to the south, and everyone craned their necks to see. Second from the front, Tullus had a great view as the contestants sprinted around the last corner and into sight. Two men led the race, first a slight, black-haired legionary, and then a tall soldier with a ground-eating stride. They were separated by no more than five paces. Behind them came the rest, a pack of more than a dozen legionaries, elbowing and shoving at one another.

'Come on, Liberalis, you can do it,' roared the soldier who had spoken to Tullus. 'Come on, the Germanica!'

Plenty of men nearby echoed his cry, while those on the opposite side of the road jeered and shouted, 'Hel-vius! Hel-vius!' or 'A-laudae! A-laudae!'

Tullus felt a tinge of disappointment that either Liberalis or Helvius – both local soldiers – would take the victory. Although the figures in the main group were bunched too close to make any of them out, he wanted either Fusco or Justus, from the Rapax, to be near the front. Failing that, a legionary from the Eighteenth would do. There might yet be time for someone to catch the leaders before they reached Drusus' monument.

His hopes were soon dashed. While the gap between Liberalis and Helvius narrowed as the pair hammered up the slope towards Tullus' position, the rest of the runners fell back a little. The clamour from the crowd grew deafening, as hundreds of men roared at the top of their voices and stamped their nailed sandals on the ground. When the pair drew alongside Tullus, Liberalis was still in the lead, but only just. Arms pumping, eyes fixed on the finishing area, he pelted by. Helvius was right on his heels, but there was a glazed look in his eyes. Getting so close to Liberalis had taken its toll, thought Tullus. Helvius had used the last of his energy. Knowing when to use that was a crucial skill for any athlete, and it seemed that Helvius had misjudged his moment.

Sure enough, Liberalis' lead began to increase. First it was three paces that he led his competitor, then six, and ten. Helvius pursued his rival up the hill with dogged courage, but it was clear that his attempt to win the race was over.

The soldiers around Tullus scented victory. 'GERMAN-ICA! GERMAN-ICA! GERMAN-ICA!' they shouted, drowning out the cries of those supporting Helvius.

The main body of runners pounded past. Tullus was pleased to spot Fusco and Justus together, and at the front. Fusco, a lithe figure, was leading, and Justus, a blocky man with thighs like small tree trunks, was tucked in right behind him. Like as not, thought Tullus, they'd been setting pace for one another since the start. They would do their legion proud, perhaps finishing in the top three.

Loud gasps – shouts of dismay from some, and of triumph from others – filled his ears, and Tullus glanced up the slope, to Liberalis and Helvius. To his surprise, Helvius was now ahead of Liberalis, who was struggling to his feet. He began to chase after Helvius, but it was clear he would not manage to catch his adversary.

'What happened?' cried Tullus.

'He looked back at Helvius, and tripped on a loose paving stone,' came the sour answer from the legionary in front.

'Stupid bastard. He had the race won,' commented a voice behind.

Every man in the main group of runners had realised that Liberalis' misfortune had afforded them a last chance. The pack's speed increased, each soldier desperate to catch the still-flagging Helvius. They soon passed Liberalis, who was now limping badly.

Because Drusus' monument lay some distance uphill, Tullus' view of the runners was better than if the ground had been flat. His excitement rose as several soldiers sprinted ahead of the rest, closing fast on Helvius. To his frustration, he couldn't make out individual men. Let one of them be from the Rapax, he prayed.

The din from the spectators at the finishing area rose to the heavens in the moments that followed. Figures darted around the monument, attempting to finish the race, and at least one fell. Two men closed in on the inscription before the rest, and the one that reached it first raised a fist in triumph. Trumpets blared to signify that the race was over, and the crowd went even wilder.

'Who won? Who won?' clamoured a hundred voices.

'HEL-VIUS! HEL-VIUS! HEL-VIUS!' shouted the legionaries on the opposite side of the road.

'Whoreson,' yelled the soldier in front of Tullus. 'He fouled Liberalis somehow, or I'm no judge.'

Arguments began over who had done what, which legionaries were fittest and who the winner should be, and continued until the trumpets sounded a fanfare that drowned everyone's voices out.

Tullus squinted as sunlight winked off gilded armour on the road in front of the monument. A senior officer was shepherding the victor forward. The trumpets' sound died away, and an expectant hush fell.

'Loyal soldiers of Rome, fine citizens of Mogontiacum,' cried the officer, whose red sash revealed him to be a tribune. 'We are here today to honour the shade of our beloved commander Drusus, whose loss we still grieve. He would be proud of the race that has just been run! Right to the end, it seemed that men from every legion on the Rhenus could snatch victory. However, one soldier touched Drusus' inscription before the rest. That man is Fusco, of the Twenty-First Legion, the Rapax.' With a flourish, he placed a wreath on Fusco's head.

Further up the hill, a section of the crowd began chanting, 'RA-PAX!'

However, the applause from the rest of the spectators was desultory – their comrades hadn't won, and their wagers had been for nought. The next thing on their minds was more wine, or a woman, or both. This was a rest day for the local soldiery and they had to make the most of it.

'Fusco did it!' muttered Tullus, grinning at the thought of the winnings he'd collect. Six hundred denarii was a sizeable sum, enough to feed and water him like a tribune, never mind a centurion. The notion of buying a horse for the rest of his journey to Vetera was now a reality, rather than the fanciful wish it had been before.

'You're with the Rapax, sir?' asked the legionary in front of him.

'Aye.' Tullus caught himself. 'Well, I was, until recent days. I've been transferred, to the Eighteenth.'

The significance of this move wasn't lost on the soldier, whose eyes widened. 'Begging your pardon for my behaviour earlier, centurion, when you, you—' His voice failed.

'When I belched in your ear!' Tullus said with a laugh. 'It was a trifle rude, I'll admit.'

'Not at all, sir,' protested the soldier, his flush worsening.

'Peace,' ordered Tullus. 'Tell me, is there a decent watering hole near here? The places I've seen are worse than the basest establishments in Castra Regina.'

'You could do worse than the Sheaf of Wheat, sir.' The soldier pointed towards Mogontiacum. 'Make for the centre of the town. There's a staggered crossroads not far from the gate. You want the street that leads towards the river, and the temple of Magna Mater and Isis. Look out for the pair of water troughs decorated with fauns. It's opposite them.' His face split into a smile as he caught the silver coin that Tullus had flipped at him. 'Thank you, sir!'

'To help drown your sorrows. May Liberalis do better next year.' Tullus strode off in the direction of the town. Once he had collected his winnings, he would visit the shrine of the two goddesses, which was famous throughout the region. Only then would he seek out the Sheaf of Wheat.

He had a strong feeling that it was going to be a good night.

Tullus adjusted the arms of his wool tunic at the point where they emerged from under his mail, and picked up his helmet. He had placed it on a shelf by the door of the shop as he'd entered. He put it on and tied the chin strap: it afforded no protection when held under one arm. Behind him, the betmaker groaned from under the wreckage of his desk.

Tullus cast him a jaundiced look. 'Count yourself lucky that I only broke your nose, you thieving cocksucker. Did you really think you could run off without paying me what was mine?'

The betmaker had the wit not to reply.

In truth, thought Tullus, it had been a close-run thing. If he had arrived a dozen heartbeats later, the betmaker would have finished locking his door and disappeared into the thronged streets. He knew from their earlier conversation that Tullus was only passing through Mogontiacum. A day or two of lying low, and he would have got away without paying out the six hundred denarii. The gods had been smiling on Tullus, though. The fool had had a beating to remember instead, and had surrendered the full monies due. Any sympathy Tullus might have felt for the man's plight – the sum would beggar him, he had whined – had vanished at the sight of the glinting aurei in the strong-box that had been hidden under the floor. The gold coins weren't that common still, yet the betmaker possessed scores of them. Nonetheless, Tullus had been careful to take only what was owed to him – twenty-four aurei.

With a final glance at the betmaker, to make sure he wasn't thinking of planting a blade in his back, or trying to follow him, Tullus walked out into the street. His plans had changed. The altercation had given him a fierce thirst. Visiting the shrine could come later, after he'd had some wine. Rather than jingle his purse, which might attract unwanted attention, he laid a discreet hand to it. Its weight, far more substantial than normal, was of immense satisfaction. Well done, Fusco, he thought. You did the Rapax, and me, proud.

A hundred paces from the betmaker's shop, his stomach began to rumble. It had been many hours since he'd eaten, and some ballast would prevent the wine going straight to his head. Tullus stopped at the counter of an open-fronted restaurant, where he took his time over a small bowl of mutton stew and kept a covert eye on the betmaker's premises. The man poked his head out of his doorway a short time later, but he did nothing more than cast sour looks up and down the street. Content, Tullus traced his way to the Sheaf of Wheat.

Tullus leaned back against the tavern wall, grateful for its support. His head spun, and there was a pulse throbbing in his throat. His ears were ringing with the noise of the shouted conversations going on around him, and the musicians to his left sounded like a mob of caterwauling felines. It was time to ease back on the wine, he decided. Since his arrival at the Sheaf of Wheat, time had become a blur. It had begun with a chance encounter. He hadn't seen Valerius, a former comrade in the Rapax, and now a centurion in the Germanica, for two years. Their reunion had been most welcome.

Drinking partner on hand, Tullus had reckoned himself set up for the night, but he had forgotten Valerius' ability to soak up wine like a sponge. They had finished six jugs, thought Tullus fuzzily, or was it eight? He focused with difficulty on Valerius, who had pulled one of the establishment's whores, a dusky Iberian, onto his lap. 'Valerius. What time is it?'

His face buried in the whore's bosom, Valerius didn't hear.

'Valerius!' Tullus hammered a fist onto the table.

Valerius broke away with evident reluctance. 'What?'

265

'How long have we been here?'

'Who cares?' Valerius cast an eye at the line of small windows that ran along the front wall. 'It's almost dark. More than that, I can't tell you.' He cupped one of the whore's breasts, and added, 'There's plenty of time for drinking and fucking! That's all that matters.'

Tullus was about to answer, when his nostrils filled with rose scent. Turning his head, he found a beautiful woman – curvy in the right places, black hair cut in the Egyptian style, eyes rimmed with kohl – seating herself on the table. Her loose-topped dress was inviting enough, but more tantalising were her open legs, which were arranging themselves on either side of him. Tullus couldn't help but gaze between them. She was wearing the scantiest of undergarments, which left nothing to the imagination.

She let out a throaty laugh, and raised his chin with a scarlet-tipped finger. 'Like what you see, optio?'

Tullus' tongue was thick in his mouth. He nodded.

'My friend is no optio,' Valerius remonstrated. 'Tullus is a centurion. Just been promoted, he has.'

'A centurion,' purred the whore, rubbing a foot against Tullus' crotch. 'I *love* senior officers.'

I bet you do, thought Tullus. Your prices just tripled. Despite his cynicism, however, he was becoming aroused. 'What's your name?'

'Hathor,' came the husky reply. 'Why don't you take me upstairs?' She leaned in close, filling his face with her cleavage.

What a good idea, thought Tullus, his lust running wild. It had been months since he had bedded a woman. In his current state, it was debatable whether he'd be able to finish the act, but it was worth a try. He shifted his legs, preparing to stand, and felt his purse – attached to his belt – move against his upper thigh. Damn, it was heavy, thought Tullus, rallying the vestiges of his self-control. If he followed Hathor, one thing would lead to another very fast. When he was done, he would fall asleep – that was the way of such things. If he wasn't up to performing, sleep would take him – this too was inevitable. It was also predictable for whores to rifle through their clients' belongings. There wasn't a whore in the world, Tullus decided regretfully, with the restraint to leave his golden aurei where they belonged. Much as he wanted to do as Hathor asked, a drunken fuck, or more like, an attempt at one, wasn't worth losing his winnings.

'Not tonight,' he said, moving her foot from his groin. Fuzzy-headed with lust and wine, he didn't notice the brief change in her posture as her toes touched his bulging purse.

Hathor pouted. 'You won't regret it.'

I *would*, Tullus thought. 'Maybe later,' he said.

'What's wrong with you, man?' demanded Valerius. 'She's the best-looking whore in the place.'

'I've got other business,' said Tullus, standing with an effort. He picked up his helmet.

'What could be more important than wine and a beautiful whore?'

'I need to make an offering,' he said remembering his resolution earlier in the day. 'Thanks for my luck earlier, you know.'

Valerius grinned and tapped the side of his nose. 'I understand. Come back when you're done. I'll still be here.'

'So will I,' said Hathor, trailing a hand down Tullus' arm.

Tullus tipped his head at Valerius, gave Hathor's arse a squeeze, and weaved his way to the door.

Neither he nor Valerius saw the faint nod that Hathor gave to the pair of tough-looking men propping up the counter nearby.

Fighting his way free of the crowd – the inn was packed – Tullus pushed past the doormen, three bruisers who bore more than a passing resemblance to ill-carved slabs of stone. After the room's pungent fug, the cool night air felt wonderful on his flushed face. He took a deep breath, and another. A walk would do him good. Once his offering had been made, he could return here if he still had a stomach for more drinking. Removed from the twin temptations of wine and Hathor's body, though, Tullus wondered if finding his guesthouse might be wiser. 'Which way to the shrine of Magna Mater and Isis?' he asked of the nearest doorman.

'That way, sir.' A massive arm pointed down the darkening street, which still had decent numbers of people on it. 'It's perhaps a quarter of a mile.'

Tullus considered his options. The temple wasn't far, but the light was fast fading from the sky. His return journey to either inn or guesthouse would be made in complete darkness, that was clear. All kinds of lowlifes emerged onto the streets after sundown. Noticing the look in the doorman's eyes, which suggested he thought Tullus was afraid, Tullus rolled his shoulders angrily, and checked that his sword hilt was where it should be. Without a backward glance, he set off for the temple.

The uneven paving was treacherous to a sober man, let alone a pissed one. Like the unfortunate Liberalis earlier, Tullus knew he could break an ankle with ease. Twenty steps from the inn, he paused to let his eyes grow accustomed to the darkness before continuing his journey. Drunk legionaries made up much of the traffic. Arms slung over each other's shoulders, they ambled along, whistling at the painted whores in dim-lit doorways, and arguing over which restaurant they should eat in. Head down, walking with purpose, Tullus passed unseen by all. By the time he had crossed several intersections without hindrance, his confidence was growing. No one would dare hinder an officer of the legions.

'Get away from me, you vermin!' The voice came from off to one side. 'Help! I'm being robbed!'

Tullus searched for the cry's source. A short distance down a side street he could make out three figures, two confronting the other. Under normal circumstances, a night patrol of Castra Regina, say, Tullus would have had six or more soldiers with him. He was ten strides closer to the trio, a challenge issuing from his lips, before he remembered that he was in fact alone. A glance up and down the street revealed none of the legionaries who had been so plentiful on the first part of his journey. It would have been cowardly to have shouted for help, or to have done an about face, so Tullus summoned all of his bravado, and drew his sword. 'Be off, you sewer rats! Find someone else's ankle to bite.'

It became clear in the next six heartbeats that no robbery was taking place. The three were acting in concert, Tullus realised with dull horror, as they spread out, two facing him and one darting around to his rear. He saw no big blades, only a knife and two clubs. That was small comfort. 'What's going on here?' he demanded in his best parade ground voice.

'Nothing at all, optio,' said the nearest, a burly man in a hooded cloak. 'Hand over your purse. Do it quick, and you'll never see us again.'

'There's precious little in it,' replied Tullus with mock sorrow. 'I've been drinking since before the race began.'

'We want it nonetheless. Now.'

The man's tone implied that he knew about his winnings, thought Tullus with alarm. Had the betmaker followed him after all? Or had he missed something at the inn? Acutely aware of the thug already behind him, he had no time to work it out. Casting a look over his shoulder, he cursed. The third man stood ten paces away, blocking his path back to the larger thoroughfare. He'd fallen for one of the oldest tricks in the book, and if he didn't give up his winnings, he would end up choking on his own blood, or with his brains oozing out of the soup pan of his skull. Yet the thought of handing over his money made Tullus' pride flare up, white hot. Whoresons, he thought. They're not getting it.

The street they were on was typical: narrow, with stone- and brick-built houses on either side. There was no one in sight, not a soul who might help, and so Tullus picked a building with a large entrance. With a few quick sidesteps, he placed his back against the door.

Hooded Cloak moved closer at once; his companions followed, like shadows. They were careful to stay beyond reach of Tullus' sword, but there was no doubting their intention. 'Are you going to break it down?' demanded the largest of the three, whose body odour was palpable at ten paces. His companions sniggered.

It was a faint hope indeed that anyone would answer – only a fool would unbar his door to a stranger after dark – but Tullus struck his sword hilt off the timbers behind him. *Thump. Thump. Thump.* 'Open up, in the name of the emperor,' he roared. 'An officer of the Eighteenth Legion demands entrance, on official business!'

'What kind of imperial officer comes calling at this hour?' asked Hooded Cloak with a laugh. 'You've got one more chance. Hand over your purse by the count of ten, or we'll kill you. One.'

Thump. Thump. Thump. Tullus stopped, listened. He could hear nothing from within the house.

'Two.'

Thump. Thump. Thump.

'Three.'

Tullus' eyes moved over the trio, assessing them. Hooded Cloak was the leader, which also made it likely that he was the most dangerous. Unless he was a fool, however, he would prefer his men to shed their blood first.

'Four.'

That meant that Filthy, the one who stank, had to be downed first. The last man, who was unsteady on his feet, was either old, or drunk. Maybe he was both. Wineskin, I'll call him, thought Tullus. He's the least of my worries.

'Five.'

Tullus hammered again on the door. 'Open, in the name of all that's holy!' Still he heard not a sound.

'I'm losing my patience,' snarled Hooded Cloak. 'Six. Seven.'

Tullus touched the phallus amulet at his neck, and removed the bronze bracelet from his right wrist, gripping the body of it in his left fist so that the decorative rams' heads protruded from his knuckles. He'd never had cause to use it so, but more than one soldier had told him it was a fearful weapon if raked across an opponent's face. It wasn't as good as having a shield, but needs must. He readied his sword arm, and blinked away sweat. If the three came at him together, things would be difficult indeed. He had to hope that Hooded Cloak would hang back a fraction.

'Eight.'

Tullus made a feint at Filthy, hoping to give him a flesh wound and take him out of the equation. The ploy was an utter failure: Filthy dodged backwards, faster than Tullus could follow, and Hooded Cloak thrust his knife at Tullus, forcing him back to the doorway.

'You dog,' said Hooded Cloak. 'Nine. Ten. Purse?'

'Fuck you!' The bracelet had made it difficult to untie the drawstring from his belt, but Tullus had managed it. With a grunt, he hurled his purse straight at Hooded Cloak. Drunk or not, Tullus was so close that the bag flew straight and true, smashing into the man's face with a satisfying *thunk*. Hooded Cloak screamed, the purse burst open, and coins fell with a musical jingle to the ground.

The unmistakeable sound had the desired effect. Both Filthy and Wineskin's gaze moved to their leader, and the fallen money. Tullus was already moving forward. Ripping the bracelet across Filthy's cheek, he felt it tear the flesh open. Filthy shrieked, and Tullus stabbed him in the belly for good measure. In, out, just enough to slice the guts. Filthy's moaning doubled in volume, and he staggered away. Tullus felt the air move by his head as Wineskin, reacting too late, brought down his club in a swingeing blow that would have dropped him in his tracks. Shuffling his feet, he retreated to the doorway.

'You whoreson,' growled Hooded Cloak, his voice muffled by the hand he was holding to his face. 'My fucking nose is broken.'

'Come closer and see what else I can offer you,' retorted Tullus, wondering if he could yet survive.

'I'm going to kill you,' said Hooded Cloak. 'No one hurts me like that and lives to tell the tale.' He glanced at Wineskin. 'Ready?'

'Aye.' Wobbly or not, there was a purposeful set to Wineskin's stance. 'Wait. I'll go at him first.'

The two others were only too glad to let Filthy limp forward, holding his stomach with one hand, but somehow wielding his club with the other.

Some men were too stupid to know when to die, thought Tullus, fighting a rising sense of dismay. With a badly wounded but still dangerous Filthy leading the attack, he still had three enemies to face. He was about to pay the ultimate price for his stupidity. I've been generous to you in the past, great Mars, he prayed. Let me take at least two of them with me. 'Come on, you dogs,' he growled. 'Who wants to meet the ferryman first?'

His threat made Hooded Cloak and Wineskin hesitate for a heartbeat, no more. They were readying themselves to rush him, Tullus saw, and when they did, it would all be over. There was no shame in calling for help, he decided. Some legionaries might be within earshot.

His mouth opened.

But before he could utter a word, Filthy came at him. Wineskin and Hooded Cloak were two steps behind.

Overhead, a shutter banged open.

Ducking under Filthy's clumsy club swing, Tullus heard and smelt the foul-smelling stream of liquid that poured from above. He stuck Filthy through the gut again, this time running the blade in to the hilt. Giving Filthy a massive head-butt for good measure, he twisted the blade and shoved Filthy backwards, off his sword and into Wineskin, who went stumbling backwards.

'Bastard!' Hooded Cloak was still wiping piss and shit from his face when Tullus stabbed him through the throat. Hooded Cloak's eyes bulged with shock; his lips moved, but no sound came out. Crimson sprayed everywhere – over Tullus, all down Hooded Cloak's front – as the sword came free. Down he went, into the mud, where he twitched a couple of times and was still.

Tullus' eyes cast around for Wineskin – and Filthy, who should have died once already. To his relief, Filthy was lying on his back ten paces away. If he wasn't dead, he would be soon. Wineskin had picked himself up, and was staring at Tullus with wary eyes, clearly torn between revenging his friends and running away.

'Go,' ordered Tullus, pointing with his bloodied sword.

With perfect timing, another pot of waste was emptied from above, spattering rank liquid just short of Wineskin's feet. Hawking a gob of phlegm in Tullus' direction, he slipped off into the night.

Wary in case fresh ordure be heaped on *his* head, Tullus shuffled forward a step and called up, 'I thank you for your assistance.'

There was a loud chuckle. 'My old bones aren't up to a fight any more, but I couldn't stand by and do nothing. Are you hurt?'

'My pride has taken a little bit of battering,' Tullus replied, 'but otherwise I am unscathed.'

'The gods be thanked.'

'I would be even more in your debt if you could bring some light. Otherwise I shall have lost the contents of my purse in spite of your aid.'

'Give me a moment,' called Tullus' benefactor.

Trying not to step on any of his coins, many of which were glinting in the mud like little gold discs, Tullus moved to stand over Filthy, who still had enough strength to lunge at his feet. Tullus kicked him in the head and then ran him through the chest. That done, he checked the alley again. There was no sign of Wineskin, yet he didn't relax. Carelessness had almost cost him his life.

Iron screeched off iron as the door bolts were thrown back. The door eased open and in the orange glow of an oil lamp, Tullus saw a slight, grey-haired man clad in an old army tunic. Understanding flooded through him. 'You're a veteran.'

The old man's back straightened. 'Aye. Twenty-five years I served, in the Germanica. And you, sir?'

'Twelve so far, in the Rapax. I've just been posted to the Eighteenth.'

'It's as well I roused myself from my bed, sir,' said the old man, saluting. 'Having a centurion murdered on my doorstep would have been terrible.'

'I'm grateful,' said Tullus, the awareness of how lucky he'd been beginning to sink in. He stretched out his hand. They shook, and the old man said, 'Can I invite you inside?'

'Thank you, but no.' Tullus explained how he'd thrown his purse, and a little embarrassed, revealed how much had been in it.

'Twenty-four aurei?' The old man whistled. 'That's a tidy sum.'

'Aye,' replied Tullus, knowing he'd be lucky to find more than half of his winnings.

In the event, he did better than that. With the help of the old man's slave, and every oil lamp in the house, they found all but two of the gold coins. Tullus pressed four into the veteran's hand, ignoring his protests. 'I insist. You saved my life. If your slave can find the last aurei once it's light, he's welcome to them.'

With the two men's blessings ringing loud in his ears, Tullus returned to the main street, and made his way to the temple without further hindrance. The guards at the entrance gave him strange looks – a moment later, in the bright light cast by the lamps hanging from two huge bronze stands, Tullus realised it was because he was covered in spatters of blood – but did not stand in his way. They were used to such sights and more, he thought with revulsion. Priests of Magna Mater were known to mutilate and even castrate themselves during sacred ceremonies. It was an odd religion by anyone's reckoning, which explained why, despite its popularity, it was still illegal.

The high-walled complex was square in shape, with a central courtyard surrounded on all sides by rooms. The largest two, which faced one another across the east and west sides of the enclosure, were the shrines proper, one each for Magna Mater and Isis. In front of both sat a large stone altar, where sacrifices were made. The rest of the rooms were given over as storage or sleeping chambers, or used to instruct students enrolled in the priesthood of either god.

The hour might have been growing late, yet the place was packed, and despite the crowd, an eerie atmosphere prevailed. The air was alive to the noise of religious chants, unintelligible cries and loud music. A cockerel squawked as it was plucked from a cage and borne towards one of the altars. Strange smells – incense, and other substances – came off numerous glowing braziers. Shadows moved in the nearby chambers, and it was difficult to know if the sounds that issued from within them were of pain, pleasure or something else altogether. In the dim light, Tullus couldn't be sure if the dark liquid oozing from the straw underfoot was just mud. He thought it best not to check.

The majority of those present near the shrine to Magna Mater were women. Old or young, well or sick, barren or pregnant, each had a request of the goddess, who was celebrated as a healer and provider of fertility. Some danced, spinning in wild circles to the sound of cymbals played by priestesses in bright-coloured robes. Others stood on the spot, wailing their devotion over and over. One woman, silent as a corpse, tore at her cheeks and face with her fingernails. Streaks of blood ran down her neck, staining her dress.

Tullus felt most ill at ease. If this was the norm for an ordinary night, who knew what went on during the goddess' festivals, when only women and castrated men were permitted to attend. With a respectful bow of his head – despite his reservations, he had no wish to offend Magna Mater – he made his way to the other side of the square. He felt more at home with Isis. She too was revered as a goddess of fertility, but she was also worshipped by sailors, and by those seeking good fortune. It must have been she who had helped him win so much money, Tullus decided. The thought of his coin made him drop a nonchalant hand to his purse. Thieves operated everywhere, even inside temples.

'Like to know your future?' The gravelly voice belonged to a skeletally thin soothsayer in a characteristic blunt-peaked hat. He sidled closer, using his lituus to open a path through the crowd. Close up, his doughy skin and pallor could not be mistaken. The man was ill, thought Tullus, hoping it wasn't catching. He quickened his pace. He had no time for charlatans, in particular ones who were sick.

'You've been in a fight. The other man came off worse. That's why you're here.'

'Wrong,' said Tullus, although he *did* want to give thanks for his luck in the alley.

'Making a journey by sea soon, are you?'

'No,' replied Tullus curtly.

The soothsayer wasn't to be put off. Despite the throng, he somehow kept up with Tullus. 'Needing to know if your newborn will thrive?'

'No.'

'Ah!' cried the soothsayer. 'Your woman wants a child in her belly!'

'Piss off,' hissed Tullus. He had no woman. The army was work enough.

'You're in need of luck then. Luck in your career. Luck with earning your superiors' respect.'

'I need nothing from you! Out of my way, maggot,' ordered Tullus.

'What a fine officer you make,' said the soothsayer in an acid tone. 'So quick to condemn, so quick to assume that every prophecy is a fake.' He retreated before Tullus' raised fist, however.

Tullus had almost reached the altar dedicated to Isis when the soothsayer's voice reached his ears again. 'Some unexpected good fortune has come your way. The goddess deserves your thanks.'

The fool has worked his way through every possible reason why I'm here, thought Tullus angrily. This had to be the last one.

'Enjoy it while it lasts. Such things are ever brief.'

The man is so predictable, thought Tullus. Luck lasts for *no one*. He cast his eye over the caged birds that were for sale as sacrificial offerings. There were no pigs or sheep – they were regarded by the priests of Isis as unclean. In the dark, and with so many worshippers about, it would be unsafe to allow cattle within the shrine, so poultry and songbirds were all that was on offer. A brace of fine cockerels would suffice, he decided.

'Mud,' cried the soothsayer.

Ignoring him, Tullus bent to examine the cockerel in the top cage of a stack arranged before a wizened crone seated on a stool. 'You have a keen eye, sir,' she wheezed. 'That's the best bird in Mogontiacum.'

'Seas of mud!' said the soothsayer, louder.

'Of course it is,' said Tullus dryly. 'How much?'

'Two denarii,' replied the crone.

Tullus had time to let out an incredulous laugh before the soothsayer's voice interrupted again. It was closer now. 'I see you and your soldiers surrounded by mud, and bog, and trees, thousands of trees. Blood. There is blood everywhere.'

Tullus' temper began to overflow. He wheeled, ready to deliver a kick or a punch. 'Your lies do not scare me. Be gone, dog, or I'll give you a good hiding.'

It was as if the soothsayer did not hear him. Spit dribbled from the corners of his mouth, and his eyes were rolled back in his head, exposing the whites. It was even more unnerving how he continued to approach Tullus without falling. The crowd melted away from him, people averting their gaze and muttering prayers.

'Mud. And rain, torrential rain, sent by the gods. There are dead

275

legionaries everywhere,' intoned the soothsayer. 'You are trapped, and so are your soldiers.'

Despite himself, Tullus felt unease stir in his belly.

'My ears are filled with men's screams. The gods have forsaken them, they cry.'

Unsettled as much by the soothsayer's trance as his words, Tullus seized the man's robe with both hands and shook him, hard. 'Stop this!'

The soothsayer's eyes twitched, then slid down to their normal position. He blinked, focused on Tullus. 'W-what was I saying?'

'You were talking gibberish about mud, and trapped soldiers.'

The soothsayer gave him a blank look.

'Trying to frighten me, were you?'

The soothsayer raised his hands. 'I don't remember what I said.'

'Don't try that on me!' snarled Tullus. 'What do you take me for – a superstitious fool, who'll believe anything?'

'If I gave offence, I'm sorry,' faltered the soothsayer. 'I cannot recall a word of what I said. May Isis and Magna Mater strike me down if I lie.'

If the man was shamming, he was doing a fine job of it, thought Tullus, releasing him. He scanned the soothsayer's face again, but could see no trace of guilt. For the first time, fear caressed the base of Tullus' spine. Was it possible that the soothsayer had been sent a vision by one of the goddesses? Don't be stupid, he told himself. The man's mad, or his brains have been scrambled by fever. 'Be off with you,' he barked.

The contrite soothsayer didn't protest; he just turned away, a pathetic figure now, all skinny arms and bony legs. Tullus felt a twinge of remorse. A swift rummage in his purse produced a sestertius. 'Here,' he called. 'Buy some food. You look starved.'

'The blessings of the goddesses be upon you,' cried the soothsayer, seizing the coin. 'Pay no attention to my ravings. They mean nothing, nothing at all.'

Concealing his disquiet – there were people watching – Tullus forced out a hearty laugh. 'I don't need you to tell me that. Now piss off before I take my money back.'

Hours later, his offering to Isis accepted, the walk back to his guest-house negotiated, Tullus lay in bed, unable to sleep. The soothsayer's words rolled around his head like stones in a musician's gourd, their endless noise disquieting and annoying by turn. He had heard many bad prophecies over the years – some directed at others, some at him – but he'd never before been so affected.

It was the wine he'd drunk that had him rattled, Tullus told himself, or else it was delayed shock caused by his near escape in the alley. The strange air in the temple hadn't helped either. Maybe it was all three. Whatever the reason, the soothsayer *had* been talking nonsense. Tullus didn't know a soul who'd ever been given a reliable prophecy – at least one that hadn't been paid for, in coin.

These certainties did not help him get to sleep.

In the end, Tullus gave up. Hiding the greater part of his winnings under a loose floorboard, he returned to the Sheaf of Wheat in search of Valerius. More wine would help him forget the crazed soothsayer and his fantasies.

So too, he wagered, would Hathor.

AUTHOR'S NOTE

The idea for this short story came to me during a research trip to Germany. I was travelling along the Rhine, visiting historical sites and Roman museums, picking up information and getting a feel for the landscape for my three subsequent books, set on the German frontier of the Roman Empire, and taking place during the years AD 9-16, entitled *Eagles at War*, *Hunting the Eagles* and *Eagles in the Storm*.

The central Roman character in the trilogy is Tullus, a man whose history has fascinated me from the first time I wrote about him. As a middle-aged veteran, he would have seen things and been places, if you know what I mean. He would have *done* things too. Usually, the confines of novels mean that I never get to experience what else a character might have done. Yet ideas about people like Tullus still come to me, and I have to live with them, half-formed things that never go away, and never get written.

However, when I set foot inside the temple to Isis and Magna Mater in the town of Mainz (Mogontiacum), I was so gripped by what I encountered that I *knew* a story about Tullus visiting this temple would happen.

The modern museum might be set in the most unlikely spot (under the central passage of a busy shopping centre), yet the shrine within is dark, mysterious and more atmospheric than I could have believed. The low-level lighting that only comes on as you enter each new section was eerie; so too was the quavering flute music and chanting that came on. Thanks to my first novel, the odd, bloodthirsty rituals celebrated by those who worshipped Magna Mater were familiar to me, but it was incredible to see original offerings of strange little clay figures (some pierced through with needles), and scraps of lead inscribed with curses written by angry or wronged people 2,000 years ago. My mind went into overdrive, picturing a young Tullus, drunk, wandering down an alleyway and finding this temple. Entering, he would hear a prophecy that he'd discount as entirely mad. Years later, it would come back to haunt him.

'The Shrine' is the result.

GLOSSARY

Augustus: successor to Julius Caesar, and the first Roman emperor.

aurei (sing. aureus): an uncommon gold coin, worth twenty-five denarii.

Borbetomagus: Worms, Germany.

Castra Regina: Regensburg.

centurion (in Latin, centurio): the disciplined career officers who formed the backbone of the Roman army.

Danuvius: the River Danube.

denarii (sing. denarius): cast from silver, these were the staple coins of the Roman empire. One denarius was worth four sestertii, or one twenty-fifth of an aureus.

Drusus: Nero Claudius Drusus was a stepson of Augustus, and an excellent military leader who led major campaigns into Germany in the years 12-9 BC. He died at the young age of twenty-nine after an accident on campaign. His monument still stands in Mainz, and reading about the soldiers' footrace to it merely whetted my appetite to write about Tullus visiting the town.

Fortuna: the goddess of luck and good fortune.

Gallia Belgica: the Roman province to the west of the Rhine, which incorporated Belgium, Luxembourg, and parts of France, Holland and the German Rhineland.

Hathor: an Egyptian goddess of joy, feminine love and motherhood.

Iberian: someone from the Iberian peninsula, modern-day Spain and Portugal.

Isis: an Egyptian goddess of fertility, newborn babies, and good fortune. She was held in special regard by women, but was also revered by sailors and slaves. Although distrusted by Augustus, her worship was widespread throughout the empire.

legion: the largest independent unit of the Roman army. At full strength, it consisted of ten cohorts, each comprised of six centuries

of eighty men, all of which were led by a centurion. The First Germanica, or 'German' legion, the Fifth Alaudae, or 'Larks' legion, and
the Twenty First Rapax, or 'Predator' legion, were units stationed on
the Rhine in the late first century BC and early first century AD.

lituus: the curved bronze badge of office carried by soothsayers. Modern
bishops' croziers are no different!

Magna Mater: a strange and mysterious goddess imported to Rome
from Asia Minor (Turkey).

Mars: the god of war.

Mogontiacum: modern-day Mainz.

optio: the officer who ranked just below a centurion; the second-in-
command of a century.

primus pilus: the senior centurion of a legion. A veteran in his forties or
fifties, he was also the third-in-command of the legion.

Rhenus: the River Rhine.

sestertius (pl. sestertii): a brass coin that was worth a quarter of a
denarius, or one hundredth of an aureus.

tribune (in Latin, tribunus): one of six senior staff officers within a
legion.

Vetera: modern-day Xanten.

EAGLES IN THE EAST

A Tullus short story

For Randy Higgins, his wife, Colleen, son, Austin and daughter-in-law, Devon. This story is also dedicated to every police officer who has paid the ultimate price while in the line of duty.
'Gone, but never forgotten.'

PART I

Near Castra Regina, on the River Danuvius, winter AD 6/7

Centurion Lucius Cominius Tullus shifted about under the scratchy woollen blanket. He wanted, *longed*, to be deeply asleep, but the amount of wine he had consumed meant that good quality rest was beyond him. Sweating, restless, having to make frequent use of the pot by the bed, he had been tossing and turning the whole night. A chance encounter with an old friend from the Rapax had turned into five jugs of the local vintage. It had been a poor decision, because now he was paying for it.

Bitter experience told Tullus that his stabbing headache would get worse before it receded. Lying back on the pillow, he stared blearily at the light seeping between the roof tiles and decided that he was too old for such behaviour. A wagon trundled by outside, axles creaking. Like it or not, he thought, a new day had dawned. With his mission of accompanying a vexillation from his legion's base at Vetera to Castra Regina completed, it was time to return to Germania. The sooner he rose, the better.

Just another hour, Tullus decided.

Blissful sleep took him almost at once.

Bang, bang, bang.

The racket wasn't anything to do with him. He rolled over.

Bang, bang, bang.

He opened his eyes.

Again the timbers shook as a fist hammered on them.

'Piss off!'

'Centurion Tullus!'

'Go away.' Every word hurt.

'I bear an official message, sir.'

He came awake in a heartbeat. Weaving to the door, Tullus pulled it open and found a smartly turned-out messenger waiting. Prevented by his pounding head and roiling stomach from doing more than accepting the proffered wooden tablet, he made for his bed. Hobnails clashed as the messenger tramped off down the corridor. Tullus lay down and closed his eyes.

Try as he might, sleep would not come.

The message might be important.

Kindling flame in a clay oil lamp, he removed the seal from the strings binding the tablet and opened it. What he read by the flickering light surprised him. He ran over the words again. Instead of returning to Vetera, he was to head south and present himself at an encampment close to Rome, 'as soon as possible'. No explanation was given. Drink-fuddled, Tullus was baffled by the summons. He did know, however, that the journey would take many days, and that meant he should get some more rest. Delaying his departure by a few hours would make no difference to anyone.

Placing the tablet by his bed, he crawled under the blankets again. They were still warm, and with a sigh of pure relief, he closed his eyes. At once sleep enfolded him in its comforting embrace.

Bang, bang, bang.

Dragged into gummy-eyed wakefulness, Tullus swore. It felt as though he had only just nodded off, but the bright sunlight lancing through the chinks in the roof told him that a couple of hours had passed. He lay there, a foul, furry taste in his mouth, wanting only to drink a little water and go back asleep.

Bang, bang, bang.

Whoever was outside his room was probably not a messenger. In decades of service, he had rarely received two official communications in such close succession. It would not be the landlord either, Tullus decided. *He* knew better than to disturb an important customer.

Bang, bang, bang. 'Tullus!'

'Gods above and below, all right!' He stamped to the door and heaved it wide.

'Still abed?'

'What does it look like?' Tullus glowered at the tall, broad-shouldered man on the threshold: his old friend Vetus with whom he had caroused all night.

A leer. 'You look like shit.'

'And your eyes resemble two pissholes in the snow.'

Vetus chuckled. 'I have never felt better.'

'Liar.'

'I am in better shape than you.'

Tullus admitted ruefully, 'My skull feels as if it is about to burst.'

'Ha! The Eighteenth has turned you soft.'

'Say that to me on the training ground, maggot,' said Tullus with a flash of his usual spirit. The benefit of not drinking as he once had meant his level of fitness was good. His old friend was no sluggard – despite his broken nose and slight squint, he looked in reasonable shape – but he had a close relationship with the amphora. Running miles in a mail shirt, and fighting in it, would soon show him up, thought Tullus.

'Challenge accepted. We shall have plenty of opportunities,' said Vetus, waving a message tablet. 'The messenger found me as well, see.'

'We have both been summoned south?'

'Aye.'

Tullus rubbed his eyes, trying to concentrate. 'What in Hades is this about?'

'My guess would be Illyricum.'

'Of course.' A short distance across the Adriatic Sea, and not much further if one travelled around the sweep of northern Italia, lay the mountainous region of Illyricum. Made up of several parts, Pannonia and Dalmatia being the largest, it had been under the sway of Rome for two centuries. Thanks to recent maladministration, however, a widespread rebellion had kindled. Troops were being mobilised all over the empire. 'So the rumours of a dilectus might be true.'

Vetus nodded. 'A levy, eh? Who would have thought it?'

'The emperor must be worried.' A conscription of Roman citizens was almost unheard of.

'He will have expected Tiberius to have quelled the uprising immediately.' The emperor's heir had been dispatched to Illyricum the previous autumn, but had failed to secure any significant victories before the end of the campaigning season.

'It isn't altogether surprising that he failed. The Illyrian tribes are fierce fighters.'

'That they are, and having bloodied Tiberius' nose, their morale will be high. The Illyrians have not invaded Italia these forty years, but they might be having second thoughts now. Aquileia lies close to the border, and from there it is no great distance to Ariminium.'

'A possible invasion of Italia does not bear thinking about,' said Tullus, frowning. 'But it explains the campaign into Germania being put on hold.' Over the previous few months, twelve legions and thousands of auxiliaries had been preparing on the Rivers Rhenus and Danuvius for a massive three-pronged attack that would sweep deep into barbarian lands. Their purpose was to overwhelm the Marcomanni tribe, deemed a threat to the empire by Augustus himself.

'And why men like you and me have been chosen.' Vetus gave him a great buffet. 'If we are not to lead our men to victory in Germania, then we shall train the conscripts who will fight with us in Illyricum!'

Vetus was right, thought Tullus. Why else would veteran centurions be sent to Italia? At once he thought of Fenestela, his trusty optio, who was with his men in Vetera. Together they had knocked into shape more wet-behind-the-ears recruits than Tullus could remember. He would have to put in a request for Fenestela to join him.

'This calls for a drink,' Vetus declared. 'I am buying.'

'Hair of the dog,' said Tullus, willing his headache away. 'Why not?'

Some fifteen days later, Tullus and Vetus were approaching Bononia. After crossing the snowbound mountains south of Castra Regina and tracking down into the plains dominated by the River Padus, they and their personal slaves had joined the paved Via Flaminia at Mutina and followed it south-east. It was Tullus' first visit to his homeland in many years, and forgetting the war in Illyricum, he was struck by frequent pangs of nostalgia. The sprawling farms and vineyards, the red-tiled houses, the golden warmth of the winter sun, drove home the stark differences between Italia and the cloud-ridden riverlands of Germania where he had spent the previous decade and more.

He had grown up some hundred miles to the south, not far considering the distance they had just travelled. His parents were long dead, but he had sisters. Not for the first time, Tullus decided to compose a letter when he got a chance, and not for the first time, wondered if his siblings had ever learned to read and write, as he had in the army. That was not an excuse, he decided. Someone would be able to read the message, their husbands perhaps, or a scribe in the nearest town.

Thoughts of family turned his mind to his own situation. Prohibited as all soldiers were from taking a wife, and in the main too busy with his men even to consider one, Tullus had long been content to seek out whores whenever he felt the need. Of recent years, however, conscious that the legions would not forever be his home, notions of settling down had appealed more than paid-for flesh. Gods willing, he would find a woman when the time came to retire. An image of Sirona, the feisty Gaulish woman who ran one of the inns in Vetera, flashed into his mind. Whether she would have any interest in an ageing centurion, he had no idea.

Tullus rode his mount, a sturdy grey, with easy grace, which was more than could be said for Vetus. He and horses did not mix. On their journey south, Tullus had had much sport from his friend's lack of skill. Vetus had given as good as he got, mercilessly ribbing Tullus' inability to keep up with his drinking. It felt just like the old days in the Rapax, and was a breath of fresh air.

'There it is.' Tullus pointed. Half a mile distant loomed the characteristic shape of a Roman marching camp: rectangular, with a gate halfway along each side. A timbered rampart ran along the top of the wall, atop which sentries could be seen. 'It's big. Full legion size, maybe larger.'

'That will hold a *lot* of conscripts,' said Vetus. 'Are you ready for them?'

'I am.' Tullus ran a hand down his *vitis*, vine stick.

'Is that fool Cedo Alteram still about?' Nicknamed 'Bring me another' because of his tendency to break his vitis on men's backs, the centurion in the Eighteenth was reviled far and wide.

'He is, worse luck. One of these days he will wake up at the bottom of the Rhenus.'

If there was one fate that he wanted to avoid, Tullus decided, it was being murdered by his own men. It was unlikely, he decided. Since his first days as an officer, his soldiers had been as close as blood kin, and within six months, his new recruits would be the same.

Later that day, Tullus' frame of mind was a great deal less positive. Conscripts were not the same as volunteers, clearly, but he had not expected a rabble. He stalked up and down in front of the seventy-odd men who had been allocated to him. Poor physical specimens, sour-faced, scared or downright evil-looking, he judged the majority to be as poor a set as he had ever seen. A glance around the parade ground made it clear that he had not been singled out: few of the prospective legionaries looked like much. The dilectus ordered by the emperor had not been a success, it seemed, and yet come the spring, these men, and Tullus with them, would have to face the fearsome Illyrians. Vetus' guess had been correct. The camp was to provide the guts of a legion; once trained, it would be deployed to bolster the units already positioned in Illyricum.

Tullus' woes were not confined to his ordinary soldiers. Instead of three junior officers, he had two. They were also the scrapings of the barrel. The optio's bulbous red nose and mottled cheeks implied intimate acquaintance with the bottom of a wine jug, while the wrinkle-cheeked signifer looked as if he should have been discharged fifteen years before.

Tullus' stony expression revealed none of his reservations. *Slap, slap, slap* went his vitis off his left palm. His boots crunched the dirt. Down the front rank, eighteen recruits in length, he strode, and around to the second line. Gaze boring into any that met his – it was not many – he made snap judgement after snap judgement.

Cowed, the marks of manacles on their wrists, and with visible scars, some men were former slaves. Others were well-to-do types with soft hands, and clearly unhappy to be here. Whether many of either group would make soldiers, Tullus could not yet tell.

This one was tall, and had broad, muscled arms. A smith, perhaps. His eyes met those of Tullus briefly before dropping away. He had spirit, but was not over-cocky, thought Tullus, pleased. He would do. A scrawny type with terrible teeth would not look at him; his feet shifted in the dirt. A possible shirker, thought Tullus, and maybe worse. Around to the third rank. Tullus' attention was drawn by the steady stare of a man halfway along the line. Cropped brown hair, almost military style, marked him out from the rest. He did not avert his gaze, even when Tullus came to stand right in front of him.

Here was a potential troublemaker, thought Tullus. 'Name?'

'Spike.' His Latin accent was terrible.

'Spike, *sir*,' grated Tullus.

Blue eyes regarded Tullus unflinchingly.

A heartbeat went by, and another.

'Sir.'

Tullus stuck his face into Spike's. '*Every time* I address you, you will answer me with a "sir".' He spun around, roaring, '*Every time* any of you maggots speak to me, you will call me "sir". DO YOU UNDERSTAND?'

'Yes, sir,' they shouted.

Tullus made them repeat it louder. And again. As content as he could be – which was not overmuch – he turned back to the crop-haired man.

'*Spike.* What kind of name is that?'

'It is a nickname, sir, thanks to this –' Spike rubbed a hand over his bristling hair – 'and also because I used an iron spike on my shield in the arena.'

This explains much, thought Tullus. 'A gladiator, eh?'

'Yes, sir.' Spike's voice was proud.

Tullus made no acknowledgement. A Gaul or a Briton from his look, the man was better quality than most of the recruits, but it remained to be seen whether he was more trouble than he was worth.

Relief filled him as he reached the fourth rank. There had been mention of veterans being drafted in to bolster the recruits, but here was proof. He stopped in front of a strongly built bald man with a long cicatrice down his right forearm. His hair was short, in the military style, and his brown eyes stared straight ahead.

'Which legion?' Tullus demanded.

'The Sixteenth Gallica, sir. Eight years' service.'

'Name?'

'Magnus, sir.'

Deciding that he had the look of a real soldier, Tullus gave him a nod.

The next man appeared to be a veteran as well. Green-eyed, amiable-faced, he grinned at Tullus. 'Sir.'

'Let me guess. You and this one –' Tullus jerked his chin at Magnus – 'are friends.'

'Yes, sir.' Another broad grin. 'We were in the same contubernium. So was Urceus.' He indicated the tall man to his left, who had ears like jug handles and a broken front tooth.

Tullus glanced at Urceus, who gave him a decent salute. 'Sir!'

Tullus turned back to the man between Magnus and Urceus. 'Your name?'

'Vibius Manlius Mus, sir, but my nickname is Smiler.' Another smile.

291

Tullus moved on, counting a total of ten veterans in his century. More would have been preferable, and it wasn't certain that they were all good soldiers, but they gave him a foundation to build upon.

It would have to be enough.

'All right, maggots,' he cried. 'Off you go. Circuits of the parade ground, until I tell you to stop. No cutting the corners, mind. I will be watching. So will the optio and signifer. Go!'

'How many laps, sir?' Smiler called out.

'I haven't decided.'

Smiler's grin lessened only a little.

Tullus' order to run revealed vast differences between his recruits. Spike and two other former gladiators, Hadrianus and a curly-haired man called Cassius, led the race from the start. Magnus, Smiler, Urceus and the rest of the veterans dogged their heels, and a race within a race began as both groups tried to maintain the lead. The remainder of the recruits straggled along behind. Some were so unfit that they had been overtaken three times by the leaders – Spike and Magnus, neck and neck – before Tullus called a halt. Ignoring the jostling going on between the veterans and the former gladiators, he roared encouragement until the last men came shambling in.

Then, lining them up again, he subjected the recruits to a measured tongue-lashing. A few men aside, they were as miserable a collection as he had seen, Tullus thundered. They were a disgrace to the legions, and to the emperor. The Illyrians would massacre them. Dismissing the recruits, Tullus called in his optio and signifer. Neither looked happy.

'This is not going to be easy,' said Tullus.

'When do we start training with weapons?' asked a voice. A moment's hesitation. 'Sir.'

Unsurprised to find it was Spike who had interrupted, Tullus gave him and his two cronies – also loitering – his best centurion's glare. 'You get weapons when *I* say so.'

Spike glanced at Hadrianus, a blocky type with a scar over one eye, and then at Cassius. Neither said a word. Spike's shoulders went up and down in an uncaring shrug. 'Yes –' again the slight delay – 'sir.'

'Quicker,' said Tullus, who knew well that such insolence had to be stamped on at once.

'Sir?' Spike's face was the picture of innocence.

Tullus barrelled over and thrust his face into the gladiator's for the second time. 'When you call me "sir", you say it nice and fast. You do not leave me hanging, waiting to hear it. Understand?'

Spike made no reply.

'Answer him,' Hadrianus hissed.

Silence.

Tullus drove the head of his vitis into Spike's midriff, as he had done to countless men before. As Spike bent over, retching, Tullus said loudly, 'We can do this as many times as you like, maggot. Understand that there will be only one loser. You. Whether it's from my stick or my boots, you *will* learn to obey. Refuse, and you will end up a bloodied corpse.' Intuiting that this might scare a former gladiator less than most, Tullus added, 'Do what you are told, however, and you will be paid well. Given respect. Try hard and you might even get promoted. At the end of your service, you will receive a farm, or a lump sum that will set you up for life. It's an easy choice in my mind.'

Spike retched again, and spat.

Tullus waited.

When Spike looked at him, it was as if he were seeing Tullus for the first time. 'Aye, sir. I understand.'

'Good,' said Tullus calmly. 'Ten laps of the parade ground, all three of you – at the double.'

Meek as lambs, the former gladiators set off at a run.

He turned back to the optio and signifer, both of whom looked impressed. 'I always find stamping out a fire when it starts is easier.'

'Yes, sir.'

Neither of you would have done that, thought Tullus. The sooner he got Fenestela here, the better. 'I know running with the recruits might be too much, but both of you need to be able to march.'

A prolonged bout of coughing took the signifer. When he had finished, his eyes and nose streaming, he promised to do his best.

The optio muttered something similar.

Tullus wasn't convinced by either.

A month passed. He now only had one junior officer – the optio had collapsed on his very first twenty-mile march, and was not yet returned from the camp hospital. Oddly, the signifer, an ancient by anyone's standards, had taken on a new lease of life, and was proving a useful aide to Tullus. His men were already in better shape, aided by two solid meals a day. All could complete a full-length training march in kit, although not at the proper pace. A nearby river served for their swimming exercises, a hill for increasing stamina. They were training daily with heavy wicker shields and wooden swords, and learning the basics of fighting in formation.

As Tullus had hoped, the veterans were solid and reliable: in particular Magnus, Smiler and Urceus. Spike, Hadrianus and Cassius were also promising, but had a propensity to pick fights with other recruits. Tullus was not altogether surprised by the confrontations: the former gladiators were regarded by the other men with a mixture of scorn and fear.

When the day's tasks were done, Tullus and Vetus had fallen into the habit of meeting up. Sitting by a fire, cups of wine in hand, eating meals cooked by their slaves, and sharing stories about their recruits made the long hours of soul-sapping training bearable. They traded tales of the battles and skirmishes they had fought too, and together lamented the quality of some of their superiors. Poor quality was not limited to the ordinary men.

One windy evening, Vetus was regaling Tullus with the tale of a recruit who had tumbled into the river in full armour that day. But for a quick-thinking comrade, who had swiftly shed his mail shirt and dived in after, the hapless soldier would have drowned.

'What did you do with them?' asked Tullus. Taking off armour was prohibited unless sanctioned by an officer.

'I tore strips off both: the one who had fallen in for being a clumsy fool, and the one who had saved him for being a disobedient one. If we had been under attack, I said, I would in all probability have lost two men, not one. Anyone who takes off his armour in future without being ordered to will receive a flogging.'

'Aye,' said Tullus. Life was tough. Dangerous. There was no point making it even worse.

Vetus reached over and refilled his cup.

They saluted one another and drank.

'What a surprise to find you drinking, sir.'

Tullus almost choked on his wine. 'Fenestela?'

A familiar, auburn-haired, red-bearded figure emerged into the firelight. Ugly as the day was long, tough as cured leather, Fenestela was Tullus' oldest comrade. What passed for a smile twitched his lips. 'Here I am.'

'Not a moment too soon.' Tullus leaped up, beaming. 'Vetus, this is Fenestela, my optio from the Eighteenth. Fenestela, Vetus, an old comrade from the Rapax.'

They all clasped hands. Vetus offered a brimming cup to Fenestela, and they toasted one another.

'You made good time,' said Tullus. 'My request must have been approved immediately.'

'It was, sir.' Fenestela jerked his head in the direction whence he had come.

'Before we settle down, a walk might be a good idea.'

Tullus knew Fenestela like the back of his hand. 'Trouble?'

'Potentially, sir.'

Vetus frowned. 'You didn't intervene?'

'No, sir.'

Vetus' frown deepened, and Tullus said, 'He will have had his reasons. Explain, optio.'

'One of the men was carping about the training. Saying it was too hard, that you were too tough on them.'

'Nothing new,' said Tullus, snorting.

'He was looking for support among his comrades,' Fenestela went on. 'There was mention of complaining to those higher up. One of his comrades, a veteran by his appearance, told the whinger to shut his mouth or he would do it for him.'

'Good,' said Tullus, wondering if he could put a name to the men involved.

'Like as not, sir, it will already have been resolved, but I thought you might want to be sure.'

Tullus got up.

Leaving Vetus by the fire, they began walking along the tents, which were pitched in a double line facing each other. Men saluted; greetings rang out.

Tullus clapped Fenestela on the arm. 'It's good to have you here.'

'Good to be here, sir.'

A meaty sound – that of a blow – carried from the end tent on the right, and Tullus increased his pace.

'Got any more to say?' growled a voice – that of Magnus.

There was no answer.

'Maybe you're not as stupid as you look,' said Magnus. 'Anyone else want to complain?'

Silence.

Tullus rounded the tent and took in the scene. Magnus was standing over a prostrate form, the recruit with the shifty eyes. *He* had what would soon be a fine black eye, and was holding the right side of his jaw. The closest three men, Spike, Hadrianus and Cassius, wore guarded expressions. Smiler, Urceus and the last soldier seemed pleased.

Ignoring the scrambling to feet and mutters of 'Sir', Tullus fixed Magnus with his gaze. 'Everything all right here?'

'Yes, sir.'

'Anything to report?'

'Not really, sir. It was a friendly tussle, nothing more.' Magnus was staring over Tullus' shoulder.

'And you?' Tullus asked the recruit, who was wiping blood from his split lip.

'What he said, sir.' The man's gaze did not lift from the dirt.

Tullus glanced at the rest.

'It were nothing serious, sir,' declared Urceus.

Smiler grinned his agreement.

Tullus gave Magnus an approving nod. Keeping order within one's own contubernium was to be commended. He indicated Fenestela. 'By the way, this man is your new optio. He and I go back a long way.'

Eight voices cried, 'Sir!' and all eyes fell on Fenestela, who returned the salutes with a stony face.

'We will leave you to it,' said Tullus.

They walked away.

'The big man had it all dealt with,' said Fenestela quietly. 'That's a good sign.' As was common when there was no one else around, he did not call Tullus 'sir'.

'Agreed. It is also promising that the fool he beat up knew better than to complain. Let us hope he keeps his mouth shut and his head down from now on. He might even grow to like army life.'

Fenestela chuckled. 'With you and me over him, how could he not?'

Tullus smiled. Gods, he thought, but it was good to have his optio back.

PART II

Noviodunum, southern Pannonia, spring AD 8

More than a year later . . .

T he sun was low on the western horizon, turning the stony peaks a glorious dark red. It was a windless evening, and the temperature was pleasant. Birds arrowed overhead, seeking a roost for the night. The relentless buzz of cicadas filled the air. Tullus was polishing off a plate of bread, cheese and olives outside his tent. He stretched his feet out before him, enjoying the sensation of just sitting down. It had been another long day.

Around him sprawled a vast camp, home to a significant part of Germanicus' army. It had been their home since the conclusion of the previous year's indecisive and frustrating campaign. After marching from Italia, his legions had faced the Mazaei tribe in central Dalmatia. Initial successes had proved impossible to follow up, because the enemy tribesmen retreated into the wilderness. Forts were built so that territory taken was not lost again, but the bulk of Germanicus' troops had withdrawn to Noviodunum for the winter. Now another campaigning season was about to begin. Orders had arrived. The legions were to break camp the day after tomorrow. They would march south towards Splonum, an enemy stronghold in the Dalmatian mountains. There would be fighting long before that, however. Lightly armed, the rebel tribesmen's favoured method of waging war was to ambush the legions.

During the entire campaign of the year before, Tullus and his men had endured countless attacks in deep narrow valleys, or on twisting paths through dense forest. Casualties were rarely heavy on the Roman side, but it was demoralising never to be able to bring their foes to bay. Often their only sight was the tribesmen's backs, for they fled after raining down a few volleys of spears and stones.

Tullus was too old a hand to let his men go drinking just before a march. Instead he had excused them all duties *tonight*. He would pretend not to notice their bleary faces and reddened eyes tomorrow. He smiled. Well, for the morning, at least. Come the afternoon, they would need to be readying kit, and sharpening blades.

'Ready?' Fenestela had crossed the avenue from his tent. Water dripped from his shiny-clean face.

Tullus was used to Fenestela's scant concessions to hygiene. 'For what?'

'You know well.'

'A drink?'

'Aye. We're not going to be the only sorry whoresons who stay in camp.'

'Just the one,' said Tullus.

Fenestela winked. 'Aye.'

'I mean it.'

'Of course you do, sir.'

Tullus snorted. A glance at the sky brought him to the decision that he didn't need a cloak. He got up, instinctively shifting his belt a little so that both dagger and sword sat right. Scooping up his vitis, he jingled his purse. 'D'you have coin as well?'

Fenestela nodded.

In companionable silence, they made their way through the growing gloom. Tents spread out to left and right, a forest of leather shapes. Fires glimmered between, illuminating the shapes of men sitting, eating, drinking. Voices mingled with the sound of pots and pans. Smells filled their nostrils: roasting lamb, wine, herbs, and a whiff of horse manure from the cavalry section.

Slipping out of the almost-closed gate, Tullus had a word with the gloomy-faced sentries, who were from Vetus' century. 'You'll get your turn,' he promised, adding, 'Be sure to stay alert.'

'Expecting trouble?' asked Fenestela on the gravelled road – laid by themselves – that led to the town.

'Not particularly.'

'Expect the unexpected, eh?' It was one of Tullus' pet sayings; Fenestela's too.

'I couldn't have put it better myself. Now, where's the best place not to be swamped by our own men?'

They bandied about a few locations.

'Not Dionysus' Table,' said Fenestela. 'The wine there is sourer than acetum. It's no better at the Vine. There's too much fighting as well.'

'The Forge?' suggested Tullus. 'The prices keep the rabble out, and its food is as good as the wine.'

'Old men, aren't we, to be as interested in our bellies?'

Tullus chuckled. 'It's better than drinking until we spew. I have done that too many times.'

Night might have been falling, but the streets of Noviodunum were thronged with legionaries eager to enjoy what would be their last night of freedom for months. Bursts of song were interspersed with shouts and laughter. Every open-fronted restaurant had a crowd before it, every inn and tavern bulged at the seams. The half-clad, kohl-eyed women standing at the mouths of alleyways were doing a brisk trade. Musicians played popular tunes on flutes, accompanied by youths on rattles. Jugglers and acrobats performed. Scrawny boys loitered, intent on lifting a purse from the drunk or unwary.

The pair's outward appearance was little different from that of the ordinary soldiers – each wore a tunic, metalled belt, sword and dagger – but their confident bearing and the vitis in Tullus' hand saw them given a wide and respectful berth. They picked their way down winding side streets, and the crowds died away. Pools of yellowish light marked an occasional wall-mounted torch; Stygian blackness reigned in between. Tullus and Fenestela kept to the middle of the street. It was early yet, and they knew where they were going, but that did not mean there was *no* danger.

Reaching the Forge without incident, they passed the up-down stare of the brutish-looking doormen, and entered. Oil lights hanging from large iron stands threw out warm golden light. The floor was simple mosaic, the plastered walls decorated with basic but well-done paintings. Run by a short, friendly woman by the name of Octavia, the inn was large, with a warren of rooms for customers. This, the bar, was full of optiones and other junior officers, as well as a sprinkling of centurions.

Invitations to join a couple of the latter rang out, but Tullus was in no mood for company. He waved and smiled, and selected a quiet table along one side wall, close to the entrance. Ordering a jug of the best local wine and a platter of roasted lamb, he and Fenestela fell to reminiscing about the Eighteenth. Both of them had been away from Vetera for over a year.

'Do you miss it?' asked Fenestela.

'A little. I don't miss the cursed cloud in Germania. Illyricum may be full of unfriendly savages, but the sun shines almost every day.'

'The food is better here too,' said Fenestela, eyeing the plate of meat being borne in their direction.

Silence descended as they fell on the lamb like starving beasts. Wiping up grease with a crust of bread, Tullus said, 'There won't be much food like this from now on.'

'You never know. Remember that ham Urceus and Cassius produced last autumn?' After a ten-day march through barren mountains and hills, the unexpected bounty had been most welcome.

'I'd forgotten,' said Tullus, smiling. 'That pair are like magicians.'

'They can appear from nowhere too, it seems.' Fenestela's gaze moved over Tullus' shoulder, towards the door.

Tullus twisted slowly to look. 'It's not just Urceus and Cassius.' Magnus, Hadrianus, Spike and Smiler were with them. There was no sign of the shifty-eyed soldier, or the eighth man.

'The prices will put them off.'

Fenestela was right. Sour-faced, the legionaries got up from the table they had briefly occupied, and made for the door.

Before Fenestela could say a word, Tullus was on his feet. 'Wait!'

Urceus heard. 'Sir?'

'Not staying for a drink?'

'Too pricey here, sir.'

Tullus waved a hand. 'Sit down. I'm buying.'

Surprise filled Urceus' eyes. 'Thank you, sir.' Quickly, he called back the others. They all filed past Tullus, delighted.

Smiler was beaming from ear to ear. 'Very good of you, sir.'

'Thank you, sir,' said Cassius. The others echoed his words, even Spike.

'It won't happen often, so enjoy it,' said Tullus, making for the bar.

Octavia herself came to serve him. Solidly built, with shoulder-length brown hair and eyes of the same colour, she had an open, friendly face and a wicked sense of humour. She was no soft touch, however. Tullus had seen her smash an amphora over the head of a troublesome signifer, and laugh while she was doing it.

'Centurion.' She inclined her head.

'Three jugs of wine for that table,' he said, pointing. 'Not the cheapest you have, but not the most expensive either.'

'As you wish. Any food – olives, cheese?' Her Latin was good, and only slightly accented.

'Aye, enough for all of them.'

She beckoned to one of the serving staff, and relayed the order. 'They must be your men.'

Unexpected pride filled Tullus. 'They are.'

'And you are off to war the day after tomorrow.'

'Again, aye. Every man in this room will be the same. Not all of us will return.'

'No.' Sadness flitted across her face.

Curiosity pricked, Tullus asked, 'Are you Roman?'

'My father was – a soldier, like you. A centurion. My mother was from here.'

'Which legion?'

'The Twentieth, based on the Danuvius.' She saw Tullus' enquiring look, and continued, 'Father's last post was here. He married my mother after retiring. They ran the place together. Plague took them both ten years ago.'

'I'm sorry,' said Tullus.

She shrugged. 'The gods give, and they take away.'

'Have you a husband? Children?'

A roll of her eyes. 'I am too busy running the inn.'

'Maybe the right man has not come along,' said Tullus, reminded of Sirona, and wondering if she would ever accept his advances.

'I won't hold my breath. Now, if you'll excuse me.' With a loud cackle, she was gone, moving down the bar to serve another customer.

'I did not expect to find vermin in here.' The voice was clipped, and distinctly upper class.

Tullus' eyes moved. A young man in a fine tunic with a narrow purple stripe was standing over his men's table. Two other tribunes stood behind him. His heart sank. All three were from the legion Tullus' century had been attached to. Lip curled, the tribune glanced at his fellows. 'They told us this was where officers drank, no?'

His companions agreed, but they looked a trifle uncomfortable. One said, 'Come, Nepos. There is a table over there, by those centurions.'

'I want *this* one.' Nepos jerked his head at the door. 'Out. The lot of you.'

Hades, thought Tullus. All I wanted was a quiet night.

'Out!'

Spike began to stand up, his fists bunched.

Hadrianus dragged him back down. 'Sit,' he hissed.

The corner of Spike's mouth twitched, but he obeyed.

'Senior centurion Tullus, sir,' said Tullus, interrupting before the situation deteriorated further. 'Can I be of assistance?'

'No.' Nepos regarded Tullus, his expression haughty. 'I am fully capable of dealing with scum, centurion.'

Little cocksucker, thought Tullus. Born with a silver spoon in his mouth, you haven't done a day's work in your pampered life, let alone fought a battle. You came straight here from Rome too, after Daddy secured you the post.

'I am sure you are, sir,' he said, continuing swiftly, 'Did these men offend you?'

'Yes, by being here.' A disdainful sniff. 'I want their table.'

Tullus held in his temper. It did not do to cross such senior officers, even if they were beardless fools. Although his men had done nothing wrong, it would be simpler to make them move. 'Of course, sir.' He jerked a thumb. 'You heard, boys. Up you get. Find another place to sit.'

Cassius, Urceus and Smiler got to their feet. Magnus, Spike and Hadrianus stayed put, a tiny act of rebellion.

'You don't seem to understand, centurion. I want them to leave!'

Tullus stiffened. Whether it was worth confronting Nepos, he was not sure, but he was struggling to contain his temper.

'Every soldier is welcome in this inn.' Octavia's voice cut across the din.

Nepos turned, made an attempt to smile. 'You are . . .?'

'The owner of this premises, sir. I say those men can stay.'

Tullus gave her a pleased wink.

Nepos spluttered, and glanced to his companions for support. Neither looked prepared to continue the argument, but Nepos' face grew even angrier.

'Give them the table, boys,' ordered Tullus. It was better to let the tribune save face than to antagonise him further.

Magnus, Hadrianus and Spike looked unhappy, but they and the rest knew when to keep silent. Taking their wine, the six moved off to the other side of the room.

'It's all yours, sir,' said Tullus, wishing he could empty a jug all over Nepos.

A venomous glare was his only reply. With the smallest salute he could get away with, Tullus walked away. I'll be back in a moment, he mouthed at a watching Fenestela.

His men were crouched over their new table, heads together. 'Gratitude, sir,' said Magnus. 'That could have turned nasty.'

'Agreed,' said Tullus. 'Nepos is one to watch out for.' He caught Spike's eye. 'Be careful. You might find me a pain in the arse, but crossing a tribune is another matter altogether.'

'Yes, sir.'

To Tullus' relief, Spike's tone was accepting.

'I'll keep him right, sir,' said Hadrianus.

Spike elbowed him, hard. 'Just you try.'

'We owe you, sir,' said Smiler.

'And not just for the wine, sir,' added Urceus. 'I seen a man put up on a cross for not much more than what just happened.'

You and I both, thought Tullus. They blow in, lord it over us regulars, treat us like shit, and piss off after a year. 'Stay well clear of him, you hear?' Satisfied by their nods, he rejoined Fenestela.

'He seems particularly odious.' Fenestela poured wine for them both.

'Nothing would give me more pleasure than to beat the shit out of the supercilious prick,' said Tullus from the side of his mouth.

'We can dream, eh?'

'Aye.' Tullus threw down the contents of his cup in one swallow.

Try as he might from that point onward, his enjoyment had been soured. He could not stop glancing in Nepos' direction. Each time he did, the tribune seemed to sense it, and glower back. His fury boded ill for the next time they met. It might have been wiser to have held back entirely and let Nepos bully his men, thought Tullus, but what was done was done.

To his relief, the tribunes did not stay long. Pausing only to throw a final scowl at Tullus, Nepos followed his companions outside.

'Good riddance,' said Fenestela.

Tullus nodded. 'I've lost any appetite for drinking. Let's give those three pricks a head start, and then leave, eh?'

Fenestela looked disappointed. ''Twould be the sensible option, I suppose.'

'Stay if you want.'

'Who would hold your hand on the way back?'

'Cheeky bastard,' Tullus said, but he was smiling.

A shout carried inside. Not a sound made to catch attention, but one of pure, unadulterated fear. Another followed. The doormen were talking urgently to each other. Tullus glanced about the room. No one else appeared to have heard. He pricked his ears. A third cry, fainter this time.

'It's the tribunes,' he said intuitively. 'Much as I don't give a shit about Nepos, we can't stay here. You get the men, fast as you can. I'll go outside.'

He made for the door, ignoring the startled faces of those he jostled past. He found the doormen peering down the alley. The gloom made it impossible to see, but the sound of fighting was plain. 'What's going on?'

'I don't know, sir. I think those senior officers are in a bit of trouble,' said one sheepishly.

Tullus shoved him. 'And you are just standing here?'

'Our job is to keep things quiet on the door, sir, not the street,' came the sullen answer. 'If we left our post, Octavia would cut our balls off.'

She would do well in the legions, thought Tullus, drawing his sword as he ran off.

'Help!' cried a voice.

They weren't all dead, thought Tullus. Slowing his pace as the light cast by the lamps outside the inn dwindled, he peered down the street. Sword ready in his right hand, vitis in his left, he shuffled forward, letting his eyes accustom themselves to the darkness. He kept silent, not wanting to give away his position. Voices speaking Latin reached his ears, and muttered orders in another tongue. He could see nothing. His skin prickled. Left and right he looked, seeing only shuttered shopfronts and doorways.

Twenty paces he went. Two score. Then, to the left and about fifty paces away, he saw a group of shadowy figures clustered around the opening to an alleyway. He padded towards them. Focused on whoever was within, no one noticed. Then Tullus made out Illyrian. The men he could see were the attackers, which suggested the tribunes had re-treated into the more defendable alley. He inched closer, counting. Six men. Seven. Bad odds.

A soft noise to his right.

Tullus ducked, and the club that would have sent him to the under-world whistled overhead. He twisted, and lashed out with his vitis. It connected with a meaty *thwack*, and his assailant yelped. A heartbeat later, and Tullus' blade was hilt-deep in his belly. He screamed, and Tullus booted him backwards, off the steel. He went down bawling.

Knees bent, ready for another attacker, Tullus ignored him. A heart-beat tripped by, and another. Leaving the gut-stuck man to scream at the sky, and distract his companions, he moved swiftly to the far side of the street.

Not swiftly enough.

Voices cried out. Shadows rippled towards him, two, three.

To look up the street towards the Forge – and its wall-mounted torches – risked losing any night vision. Praying that Fenestela was coming, Tullus put his back against the wall of the nearest building. Memories of a similar clash years before, when he had been carrying a purse laden with gold coins, flooded back. I survived that, he told himself. I can survive this.

As the Illyrians drew nearer, Tullus was able to make them out better. He changed his mind. All three were young and lithe, and they had spears. He might take one down, maybe even two, but he *would* die. With nothing to lose, therefore, attack was the best form of de-fence. Picking the closest one – the others were a few paces behind – he hurled his vitis at head height. Twirling like a spinning top, it struck the Illyrian smack in the face. Tullus came swarming in behind it, his shoulder barge sending the warrior flying.

Most men would have done the wise thing then and fled, abandoning the tribunes to their fate. I am a fool, thought Tullus, aiming straight for the alleyway in which the senior officers were trapped. Gambling that the Illyrians there would not expect him to come haring over like a fox with its tail alight in the Cerealia, he crossed the street in three strides. A shocked face loomed before him. Tullus' sword point rammed into its mouth. Out it came. Hot blood spattered Tullus' face.

Figures closed in from both sides. Air swished, spears lunged at him.

I'm done, he thought.

'Roma!' cried a voice from the alley. A shape emerged, a short blade in one hand.

From down the street came an answering call.

'ROMA!' Tullus repeated. He thrust left to force his enemy there back, then advanced right, towards the inn *and* the second warrior. His belly was tight with the expectation of a spear thrust. 'ROMA!'

Whether his cry did it, or the impending approach of Fenestela and his men, he would never know. The Illyrians vanished into the night. The sound of running feet was replaced by Tullus' breath, sawing in his chest, and then, from the alleyway, a low moaning.

Calling out his name and rank, he walked towards the figure with the knife. 'I am Roman,' he said loudly. 'I am here to help.'

'Thank the gods,' a voice answered. It was not Nepos.

Sure that the man was one of the tribunes, Tullus asked, 'Are you all right, sir?'

'I am, but one of my companions is wounded. How badly, I am not sure. The other is as well, I think.'

Fenestela's arrival a moment later with six men, and flaming torches, was opportune. The tribune Tullus had spoken to pale-faced but determined, and his tunic a patchwork of bloodstains. 'Not mine,' he explained. 'I helped Antonius into the alley. Some of it might be Illyrian too,' he added with a flash of pride. 'I stuck one.'

Ordering Fenestela to pursue the warriors with four men, Tullus took a torch and with Cassius and Urceus, followed the tribune into the alley. There they found Antonius, unconscious, his tunic more crimson than white. Nepos crouched beside him, cradling his left arm. Tullus had hoped to find him unhurt, hiding in the alley from cowardice, but Nepos had a through-and-through wound from a spear. Despite his vociferous complaints, *he* was the lucky one. Antonius had been stabbed in the guts. He would not last more than a few days.

Poor bastard, thought Tullus as he ordered Cassius and Urceus to carry him between them. 'Did they try to rob you, sir?' he asked the third tribune, whose name was Iulius.

'That was the strange thing. They didn't.'

Unease tickled Tullus. 'Then it was an assassination attempt, sir.'

'Who would want to kill us?'

Tullus ground his teeth. Jupiter, they send babies out to command

306

us, he thought. 'It'll be one of the enemy leaders, sir, trying to weaken our legion. The chain of command would be splintered with three tribunes gone.'

'Of course. Praise the gods that you came when you did, centurion.'

'Why are you thanking him?' cried Nepos before Tullus could answer. 'It's *because* of this idiot that Antonius and I are injured! He should have got here far sooner. Better still, offered us an escort at the inn.'

It took all of Tullus' self-control not to turn on Nepos with bloodied blade. Grateful for the poor light, which gave him time to mask his fury, he was also thankful for Iulius' swift response.

'Come now! Noviodunum is safe, or *was*. No one has been attacked in this manner all winter. But for this fine centurion and his men, we would all be dead.'

Nepos subsided, muttering, and they bore Antonius back to the Forge. Octavia was waiting at the threshold. She took one look and beckoned them inside. Sweeping cups off the nearest table so they could lay Antonius down, she called for bandages, hot water and acetum.

'It's bad, isn't it?' muttered an ashen-faced Antonius as Tullus slit his tunic open.

'A flesh wound,' said Nepos, who was standing alongside. 'A little bed rest, and you will be fighting fit again.'

Antonius' eyes, full of hope, moved from Nepos to Tullus.

'It is bad, sir. Very bad,' said Tullus, only too familiar with wounds like the oozing, wet-lipped slit in the tribune's belly.

Antonius groaned, and one hand crept down towards the hideous injury.

'I wouldn't, sir.' Urceus gently took Antonius' hand in his own. 'Squeeze, sir, hard as you can. It will ease the pain.'

Tullus gave Urceus an approving nod.

The serving girl arrived, arms full. Taking charge, Octavia cleaned and dressed the wound with rough linen wrappings. 'That should stem the bleeding a little,' she said to Tullus. 'Until you get him to the hospital.'

'Your father taught you?'

'I used to help the surgeons when I was a girl.' She lowered her voice. 'I have no poppy juice, sadly. That is what he needs most.'

'They will have it in the camp,' answered Tullus quietly. 'My thanks.'

'I wish I could do more. He—'

'I know.'

'Of course. You must have seen men hurt like that before.'

'Too many times.' Tullus couldn't even put a figure on it. Why could Nepos have not been the one, he thought again. 'Can I trouble you for some blankets to fashion a stretcher? The sooner we get him to the camp, the better.'

'At once.'

Tullus watched as Octavia hurried away, shouting orders.

'She's as good as many an orderly, sir,' said Urceus.

'And she sells wine,' added Cassius, grinning.

Tullus saw where this was heading. 'Don't even think it. She would not be interested in the likes of you. Plus, she is hard as nails.' He related the tale of the signifer and the amphora.

His men nodded in acceptance.

They were about to leave when Fenestela returned. He had found no sign of the warriors. 'Vanished like rats down a hole, sir,' he reported with disgust.

'No surprise. Come the dawn, we can search the town properly, and send out patrols.' These would be face-saving gestures, thought Tullus, but necessary ones. Antonius' impending death would affect morale.

It was a bad start to the year's campaign.

PART III

Tullus cursed. A tiny stone had flicked up and into his left boot, and then worked its way under his foot. He had been marching with it for half a mile, maybe more, trying without success to shift it to a place that didn't hurt. He fell out of line, ordering Magnus, the new signifer, to keep the same pace. Magnus, still delighted by his promotion, gave him an enthusiastic nod.

Ten days after the attack on the tribunes, and six after Antonius' lingering death, the army was on the march. No one had been caught for the murder, even though the army had turned Noviodunum upside down. Several locals had been beaten to death by over-enthusiastic search parties. The resulting tide of unrest had expedited the legions' departure. Tullus had been relieved by Germanicus' decision, because soldiers with nothing to do are prone to seek out trouble. More civilians would have died.

Leaving the lowlands behind, the army had entered the mountains that formed the spine of Dalmatia. Roads had dwindled to tracks, and now Tullus found himself on a goat path in a narrow valley bounded on both sides by almost vertical stone cliffs. Glaringly white under the spring sun, they were bare of vegetation apart from the occasional stunted tree clinging to a tiny ledge. Today his legion was in the vanguard, with his cohort at the very front. The auxiliaries were further out, as was the custom. Currently, there was no sign of them, which might be of concern or might not. Some days the enemy attacked, and others they didn't.

It left a man feeling on edge, thought Tullus, finding a patch of grass alongside the track. As if malevolent eyes were on him all the time. He glanced casually behind him into the scrubby bushes. Nothing. This was as much concern as he could show. Any more, and his men's spirits might be affected.

Shield set down beside him, he began to undo his boot, a process which required the loosening of at least four loops of the immensely long laces. Eager to avoid any re-lacing, he was careful to keep the ends from slipping out of the holes.

Inevitably, the comments started.

'Lost a hobnail, sir?' Hadrianus was passing. He held out a leather bag, the same as every soldier carried.

'No,' said Tullus, sure that Hadrianus was trying not to smirk. 'Thank you.'

'You should march without boots, sir,' said Spike, who never failed to let his comrades know how tough the soles of his feet were, courtesy of years fighting on the arena's sands.

Others joined in. 'The centurion has a blister!' 'Sore feet, sir?'

Hoots of laughter. The men did not often get a chance to make fun of him.

Tullus grimaced and waved a dismissive hand. 'It's just a stone.'

'Sure you're not tired, sir?' called a voice. 'Have a rest. We won't march *too* fast.' Roars of delight.

Tullus was sure it was Smiler, but he couldn't see. 'I may be an old man, but I can march further than any of you maggots!' he shouted.

They cheered, which was precisely what he had hoped for.

Distracted by the banter, he had only just taken off the boot. Turning it upside down, he watched with satisfaction as a stone chip fell out. It was amazing how something tiny could be so cursedly uncomfortable. Easing the boot back onto his foot, Tullus tugged on the first set of loops that would tighten his laces.

A cry of pain from down the track.

Tullus' head twisted. A shout like that meant a man had fallen and broken an ankle. Or—

A scream. Shouts. An officer roaring commands.

'We're under attack!' cried Tullus. 'Shields off your backs! Eyes left and right!'

Spears hummed in from behind him, one, two, half a dozen. Men cursed. Someone screamed. Confusion reigned. In the narrow marching column, it was difficult to unsling the massive shield without hitting a comrade.

Tullus himself was dangerously exposed, but he could go nowhere without his boot. Skin crawling, sure that a spear would take him in the neck, he tied the laces as fast as possible. Job done, he offered swift thanks to Fortuna and snatched up his vitis and shield. Keeping the latter faced to his left, the direction the spears were coming in from, he rejoined the column. His men were a mess. Some had obeyed his orders, but others were still trying to get their shields off their backs, or arguing with one another. War cries carried from tree-covered area on the left. Tullus tried to gauge the enemy's strength, but it was an impossible task. He returned his attention to his men.

'Shut your mouths! Javelins down! Shields off your backs! Those closest to me, face left! Those on the other side, face right! Form a line! The rest of you, shields over your heads!' Ignoring the enemy completely, he walked up the century, clattering his vitis off helmets and shield rims. He was pleased to find Magnus had rallied eight or ten men. Giving him an approving look, Tullus walked back down the line, repeating the same words. Spears continued to land, but not in great numbers.

His calm was infectious. By the time he had reached Fenestela in the last rank, the century was a solid wall of shields, left and right, with a protective roof. Casualties were acceptable: one death, and two minor wounds. One of these was a man with a broken cheekbone, caused by the swinging edge of his comrade's shield as they had tried to obey Tullus' command. The abuse he was getting from his comrades, not all of it good-natured, was audible from some distance away.

Content that the enemy were not about to charge, and that his men were as safe as could be arranged, Tullus stepped a few paces away from the column to get a better view.

'They'll aim at you, sir,' said Fenestela.

'I know.'

Ignoring Fenestela's mutter, and trusting that the warriors could not throw well enough to hit his cheeks or feet – the only parts of him not protected by shield, helmet or greaves – he stared down the track. A spear landed behind him, how close he could not tell. Another followed. Tullus did not turn his head. To his relief, the attack appeared to be confined to a short section of the track, that which was overlooked by the stand of trees.

The danger to his men and those of the century behind, however, continued. Emboldened by the Romans' lack of response, more and more warriors were leaving shelter so they could throw from closer range. Things could easily get worse, thought Tullus. The enemy might come down onto the track and attack his soldiers head on. He could not wait for orders – Germanicus was a long way to the rear, and the senior officers miles further back.

An attack up the steep slope was risky. He had no way of knowing how numerous the warriors were. Go too far from the column, and they might be overwhelmed. Do nothing, however, and more men would be injured. Lives might be lost. And if the enemy's plan was to halt the legion while the track ahead was being blocked, every moment wasted was increasing the likelihood of disaster striking.

It was clear Fenestela wanted to be part of Tullus' plan, but someone had to stay in overall command. He glowered, as was his wont, when Tullus issued his orders.

'I'll be back,' said Tullus.

'See that you are, sir.'

They exchanged a look, as they so often had in such situations, and then Tullus strode off to the front of the century. 'Magnus, you're in charge here.'

Tullus called out names – Spike, Hadrianus, Smiler, Cassius, Urceus and fourteen others – and Magnus' grin faded.

'If the enemy comes haring down the track, I am relying on you to stop them,' said Tullus.

Magnus nodded, appeased. 'I will, sir, you can be sure of that.'

Twenty men in total. Fewer, and he would not have enough, thought Tullus. More, and he risked his still inexperienced soldiers breaking.

'Those whoresons need to be driven back,' he explained. 'They might run, but they could also stand and fight.' His gaze roved. Spike, Hadrianus, side by side. Smiler, smiling even now. Cassius and Urceus giving each other a grim look. He saw uncertainty in some faces, fear in others, mad eagerness in the former gladiators'. Where he led, Tullus decided, his men would follow. How they would fare if the fighting grew heavy, he could not tell. It was in the gods' hands.

Placing himself at the right of the front rank, with Spike, Hadrianus, Smiler and Cassius to his left, he had the rest form in fives behind. It would be madness to try and run up the steep gradient, so he walked, all the time talking. 'Stay close to one another. Ranks two to five, hold your shields over your heads until I say so. All of you, watch your footing. Look out for incoming spears.'

Angry howls. Spears, which missed. They had been seen.

312

Tullus kept low, peering up at the enemy from behind his shield. He counted. 'Thirty-odd of them, I can see. There could be more, though. All right with that, boys?'

The answering roar made him smile.

They climbed. Sparks flashed as spears rang off rocks. Stones shifted underfoot. Lizards that had been basking in the warm sun darted away into crevices. The air was ripe with the smell of wild herbs. Satisfied that those with him in the first rank were holding a line, Tullus glanced over his shoulder. 'You at the back! Keep up!'

'Spears, sir!' shouted Cassius.

Tullus' gaze shot back to the front, and he cursed. The warriors had grouped together, and a volley was heading in their direction. 'Spears!' He ducked below the rim of his shield.

Air moved. Men muttered prayers. Tullus heard someone moaning in fear.

With a sickeningly familiar sound, the enemy missiles landed. *Thunk, thunk* into shields. Crash off rocks. A softer, innocuous noise – followed by a scream – into flesh.

'Who's hurt?' bellowed Tullus.

'Gaius, sir,' came a voice from behind.

'Badly?'

'He's dying, sir.'

Tullus' only solace was that Gaius was one of the weakest men. 'Shields hit?'

'Mine, sir.' 'And mine, sir.' The chorus went on. Six shields.

Tullus ordered someone to take Gaius' shield. Then he had the men without spears embedded in their shields pass them forward so that every man in the front two ranks was unencumbered. All the while, fresh spears rained down. Another man's shield was hit. Trying to remove the enemy shafts would take time, time he did not have. There was only one option, Tullus decided.

He took a deep breath, and gave the order to draw swords and advance.

Up. Up. Leg muscles screaming, sweat stinging his eyes, fist tight upon his weapon's hilt. Someone slipped, cursed, got back on his feet. The warriors stopped throwing, lest they have no weapons to fight with. The bolder among them advanced towards Tullus and his men, faces contorted with battle rage. Come on, he thought. Break your own line.

'With me?' Tullus shouted.

A rolling chorus of 'Ayes'.

The warriors facing them were lightly armed, as was their custom. Perhaps half had bronze or iron bowl-like helmets. All had shields, oblong or hexagonal, and faced with leather. The primary weapon was the spear, which had a leaf-shaped blade. Wealthier men had swords. A few individuals wore mail shirts.

Twenty paces. Three warriors, youths, glanced at one another and charged.

Tullus grinned a wolf-smile. 'Halt! Pick your target!'

The trio scrambled down the slope, yelping like dogs on the trail of a boar. An arrowhead of mad bravery, they rushed at Tullus and his men.

Being on the very right, Tullus could only watch, and trust in his soldiers.

Ten paces. The first warrior's eyes were bright blue. One of his companions had black-and-white lines painted on his shield. The third had a straggly beard.

They hit, spears lunging forward.

Hadrianus struck first, his blade lancing out from behind his shield to take Blue Eyes in the throat. Smiler killed Painted Shield the same way. Cassius broke Straggly Beard's nose with his shield boss and then, as he reeled away, screaming, spitted him in the belly. Spike stepped forward and finished him off.

'Back into line!' cried Tullus. Pleasingly, Spike obeyed at once.

As he had hoped, the death of the three youths dented the enemy's confidence. A few spears shot overhead, or glanced off shields. The warriors' line was longer than Tullus' short one, but there were gaps in it, and some of the faces he could see were unhappy. Good, thought Tullus. 'Forward!' he roared. 'Forward!'

They hit the enemy at walking pace. Shields battered off one another. Oaths in Latin and Illyrian shot back and forth. Men shouted. Screamed. Fell.

Tullus killed a warrior, and then helped Hadrianus to down another.

Another Illyrian drove his weapon at Tullus. He ducked, and the spear blade drove through the timbers, its tip stopping two fingers' breadth from his face. He and the warrior pushed and pulled, Tullus trying not to lose his shield, the other desperate to free his spear. The contest ended when Tullus gutted his opponent, but his shield remained useless. 'Urceus!'

'Yes, sir?' from right behind him.

'My shield is fucked. Take my place.'

'Sir!'

Using the training-ground move, Urceus angled his shield side on to come around Tullus' midriff. As Tullus dropped his own shield and twisted around to the right, Urceus slipped in to his left and assumed his place in the front rank. Almost at once, an enemy warrior attacked.

Trusting Urceus, Tullus glanced about, assessing their situation. His heart leaped. Although it was an obvious move, no warriors had thought to flank them. He could see none emerging from the trees either, to back up their comrades. Best of all, the ones facing his men were wavering. 'Forward!' Tullus shouted.

He followed Urceus, who was humming to himself. 'You all right?' Tullus asked.

Urceus laughed a little. 'Me, sir? Aye, never been better.'

'You are singing.'

'It's something I do, sir, when I'm excited.'

'As long as you're paying attention to those savages . . .'

'Oh aye, sir, I am.' Urceus buried his blade in the side of a warrior who had turned to run.

He's a cool one, thought Tullus.

Soon after, the warriors broke. Spike and Hadrianus tensed, as if to charge after them, but Tullus roared, 'Hold the line! We have done our job.'

A growl of frustration, but they obeyed. They'll be all right, thought Tullus with satisfaction.

The rocks were carpeted with enemy dead and wounded. Tullus' men had not escaped unscathed. As well as the slain Gaius, three men were injured. Hadrianus had had his cheek opened by a spear blade. Covered in blood, he protested loudly that it was but a flesh wound. 'Spike says he can't see my teeth through it!'

Cassius was nursing a broken nose, courtesy of a smack in the face from an enemy shield. The size of an overripe plum and the same colour, it was already the subject of loud comments from his comrades. Cassius muttered and swore back. The last injured man was Spike, who had twisted an ankle. 'It's nothing, sir,' he said to Tullus, but his ginger steps and wincing face gave the lie to his protest.

They were light casualties, however. Tullus was well satisfied as they withdrew down the slope. The enemy had vanished into the trees, and with no sign of any more on the track, the legion was free to continue its march.

Later that evening, Tullus was tucking into a bowl of rabbit stew cooked up by his slave. The rabbit had been provided by the resourceful Urceus, who was lethal with a sling. Since the previous year, Tullus had taken to letting him head off at the end of a day's march. Army supplies kept them going, but a man soon grew tired of flat bread and cheese. Urceus almost never returned empty-handed, and oftentimes came in, grinning, with half a dozen rabbits dangling from thongs around his neck. Cassius always accompanied him – the two were firm friends. Tullus tended not to demand a share, thinking it better to let Urceus share with his comrades.

'What's this for?' he had asked an hour before, when Urceus arrived with the gift of a rabbit.

'Just a thank you, sir.' Urceus smiled, revealing his broken front tooth.

'For what?'

'Sending me into the front rank, sir.'

'I had to – a man without a shield is dead.' It wasn't as simple as that, of course, and Tullus had given him an approving nod. 'You did well.'

Urceus' grin almost split his face. 'Thank you, sir.'

'You can't sing to save your life, however.'

They had both laughed.

Tullus scraped the bowl with his spoon, gathering up the last of the juices.

'That smells delicious. Is there any left?' Fenestela was approaching from the direction of the eastern rampart, where some of their men were on sentry duty.

Tullus peered into the clay vessel sitting close to the fire. 'A little. Move fast, though, or I'll have it.'

Fenestela sat beside him, and produced a spoon from his leather purse. He dipped into the pot and tested the stew's heat with the tip of his tongue before swallowing. 'Ah, that's good. Just what I needed.'

When Fenestela was done, Tullus asked, 'Any sign of the Illyrians?' There had been two further attacks on the army since the first ambush, and the enemy had stayed in sight along the heights right until the site for the camp had been reached.

Fenestela wiped his lips with the back of a hand. 'Not even a shadow. They're still out there, though.'

'Of course. And the men?'

'Alert. Alive to the fact that you or I will be checking on them regularly.'

Satisfied, Tullus poured them both wine. He raised his cup. 'To Gaius. May the gods of the underworld watch over him.'

Fenestela's cup went up in salute. 'To Gaius.'

They drank deep.

Fenestela made a face. 'It's only a shade better than piss, eh?'

'Better than having no wine at all.'

'I'll drink to that.'

They saluted each other again.

'I have an idea where you might get a decent drop, sir.'

Annoyed, Tullus turned his head. Cassius, who had been passing, bobbed his head in apology. 'I couldn't help hearing what you said, sir.'

Interest replacing his irritation, Tullus beckoned. 'You're supposed to be in the hospital tent overnight.'

Cassius walked into the firelight. 'I'm all right, sir. I want to be with my comrades.'

Pleased – it was a very good sign when injured men preferred the company of their fellows than the relative ease of the hospital – Tullus nodded.

'How's the nose?' asked Fenestela. Cassius' face was now bruised from below both his eyes almost to his chin.

'It's all right, sir. Hurts to eat, but I can drink!'

'As long as you don't overdo it,' warned Tullus. 'Hungover soldiers are easy to kill.'

Cassius' expression grew serious. 'Aye, sir.'

'So, this this supply of wine you mentioned,' said Tullus. 'Where is it?'

'Remember the Forge Inn at Noviodunum, sir? The woman as runs it, Octavia, she's with the supply train. Sets up a tent every evening. Does a roaring trade, sir.'

It was common enough for male innkeepers to follow the army with a train of laden-down mules, but Tullus had never known a respectable woman to brave the dangers of a campaign. He glanced at Fenestela, who shrugged. 'I didn't know.'

'Gratitude. I might investigate,' said Tullus to Cassius, who grinned. 'I'll join my comrades on the wall, sir, if that's all right?'

Granting permission, Tullus dismissed him, and he and Fenestela chewed over the day's events. Gaius' death was unfortunate, but the men had done well. It was a relief, because Splonum, the army's destination, would be a much greater examination of their mettle. Heavily defended and with strong fortifications, it would be a test for all. They talked too of their old life with the Eighteenth, and how it would be good to return to Vetera when the war had been won.

'Never thought I'd say it, but I miss Germania,' said Tullus.

'Winter never ends, remember. Which do you long for, the cold, or the damp?'

Tullus chuckled. 'I like that time of the year. Warm barracks, fires of an evening, the vicus to wander around.'

'You're forgetting the mud, and the endless rain,' said Fenestela with a snort. 'Not to mention the frost and ice. Patrols through the snow. Nights on sentry duty when you can't feel your fingers and toes.'

'You don't have to do the latter,' retorted Tullus.

'Checking on the men is bad enough.'

'You're getting old.'

'Says the man who likes to sit on his arse in an inn with a mug of beer in his fist. Is it the Ox and Plough where you'd like to be, by any chance?' Fenestela winked, and added, 'Talking to Sirona.'

Tullus found his cheeks were a trifle warmer than they had been. He opted to say nothing.

'Sirona is a fine woman. A man would have to be blind not to see that.'

Tullus shot him a sharp look. 'Do you have your eye on her too?'

'Me? No. I would never stand in your way.' Fenestela scowled. 'Not that she'd have me anyway.'

'A wife wouldn't suit you. Telling you what to do, tidying everything up so you don't where it is, giving you the evil eye after a night on the wine.' Saying it out loud made Tullus wonder if he could ever contemplate marriage either.

'Aye, you're right,' said Fenestela. 'When I retire, it'll be me and a few dogs.'

Tullus lifted his gaze to the sky, brightened by a multitude of stars. The moon had risen, its silver-white light outlining the peaks around the camp. 'Speaking of sentry duty, I had best do the rounds.'

'I can do it,' said Fenestela, moving as if to stand.

'Stay where you are – I need to stretch my legs. Don't finish the wine.'

Fenestela leered at him.

Tullus ducked into his tent. He had taken off his armour earlier, deeming the risk of a night attack at night to be small. There was no need for his helmet either. Replacing his metalled belt with a simple one of leather – having no decorative dangling strips, it would not give him away – he adjusted his scabbard until it sat just so on his left hip, and donned his cloak. Bidding Fenestela farewell with a wave of his vitis, he walked quietly towards the rampart.

The camp was peaceful. A few diehards lingered around their fires, talking and drinking, but most men had turned in. Tullus padded by, escaping notice, just as he wanted. Halting by the last tents, he stared across the open space that lay before the earthen ramparts. The section manned by his soldiers, a quarter of the length of the wall, was directly opposite. Eight men, an entire contubernium, were on duty. One man every twenty-five paces or so, a far denser arrangement than was normal. Finding the fresh-made wooden ladder that marked the start of their position, he lifted his eyes. There was the first man, shifting about. And the second, motionless apart from a tapping foot. Three men, four. Five wasn't where he should have been, because he was talking to six. As Tullus watched, however, six turned around and tramped back to his position. That was acceptable. The seventh and eighth men were where they were supposed to be. Content, he padded towards the ladder.

Something made him look up again at the last two men. The seventh had shifted, but the other hadn't budged an inch. A dozen steps closer to the rampart, now Tullus could see that his head was bent forward. Hades, he thought. Don't let the fool be asleep.

The punishment for such an infraction was the fustuarium, being beaten to death by one's comrades. Tullus had witnessed two. Brutal, bloody, gut-churning, they lived on in the dark corners of his mind.

Thankfully, neither victim had been one of his soldiers. Resolving to make more noise than usual as he neared the last sentry, he told himself that if indeed the man was dozing, he would wake in time.

Try as he might, his hobs made a little noise on the ladder. The first man, Spike, gave him a crisp salute. Tullus wasn't annoyed. Spike's clear, bright eyes showed he hadn't been even close to nodding off. His twisted ankle was a little stiff, he said, but it took his weight. With a 'carry on' nod, Tullus proceeded down the walkway, grateful for the packed earth that absorbed the sound of his tread.

Peering into the darkness beyond the defences, Hadrianus didn't hear him until the last moment. Despite being startled, he remembered his training, to acknowledge Tullus with only a salute. To speak aided the enemy; it also alerted any potentially sleeping sentries to the presence of an officer.

'Seen or heard anything?' whispered Tullus.

'No, sir.'

'Good. Stay alert. The enemy *is* out there.'

Tullus moved on. He was unsurprised to see Magnus watching him approach. The big man saluted.

'A fine night,' muttered Tullus.

'It is, sir. Not too cold.'

'Anything to report?'

'It's peaceful beyond the rampart, sir, but either Hadrianus or Spike is letting off the loudest farts. The noise would wake the dead.'

Tullus had to bite back a laugh. 'Let me guess. You cooked tonight.'

'Ah, now, sir.' Magnus sounded hurt.

'Am I right?'

Magnus' teeth flashed in the gloom. 'Yes, sir.'

'Don't complain to me then. Be grateful you're far enough away from the smell.' Tullus clapped Magnus on the shoulder and left him to it.

Smiler also heard him. Unusually, however, he wasn't smiling.

'What's wrong?' asked Tullus at once.

'I heard a few birds calling a while back, sir. Not owls either.'

The fine hairs on the back of Tullus' neck prickled. Nocturnal birds other than owls were uncommon. 'Enemy scouts?'

'That was my thought, sir.'

'When was the last call?'

'Some time ago, sir. I wondered if they came to have a look at the camp, and then thought better of it.'

'That is one possibility.' The other, thought Tullus, was that the bastards were creeping towards the defences in silence, or waiting until later in the night. He stood still, staring into the darkness. Open ground ran away from where he stood. A hundred paces off, a narrow stream pattered quietly over rocks. Past it were the outlines of trees on the nearest slopes, and above them, the peaks, sharp-edged in the moonlight.

Tullus counted two hundred heartbeats. No bird called. Nothing moved.

Advising Smiler that he would return, and to call a comrade if he noticed anything further, Tullus went to check on Urceus. He too had noticed the odd calls.

'They weren't no birds I've heard before, sir.' Encouraged by Tullus, Urceus went on, 'I knows my birdcalls, sir. It was men as made those noises.'

Again Tullus peered into the night, and once more he saw nothing. Heard only a fox's bark. Unease tugging at him, but unable to justify sounding the alarm, he continued his circuit. The sixth man was Cassius.

Tullus paused beside him. 'You heard anything?'

'No, sir.'

It was no surprise, thought Tullus, considering Cassius' stertorous breathing through his broken nose. 'They are out there, nonetheless.' He related what Smiler and Urceus had heard, and told Cassius to be on the lookout for anything unusual.

Sentry seven was the shifty type whose name Tullus could never remember. He seemed nervous. Tullus told him to settle down, that everything would be all right. He lingered a while, hoping that their muttered conversation would wake the eighth sentry (if he was indeed still slumbering). Finally, making no real attempt to be quiet, he walked towards the last man, Vindocomus, a short individual with a nervous laugh.

Vindocomus seemed oblivious to his approach. A dozen paces out, and Tullus' worst fears were realised. He was propped up by his shield, arms crossed under his chin. Fast asleep.

Tullus cleared his throat.

No response.

Right below them, inside the camp, armour jingled. Hobnails crunched the dirt. Tullus paid no heed. Closing in, he prodded Vindocomus with his vitis, hard.

The unfortunate soldier came awake, eyes unfocused, mouth agape.

'You maggot!' hissed Tullus. 'I could have been an enemy warrior!'

'I-I-I'm sorry, sir.' Realising his predicament, Vindocomus looked terrified. 'I've not been feeling well.'

Feet climbed the nearest ladder, which was just beyond where they were standing.

Tullus rammed his face into Vindocomus'. 'Expect me to believe that?'

'No, sir, I really am ill.'

'You fought today without complaint.'

'I shat myself during it, though, sir.'

'Aye, well, you wouldn't be the first.'

'No, sir, it wasn't that. I have the shits, really bad.'

There was a ring of truth in Vindocomus' words, thought Tullus. His nostrils twitched. And a whiff of certainty in the air. He decided merely to deliver a severe dressing down. When Vindocomus had recovered, he could spend a month digging ditches or the like.

Tullus' mouth opened.

'Here he is!'

Horrified, Tullus found himself confronted by the tribune Nepos, who had clambered up onto the walkway. A pair of staff officers trailed in his wake.

PART IV

'It is customary to salute a senior officer,' snapped Nepos.

Furious, feeling like a new recruit, Tullus obeyed. Vindocomus, looking even more scared than before, made a sloppy attempt at one.

'My apologies, sir,' said Tullus. 'I didn't expect you at such a late hour.'

'You got to him first,' said Nepos, prowling towards them, still favouring his bandaged arm.

Suddenly, Tullus had a nasty feeling in the pit of his stomach. 'First, sir?'

'I was taking the air, checking on sentries, you know. I also spied this lowlife.' Nepos glanced over his shoulder at his staff officers, who nodded. 'He was clearly resting on his shield, and he didn't move for the space of four score heartbeats.'

The poor bastard is sick, thought Tullus, but he couldn't say it. The regulations were black and white. Nonetheless, he could not keep silent. 'Sir, I—'

'He *was* asleep, *was* he not, centurion?'

Tullus hesitated. Vindocomus' fate was already sealed. For him to go against the word of three senior officers was therefore madness. He too would be punished. Not the fustuarium, he thought. Demotion was more probable, and regaining his former rank would become an insurmountable climb.

'Well?' demanded Nepos.

Tullus squared his shoulders. 'He was asleep, sir, yes.'

'As I thought!' crowed the tribune.

'He is ill, sir,' said Tullus, unwilling to give up even now.

A snort. 'If he is well enough to stand sentry duty, he is well enough to keep the camp safe from the enemy.'

It was a valid point, thought Tullus, his heart heavy. 'Yes, sir.'

'He is a miserable piece of shit. The fustuarium should be straight after the morning parade, I think.'

'Sir,' said Tullus from between gritted teeth.

Looking like the cat that got the cream, Nepos strode past, his purpose clearly to check on the rest of Tullus' men.

A rank smell laced the air.

'Sorry, sir.' Vindocomus' voice wobbled. 'I couldn't hold it in.'

'It's not your fault,' said Tullus gruffly. His mind raced, trying to think of ways out of the hideous situation. Nothing presented itself. Vindocomus was doomed, and it was Magnus, Spike, Hadrianus and the rest who would have to kill him.

Vindocomus began to cry quietly.

The wretch deserved some dignity, Tullus decided. 'Come on. I'll escort you to the latrine trench. You can get cleaned up after.'

A snuffle. 'T-thank you, sir.'

They walked along the rampart, past the rest of the contubernium. It was plain from their dismayed expressions that Nepos had explained what they would be expected to do come the morning. His face stricken, Urceus clasped Vindocomus' hand. Cassius offered him his wineskin. Magnus and Smiler both whispered something in his ear. Hadrianus and Spike, the former gladiators, looked outraged. It wasn't surprising, thought Tullus. Join the army only to be treated worse than in the ludus.

Down the ladder they went, and in silence, made their way to the latrine trench, which lay close to the east gate. Vindocomus walked with sloped shoulders, his posture that of a man who has given up all hope. His was a cruel fate, thought Tullus. If only Nepos had not seen Vindocomus dozing. If only the tribune was not such a vindictive bastard. If only there was a lesser punishment. If only a swifter death could be given him.

The stench of the latrine trenches, rich and acrid, clawed the back of Tullus' throat. Long ditches deeper than a tall man, they were normally found outside camp walls. In hostile territory, this was too dangerous, so the soldiers had to live with the smell. At this hour, they were abandoned.

Inspiration struck Tullus. It was a grim choice, but better than the fustuarium. He steeled his resolve; he had to act fast, without hesitation. 'Got any family?'

'My mother, sir, and a couple of sisters.'

After getting Vindocomus to tell him where they lived in northern Italia, Tullus said, 'I'll see to it they get your pay and personal effects. If I can visit when the war is over, I will. Tell them you didn't deserve this.'

'Thank you, sir.' He was pathetically grateful.

They reached the latrine trench. Vindocomus glanced at Tullus for permission, and then with a speed born of desperation, squatted at the edge, hoiked up his tunic and pulled aside his undergarment. Liquid shit exploded from his rear end.

Tullus stepped in, his dagger reversed.

Vindocomus looked up in confusion.

'I'm sorry,' Tullus muttered, and struck him in the side of the head with all his strength. A surgeon had once shown him the weak spot in the skull two fingers' breadth back from the eye socket. Hit a man there hard, the surgeon had said, and he was dead before he knew it.

Vindocomus let out a surprised gasp, and toppled backward into the latrine trench, which was already deep in shit and piss. A soft splash rose. He sank fast, vanishing into the foul-smelling liquid without a trace.

Racked with guilt, Tullus stood, watching a few bubbles rise. It was an ignoble death, he told himself, but a better one than that which awaited him the next morning. With a sigh, he turned away.

Fear creased through him. A soldier stood not ten paces away. Tullus strode forward, ready to knife him. He was not about to face execution himself for the merciful end he had given Vindocomus.

Bright blue eyes held his gaze. The soldier had a crooked nose; Tullus thought he recognised him.

'I'm in Vetus' century, sir. He speaks well of you.' The man made no move towards his own blade.

Tullus halted, his dagger yet ready to do its work. 'What did you see?'

'Nothing, sir. Not a thing.'

Tullus gave the man his hardest centurion's stare, and was pleased that it was returned. 'He was one of my men,' grated Tullus. 'Tribune Nepos caught him asleep on sentry duty just now. Sentenced him to the fustuarium. I saved him that agony.'

The soldier nodded.

'You have seen men beaten to death?'

Pain flashed across the blue eyes. 'Aye, sir.'

'I couldn't think of any other way,' said Tullus, bizarrely relieved to share what he had done with someone.

'Vetus would have done the same, sir.'

Tullus nodded jerkily. 'What's your name?'

'Maximus, sir.'

'You're a veteran?'

'Yes, sir.'

Tullus gave him another jerky nod, and walked away. His mind screamed a warning: send Maximus the same way as Vindocomus.

He could not do it.

Night passed without an enemy attack. Summoned by trumpets not long after dawn, the legion had assembled, cohort by cohort, on the open ground inside the walls. After a short address by the legate, about how they would continue the march to Splonum, Nepos had announced Vindocomus' crime, and his punishment. Heads craned in Tullus' direction; muttering was audible everywhere. The threat of the fustuarium was such that it rarely needed to be imposed.

Nepos came striding over to Tullus' century, his face pink with self-satisfaction and bloodlust. His eyes roved left and right, over the legionaries. 'Where is the spineless worm?'

Tullus stared straight ahead. 'He's dead, sir.'

'What?' Nepos' tone was shrill with disbelief. 'How?'

'He asked to go to the latrine trench soon after you left us, sir. I left him to it: there was nowhere for him to run, what with the gates being shut. When he didn't come back, I went to look for him. He was floating face down in the shit, dead as a ten-day-old corpse.'

Nepos frowned. 'He drowned himself?'

'I suppose so, sir. That, or he slipped in by accident, and couldn't get out.' The pits were deep, their steep sides slick with ordure. Not a day out of Noviodunum, a drunk legionary had perished in this manner. Nepos would have heard, surely, thought Tullus, his nerves biting at him.

'It seems altogether too *convenient*.'

''Tis most unfortunate, sir,' said Tullus in a regretful voice. 'The men should have seen justice meted out.'

'Where is his body?'

'By the latrine trench, sir. I thought you might want to see it.'

Nepos glared at him. 'Go and wait there until I come.' He stamped off in the direction of the legate, who was waiting for the punishment beating to begin.

Tullus imagined the legion commander's face when Nepos told him that Vindocomus was dead. It would not look good for the tribune; but that was small satisfaction for the unnecessary death of a good soldier.

He had a word with Fenestela, who knew what he had done to Vindocomus, and ordered him to ready the men for the day's march. Tullus was about to leave when Cassius leaned towards him and whispered, 'Thank you, sir.'

Tullus gave him a look. 'For what?'

'Vindocomus, sir.'

'I have no idea what you're talking about.'

'Course not, sir,' said Magnus, who was standing beside Cassius.

Tullus' eyes moved along the front rank. They were all watching him with knowing expressions. Magnus, Cassius, Smiler, Urceus, Hadrianus, Spike, and the shifty man whose name he could never recall. They *knew*, he decided, or they had a good idea. And they were grateful, he could see it. Moved and relieved, Tullus muttered, 'The maggot slipped, that's all.'

He marched away to begin his vigil by Vindocomus' corpse, his step a little lighter than before.

That evening, Tullus had more need than usual for a drink. Ordered by Nepos to leave Vindocomus unburied – 'The filth deserves no better,' the tribune had declared – he had been able only to say a few words over the corpse before marching out. Soon after leaving the camp, the enemy had attacked. The advance came to a halt until the warriors were driven off. A raging mountain stream slowed progress later in the morning. Standing around as the engineers felled trees to use as a makeshift bridge was boring, and dangerous. A second Illyrian attack came, heavier than anything previous. It too was repelled, but half the day had been wasted.

By the time Tullus reached the day's encampment, the army had covered a paltry six miles.

Having checked on his men, and ensured they were all fed, and content as could be expected, Tullus summoned Fenestela. Together they went in search of Octavia's temporary 'inn'. As with the latrines, army rules had been bent. Civilians were banned inside camps, but the alternative when at war, to leave them outside at the mercy of the enemy, was madness. A blind eye was turned, therefore, when trades-men and innkeepers quietly set up shop each afternoon beside the auxiliary tentlines.

'That must be it,' said Tullus, pointing. An anvil sat outside a tent triple the size of that which would hold a contubernium.

Fenestela chuckled. 'The Forge, eh?'

It wasn't the only 'inn'. Four others had been allowed as well. A long line snaked away from each. Everywhere off-duty legionaries stood, talking, laughing, queuing.

Tullus and Fenestela bypassed the legionaries waiting to get into the Forge. A few resentful glances came their way, but no one protested. The same brutish-looking doormen from Noviodunum stood guard at the entrance. Recognising Tullus, they stood aside.

The interior was jammed with soldiers, snug as the stone ballast in a ship's belly. The fuggy atmosphere was a rich mixture of sweat and wine. Songs beloved by different units were being hurled to and fro. Shouted conversations, lewd jokes and laughter filled the air. Followed by Fenestela, Tullus made his way through, asking, shoving and if nec-essary ordering men to get out of his way. Finally reaching a wooden counter, the only furniture, he planted his elbows on its rough surface.

Amphorae lay stacked six high, up to the tent's leather roof panels. Octavia and two barmen paced up and down, tending to the thirsty customers. She caught Tullus' eye, and smiled. 'Centurion.'

'Octavia.'

She came to the other side of the counter. 'This must be your second-in-command.'

'Aye, Fenestela. He and I go back a long way.'

'It's a pleasure to meet you,' said Octavia.

To Tullus' surprise, Fenestela blushed to the roots of his red-grey hair. 'My lady,' he muttered.

Her smile broadened. 'You must be parched. It was a tough day.'

A jug and two cups appeared in front of Tullus, and he muttered his thanks. 'You heard about the ambush at the stream?'

She made a face. 'Eventually.' Always towards the very rear of the miles-long column, civilians and the mules carrying supplies and equipment were among the last to receive news, as well to reach each day's camp.

'Better late than never,' said Tullus.

'True, but tell that to the customers. We were hours late arriving.' She rolled her eyes. 'There were already men waiting as we pulled in. They were so eager that they helped to erect the tent. Gods, but that would be useful every day.'

'Did you give them a free drink?' asked Fenestela.

Octavia snorted. 'Do I look as if I came down with the last rain shower?'

Fenestela buried his nose in his cup.

'That's a fine vintage,' said Tullus, swirling his wine appreciatively.

'Only the best for you, centurion.' Octavia's smile was genuine.

Tullus raised his cup in a toast.

She leaned over the counter and asked quietly, 'Have you seen that tribune recently?'

Tullus mind filled with images of Vindocomus, terrified, weeping, staring at him as he toppled into the latrine trench.

'Centurion?'

Tullus realised that Fenestela and Octavia were staring. 'I have had quite a lot of dealings with him, unfortunately.'

Her eyes rested on him. When he did not explain further, her expression grew serious. 'You cannot speak of it.'

'I would rather not.' With a flick of his chin, Tullus indicated the soldiers packed around him. 'You understand.'

A brisk nod. 'Military matters should be left at the door.'

'Let us drink to that,' said Tullus to Fenestela.

Someone shouted Octavia's name, and she went to serve other customers.

'Nepos, eh?' said Tullus.

'He's a cocksucker, and that's no mistake,' replied Fenestela.

'Gods willing he starts to act like most tribunes and leaves us well alone.'

Fenestela growled in agreement.

'So I said to the centurion, I said, "It's not my turn to dig the trench, sir."' The loud voice came from over Fenestela's left shoulder.

'Oh aye? And what did he say to that?' asked a second voice.

'The prick hit me a mighty belt with his vitis, and he told me it was my cursed turn whenever he said so. Then the optio slapped me about for making trouble.' More oaths.

'It's always the same,' said the second man. 'Always has been, always will be. Let's just get pissed and forget about the pair of them.'

'Until tomorrow, eh?'

Another curse.

Tullus glanced at Fenestela. 'D'you think they talk about us like that?'

A smirk. 'Probably.'

'I'd say you're right,' admitted Tullus with a rueful grin. 'But our men respect us too.'

'They wouldn't follow you into battle the way they do otherwise.'

Fierce pride swelled in Tullus' chest. 'Now *that* is something worth drinking to.'

They saluted one another and threw back their wine.

'To victory over the Illyrians,' Fenestela said.

Refilling their cups, Tullus said loudly, 'Roma Victrix!'

In a heartbeat, his cry was taken up. Reverberating shouts filled the tent. 'Roma Victrix! Roma Victrix!' Arms round each other's shoulders, men danced about. Wine was spilled, cups smashed underfoot.

Fenestela staggered as someone collided with him. 'Just like the old days, eh?'

Tullus grinned.

'See what you've started?' Octavia's tone bordered on disapproving. 'I'll not have an unbroken cup at this rate.'

Tullus met her unblinking stare. 'This must happen every day, and your prices take breakages into account, I am sure.'

Her lips twitched. 'Perhaps.'

Tullus slapped down a handful of silver. 'This is for any extra costs.'

'There was no need.' Even as she spoke, however, Octavia swept the coins off the counter.

'That will also pay for another jug,' said Tullus. 'And a third if need be.'

'Of course, centurion.' With that, she was gone, shouting at one of her staff to take his finger out of his arse and do some work.

'I swear she batted her eyes at me,' said Tullus.

Fenestela snorted. 'Talk about an overactive imagination. Drink up.'

They busied themselves with finding the bottom of the jug, and then with tackling the third. The world seemed an altogether finer place by then. The singing had grown louder, and the general atmosphere more festive. Octavia produced food: cheese and bread, and fried sausages. Tullus' and Fenestela's position at the counter could not be bettered, and they attacked the platters with vigour.

'I need a piss,' said Tullus.

'Me too.'

'We'll never get back in once we have left. Shall we call it a night?'

'That sounds good,' said Fenestela, adding, 'We are definitely getting old.'

Farewells made to Octavia, they shouldered their way outside. After the humid, sweaty atmosphere of the previous few hours, the cool air felt fresh and sweet. Above the western rampart, the darkening sky was an incredible shade of burnt orange. A few stars twinkled overhead. There was not a breath of wind.

Tullus, who had no cloak, shivered. 'There could be a nip of frost in the morning.'

'As long as there's no snow, I don't care.'

They paced along the side of the 'inn', taking the quickest path towards their century's tents. The latrine trenches were on the way, and the thought made Tullus think of Vindocomus. He cursed Nepos again, and decided that if an opportunity to hurt the tribune ever presented itself, he would seize it with both hands.

'Give us a kiss,' said a loud voice from around the rear of the tent. 'Me and my mate.'

'Take your dirty hands off me, filth!' cried a woman – Octavia.

Tullus and Fenestela exchanged an alarmed look, and then they were both running. Around the corner they tore.

Octavia was backed up against a pile of empty amphorae, with two legionaries blocking her escape. The neck of her dress had been ripped, and her face was red with anger. 'Piss off,' she shouted.

'Don't be like that, sweetie,' said one legionary, reaching out a hand.

Octavia slapped it away. As he lunged for her again, she twisted around and seized a small amphora. Whirling, she smacked the first soldier in the face with it. He dropped like a sheep before the sacrificial altar. His companion snarled and grabbed hold of the amphora, trying to wrestle it from her. 'You bitch!' he cried.

Tullus and Fenestela came in at his back. Fenestela seized the man's elbows and wrenched him away. With a heave, he turned him to face Tullus, who promptly punched him in the solar plexus, *one-two*. There was an *ooof* sound as the soldier's lungs emptied; only Fenestela's grip held him up.

'I needed no help,' said Octavia, who looked more furious than scared.

It was a debatable point, but Tullus decided not to argue it. 'Are you all right?'

She pulled up the neck of her dress. 'I am.'

'My apologies for this pair.' Tullus kicked the man she had cracked with the amphora, who was unconscious. 'They will be severely punished.'

'I know.' She gave him a warm smile. 'I must get back to work. The customers are waiting.'

Impressed by her cool, Tullus watched as Fenestela dumped the man he had punched on top of his comrade. The latter did not even stir, and the former merely groaned. 'They will lie there long enough for us to find someone who knows them,' said Tullus.

'Centurion.'

He turned his head. Octavia had paused at the back entrance to the tent. 'Yes?'

'Thank you.' And then she was gone.

A fine woman, thought Tullus.

He identified Octavia's two attackers easily enough, by hauling soldiers around from the 'inn' in twos and threes to look at them. This done, Tullus had the pair dragged back to their tentlines, where he spoke with their centurion. Embarrassed that another officer should appear with two of his men in such a manner, the centurion promised that they would suffer long and hard. Tullus gave them a couple more belts to remember him by, and took his leave.

Spying Nepos on the way back to their century's position, they had to take another route. Accompanied by his usual gaggle of staff officers, the malevolent tribune appeared to be making an inspection of various units' tents.

'Hades, but he is a stickler,' said Tullus.

'Not seen his like in a while,' said Fenestela.

Tullus glanced about. 'He needs cutting down to size.'

Fenestela raised an eyebrow – this was extremely dangerous talk – but made no reply.

'If we get a chance, eh? Something sly that he'll never know about.'

Fenestela leered. 'It would be a pleasure.'

PART V

O ver the following days, Tullus had little time to consider his revenge on Nepos. Beating off enemy attacks daily, the army made slow but steady progress towards Splonum. Moving further and higher into the mountains, and with supplies impossible to find, the soldiers existed on little more than bread and wine. Urceus' skill at hunting became so useful that Tullus excused him from all extra duties, and sent him out every afternoon with a few others as protection.

The walls of Splonum proved little match for the legions' siege engines, which had been hauled up, dismantled, in wagons. Thus reduced, and thousands of prisoners taken, the army moved on to the next stronghold, some miles to the south. A routine developed. Surround an enemy fort. Reduce its defences to rubble. Attack. Kill those who fought, enslave those who surrendered. Plunder everything that could be eaten or sold later. March on. After some half dozen enemy strongholds had fallen, Raetinum had become the main topic of round-the-fire gossip, and what officers spoke about when they were alone.

It lay to the south, on the edge of the territory of the Liburni, a tribe whose fast ships had long since been adopted by the Roman navy. Its garrison swelled by those who had escaped the army's clutches, Raetinum was nonetheless the last fortress of any size in the area. Take it, the talk went, and the end of the rebellion might be in sight. That achieved, Tullus would say to Fenestela, they could return at last to Vetera.

The walls of Raetinum came into sight late one sunny afternoon, causing much anticipation. Perched atop a spiny ridge, it was surrounded by vertiginous slopes fit only for mountain goats. The approach was via a winding track that led to a semi-circular curtain wall that backed onto a narrow but dizzying chasm. Its gate was protected by a pair of strong towers. Behind these defences was a wooden bridge, and beyond that lay the fortress proper, which was surrounded by its own high timber rampart. The difficulties of quarrying and transport meant that only the outer defences had been built with stone.

Germanicus did not waste any of his men in a pointless attack, and so Tullus and his men, who were among the earliest to reach the first line of enemy defences, took their ease as they waited for the siege engines. Warriors watched them from the towers and the curtain wall, hurling abuse and the occasional spear, which skittered harmlessly off the rocks in front of their position. Few of Tullus' soldiers bothered to reply. Two exceptions were Smiler and Cassius, who between them had learned a little Illyrian. Catching the attention of a warrior with a fine bronze helmet, they traded insult after insult. The contest culminated with the Illyrian baring his genitals at Smiler and Cassius, who, to the amusement of their comrades, promptly did the same.

'Feel better?' asked Tullus when the pair rejoined them.

'Aye, sir.' Smiler's grin was broader than ever, and Cassius couldn't have looked more pleased.

It took until nightfall for the siege engines to reach them. Assembled by firelight, they were ready and in place by dawn. Legionaries who would not be part of the assault hauled rocks up for ammunition, while Tullus and his men watched. Without artillery of their own, and intimidated by the hundreds and hundreds of waiting legionaries, the defenders had fallen silent.

Hadrianus cupped a hand to his mouth. 'Not so cocky now, are you?'

There was no reply.

'We'll soon make 'em sing, eh?' said Hadrianus to Spike.

Spike's answer was a grim nod.

Tullus, who was observing from the corner of his eye, was quietly satisfied. Like Cassius, the two former gladiators had become fine soldiers, disciplined, obedient and fierce in combat. Magnus, who had grown into his new role perfectly, was muttering encouragement to the men on either side of him, and to those in the ranks in front and behind. Tullus cast an eye over the rest of his soldiers, who were ready to attack the moment the enemy defences were breached, and was pleased by what he saw.

'When is the artillery going to start shooting?' Cassius asked.

'Any moment,' replied Urceus. 'There's no reason to wait any longer.'

'The sooner we get in there, the better,' said Magnus. 'Isn't that right, boys?'

There was a rumble of assent, and Tullus had to hide a smile, so similar was Magnus' delivery to his own. Imitation was the finest form of flattery, he thought, remembering the saying. Cassius' question was a good one – the artillery officers had no reason to delay their barrage.

'Look who's here,' muttered Fenestela.

Spying Nepos, Tullus understood. The tribune wanted to be the one who gave the order. How much he had had to brown his nose for this privilege was unclear.

'A pity we can't get the prick to lead us,' Tullus said quietly. 'Show us all what a coward he is.'

'Shall I ask him?' Fenestela's eyes were glittering.

Tullus chuckled.

So did someone in the ranks of men behind. Tullus spun, but every man's face was blank.

Nepos had a word with the officer in charge of the two large catapults, who shouted to his men. Well-drilled, standing by the weapons, they went to work. A pair of men wound the arm of each back, using lengths of wood inserted into the ratchet mechanism. The instant the arm had come to rest, two men heaved a large stone into the leather pouch that dangled from its end, and stepped out of the way. A junior officer pulled the release rope, and the arm shot upright, flinging the stone into the air.

Tullus' gaze followed both missiles high into the blue sky, and back down again. They smacked into the wall left of the gate, just below the rampart and about twenty paces apart. Chips of stone flew, and several defenders were knocked from their feet by the impact. The bolder among them shouted their contempt. Nepos scowled, but the artillery crews paid no heed. Slight adjustments were made to the angle of the throw, and two more stones were hurled skyward.

These hit the wall much closer together, and a small chunk of masonry tumbled to the ground. Tullus' men shouted with excitement. Nepos all but preened himself.

They're not cheering you, cocksucker, thought Tullus.

As the barrage continued, the enemy defenders retreated to the towers. The artillery crews loaded and shot, loaded and shot, concentrating their aim on the same spot. A dozen efforts and they had smashed a man-sized cavity in the wall. Thirty shots, and a section of walkway the length of a wagon had collapsed.

Nepos came stalking over to Tullus. His armour gleamed; the feathers on his helmet stood straight and tall. Not a speck of mud dirtied his freshly polished boots. Even the bandage on his arm was spotless.

Tullus called his men to attention, and saluted.

'Ready for the assault, centurion?' asked Nepos, his tone somehow suggesting that Tullus was not.

'Just waiting for the order to advance, sir,' said Tullus, staring over the tribune's shoulder.

'You will be with them?'

'Of course, sir.'

'I shall expect you to succeed at the first attempt then.' An unpleasant smile.

'We'll do our best, sir.'

'Fail, and you shall have me to answer to.'

'Sir.' Stung by the insult, Tullus could say no more.

'Why don't you lead us, Tribune, sir?' called a voice from behind him.

A chorus of ayes rose. 'You lead us, sir!' cried another voice. 'With feathers like that, you'll be sure to drive the enemy back!' Snorts of suppressed laughter followed.

Nepos' face had turned puce. 'Who said that? Stand forward, those men!'

It was Cassius and Magnus who had spoken – Tullus was almost sure. He would go to Hades before naming them to Nepos, however. 'Who was it?' he shouted, but with none of his parade-ground heat.

No answer.

Nepos jumped up and down like a small boy having a tantrum. 'This insubordination is unacceptable!'

'Yes, sir,' said Tullus, thinking: it's jokes like that which help men to charge into battle.

Then Nepos was in his face. Spittle flew, hitting Tullus' cheeks. 'Think you can get away with this? Find those men or I will see you stripped to the ranks, you and your ugly brute of an optio!'

'The wall, sir.' Tullus pointed. The catapults' intense barrage had now broken a 'V' shaped hole that reached almost to the ground. Any moment, and the breach would be scalable.

'I don't care about the cursed wall!' screamed Nepos. 'I want the men who insulted me, and I want them now!'

Tullus' eyes met his, and then, drawn by movement behind Nepos, focused on a pair of archers who had emerged from the nearest tower. Running to the edge of the breach, they drew out arrows from their quivers and nocked. Tullus' breath caught in his chest. They weren't looking at him, but at Nepos. His fine armour and stunning crested helmet were too attractive a target to ignore.

'I don't know who they are, sir,' said Tullus, playing for time.

'Well –' Nepos' forefinger jabbed him in the chest – 'get in among them –' another jab – 'and find out!'

The archers stared down their arrows.

Tullus' skin crawled. If they missed, he would be hit. It was worth the risk, he decided. 'What about the attack, sir?' he asked in a confused-sounding voice.

'Do what I say, you foo—' Nepos' mouth worked, but no sound came out.

Tullus stared at the barbed head protruding from Nepos' neck. It had come through shallowly, and was not a mortal wound, unfortunately. A finger's breadth to the right, however, and it would have skewered Tullus, or perhaps a man behind him.

Ssshhhewww. A second arrow shot in, missing Nepos and Tullus, and *thunk*ing into a man's shield behind them.

Nepos' left hand came up. He touched the arrow, and his fingers came away bloody. He staggered, and gestured weakly at Tullus to help him.

'I'll see to the tribune,' Tullus roared. 'Magnus, you lead the attack. ATTACK!'

His men swarmed forward, running towards the breach in a flowing tide of unbridled fury. Between them they carried bundles of brush and scaling ladders.

Tullus discarded his shield, and slipped his right arm under Nepos' left, and around the tribune's shoulders. 'Let's get you back, sir, out of range of the archers.'

Nepos could no longer respond. Blood ran, *drip, drip, drip* from the end of the arrow, and from around the shaft, down his neck. His legs were buckling; Tullus had to half carry him.

A quick glance at their own lines told Tullus no one was watching. He reached up with his left hand, and wrenched on the arrow. Nepos mewled with pain; his hand flapped at Tullus' face.

'It's all right, sir,' said Tullus. 'The surgeon will soon have you right.' Gripping the arrowhead, he shoved it backwards, into Nepos' flesh.

Another cry of agony. The tribune's fingers clawed weakly at his cheek.

'You can't walk, sir?' Tullus released his grip and let Nepos fall. 'Better have a rest, eh?'

Nepos was coughing, choking. The impact with the ground had driven the arrow forward again. Now almost its entire length protruded from the front of his neck. Blood was gouting around the shaft. Nepos' eyes were full of terror and rage. He tried to speak, but all that came out was an unintelligible moan.

Tullus knelt down. 'Hurts, doesn't it, sir?' he hissed. Another look over his shoulder. No one was paying any attention. Swiftly, Tullus rolled Nepos onto his side. Grabbing the feathers on the end of the arrow, he pulled it backwards. A thin scream filled his ears, and Nepos thrashed about. 'There now, sir,' said Tullus, and ripped the barbed head back, deep into Nepos' flesh. It lodged, as he had hoped, and he twisted the shaft first one way, then the other. Again and again he worked it around, until at last a spray of bright red blood came. Satisfied, Tullus leaned back on his knees, and watched the crimson mist the ground before him.

'That, you cunt, was for Vindocomus,' he said.

Nepos' eyes widened. He had heard. Understood.

Tullus waited until the tribune was dead. Then, standing, he retrieved his shield and joined the attack. Despite the chaos, the screams and shouts, he felt an overwhelming sense of calm. The injustice of Vindocomus' fate, and his mercy killing by Tullus, had been set right. Nepos would never terrorise anyone again.

The breach was swarming with legionaries. Not an Illyrian could be seen on the rampart. Tullus waited his turn, and clambered up the broken masonry, using his sword hand for balance. At the top, he paused. What he saw made him want to cheer. Instead of doing the sensible thing and destroying the bridge, the Illyrians had opted to leave it in place – doubtless to let their men retreat if needs be. What they had not counted on was the speed with which the Roman catapults would breach their wall, and the unstoppable force of the legionaries' attack.

Knots of warriors were still fighting – around the base of the towers, at the bridge, but there was no unity, no cohesion to their formation. Even as groups of legionaries surrounded them, more were pounding over the bridge towards the main fortifications – the prize that had to be taken. A number of ladders had already been thrown up; men were clambering up them.

It was impossible to make out individuals at this distance; Tullus had no chance of spotting Fenestela and the rest. He made his way down onto the flat ground, and on his way to the bridge, studied every face. There was no sign of his century, and he pressed on, clambering over the injured, the dead and dying.

Smoke tickled his nostrils, and he looked up. On the other side of the bridge, black tendrils were rising from all along the rampart. It made no sense for fires to be burning inside the walls, but he had no time to ponder its relevance. Attacked by a pair of warriors who had been attracted by his transverse-crested helmet, he fought a brutal two-on-one battle. Unluckily for the Illyrians, farmers from the look of their shoddily made shields and rusted spears, they were facing not just a veteran, but a man who had come out the other side of dozens of such clashes. Tullus left one gasping his last breaths, and the other face down in the dirt.

The brief encounter had delayed him, and he cursed. A foothold had been gained on top of the defences; more and more legionaries were ascending the ladders. By the time he reached the bottom of one, his men would have vanished into the maze of streets that would lie on the other side. It was dangerous, even foolhardy, to venture alone into the madness of a fortress that was being stormed. Tullus discarded the notion of staying where he was. He was not prepared to keep his hide safe while his men were risking their own. If needs be, he would join ranks with whatever Romans happened to be nearby.

Again, he noticed the smoke. It was billowing now, great plumes rising from just behind the ramparts. Licks of flame were visible too.

'Hades,' Tullus said, realising. 'They're firing the town.'

His gaze shot left and right, behind him. No one was paying any notice to the heat and smoke. Consumed by battle lust, the desire to pursue the fleeing enemy, to search for women and booty, wave after wave of legionaries charged headlong over the bridge. Standing in their path would not work – he needed to make their officers aware – and when that was done, he *had* to find his men.

Tullus made a beeline for every optio, signifer and centurion in sight. He didn't know all by name, but he recognised them, and they knew him. Pointing at the smoke, he explained that he thought it was a trap. Once they had crossed the bridge, the legionaries should wait at the bottoms of the ladders until the situation was better assessed. Persuaded by Tullus' determined tone, the officers agreed to his suggestion.

He then ran to the base of the wall, and spoke to the officers there. By the time he had managed to bring the attack to a virtual halt, the crackle of burning wood was audible from the other side of the fortification. With a bad feeling in his belly, Tullus went up the nearest ladder as fast as he could. One-handed climbing – thanks to his shield – was not easy, but Tullus gave no thought to the danger.

Finally at the top – which was empty of legionaries and defenders – he was horrified to find that it was not only buildings that were burning, but the timber rampart itself. He could see flames beyond the main gate too. The Illyrians had panicked, and set fire to their own town, he decided, in an effort to thwart the Roman attack. His hunch had been correct, and the danger to his men was even greater than he had thought. Tullus relayed what was happening to officers at the foot of the ladders. The assault was not to continue until he or someone carrying word from him had declared it safe.

A gust of wind carried a wave of heat to Tullus that made his eyes water. Soon the flames would reach where he was standing, and if the entire rampart began to burn, there would be no way out of the town. Quickly, he scrambled down the nearest set of stairs. Chaos greeted him: crimson-spattered corpses, a mule with its guts hanging out, a cart lying on its side, wheels turning idly. A legionary sat gazing stupidly at the blood pumping from the stump of his wrist. Those with more grievous wounds wailed and screamed, or thrashed about. None of the nearest casualties were Tullus' men, which relieved him. He cast about, wondering which of the streets facing him to take.

The sound of fighting came from the largest. Sword drawn, Tullus put his head down and began to run. Narrow, bounded on left and right by low-roofed, single-storey houses, some with pens for livestock, it was paved with beaten earth. Alleyways loomed on both sides, potential places for ambush. Although it was dangerous, he paid them little heed. The fire had spread – it almost felt as if it was pursuing him. Finding his men had become imperative.

He came to a larger left turn, and hesitated. About fifty paces away, a large group of legionaries faced a similar number of warriors across a just-thrown-up wooden barricade. Tullus went close enough to determine that they were not his men, and then turned and sped back to the main thoroughfare. He reached it at the same time as a trio of warriors emerged from a lane opposite.

They stared at each other.

Roaring at the top of his voice, Tullus charged.

The warriors took to their heels, and he spat after them.

He continued his journey, here and there passing bodies, discarded spears and shields, ground stained with blood. In normal circumstances, Tullus would have been pleased – the scarcity of Roman dead meant that all the momentum was with his side – but the loud crackle of flames behind him, and the all-enveloping smoke visible each time he looked over his shoulder, were now of major concern.

Soon after, he found his men and several hundred others gathered in front of a small, timber-palisaded citadel. The stronghold sat on a great manmade mound, and was surrounded by a thorn-branch-filled ditch. Scores upon scores of warriors jeered from the battlements. An occasional spear came arcing down, landing close to the legionaries, who were milling about, unsure what to do next.

Spying Fenestela, Tullus felt a wave of relief. He at least had not been hurt or slain. He marched over. 'Fenestela!'

The optio's head turned. He grimaced – his smile – and saluted. 'You made it, sir!'

'I did.'

Some of the men saw Tullus. Cheers erupted. 'What took you so long, sir?' Cassius shouted. 'We thought you had abandoned us, sir,' added Hadrianus, grinning.

Tullus waved acknowledgement, and bent his head to confer with Fenestela.

'Nepos?' asked Fenestela in an undertone.

'Gone.' He didn't explain further.

'Good enough for him.'

'Even so. Casualties?' Tullus' eyes were wandering, trying to see if any faces were missing.

'Two dead, three walking wounded.' Fenestela listed the names, which did not include any of the veterans or former gladiators.

'Light losses – you did well.'

'Magnus kept his head, and made them keep formation. He's solid.' Fenestela had been at the back, his normal position – to make sure that no one dragged their heels during the attack.

Tullus caught Magnus' eye and gave him an approving nod. The big man saluted. 'And the enemy?' asked Tullus.

Fenestela indicated the citadel. 'They're all in there, sir, bar a few stragglers. Once we bring up the ladders, and a few catapults, it will be over in a couple of hours.'

'That's the least of our worries.' Tullus pointed in the direction he had come, and explained what the enemy had done. 'The whole cursed place is aflame, or soon will be. We need to retreat.'

Fenestela swore. 'This I had not expected.'

'Nor I. Organise the men. I'll tell the other officers.'

It didn't take long for Tullus to explain the situation. He needed no powers of persuasion. A thick blanket of smoke now filled the air over the town, and it was moving in their direction. The roar of flames was loud. The Illyrians had heard it too; they were cheering, and hurling volleys of spears.

Tullus had the men form up six wide, broad enough to punch through the enemy, but still able to manoeuvre should the need arise. He picked Magnus to stand on the far left, with Smiler, Spike, Hadrianus and Cassius. He himself took the right-hand-most place, with Urceus behind him. 'We move fast, boys,' he said. 'The moment the filth see us withdraw, they'll be after us like a pack of hounds. Ready?'

A full-throated roar.

Tullus gave the order to draw swords. They broke into a half walk, half run. Hobnails crunched the dirt; shields knocked together. Orders rang out behind; the other centurions were following his lead. A baying cry issued from the citadel, its words unintelligible, but its meaning crystal clear.

'They're coming after us, boys,' said Tullus. 'Eyes left and right.'

The first attack came halfway down the main street, a gang of ten warriors who came screaming out of an alley. A well-thrown spear caught a legionary in the third rank, and he fell, screaming. Tullus called the halt, and had the closest soldiers face the enemy. They beat back the warriors, killing half, and sending the rest packing. More were visible in the alleyway, however, and loud whoops and cries told him that his fear of the citadel emptying had come true.

He led his men on.

Recognising the street where he had seen the fight at the barricade, his heart lifted. They were drawing close to the outer wall, and beyond it, with luck, safety.

Round a slight bend, and Tullus' heart missed a beat. Again he called the halt.

A hundred paces further on, their path was blocked by a wall of orange-yellow flame. Even at this distance, the heat was greater than that of a bath-house furnace. Sweat began to bead on his face. He stared, puzzled how the street – bare of wood or buildings – was burning. Then, making out the shapes of wagons and carts, he cursed. While he had been trying to find his men, the enemy had been busy.

'What do we do, sir?' asked Smiler. Incredibly, he was still smiling.

Tullus could feel the weight of everyone's gaze.

Shouts from one side, and then the other. Warriors were massing, preparing for an attack.

He stared at the conflagration in front of them. The burning carts left no way through – not unless a man wanted to be cooked alive in his armour.

Another century arrived, and Tullus went to talk to its centurion, who was none other than Vetus.

'Out of the frying pan, eh?' Vetus' light tone could not quite conceal his alarm.

'The side streets are jammed with the enemy. There's only one way through.' Tullus gazed at the wall of flame, and imagined his men burning to death.

The first spears came humming in. Scores of warriors were massing at the entrances to the side streets, but they had not yet mustered the courage for a charge. Tullus judged that Fenestela and Magnus had the men in hand, so he pulled Vetus into the doorway of a house. 'We need a plan.'

'If there was another wagon, anything on wheels, we could use it to smash through.' Vetus cast about, but the street was empty.

An idea hit Tullus. 'There's a well in that yard opposite. Men who had drenched themselves and their shields with water might be able to push a way through.'

'It's not much of a plan.'

'Have you got a better one?' snarled Tullus.

Vetus shook his head. 'Me and my lot will do it.'

'No,' said Tullus. 'It's suicide.'

'My choice.'

They locked eyes. Neither would look away.

Flames crackled. Fenestela shouted an order. Spears landed. Men screamed.

Vetus cursed, and pulled a silver denarius from his purse. 'Augustus, or a bull?'

'That's easy,' said Tullus. He was loyal, but no arselicker. He would never choose the emperor's likeness in a wager. 'The bull.'

Metal flashed as Vetus spun the coin high. Catching it, he smacked it onto the back of his hand and lifted his fingers away. A broad-chested bull with horns stared back at them, the word AUGUSTUS stamped above it. 'You win.'

'I get to choose,' said Tullus, walking away. 'Fenestela!'

A hand gripped his shoulder. Vetus twisted him around. 'No, my old friend. You won. I lost.'

Tullus wondered if he could smash Vetus in the side of the head with his sword hilt, and order his optio to take command. He raised his right arm a little.

'Tullus!'

He came back to the moment. Vetus was staring, no, glaring, at him.

'This is *my* fate, brother. Do not take it from me. Gods willing, I will see you on the other side.'

Tullus' nod was jerky. 'On the other side.'

While Vetus quickly led his men to the well, Tullus split his century into two halves and held off the enemy on each side of the street. He sent Hadrianus and Cassius to pass the word to units behind theirs. The centurions were to be ready to charge with their men through the gap the instant Vetus' century had done its work. Tullus made no mention of the attack failing, because it was plain to a blind man that if it did, most, if not all of them, would die.

The Illyrians' attacks grew more determined. Swarming out of the side alleys, clambering through the livestock pens, they threw themselves at Tullus' men like wild beasts that have not eaten in a month. Volleys of spears flew out of the smoke. Youths with slings perched on roof tops and shot at the Romans with impunity. Men fell, or were wounded, and could no longer fight. Hundreds and hundreds of warriors faced Tullus' legionaries on both sides. Step by hard-fought step, they were pushed back into the centre of the street.

'Vetus! Vetus! Jupiter, where is he?' Tullus craned his neck. If his former comrade didn't make his move soon, there would no need.

'Here he comes, sir,' cried Smiler.

The feathers on Vetus' helmet straggled down to either side. Water streamed down his nose, and his mail had a dark silver sheen. The painted motif on his shield was running a little at the edges – he had immersed it in the well, Tullus judged. Behind him the forty-odd men he had chosen were as wet, their shields in particular saturated, for these would be their best protection against the flames and raging heat.

Vetus caught Tullus' eye. They gave each other a nod. 'On the other side!' yelled Vetus, and then, 'Testudo!'

The instant his legionaries had obeyed, he gave the order to advance. Shields facing left and right, front and back, with a 'roof' made of more, the testudo left only the legionaries' lower legs exposed. A small gap between the top of each shield in the first rank and those in the 'roof' allowed these men to see, and to guide their comrades. It was also, Tullus thought, another place that fire could lick in to scorch flesh.

Designed as a static formation to withstand arrows, or to advance slowly to the base of town walls so that engineers could undermine the defences, the testudo was not meant to be used by running men. Yet without momentum, there would be no chance of pushing aside the barrier formed by the wagons and carts. Vetus shouted an order, and his men picked up their pace. A fast walk, and they were fifty paces from the pulsating, yellow-orange wall of flame. Half walk, half run, and they had closed to twenty-five. Then it was a dozen.

Sparks showered down on the upturned shields. Lengths of red-hot timber shifted beneath the men's sandals; one twisted and flicked upright. A man screamed. Suddenly, the feathers on Vetus' helmet were burning. He roared another command.

Without slowing down, the testudo entered the firestorm.

Flames caressed the shields, the faces of those in the first rank. They licked at men's legs. Agonised wails ripped at Tullus' ears; he wanted to look away, but he could not. He willed Vetus and his heroic men onward, before they were reduced to scorched lumps of flesh. Already, however, their speed had slowed to a virtual standstill. Steam rose as the water on the soaked shields boiled. Part of the 'roof' collapsed as men inside stumbled or collapsed.

A dull crack. Somehow the testudo had reached the wagon occupying the central portion of the burning barricade.

A three-year-old child could have pushed harder, thought Tullus, despairing. Unable to block out the screams of Vetus and his men as they were reduced to living torches, he turned away.

'Sir!' Spike's voice, hoarse with tension.

Tullus looked. Blinked in disbelief. Laughed madly.

'There's a gap, sir!' cried Hadrianus.

The wagon Vetus had hit must have been charred through and through, Tullus decided. There could be no other explanation for the way it was crumbling into a pile of blackened timber and ashes. Already he could see through the barrier to the other side.

'We have a chance, boys,' he shouted. 'A chance!'

He had forgotten about the second half of Vetus' century. Commanded by his heroic optio, and shaped into a second testudo, it now advanced into the conflagration.

The men in it also burned.

Screamed.

Died.

But they shoved the remnants of the wagon further to one side, widening the way through the flames.

Soaking their own shields in water would offer them a better opportunity to get through unscathed, thought Tullus, but the enemy's attack had redoubled. War cries ululated, spear shafts clattered off shields, feet stamped the earth. Even as he hesitated, an arrow took Urceus in the throat. Blood bubbling from the wound, he dropped his shield, and then, oddly, folded to his knees as a man might before a statue of a god.

Grief tore at Tullus. He reached out a hand, but Urceus was already on the ground, his eyes staring at nothing.

'Form up, four wide, twenty deep! Testudo!' Tullus bellowed. The width of the gap meant it was a narrower formation than usual. Consequently, it was a great deal longer too, which worried him. No one could be left behind, however.

Again, he put himself at the very right, in the front. Smiler was on the far left, with Spike and Hadrianus between them. Magnus and Cassius were in the second rank, on the sides. Fenestela would be at the rear, urging any laggards on. A grim smile played across Tullus' lips. The chances of anyone dragging their heels were slim indeed.

'If a man falls, leave him,' he said. 'Forward, at the double!'

Tramp, tramp, tramp. The ground was covered in burning ash and pieces of wood. Heat like Tullus had never felt cut at his face and lower legs. The leather of his boots was burning up. He ducked down behind his shield for two paces, just for a respite. Then up again, his gaze shooting left and right. They were ten paces from the flames. 'Keep moving!'

A familiar sound, that of spears rushing in, almost silent, from their rear. Tullus' skin crawled. He heard the impacts as they landed, hitting shields, helmets, flesh. A heartbeat's delay. Screams. Curses. Thuds as men fell.

Tullus' eyelashes frizzled. Under his helmet, his arming cap was uncomfortably warm. His left fist was hurting – glancing down, he saw with dismay that the metal boss of his shield was starting to glow. A lump of burning wood struck the top of his right boot. Instant pain lanced from his foot; he kicked out savagely, sending the orange-red chunk flying. 'Forward!'

The heat was unbearable now, a solid wall that threatened to suck the very air from his chest. The flames were on both sides, dancing high as a building. Underfoot, there were charred bodies – Vetus and his men. Eyelids reduced to slits, forehead feeling as if boiling water was being poured on it, feet burning inside his boots, Tullus drove on.

One step more, he told himself. Two. Three.

A man to his left staggered. Fell. Someone shouted.

To turn his head was to falter. To die. Tullus forced his left leg forward, then his right.

The heat lessened. His boots crunched again on dirt. He dared to hope, for the fire on either side was lower than it had been. There were no warriors in sight. Ten paces Tullus led them, and then another ten. He tried to speak, but all that came out was a harsh croak. Tullus risked a glance to his left. Shock lanced through him. Spike was not there. He kept walking – the rest of the century needed to get clear.

Hadrianus was muttering and crying at the same time, 'I've got to go back.'

'He's gone,' said Smiler, his voice gentle.

'NO!' Hadrianus burst free of the rest, and raced around to the right. He came within touching distance of Tullus.

'Stop!' Tullus said, as loud as his parched throat would allow.

Hadrianus checked. His eyes met those of Tullus. 'He saved my life in the ludus once, sir.'

'I am ordering you to stay *here*.'

'Sorry, sir.' Hadrianus ducked his head and ran back, towards the flames.

Tullus' curse would have whitened a man's beard. He spun to his right and faced down the street. The last of his men were emerging from the gap made by Vetus. 'HADRIANUS!'

There was no answer. Hadrianus vanished into the blaze.

He did not return.

Grief beat at Tullus. He felt tired. Old. Burnt to a crisp. From somewhere, though, he found a little more strength. They were not out of danger. 'Fenestela!' he cried.

'Here, sir!'

Thank you, Fortuna, thought Tullus fervently. That loss I could not have taken.

'Sir!' Magnus' voice. 'On the left!'

Tullus' head turned. Out of an alley spilled five, ten, a score of warriors. Clearly waiting for any Romans who made it through the burning barricade, they charged straight at them. 'Wheel left,' Tullus cried. 'Shield wall!'

His burned, exhausted soldiers obeyed, but their line was incomplete. Men had fallen in the flames. Others were dazed, panic-stricken. Tullus found himself in the second rank with Cassius to his left. Magnus was almost directly in front of them; so too was Smiler.

The Illyrians hit. Spears came thrusting over the tops of shields.

Blood sprayed. Warriors shoved their way into Tullus' century, screaming at the tops of their voices. Men fell.

'Hold them,' Magnus roared. 'HOLD THEM!' He plunged his
sword into a warrior's chest, and with a great shove, heaved him into
the man behind. He stumbled, and Smiler's right arm went out, lightning fast. Down went that warrior, frothing and choking.

The legionary in front of Cassius collapsed, and he swarmed forward
into the space. 'ROMA!' he shouted. 'ROMA!'

Tullus' chance came a heartbeat later. He smashed a warrior's nose
with his shield boss, and as the man reeled back, blood pumping, he
stabbed him in the throat. He roared his fury at the next enemy, who
flinched. Tullus gutted him. The nearest warriors took a step back.

'The centurion is here,' Magnus shouted. 'Tullus is here!'

His men cheered, and like that, their morale rose. They slew every
Illyrian within reach, and closed the gaps. The enemy retreated, and
Tullus' soldiers advanced in a solid line. 'That's it, boys,' he said. 'Nice
and steady.'

When the warriors broke and ran, he did not let his men give chase.
More important was to keep the area secure, so that the legionaries
still trapped behind the barricade could pass through unhindered.
'Magnus.'

'Sir?'

'That was well done.'

Magnus flushed. 'Just doing my job, sir.'

'Aye. Keep doing it.'

'Sir.'

'You too, Cassius,' said Tullus.

Cassius bobbed his head. 'Thank you, sir.'

Movement in the alley caught Tullus' eye. He looked. A lone warrior had come back. Cocking back his right arm, he hurled his spear.
Tullus' eyes followed its possible path.

'Cassius!' Tullus lunged, but too late.

The spear entered Cassius' left eyesocket. He dropped like a stone
down a well.

An animal scream left Tullus' lips. It took all of his strength not to
charge after the fleeing warrior. He cared nothing for himself, but his
men still needed him. With gritted teeth, he split his century into two
equal groups. He and Magnus guarded the left side of the street, and

Fenestela, with Smiler and the rest, kept watch over the right.

Legionaries were streaming through the gap in the barricade, but not in the numbers he had hoped for. Tullus beckoned to the first officer he saw. What he heard was troubling. The enemy's attack continued, causing heavy casualties among those left on the other side. More buildings had been set aflame, threatening to encircle them.

Against his better judgement, Tullus was starting to consider leading his men back to help their stricken comrades. Then, as if the gods had intervened, another burning wagon collapsed in a stream of spark and flame. The ground was far too hot to walk on, but he had had an idea. Grotesque though it was, he gave the order to find every corpse that could be found. Illyrian first, then Roman, it did not matter. Lifting, dragging, he and his soldiers heaved the bodies down one after another, laying a wall of armour and flesh on top of the wagon's remains.

Their efforts were an unqualified success, widening the gap enough for a tide of their comrades to come through.

It was a price worth paying, Tullus decided. A complete massacre had been avoided.

This awareness did not stop his heart from aching.

Despite Tullus' achievement, Roman casualties were heavy. Twenty-three men of his century had died, while other units, such as that of Vetus, had been entirely wiped out. The number of dead came to more than five hundred, with a similar total suffering severe burns. The losses did not stop Raetinum falling the next day. Once the fires had burned themselves out, there was nothing to stop the Romans from returning to the citadel, the defences of which had also been consumed by the flames. The Illyrian garrison, which had hidden in subterranean chambers beneath their stronghold, put up little resistance. Grief-stricken, the legionaries slaughtered scores of them before the officers intervened. Mourning still for Urceus, Spike, Hadrianus, Cassius and all his other dead, Tullus would have let the killing continue. As Fenestela said, however, dead Illyrians were worth less than live, enslaved ones.

The taking of Raetinum broke the local tribesmen's spirit. Germanicus' army swept all before it, as did that of the general Silvanus in the south-east. A full month before the harvest, the Pannonians surrendered. Although the Daesidiates, a southern tribe, continued the struggle, the rebellion was nearing its end.

Despite the clamour of singing, shouted conversation and ribald laughter, the cicadas' buzzing chorus could still be heard. It was a clear, warm night, illuminated by thousands of twinkling stars. The fine weather had allowed Octavia to stop using her tent, and thereby serve far more customers. Hundreds of off-duty legionaries had congregated by her wooden counter, behind which were stacked countless amphorae. Tullus was there with Fenestela. They had been drinking since midday, and were decidedly the worse for wear. Octavia had been topping up their jug every time it neared the halfway point, and would accept no payment. 'Repaying my debt,' she said any time Tullus tried.

'There'sh Magnush,' said Fenestela. 'Magnush!'

'And Smiler,' said Tullus. 'Come here, both of you.'

The pair elbowed past a couple of legionaries. They saluted, grinning. 'Sir. Sir.'

'Want a drink?' asked Tullus, waving at the jug on the counter. 'Help yourself.'

'Thank you, sir.' Smiler poured for Magnus, then himself. They raised their cups to Tullus and then Fenestela.

'To fallen comrades. Dis manibus,' said Tullus thickly. 'Vindocomus.'

'Vindocomus.'

'To Urceus,' said Smiler.

They drank.

'Spike and Hadrianus.'

They drank.

'Cassius,' said Magnus.

They drank.

'All good men.' Tullus nodded ponderously. 'Good soldiers. Dis manibus.'

'Dis manibus,' they all repeated.

Silence descended as they remembered their comrades.

Tullus caught Octavia's eye.

'Another jug?' she called.

'Aye. Gratitude.'

With everyone's cups refilled, Tullus made a toast to the war's end. 'It won't be long now, boys,' he said. 'Spring by the latest.'

'You'll be returning to Vetera then, sir,' said Magnus, looking a little downcast.

'Or before that, if the rumours are to be believed,' said Tullus. 'Germanicus and the other generals don't need ten legions to finish this affair.'

'The Eighteenth, isn't it, sir?' Smiler also looked sad.

'That's right.' Although these men and the rest of his century had grown dear to him, Tullus was glad. It was time to go home.

Smiler grinned. 'Maybe we'll be transferred to the Rhenus one day, sir.'

'Gods willing that comes to pass,' added Magnus. 'It would be an honour to serve under you again, sir.'

Touched, Tullus reached out to grip first Magnus' great paw, and then Smiler's hand. 'The honour would also be mine.'

'Let's drink to that!' roared Fenestela, his beard bristling.

AUTHOR'S NOTE

The battles in this tale are part of the 'War of the Batos' (two un-related chieftains of the same name), which took place between AD 6 and 9 in Illyricum, an area roughly equivalent to modern-day Slovenia, Croatia, Bosnia and Herzegovina, and parts of Serbia and Montenegro. Sparked by the Romans' harsh rule, the insurrection spread rapidly throughout the region, with the rebel armies numbering in the region of one hundred thousand warriors. Alarmed by the scale and ferocity of the uprising, and by his generals' failure to put it down immediately, Augustus resorted to conscription. It seemed a gift for Tullus to be one of the officers drafted in to train the new recruits. The campaign of AD 8 included the attacks on Splonum and Raetinum. The burning of the latter, the heavy casualties suffered by the Romans there, and the way they had to escape using the bodies of the slain, were recorded by Cassius Dio. For more details of this fascinating war, I refer you to the excellent text *Germanicus*, by my friend Lindsay Powell (Pen & Sword Books).

No less than seven of you lovely people feature in 'Eagles in the East'. It's been great fun talking with you by email, working out names and so on. I hope you like my portrayals – apologies to those of you who died! (You had to, in case I write more stories about Tullus in the future, and I need more characters for readers. Two of those who made it – Magnus and Smiler – also *had* to, because they feature in 'Eagles in the Wilderness'. Octavia lived too – maybe she will appear in another short story in the future.)

Randy Higgins, to whom this story is dedicated, stars as Magnus. Thank you, Randy, for your unwavering support and enthusiasm. It's been a pleasure. Big thanks for your support as well, Andrew Cartlidge (Smiler), Chris Lyle (Spike), Adrian Tyte (Hadrianus), Krystal Holmgren (Octavia), Tony Estabrook (Urceus) and Gary Bentley

(Cassius). It was great fun writing you all into the story. I actually didn't want to kill any of you, but it had to be. Sorry!

Huge thanks to the legion of fantastic people who made the Kickstarter campaign into such a success – THANK YOU! Thank you also to the amazing Pete Simpson, who did the artwork, as he did for 'Eagles in the Wilderness'. In no particular order then, thank you to: Neal Aplin, Karen Atter, Sergio Bannino, Steve Blake, Dominic Bronk, Robin Brown, Rob Buntin, Will Cee, Vincent Cenni, James Cleave, Phill Clegg, Frances Cripps, Mark Downing, Ollie Drake, Gill Eagles, Dan Fundal, Michal Fišer, Lothar Fischer, Garry Fitzgerald, Martin Gander, Ruben GH, Pawel Ginter, Steve Glüning, Nigel Graham, Daniel Grave, Dilys Guthrie, Stephen Harman, Nick Harpin, Debra Hayward, Phil Hendry, Taff James, Roger and June Jarrold, Daniel Kelly, Patrick Krippendorf, Alan Laws, Ellis Lewis, Mark Lewis, John Lodge, Daniel Loose, Jonathan Lowe, Mark Mahoney, Stephen and Ruaridh McIntyre, Wullie McMartin, Jay Mead, Cliff Moon, Derek Moss, Andy Noyce, Marie A. Parsons, Ben Pickersgill, Brent Quigley, Martin Rea, Jonathan Redman, Charlene Robertson, Phil Robinson, Edna Russell, Cris Samways, Mark Seccull, John Sibley, Sean 'Bear' Sickler, Anthony Smart, Maureen Smith, Vic Smith, Bryan Spencer, John Stock, Joseph Tartaglia, Maurits van der Vegt, Rick van Strien, Daniel Vaupel, Sara Waddington, Anthony Ward, Daniel Ward, Samantha Wilkinson, Anne Willis, Milca and Andy Wilson, Monique Zwaenepoel and Guest 295967145 (no response to my messages, sadly).

Every one of you is fabulous, and I appreciate your support. Sorry that I couldn't write all of you into the tale.

GLOSSARY

Aliso: a Roman fort that lay a short distance east of Vetera; possibly modern-day Haltern-am-See.

Amisia: the River Ems.

Flevo Lacus: the Zuiderzee, now the Ijsselmeer.

German Sea: the modern-day North Sea.

Mare Nostrum: the Mediterranean.

Rhenus: the River Rhine.

Saltus Teutobergiensis: the Teutoburg Forest (or defile), location of the Varian disaster in AD 9, when three legions were annihilated by German tribes. Want to know more? Read *Eagles at War*!

Venedi: a tribe recorded as having lived east of the German tribes, in what would be modern-day Poland.

Vetera: modern-day Xanten. I cannot recommend a visit to the Roman archaeological park here enough. Roman Germany makes for the most fantastic trip – see the author's note in any of my Eagles of Rome trilogy, or email me (ben@benkane.net) for the details.

Other stories of mine that you might not have read:

'The Patrol' – a short story that fits between *Hannibal: Enemy of Rome* and *Hannibal: Fields of Blood*.

A Day of Fire – my story is one of six, all set during the eruption of Vesuvius in AD 79.

THE ARENA

A prelude to *Hunting the Eagles*

OUTSIDE THE ROMAN FORTRESS OF VETERA, ON THE GERMAN FRONTIER, AUTUMN AD 12

Together with several of his comrades from the Fifth Legion, legionary Marcus Piso was rambling towards the settlement outside the massive camp in which he lived and served. It was early afternoon, and a watery sun could do little to dispel the chill in the air. Piso was drunk. Not pissed out of his head – that would come later – but in that fuzzy, pleasant state which made him feel goodwill towards all, and when the world seemed a better place. A tall man with spiky black hair, Piso had been in the army for four years – five come the following spring. Vitellius, his acerbic best friend, had been in far longer, and the rest had served for periods in between the two. Of the group, only Piso and Vitellius had been in the Eighteenth, one of the three legions wiped out by German tribesmen some years before.

It was payday for the legionaries, a happy event that occurred every four months, and a cause of much revelry and drunken behaviour. The great majority of the camp's garrison of two legions had been off duty since the morning's parade and disbursement of monies. A couple of hundred unfortunates from each legion, selected by lot, remained in the camp as sentries, orderlies and messengers, but the rest, like Piso and his comrades, had been enjoying themselves from the moment they'd exited the fort's massive gateway. Everyone's destination was the vicus, the sprawling village that lay a short distance along the road north.

Well aware of the day's importance, local shopkeepers and inn proprietors had been hard at work since dawn. Temporary stalls – forbidden under normal circumstances, but ignored three times a year – had sprung up right outside the fort's main gate, and lined the way towards the vicus. Wine of every kind was on offer, from burn-your-throat Gaulish and headache-inducing Iberian, to the finest Campanian and silk-smooth Falernian. Rosy-cheeked women were selling fried sausages and fresh bread. Bakers competed with one another over whose pastries and cakes were the best. One enterprising individual even had a roasted piglet on a platter, complete with an apple in its mouth. 'A copper for a thick slice,' he roared. 'And the crackling's free!'

The legionaries had been paid cohort by cohort. Being in the seventh, Piso and his comrades had emerged after more than half the legion. They had grumbled with the rest as they'd shifted from foot to foot, their gaze fixed on the paymasters' tables far in the distance. Their eagle-eyed centurion Tullus had been watching, however, so it had been under their breaths. Nothing to be done but wait, Vitellius had muttered. It was shit, Piso had replied, but at least the initial mad rush would be over once they'd had their coin.

He was right. By the time the group had walked outside, the deluge of thirsty soldiers had washed over the first stalls and moved on to the more plentiful delights of the vicus, leaving shorter queues and quicker service. Piso and the rest had parked themselves by a stall run by a wall-eyed reprobate known to one and all as Verrucosus, thanks to the large wart on one of his florid cheeks. A man wouldn't have known it from the clean tables and benches on display today, but Verrucosus ran one of the sleaziest dives in the vicus. His wine was drinkable, though, which was more than could be said for most of his competitors.

The huge demand from six cohorts had seen Verrucosus' stock almost drained – 'Head to my inn – there's plenty more where this came from!' he'd cried as Piso and his companions threw back their third and final cups of wine. Promising they *would* call in, the still-thirsty legionaries had instead made straight for the stall next door. Not until they'd had perhaps half a dozen more did they even consider moving on.

Progress had been slow since, thought Piso fuzzily. He had stopped to have some sausages and bread. One of their group had wandered beyond the tents to empty his bladder, and still hadn't returned. Vitellius was the latest to stray. Casting about, Piso spied him by a baker's stall. To Piso's amusement, Vitellius was buying two pastries *and* a slab of almond cake, which he devoured on the spot.

'How can you even want something sweet now, let alone that quantity of it?' Piso demanded.

Vitellius, his usual sour expression absent, shrugged. 'It's payday. I haven't eaten something sweet for a month and more.'

'When a man's drinking, it's savoury food he needs,' said Piso, shaking his head in distaste as the baker proffered some kind of sticky confectionery. 'Come on, or we'll never get there.'

'Where's "there"?' asked Vitellius, wiping his mouth on his sleeve. Like Piso, he was dressed in a tunic, metalled belt with attached dagger, and studded sandals. 'The Ox and Plough?'

Piso, who hadn't actually decided, gave bleary consideration to the idea. The Ox and Plough was one of the most popular establishments in the vicus. Run by Sirona, an attractive, middle-aged Gaulish woman, and her hulking sons, it was clean, and served good wine and food. Its main disadvantage was that Sirona was friendly with Tullus. Artio, the girl Tullus had rescued during the bloody ambush on their legion, also lived at the inn. 'Not today,' said Piso. 'We'd have to be on our best behaviour.'

There were rumbles of agreement from the others. 'Tullus might appear,' said one.

'True enough. We'd best avoid it,' said Vitellius. 'It's payday, for Jupiter's sake. We don't want to have to look over our shoulders the whole time.'

'Where then?' demanded Julius, a beefy man from Capua.

'How about a whorehouse?' suggested Vitellius, adding with a wink, 'Before Bacchus has done his worst?'

A couple of 'ayes' met this proposal, but most of the group disagreed.

'Speak for yourself, old man. I can get it up no matter how much I've drunk,' said Piso. He leered at Vitellius, who was more than a decade older than he. 'Benefits of youth and all that.'

'Wine reduces every man's ardour, you dog. Unless you're Priapus' son?' retorted Vitellius, giving him a sharp elbow in the ribs.

'Maybe I am! What's more important is that I'm still thirsty.' Truth be told, Piso was averse to most of the local whorehouses, which tended to be populated by raddled creatures carrying a variety of transmissible diseases. There was *one* premises he liked, the home of a beauty who went by the name of Diana, but its prices were eye-watering. Piso wasn't sure if the fistful of coins weighing down his purse would buy Diana's services for an hour. If they did, he'd be flat broke once the deed was done, and the next payday was a *long* way off. 'There'll be time for whores later,' he declared. 'It's wine we need!'

The others cheered. Scowling, Vitellius subsided.

'To the vicus then,' said Julius. He caught Piso eyeing the betmaker's stall, where several legionaries were rolling dice. 'You can waste your money later. No lagging!'

Piso, who was fond of every kind of gambling, obeyed. If they didn't get a move on, they would still be here at nightfall. Better to be in the vicus, where the variety of entertainment was greater. He had another reason too. The earlier he managed to get his comrades to the settlement, the more chance there'd be of persuading them later to go to the local arena, where gladiator contests were to be staged. A contact of Piso's – one of the heavies who worked for the itinerant gladiator trainer supplying some of those fighting today – had given him the nod about a new, unknown murmillo. If Piso could refrain from pissing away too much of his pay, he might be able to multiply it into much more substantial funds. With this happy idea uppermost in his mind, he strode after the rest.

A couple of hours later, Piso remained in good humour, but he was a great deal the worse for wear. He and his comrades had patronised several taverns, and consumed more wine than he could remember. There had been a meal of stewed beef at an open-fronted restaurant, and a visit to an armourer's. In the latter, Vitellius had ordered a new belt, and Julius a dagger, both slapping down their deposits with the ponderousness of the very drunk. As was inevitable during such drink-fuelled celebrations, their group had splintered. Men had been distracted by cock-fighting down alleyways or chance encounters with former comrades. Piso wondered if one of their number had sloped into a brothel beside the last inn they'd left, but he couldn't be sure. Whatever the reason, only he, Vitellius and Julius had made it to the arena, which lay south of the fortress.

The walk from the settlement, some mile and a half, had been welcome, the fresh air and break from drinking affording a chance to sober up a little. The quickest route to the arena, through the fort, had not been without risk. A minority of officers were disciplinarians, even on days such as this – yet the thought of having to walk around the camp, risking a drunken tumble into the ditch, had been worse. Adopting the soberest faces they could and taking an avenue parallel to the main one, Piso and his two comrades had made the journey without incident.

Heartened by the shouts and cheers floating through the air, they pressed on towards the brick-built amphitheatre, which was positioned at the bottom of the gentle south-facing hill below the great legionary fortress. There were fewer soldiers here than in the vicus, but the crowd milling around the shops and stalls still numbered in the hundreds, and Piso had no doubt there would be many more inside the theatre.

'Let's go inside and get seats,' said Vitellius, slurring his words. 'My legs are killing me.'

'Never happy, are you?' mocked Julius.

Vitellius scowled as Piso and Julius laughed. 'I don't complain that much,' he muttered.

'I want to sit down too,' Julius admitted. 'The wine's getting to me at last.'

'At last?' cried Vitellius. 'This from the man who proposed marriage to a serving girl with fewer teeth than a grandmother!'

'What can I say? I'm a lover of the female form,' retorted Julius with a filthy grin.

'You'd hop up on a she-ass if it let you. Asina!' cried Piso, using the derogatory term.

'I've got standards,' protested Julius, wagging a finger. 'Not many, but some – and they don't include that kind of relationship. Now, are we going inside?'

'What about placing bets?' demanded Piso.

Vitellius made a face. 'I always lose. Better to save my money for wine and whores.'

Julius was also shaking his head, no, and Piso sighed. 'Go on in. Use gates one, two or three. I'll find you.'

'Let me guess – you've got a tip for one of the fights,' said Vitellius.

'That's right,' Piso replied over his shoulder.

'You'll lose all your money – again,' warned Vitellius, but Piso wasn't listening. He racked his brains for the name of the murmillo. Was it Avilius? Aulus? Aquila? He was cursed if he could remember. His good mood evaporating, Piso stamped from betmaker to betmaker, reading their boards, which detailed the fighters paired off against each other in the day's contests. From what he could make out – this was confirmed by one of the betmakers – only two contests were left, both with murmillones. Neither had a gladiator whose name began with 'A'. Wary of arousing suspicion – if one of the sharp-eyed betmakers suspected

he had inside knowledge, they would *all* refuse to take his money –
Piso refrained from asking detailed questions about the fighters. With
building frustration, he heard the next bout being announced. Soon
the betmakers would stop taking wagers, and he would miss his chance
– if the gladiator he'd been told about was even in this cursed contest.
Piso swore under his breath. What to do?

Fortuna must have been in a good mood, because his attention
was then drawn to the loud conversation of three nearby legionaries.
'What's the point of putting money on a fighter no one's heard of?'
demanded one.

'You'd be better pissing it up against the wall,' added the second.

'I like the sound of his name,' protested the last soldier. 'And it's my
fucking money, last time I checked.'

'Spend it on wine instead – a denarius will buy you enough for the
rest of the night, and more,' advised the first man.

'Piss off,' grumbled the prospective gambler. 'My father had an old
friend called Longus. He was like an uncle to me.'

What was I thinking? Longus, thought Piso in delight. The murmillo's name is Longus!

The legionary eyed the closest betmaker, a lank-haired Gaul. 'Ho,
friend. What odds on Longus in the final contest?'

'He's to fight Donar, the local champion. Twenty-to-one against,'
said the Gaul.

'Donar – the German who fights as one of your kind?' asked the
legionary.

'He had to choose one of the classes. Better to be a Gaul than a
Thracian or a provocator. Besides, presenting himself as a German in
the arena here wouldn't go down too well after what Arminius did,'
declared the Gaul. 'How much are you wanting to wager?'

'A denarius.' Silver glinted in the legionary's hand.

'Bet accepted.' The coins vanished into the depths of the Gaul's
capacious purse.

Piso didn't stay to hear any more. Longus *was* the murmillo he'd
been told about. Acting casual, he managed to place two different-
sized bets on Longus, securing similar odds, and without causing any
of the betmakers to have misgivings. Praying now that his tip was accurate, he picked his way to the nearest entrance. As he jostled through
the crowd, he bumped into Degmar, the wiry Marsi tribesman who

364

served Tullus. Piso gave him a friendly nod. It was Degmar who had saved him, Tullus and a dozen or so others after the terrible ambush three years before. Degmar, who was with a couple of other tribesmen, muttered a greeting in reply, and then they were swept apart.

Vetera's timber and stone amphitheatre was no grandiose structure like those in Rome and other cities, but it had numbers inscribed over the various entrances. Piso opted for the more central second, the best option for finding his friends. Inside the narrow staircase that led up towards the banked seating, the clamour from the spectators was deafening. The timber planking above Piso's head shook with the impact of hundreds of hobnailed sandals, and the air rang with cheers, ribald comments and laughter. There wasn't a fight going on, he thought. Too many men were laughing. As he emerged into the open air again, his gaze fell first – as it was supposed to – on the circle of sand that formed the amphitheatre's centre. Half a dozen dwarfs in ornate, fantastical armour and carrying weapons were chasing a flock of clipped-wing cranes around the arena. Ridiculous and outlandish, Piso couldn't help but chuckle.

'You can do better than that!' roared a soldier several rows of seats away. 'Kill them!'

'What's crane taste like?' shouted another.

'Never mind crane, my friend here wants to eat dwarf!' retorted a wit to Piso's left.

Spotting his friends several rows back, Piso worked his way towards them.

'Happy?' asked Vitellius.

'Aye. I placed a couple of bets.'

'Please tell me you didn't throw away all of your pay,' said Vitellius, rolling his eyes at Julius.

'Not all, no.' Piso's fingers cupped his much lighter purse.

'You're not borrowing money from me for the next four months,' warned Vitellius.

'Or me,' Julius was quick to add.

'What kind of friends are you to doubt so fast?' cried Piso. 'If I win – when I win – you're the ones who'll be looking for loans, not me.'

Julius scoffed, but Vitellius raised a placatory hand. 'You do come out on top sometimes, it has to be said. I will hold my counsel until the fight's over. When is it on?'

'It's the last bout. I've bet on a murmillo who's to face the local champion.'

Vitellius groaned. 'I take it back. Your money is good as lost.'

Julius hailed a passing drink-seller. 'Over here! My friend needs to get even more drunk.' He cast a wicked look at Piso. 'Best to be out of it entirely by the time you lose.'

'Screw you, Julius,' retorted Piso, but without heat. 'Just get the wine in.'

Slurping the vinegar-like liquid, they watched the cranes being pursued and hacked to pieces one by one. Much hilarity ensued as several dwarfs smeared blood on their faces and, using cut-off wings, proceeded to flap around the arena's perimeter. Coins and pieces of bread rained down on the little performers; one soldier even lobbed a skin of wine down. Desultory applause rose from the audience. Bowing and scooping up their scant rewards, the dwarfs made another circuit before vanishing into one of the doors that gave onto the circle of sand.

The master of ceremonies, a paunch-bellied veteran and sot nick-named Rufus because of his blotchy purple nose, took to the sand without delay. Spectators' patience in general was poor, and legionaries were no different. Cries of 'Bring on the next act!' and 'Where are the gladiators?' were already filling the air.

'Brave soldiers of Rome!' cried Rufus as slaves began clearing up the bloody, feathery mess that comprised the cranes' remains. 'After the delights of the dwarfs—'

'Delights?' bawled a legionary in the front row, his position only a man's height above the sand. 'It was a fucking stupid display!' Scores of men yelled in agreement, and with expert precision, he hurled a ripe plum, which split as it struck Rufus in the midriff, staining his already grimy tunic. 'Show us some decent fighters, and quickly!' threatened the legionary.

Rufus retreated to the centre of the arena as a barrage of fruit, hunks of bread and clay cups were hurled in his direction. Impossible though it seemed, his face turned a darker shade of red. 'Abuse me, and there will be no more contests,' he shouted.

A baying sound of anger and disapproval drowned out what he said next. More objects were thrown, and menaces made. One legionary even jumped down onto the sand and began walking towards the now-worried-looking Rufus.

366

'Not again,' snarled Piso. 'Get out of there, you fool!' he shouted at the legionary, who had been joined by a comrade. They didn't hear, or ignored him, and he ground his teeth. Public disorder and fights were common on payday, and on occasion riots broke out. There hadn't been a full-blown one for two years, but it had also been at the amphitheatre, and caused by unhappy, drunken soldiers. Piso wasn't that interested in the day's contests, but if they were abandoned, his bets would be void. The likelihood of the betmakers trying to keep his money was low – he had a token from each marked with the value of his wagers – but they'd vanish the moment trouble erupted. A considerable delay was probable before he managed to retrieve his money.

Relief filled Piso as five legionaries appeared on the sand, led by a furious-faced optio. He launched a ferocious attack with his staff on the pair who had invaded the arena. *Thwack! Thwack!* The long piece of wood, decorated with a ball of bronze at one end, was a weapon every bit as fearsome as the vine sticks wielded by centurions. Howling with pain as the staff connected with their heads, shoulders and backs, the two interlopers fled. 'Out, curse you!' roared the optio, swiping still as they clambered up the wooden sides of the arena with the help of comrades above.

The audience's mood, which had turned threatening for a moment, changed in a heartbeat. No one could fail to find the spectacle of the legionaries having their backsides thrashed amusing. Piso laughed and jeered with the rest.

'Count yourselves lucky to have escaped so easy,' shouted the optio. 'The next troublemakers I catch, on the sand or anywhere else, will get a beating they'll not forget, as well as a *month* of forced marches. Keep your arses on the seats. Drink your wine. Enjoy the gladiator fights, and then fuck off back to your barracks.' He turned in a slow circle, jabbing his staff at anyone foolish enough to meet his eye. An awkward silence fell, and content that the soldiers had been cowed, the optio signed to Rufus that he should continue, before leading his men out of the arena.

'Shame,' said Julius. 'A good fist fight would have been fun.'

'You're pissed out of your head,' replied Vitellius in a low tone, indicating with his eyes the legionaries behind them. 'And we're almost surrounded by men from the Twenty-First.'

Julius stared, and was ordered by the soldiers – who'd heard him – to turn around if he didn't want a new arsehole torn for himself. Unsettled, he coughed, splattering wine over Piso. 'For Jupiter's sake!' Piso cried.

'Sorry,' muttered Julius, trying not to look at the men to their rear. 'Me and my big mouth.'

'Ignore them, and keep your voice down from now on,' said Piso, snorting at Julius' slow realisation. He'd been aware of the soldiers from the moment they'd sat down. Brawling between the men of different legions was an everyday occurrence. Fatalities were rare – no one wanted to face a possible death sentence if caught – but black eyes and broken bones were common sequelae. If he or his comrades returned to barracks in such a state, their pain wouldn't end there: Tullus, wily as a fox, would winkle out the reason for their injuries, and heap on additional punishments as a deterrent to repeat offending.

Although the unrest had been nipped in the bud, Rufus was quick to announce the next fight, and without his usual florid turn of phrase. 'I give you, Celadus, thraex, with nine victories, and Asellus, retiarius, with two wins and a draw.'

Feet drummed off the flooring again as the fighters emerged onto the sand.

Celadus was short and squat; some would have said that he was running to fat. A magnificent griffon-crested helmet hid his face from view. Polished bronze greaves covered his lower legs, a shaped piece of armour his right shoulder and he carried a small, rectangular shield. His weapon was a Thracian sica. With head held high, he stalked to the centre of the arena and bashed his curved sword off his shield, eliciting a deep-throated roar from the audience.

Asellus was a muscly, brown-skinned Iberian clad only in a loincloth. His left arm was covered in padding and a ridged piece of bronze protected his left shoulder. He swaggered about the edge of the arena, raising his net and trident and encouraging the crowd to cheer for him. Few did so, and Piso's interest in him surged. Retiarii were expected to lose to their more heavily armed opponents, but that didn't mean it always happened. He signalled to one of the betmakers still working the stands. 'What odds on the retiarius?'

At once derisive comments rained down from those around Piso about Asellus' ancestry, lack of skill and rapid expectation of defeat or death. The betmaker shrugged, as if to say, 'Listen to them', before replying, 'Thirteen-to-one against a win.'

'Here.' Piso proffered a denarius.

The betmaker took his name and handed him a stone inscribed with the lettering 'D I R', meaning one denarius bet on the retiarius. 'Good luck,' he said with a sly grin and clambered into the next row. 'Bets! Anyone still wanting to place a bet?'

'Just give *me* your money,' pleaded Vitellius as Piso resumed his seat. 'At least a friend would have it then, instead of that pox-ridden lowlife.'

'I'm happy to take it too,' said Julius.

'You're both offering the same odds?' Piso shot back. Vitellius and Julius sneered, and he laughed. 'In that case, you know where to go.'

Trumpets blared, forcing silence. The referee waved the two fighters closer to each other. 'For the glory of the emperor, Tiberius, and our general, Caecina!' he shouted, bringing his staff down between the gladiators until it touched the sand. 'Begin!'

A mighty roar went up, and Celadus and Asellus closed.

The pair traded blows and circled around for a time, gauging each other's skill, keeping Piso's hope of Asellus winning alive. To Piso's delight, the retiarius began well, striking with his trident early on and drawing blood from Celadus' left calf. Celadus' response was savage, pushing Asellus backwards with a flurry of short charges. He let out a triumphant cry during the last as Asellus skidded and tumbled onto his arse. Although the retiarius managed to convert the fall into a roll and get to his feet again, Celadus' sica flashed in, opening a long, shallow cut on his back. The crowd bellowed in appreciation. Celadus didn't follow up on his success, however, and Piso came to the unhappy realisation that the thraex was playing with the retiarius. Like as not, his money was lost.

Undeterred, Asellus managed to snare the thraex soon after, but the net didn't envelop Celadus' sword arm. Asellus tried to spear his opponent nonetheless, even as Celadus was swarming forward, sica at the ready. Asellus had to beat a hasty retreat in order not to be gutted, in the process losing his net. Celadus halted, stripped the knotted mesh from his helmet crest and hurled the thing behind him, to the far side of the arena. 'Give up now!' he roared.

Asellus must have known that his chances of winning were fast vanishing, but he was a brave man. He responded with an obscene suggestion and a savage lunge of his trident.

Celadus ducked to the side and darted forward, slamming his shield into Asellus' belly. The *whoosh* of air leaving Asellus' lungs was audible from Piso's seat. Despite being winded, he did not fall, but staggered backwards, somehow keeping his trident between him and Celadus. Angry, the thraex swatted at the pronged weapon, but Asellus kept raising and lowering it to prevent it being smashed. He tried next to move towards his net, but Celadus saw his purpose and blocked his path.

By unspoken consent, the two took a short break to catch their breath. Insults and demands for blood rained down from the audience, and Celadus resumed the fight to loud cheers. Expert at deflecting Asellus' trident up by angling his shield just so, he made a series of darting lunges *under* the weapon's shaft, each time thrusting his sica at the retiarius' belly, flank or legs. Without his net, Asellus was forced to retreat from each attack or risk suffering serious injury, and his luck ran out in the end. Blood spattered the sand as Celadus' blade sliced open his right thigh. Asellus bellowed with pain, and shuffled backwards.

Swift as a hound on a deer, Celadus was after him. *Clack. Clack.* His sica hammered off Asellus' trident, which was still keeping them apart. *Clack.* With a mighty swing of his right arm, Celadus whipped the sica upwards, forcing the trident into the air and exposing Asellus. Celadus charged forward, punching his shield into the retiarius' midriff for the second time. Down went Asellus onto the flat of his back, Celadus stamping the trident from his grasp as he landed.

The legionaries thundered their approval. Vitellius glanced at Piso, who affected not to notice. Thank the gods I only wagered one denarius, he thought.

Asellus didn't try to resist any longer. Wounded, down, with Celadus' blade touching his throat, he had no chance. Of even more concern, plenty of men wanted him to die – the chant of 'Iugula! *Kill!*' was echoing around the amphitheatre.

Piso didn't join in. It wasn't just because he'd bet on Asellus – the man had fought to the best of his ability. He deserved another chance.

Asellus lifted his right hand high, the two first fingers pointing at the sky in the gladiator's request for mercy. A chorus of jeers and taunts met his appeal. 'Kill him!' demanded one of the legionaries who'd been chased out of the arena. 'Go on!'

Pounding hobs shook the timber flooring. Hundreds of men jabbed their thumbs at their throats, and the shouting grew even louder. 'Iugula! Iugula! Iugula!' A small number of soldiers were calling for mercy, Piso among them, but they couldn't be heard.

Keeping the point of his blade on Asellus' throat, Celadus raised his gaze to the dignitaries' box, a position in clear sight of Piso and his comrades. Although the provincial governor Caecina was paying for the entertainment, he hadn't bothered to appear, which meant that the staff officer sitting there had been deputised to take his place.

A gradual hush began to descend, and the officer's bored expression slipped away as he caught Celadus' eye. He got to his feet, and the watching soldiers fell silent altogether. 'Have you enjoyed this contest, legionaries of Rome?' he asked.

'NO!' they yelled back.

A trace of irritation flashed across the officer's face. 'Did Celadus fight well?'

'YES!' came the answering roar.

'And Asellus?'

'NOOOOOO!'

Poor bastard, thought Piso.

'So Asellus should die?' asked the staff officer, regarding each part of the stands in turn.

'YESSSS!'

'It's your day, legionaries,' said the officer. Looking down at the two fighters, he jabbed his right thumb towards his throat. 'Finish it,' he ordered.

The chanting and thumb jabbing resumed. 'Iugula! Iugula! Iugula!'

Celadus stepped back and allowed Asellus to get up. The retiarius made no effort to retrieve his trident, which lay within reach. Instead he knelt, white-faced, before Celadus. After a moment's hesitation, he lifted his chin, exposing his neck. The crowd went wild.

'I wouldn't go out like that.' Vitellius' lips were by Piso's ear. 'I'd make a grab for my weapon. Die like a man.'

'He *is* dying like a man,' retorted Piso. 'It takes balls to let yourself be executed like that.'

'The gladiator's oath is a powerful sacrament,' said Julius. 'I wouldn't want to be the one who broke it and angered the gods.'

With great care, Celadus placed his sword tip in the hollow just above the top point of Asellus' sternum. He cast a look at the staff officer, who nodded, another at Asellus, who indicated his readiness. There was no pause. Celadus thrust down with savage force, sinking his blade more than a handspan into Asellus' chest cavity. Asellus stiffened; his arms twitched violently, and a faint choking sound left his lips. Blood gouted into the air as Celadus tugged free the sica. It showered the sand in great fat droplets, covered Asellus' falling body and Celadus' lower legs and bare feet.

'Habet, hoc habet!' shouted the legionaries. 'He's had it!'

Asellus slumped to the ground, and his limbs jerked to and fro. More blood poured from the red-lipped wound made by Celadus' sica, ran down the sides of his neck and spread outwards around his body, a graphic crimson offering to the gods.

He died well. Let him enter the underworld with honour, Piso prayed silently.

Celadus paced around the perimeter of the arena, holding his gore-stained blade aloft in triumph, and another massive cheer went up. Coins showered down from the stands aplenty as the legionaries showed their appreciation, and a slave was dispatched from the dignitaries' box with a heavy purse – Celadus' reward for the victory. Soon after, he bowed as two figures appeared and stood beside the gate through which Asellus' body would be taken. One was dressed as the underworld demon Charon, and armed with a hammer, and the other as the god Mercury, the conductor of souls. Soldiers cried out in mock fear at the sight of Charon, and the inevitable jokes about men having wet themselves were heard.

For his part, Piso could think only of the comrades he'd lost in the forest three years before, and how busy Charon must have been then.

Slaves bundled Asellus onto a stretcher and bore him to Charon, who struck him on the head to prove he was dead, before he was taken from sight. The circular red stain on the sand which proved that he'd died there was soon covered over as Rufus re-emerged to direct other slaves with brushes to sweep the sand clean. 'An exciting contest, legionaries, with a fitting climax,' he cried. Most men ignored him, and with a scowl, he raised his voice. 'Before the final, thrilling bout of the day, Caecina has laid on for you –' Rufus paused for dramatic effect – 'acrobats and jugglers from Iberia!'

'So fucking what?' cried a soldier, causing widespread laughter.

Rufus knew when discretion was the better part of valour, and retreated from sight.

Piso had no interest in acrobats either. 'Another drink?' he asked.

Vitellius' and Julius' faces lit up. 'Aye!'

'Wine!' Piso shouted at the nearest seller.

'Come on, you can do it!' Piso was on his feet, fist punching the air. In the arena below, the last fight was in full flow, and Longus had just cut Donar for the third time. The first, surprising wound had pleased Piso, and given him hope that his wagers might prove fruitful. The second – still unanswered by Donar – had proved the initial one hadn't been down to luck. Donar had fought back hard, however, and given Longus a nasty slice down the side of his face. Rather than intimidate Longus, the setback seemed to have goaded him on. Spinning like a trained dancer around Donar, he launched attack after attack, often without answer. It was fortunate for Donar that he had the protection of a mail shirt. Dressed as a 'Gaul', he also bore a hexagonal shield and long spear typical of his kind.

Longus' third wounding of the champion had Piso feeling his purse already weighed down with winnings. Exhilarated, he clapped Vitellius on the shoulder and yelled until his voice cracked. A big swallow of wine helped, and he resumed cheering. The audience, which had watched the unexpected turn of events with initial disbelief, was also starting to get behind Longus. 'Long-us! Long-us!' roared the legionaries behind Piso and his comrades.

'People love the underdog,' declared Piso.

'I wouldn't discount Donar just yet,' warned Julius, pointing.

Looking down, Piso's cry died in his throat. Using the extra reach of his spear, Donar had pushed Longus back with a flurry of vicious blows to the shield. Longus could do little but duck down behind it and shuffle away. In a similar tactic to Celadus, Donar checked his spear arm and charged forward to smack his shield into that of Longus, forcing him backwards at speed. The fast-changing balance of power made the audience bay with excitement.

With great skill, Longus managed not to fall, as Asellus had. Somehow he brought his sword around behind Donar. This close, there was no way of trying to strike a proper blow with the blade – nor would it penetrate his opponent's mail shirt, so Longus smashed his sword hilt into Donar's back. The blow distracted Donar enough to check his advance. With a mighty shove, Longus propelled himself backwards, away from danger. Rather than retreat further, which Piso and every man watching expected, he bounced off his rearmost foot and launched himself straight at Donar again. The move caught Donar off guard, and unable to use his spear.

Face to face with his opponent, Longus delivered a powerful headbutt. Both the griffon crest and the bowl of his helmet struck Donar on the forehead. With a howl of pain, he stumbled away, blood pouring from the upper wound. He had the sense to try and keep his spear between him and Longus, but half-blinded, he didn't point it in the right direction. Bent-kneed to present less of a target, Longus darted in and rammed Donar again with his shield. This time, the impact was enough to knock the champion down.

Flat onto his back he went, and the crowd, now wholly supporting Longus, bayed their approval.

It's over, thought Piso in exultation.

Not for nothing was Donar the champion, though. Discarding his spear, he grabbed at the lower edge of Longus' shield as the murmillo moved to stand over him. He wrenched it down, unbalancing Longus, and then pushed it up again, catching him a stinging blow under the chin. Longus' attack checked, Donar rolled away to the side, grabbing his spear. He still had his shield too. On his feet again, he began hurling abuse at Longus.

Blood dripped from under Longus' helmet – his nose must have been injured or broken – but he ran at Donar, keen to continue the fight.

The pair jabbed and thrust at each other, both appearing enraged by the other's successes. The tension was palpable, and had many in the audience on their feet, cheering and whistling. Even the once-bored staff officer was watching with fierce concentration.

Vitellius leaned close. 'Still think you're going to win?'

Startled, Piso glanced at his friend. 'Of course,' he grated, although he was no longer quite so sure.

Peeeeep! The referee blew his whistle. Neither fighter acknowledged his intervention, and he had to sound it twice more before they heard and lowered their weapons. Boos and catcalls rained down on the referee as he gestured a slave forward to retie the lower leather retaining strap on Donar's solitary greave, which had come loose.

Work done, the slave retreated out of harm's way. Longus and Donar looked to the referee, who whistled at them to begin.

The fight continued for some time, with both fighters giving their best. Longus fell once, but the referee intervened because he judged him to have slipped. A while later, Donar landed a powerful but glancing blow on the front of Longus' helmet, denting the cheekpiece and inflicting an unseen injury. Nonetheless, it was Donar who began to weaken first. Whether it was because he had more flesh wounds or wasn't as fit as he might once have been, Piso wasn't sure – nor did he care. What mattered was that Donar was now retreating more than he was attacking, that Longus' sword was weaving a constant, deadly arc around the champion, and causing damage. First it was a stabbing probe to one of Donar's feet, then a delicate, surgeon's cut to his right cheek.

In the end, it was another shoulder charge that secured victory for Longus. As chance would have it, the pair were closer to the perimeter of the arena than they'd been for most of the contest. Driving Donar backwards – he didn't fall – and staying inside the reach of his spear, Longus shoved until the planking was almost within touching distance. Realising what would happen if there was nowhere to go, Donar made frantic efforts to slow down and stop. All the momentum was with Longus, however, and a moment later, Donar's back struck the wood with a loud thud. Excited shouts went up from the soldiers just above the fighters, and men leaned over the edge for a better view.

Aware that his opponent was still dangerous, Longus head-butted Donar again and again, mashing his nose to a pulp. Drawing back his shield, Longus punched his opponent with it one, two, three times. He stepped back then and before Donar, half stunned, could do anything but groan, hacked in under the bottom rim of his shield. Blood fountained; Donar screamed, and his right, unprotected leg buckled.

Longus wheeled away, and his sword slashed the air in a crimson-tipped gesture of delight. Piso and the rest cheered, and Longus spun in a complete circle to face Donar, who had dropped to his good knee.

Despite his gritted jaw, bloodied face, and ruined leg, he managed to raise his spear towards Longus.

'Yield!' Longus' voice was muffled by his helmet, but there was no mistaking what he was saying. 'Yield!'

The chant began at once, from every part of the amphitheatre. 'Iugula! Iugula!'

Rather than answer, Donar thrust with his spear. Longus batted away the blow with ease and began hammering blows on Donar's shield, first cracking it and then smashing it in two. Chest heaving, he withdrew ten steps, out of spear range. Defenceless, Donar glared at him.

'Yield now, or die,' ordered Longus.

'Iugula! Iugula!'

Piso was grinning like a fool. He suspected that his drink-fuddled mental calculation was out by a margin, but he stood to collect at least two hundred denarii. 'The wine's on me tonight, brothers,' he muttered to Vitellius and Julius, thinking that he might indulge *himself* with a visit to Diana.

'Make your choice!' shouted Longus, approaching Donar, his sword at the ready.

With an oath, Donar threw down his spear. Longus nodded, watching as his defeated opponent made the signal requesting mercy at the staff officer.

Piso was on his feet before he knew it. 'Mitte! *Mercy!*' he shouted, indicating to his friends that they should do the same. His cynical side might have said they did it just to ensure a flow of unlimited wine, but they did as he asked. For a dozen heartbeats, few men joined in, but Donar's fine previous record must have occurred to some – and perhaps Piso's enthusiasm helped too. 'Mitte! Let him live!' roared the fool who'd been beaten out of the arena by the optio. His companions added their voices to his. So did the soldiers behind Piso. The chant spread as fast as the demand for Asellus to die had in the previous fight.

'MITTE! MITTE!'

The staff officer regarded the crowd. Almost the entire audience was now demanding that Donar should be spared. With a shrug, the officer stuck up his right thumb, raising a mighty cheer.

Longus dipped his chin towards Donar before parading around the arena to receive the legionaries' adulation.

'Let's go,' said Piso.

'Wanting to collect your winnings?' asked Vitellius with a wink.

'The quicker we leave, the faster my purse will be full, and the wine will flow.' Piso stood and began making for the nearest set of steps. 'Coming?' he called.

Emerging from the amphitheatre, Piso saw Degmar again – they nodded at one another in passing – as he made a beeline for the first betmaker with whom he'd done business, the lank-haired Gaul of earlier. The betmaker was none too pleased at Piso's appearance with a token marked, 'D 5 M U', indicating a bet of five denarii on the last murmillo. Muttering about the contest having been fixed, he paid out the one hundred silver coins with the speed of an arthritic greybeard. His heavies, a pair of broken-nosed, gap-toothed hulks, glowered at Piso, and greedy eyes aplenty saw the small fortune being handed over. He was more than glad of his comrades' presence at his back, and kept a tight grip of his purse as he sought out the second betmaker, a fleshy-lipped Sicilian.

Piso handed over his token, which was marked much as the first had been, except the seven denarii had been denoted as seven individual lines rather than 'VII'. Pursing his lips, the Sicilian peered at it long and hard.

'Where shall we go first?' asked Vitellius.

Piso glanced around. 'Sirona's place. I want some really good wine.'

'And if Tullus is there?'

'I'll buy him some too!' Cheered by the prospect of standing his centurion a drink, Piso turned back. The Sicilian was grinning at him now, which did not feel right.

'You've been drinking since this morning?' The Sicilian's tone was jocular, even honeyed.

'That's what legionaries do on payday,' retorted Piso. He held out his hand. 'My money.'

'Of course.' The Sicilian's fingers were fluttering over the little piles of coins on his table. 'Three denarii was a big bet. At eighteen-to-one odds, your winnings will come to . . . fifty-four denarii.'

'Three?' screeched Piso. 'There are seven lines on my token, you blind whoreson! Seven!'

'I can only see three,' said the Sicilian, jerking his head at his body-guard, a horse-sized German tribesman with a long beard. Horse stepped in front of his employer, his ham hands gripping a nasty-looking club. 'Three lines,' he rumbled in bad Latin. 'Three denarii bet.'

'You prick!' roared Piso.

'Here.' The Sicilian was proffering a token. 'See for yourself.'

Piso snatched it, cursing his stupidity for twisting around to talk to Vitellius. Sleight-of-hand was one of the Sicilian's many skills, no doubt. Staring down at the three lines, he let out a bitter laugh. 'This isn't my token. You've switched it!'

The Sicilian's face took on a wounded look. 'That's the one you gave me. You saw, didn't you?' He looked at Horse.

'Soldier give you that one,' agreed Horse.

Piso's urge was to punch Horse and attack the Sicilian. Even if he had been sober, however, he wasn't sure that particular contest was winnable. Vitellius and Julius would help, but they were as pissed as he was. So angry that he was giving the notion serious consideration anyway, he hesitated as the Sicilian whistled, and a second guard – also enormous – appeared from behind his stall. The new arrival stamped over to stand beside Horse, almost blocking sight of the Sicilian behind them.

Piso's spirits fell. 'You're robbing me blind,' he snarled through the gap between the heavies.

'I'm an honest man,' came the reply. Coins clinked, and a small leather bag was shoved at Piso. 'Here. Fifty-four denarii. A decent sum for any man to win.'

Piso glanced at his companions – their nods told him that if he attacked, they would too – and then he sighed. Even with their dag-gers, they were so drunk that overcoming the two man-mountains would be doubtful at best. He counted the purse's contents, finding that the Sicilian had not lied in that respect at least. 'You owe me another seventy-two denarii!' he cried, tossing the three-lined token at the Sicilian.

'I've paid you what's owed.' The Sicilian's voice was hard now. 'Be gone, or my men will move you on.'

Boiling with fury, Piso squared up to Horse, who gave him a happy leer.

'Want to fight?' Horse tapped the business end of his club off a meaty palm. 'I'm ready.'

'Piso.' Vitellius' hand was on his shoulder. 'It's not worth a broken arm or leg – or worse. Come on.'

Piso wheeled. 'Seventy-two denarii! Seventy-two fucking denarii!' he hissed. 'That's almost four months' pay!'

'I know it, brother. So does Julius.' Sympathy mixed with the anger in Vitellius' eyes. 'It's not worth a cracked skull, though, and that's all that is on offer here.'

'We'll go and get Tullus, or Fenestela,' said Piso, clutching at straws.

'Without the token, you can't prove a thing,' said Vitellius.

'I'll tell this lot what the whoreson's done,' declared Piso, waving a hand at the legionaries disgorging from the amphitheatre. 'They'll help.'

'Do you recognise any?' asked Julius. 'I can't see a single one from the Fifth.'

Piso looked, and ground his teeth because all he could see were men of the Twenty-First. The relationship between its soldiers and those of their legion varied between rivalry and outright hostility. Rather than providing some much-needed muscle, Piso decided, his situation would be a cause for hilarity and humiliation. Degmar might have helped, but he was nowhere to be seen.

'Let's go,' said Vitellius. 'The first round's on me.'

Even this startling announcement – Vitellius had a tendency to be stingy – could not drag Piso's mood from the mire. Calling the Sicilian every filthy name he could think of, and promising to get his own back, he walked away.

'Should we try and round up men to sort this out?' he muttered.

'Under normal circumstances, yes, but today's payday,' said Vitellius. 'Our cohort will be spread over every drinking den and whorehouse in the vicus. That bastard's no fool either. He and his apes will be on the road as soon as they can take down their filthy stall. By the time we got back, if we managed it, they'd be long gone.'

'Imagine that you had only wagered three denarii with the prick,' advised Julius. 'With the hundred denarii you took from the other betmaker, you'd be over the moon.'

'That's easy for you to say,' said Piso.

'You can't do anything more about it, and your purse is full,' said

Vitellius, slapping him on the back. 'Forget about the rest.'

'Aye.' Piso smiled, but inside him, a white-hot rage burned.

Piso had no idea what hour it was. Darkness still blanketed the vicus, but dawn couldn't be far off. He and his comrades had been in Sirona's tavern for a long time – since they'd left the amphitheatre, in fact. She had thrown everyone out of her inn a short time before, saying she had a bed to climb into, even if they didn't. Nothing would make her serve another drink, not even the handful of denarii that Piso had proffered. 'Save it for another night,' Sirona had said with a smile, while pointing at the door. 'Now go *home.*'

Vitellius and Julius were weaving alongside Piso, arm in arm, and singing as they went. So inebriated that they could only remember the first verse of a popular drinking song, the pair roared it over and over again. Piso snorted with amusement when the first-floor shutters of an adjacent building opened and a man's voice screeched, 'Shut up and fuck off, you noisy bastards!'

He laughed even harder at Vitellius' and Julius' response, which was to stand beneath the window and serenade the irate householder. Only when the contents of a night-soil pot came spattering down, narrowly missing them, did they beat an undignified retreat.

'What a night,' slurred Vitellius, swinging an arm over Piso's shoulder. 'Eh?'

'Aye,' replied Piso, reminded again of the swindling Sicilian. 'It was one to remember, all right.'

'Shame we didn't get to a whorehouse,' said Julius.

'None of us could have managed it.' Piso curved one of his little fingers to face the ground. 'Would have been a complete waste of money.'

'Our next night off duty, we'll hit the brothels,' declared Vitellius, stumbling and almost dragging Piso down with him.

Piso grunted, his imagination running riot. Despite the quantities of fine wine they'd consumed in Sirona's, most of his winnings still sat in his weighty purse, which meant an entire night with Diana was possible if he wished it. Come the morning, Piso decided blearily, he would have to deposit the money with the quartermaster, or face having it thieved from the barrack room he shared with his comrades. Seventy-two denarii more would have given him enough to visit Diana *and* to send a large sum home to his aged mother. Picturing the Sicilian leaving the vicus with his coin, Piso was again consumed by anger. I hope the whoreson dies a slow, painful death, he thought.

He jumped as Degmar materialised out of the darkness, flanked by his two companions. 'Greetings,' Piso muttered as his composure returned.

'Greetings,' came the amused reply.

'Degmar!' cried Vitellius. 'Well met.' He whispered an explanation to Julius, who didn't know the warrior, and Julius' suspicious expression eased. Attracted by a still-open restaurant, the pair ambled towards it, saying they'd be back soon. Piso was about to follow, but Degmar caught at his arm.

'What is it?' demanded Piso.

'Drunk?'

'Very. You?'

'No. I had a nip earlier, but nothing since. I'm thirsty, though.'

'I would have bought you a drink – several – if I'd seen you,' said Piso, feeling bad. Like as not, Degmar didn't have much coin.

'I wasn't in the vicus.'

Even more confused, Piso searched Degmar's face for a clue. 'What were you doing?'

Degmar rummaged under his cloak. 'Here,' he said, stretching out his arm.

Piso goggled at the proffered purse. 'What's that?'

'Seventy-two denarii.'

'Seventy-two denarii?' repeated Piso like a fool.

'From the Sicilian. That's what you were owed, isn't it?'

'Yes,' said Piso, even more confused. 'How did you know that?'

'You were protesting loud enough by his stall,' said Degmar with a brief smile.

'But how could you—? What did you—?'

'He owed me money too – and wouldn't pay. We –' Degmar indicated his comrades – 'stayed and watched him load up his cart after your confrontation. The filth headed south with his guards, so we followed.'

'You ambushed them?' asked Piso, incredulous and delighted.

'Something like that. Got my money, yours and more.' Coins chinked off each other as Degmar shook the bag at his waist.

'And the Sicilian?'

'He won't be cheating anyone else this side of the underworld. Nor will his heavies.'

Piso let out an incredulous laugh. This was far more than he could have hoped for. 'I'm in your debt. Thank you.' He wrung Degmar's hand.

Degmar's face split into a rare grin. 'Maybe you can pay me back one day.'

'If I can, I will,' swore Piso. 'On my life.'

'We're off to find a tavern that's open,' said Degmar. 'Sleep well.'

With that, he and his companions slipped away into the gloom. For several moments, Piso stood there, not quite believing what had just happened, and yet the new, heavy purse in his fist offered plenty of proof. Happiness washed over him. His mother *would* now receive the monies he'd wanted to send her, and the tombstones he had long wished to erect for his tentmates who'd died three years before could also become reality. There would even be enough to start saving for himself, a wise plan if he wanted to leave the legions and fulfil his dreams of setting up as an importer of German furs and the like. I'm rich, thought Piso with elation.

'Hungry?' Vitellius was calling from the restaurant.

'Aye.' Clutching the bag tight, Piso charged across the street. 'You're in luck too, because I'm buying!'

AUTHOR'S NOTE

This story was written as a free digital-only 'taster' before the publication of *Hunting the Eagles*. Outside the UK, however, readers could only access it (and 'The Shrine') on the writing platform Wattpad. It is a great pleasure, therefore, to see it in print, available to all.

The location of the story, the arena outside the legionary fortress at Vetera, modern-day Xanten in Germany, can still be visited. Set in the midst of fields a short walk from the wonderful Fürstenberger Hof Hotel, it is a deeply atmospheric place, not least late on a warm summer's evening, when a number of beers have been consumed. Such was my opinion anyway. Anthony Riches, fellow Roman author and good friend, who was there, and may have had a similar amount of beer, agreed!

EAGLES IN THE WILDERNESS

A Tullus short story

For Clive May, with huge thanks for his generous support. This story is also dedicated to every SME that is fighting injustice received from the banks – massive businesses bailed out by the UK taxpayer in 2007/8.

PART I

In the settlement close to the fort of Vetera, on the Roman frontier with Germania, spring AD 19

A short distance from the southern gate, a pair of carters travelling in opposite directions traded insults, each blaming the other for blocking the street, both refusing to admit he was to blame. Neither man paid the slightest attention to the indignant cries of the shop-keepers whose premises were now inaccessible, or to the disgruntled comments of the pedestrians forced to squeeze past their wagons. Former senior centurion Lucius Cominius Tullus, a cloth-wrapped bundle under one arm, was one of the latter. Time was he would have knocked the arguing men's heads together and directed one to reverse his cart to a wider part of the street, but no longer. Life was too short to bother with fools.

It was a dry afternoon, and warm for the time of year, but heavy rain over the previous month meant the unpaved surface beneath his feet was a disagreeable, rank-smelling morass. Tullus had taken to wearing his military calf-high boots again. The jokes from some of the inn's customers – had he rejoined the legions, he was so dressed up, had the emperor summoned him to Rome? – were easier to ignore than shit and piss on his toes.

The familiar tramp of marching feet filled his ears. A heartbeat later, a loud voice announced that the patrol might be almost over, but they were not stopping in the settlement. Moreover, the voice continued, if anyone so much as stepped out of line, they'd regret it for the rest of their miserable days. Lips twitching, Tullus moved aside to let a half century of legionaries past. Their shield motifs told him they served in the Fifth, the legion in which he had ended his career. A lifetime of habit saw his eyes rove over their equipment and weapons. Many men recognised him, giving him friendly nods or grins. Their acknowledgements made Tullus proud but also a little sad, for he missed the comradeship that had been his entire existence until two years before. He glanced down at the silver band on the ring finger of his left hand, telling himself that life moved on, that there was more than one type of companionship. He had done well to persuade Sirona, the formidably attractive owner of the Ox and Plough, to accept his offer of marriage. If he'd stayed in the army, taking a wife would have remained out of his reach.

'Well met, sir.'

The officer, who'd been pacing at the back of the column, was a gaunt-faced optio familiar to Tullus. Barking at his men to continue towards the fort, and in a lower voice telling the tesserarius to keep a good eye on them, he stopped beside Tullus. 'All well, sir?'

'Oh aye.' Tullus revealed the package under his arm. 'Buying cheese is hard work. So many varieties to choose from. Ensuring that it's not about to turn, and that I don't get fleeced over the price.' He rolled his eyes.

'D'you miss the legion still, sir?' The optio's tone was sympathetic.

'Every day.' Tullus hesitated, then added, 'But truth be told, I'm also glad to have hung up my harness. More than thirty years I served, and there isn't a single hour that some part of my body doesn't tell me about it. It's good to hear the rain drum off the roof at dawn too, and know that I can stay under the blankets, instead of leading out a patrol, or having to drill the men on the parade ground.' He jerked his chin in the direction of the Rhenus. 'Were you over the other side just now?'

'Yes, sir. Me and my boys have come back from Aliso.'

Tullus had trodden the road to that fort countless times. He'd ended up there ten years before too, after the ambush at the Saltus Teutobergiensis. He and the few men he'd managed to save had holed up inside Aliso. Besieged by thousands of drunk-with-victory German tribesmen, things had looked bleak, until a thunderstorm had come to their aid. Together with the small garrison, he and his men had managed to escape as the storm raged overhead. Tullus would remember the relief he'd felt at the sight of the bridge over the Rhenus to the end of his days. 'See anything out of the ordinary?'

A snort. 'No, sir. Things are quiet. The savages are ploughing their fields, like the farmers on this side. Some have let their cattle out, presumably the ones whose winter feed has finished, while the rest have put sheep onto the pasture.'

'No one wants trouble this close to the river.' So it had been for a couple of years, and no surprise, thought Tullus, with tens of thousands of legionaries just a short distance away – here and in the other forts along the western bank. 'Doubtless the tribes a little further east will be up to their tricks before long, though, eh?'

'As they always are, sir,' said the optio, spitting. 'A shame that Germanicus didn't get to finish the job.'

'It is,' said Tullus with feeling. The recovery of the Eighteenth Legion's eagle two and a half years before had been the finest moment of his life, but Arminius, the mastermind of the ambush, had not been brought to justice. Nor would he. A directive from the emperor in Rome had seen the provincial governor Germanicus' operations come to a sudden and unwelcome halt soon after the legions' return with the eagle. 'I'd have stayed in the Fifth to my dying day if we'd kept after that bastard Arminius,' Tullus went on. 'But it was pointless remaining in the legions with no chance of catching him.'

'Aye, sir, and with Germanicus away in the east a year and more, it doesn't seem he'll return to these parts.'

Wanting to put Arminius from his mind, Tullus joked, 'Can't say I blame him. Winter drags on forever here, or so it seems. An old man like me appreciates sunshine every day, and heat that warms your bones. Those are never lacking in the east.'

'You're no greybeard, sir,' protested the optio. 'Set you in charge of my men, and you'd still do a finer job than I could.' Promising to call soon into the Ox and Plough – the inn Tullus ran with Sirona – he tramped after his men.

The optio was being kind, thought Tullus with regret. Soldiering was a job for the young, and at least fifteen years separated him from the optio. Put the two of them on a forced march, and only one man would come in first. If it came to a fight, well, he might still have a chance. He had forgotten more combat tricks than most men ever learned. Smiling at himself, and his inability to fully step away from legion life, he set off in the direction of the inn.

A rich, herb-laden, meaty aroma wafted from an open-fronted restaurant on his left. The place was a favourite of Tullus', and his pace slowed. He hadn't eaten since dawn, and the food here – the lamb stew in particular – was better by some margin than anything Sirona ever conjured up. His hesitation was brief. Refusing his wife's cooking with a protest of not feeling hungry he could get away with now and again, but the last occasion he'd tried it – having visited this exact establishment to sample its roast pork and crackling – had been just two days prior. Test his luck too far, and Fortuna would cackle, and set a suspicious gleam in Sirona's eye. Women, Tullus had learned, had an unerring nose for sniffing out a man's secrets, even if in his case, they were only to do with food. Better to eat whatever Sirona had prepared, he decided, and smile and tell her it was delicious.

Passing the restaurant's threshold, he glanced inside.

Two men were leaning up against the counter, cups of wine in hand. One was tall and blocky; an unusual tribal tattoo marked his right arm. The other, with dark red hair and a beard, was shorter but as solid. Veterans, both of them, Tullus decided: no one else cut their hair that short, or wore tunics that had once been military.

'I tell you, it was the largest bear I ever saw. This big, its head was.' The shorter man gestured with his hands.

'Course it was,' retorted the other. 'Like the fish I caught last summer.' He held his hands half a man's height apart.

'Curse you, I'm not lying. An ursarius, I was, you know.'

'Aye, Bear, you never cease reminding me.'

'*You* are forever bending my ear about your Roman father, Cato,' the ursarius threw back. 'How he raised you after your mother died – or should I say, paid for you to be raised.'

'He was in the legions. How could he look after me?'

'Getting back to the bear—'

A derisory snort.

Tullus had heard rough-humoured banter like it a thousand times; he walked on. Soldiers hadn't changed since the dawn of time, he thought. They never would. Tongues loosened by drink, the pair would still be making fun of each other at the night's end. That, or singing out-of-tune marching songs, or punching seven shades of hell out of one another – and whoever got in their way.

His new occupation of innkeeper meant that Tullus faced men in their cups every single night, but things rarely got out of hand. Sirona had ruled over the Ox and Plough with a rod of iron long before he had arrived on the scene, and things hadn't changed. Two of her four adult sons, all strapping examples of the Gaulish race, always worked in the tavern at the same time. More often than not, a deep-throated warning from one of them served to quieten any rowdy customers; when it didn't, they used their fists and feet to good effect. It was uncommon for the cudgels under the counter to be needed; still less for Tullus to be required.

The presence of young muscle didn't mean that he shied away from confrontation: far from it. Deprived of real combat, he relished the occasional tussle. Heaving drunks out the door who were half his age and twice as fit as he was went some way towards proving that he wasn't altogether past it. Sirona didn't approve. Let the boys do it, she often said, pursing the lips that Tullus so loved. One day, he would come unstuck, she said, and end up with a broken nose.

You'll love me even more like that, he told her every time, before grabbing her for a kiss. Grumbling that people were watching, she would push him away, but not too hard. She knew better than to say more: the one time she'd really complained, Tullus had folded his arms and said, 'You and your boys might have knocked plenty of heads to-gether, but it's been my life to let soldiers know who's in charge. I have a *way* that's very . . . effective.' Threatening to cut a man's balls off, delivered in the same tone that Tullus had used to terrify a thousand new recruits, was the tried and tested way. It rarely failed – and when it did, he used his vitis, the vine stick that had been one of his badges of office. Driven deep into the solar plexus, or cracked across a man's head or shoulders, most saw the error of their ways. If things got serious – and they never had thus far – his sword and dagger were under the bar.

Sirona was a stubborn woman. 'And if you get hurt?' she'd demanded.

'I'm a soldier, wife. A soldier. Fighting is part of what I am. Stop me from doing that, and you might as well kill me now.' She had heard the truth in his voice, had seen it in his stare, and let it be.

It was a shame, thought Tullus, increasing his pace past another of his favourite restaurants, that his vitis couldn't be applied with regard to his other business dealings. After leaving the Fifth, he had hardly considered his sizeable pension. He was a man of simple needs; with the inn, Sirona didn't need it either. Ears full of the ventures his former comrades were involved in, however, he had gradually decided some-thing had better be done with the money.

Wary of setting up business himself – what did he, an ex-career soldier, know? – he had invested with a wine merchant, and also a builder. He should have been suspicious from the start, thought Tullus. Once he'd handed over the coin, both men had become elusive. They were always too busy to see him, or finding reasons to cut short their meetings.

So it had gone on for some months, until Tullus' temper had frayed, and he'd demanded evidence of where his monies had gone. Finally the books had been produced, but to his frustration, he had been baffled by the dense columns of expenses, debts, and ongoing costs. Tullus wasn't fond of figures, and it seemed both the wine merchant and builder knew it. Grumbling, suspicious that the wool was being pulled over his eyes, but unable to prove it, and reluctant to resort to physical violence with civilians – it wasn't unknown for soldiers to be dragged into the courts by unhappy citizens – he had had to satisfy himself with the wine merchant's promise of 'better times to come' and the builder swearing that business would soon pick up.

'See that it does,' Tullus had snarled, 'or someone will pay.' The threat had had some effect – some dividends at least had started coming his way. Not the amounts he'd been promised, but it was a start. Whether he would ever get back what he'd spent, he had no idea. Angry with himself, and a little embarrassed, he hadn't breathed a word of it to Sirona. At least, he thought, he had only invested a quarter of his wealth. The rest, buried under the floor of his and Sirona's bedroom, would see him to the end of his days if he was prudent, as well as leaving a decent lump sum for Artio. A smile creased his face at the thought of his adopted daughter.

It was as if the gods heard.

Tullus had neared the Ox and Plough; a heartbeat later, Artio came out of the front door of the tavern. She didn't spot him at once, which allowed him to study her. She was almost a woman, he thought. Twelve years old, or near as, tall for her age, and striking too. There was a confidence about her – he could see it now in the set of her chin, and the fearless way she looked around – that reminded Tullus of himself when he was young. Whether he'd helped to instil it in Artio, or whether it had been in her from birth, he didn't know or care. Literate, self-assured and financially secure, and with Sirona and Tullus to guide her, she would make a fine businesswoman. She would marry, gods willing, and have children too, but any man who wanted Artio's hand would have to prove himself first to Tullus.

'Father!' Artio had seen him. All her poise disappeared; she ran over, a little girl again.

Tullus didn't care that there were soldiers who knew him ten paces away. His heart swelled, and he grabbed her in a great bear hug. 'Looking for me?'

'No.' She pulled back a little and gave an expressive roll of her eyes. 'Mother has sent me to the butcher's. We need more meat in the kitchen, apparently.'

'Best get on then. You don't want to keep her waiting. Scylax not with you?'

'He's asleep by the fire.'

Tullus smiled. 'I should have guessed.' The dog he'd rescued at the same time as Artio was now their pet; his favourite spot was by the great hearth in the inn. 'Shall we take him for a walk later?'

'I'd like that.' Artio waved a hand and skipped off.

Tullus watched her run. She wasn't his blood, but he loved her as if she were. He had adopted her as his daughter more than a year before; she was the sole beneficiary of his will. He'd always thought to have had sons, but with Sirona long past childbearing age, it wasn't to be. And yet Tullus was content with Artio, more than he'd have believed possible. She and Sirona were, if he admitted it, the lights of his life, while his remaining men from the Eighteenth were like his sons.

Gods but I'm getting old and soft, he thought, pulling wide the door and stepping inside the Ox and Plough.

A wave of warm air hit him, the familiar mixture of men's sweat, wine, wood smoke and cooking meat. The place was full, almost every table occupied. The customers were the usual mixture of legionaries and veterans, with a smattering of local tribesmen thrown in for good measure. Tullus' head turned, assessing the mood, and searching as always for signs of trouble. Seeing none, he aimed for the bar, a long wooden counter on the right of the room. Behind it lay the cooking area, where the inn's food was prepared.

Pausing by the fire, he bent to stroke Scylax, who gave a sleepy wag.

'Call that a scar? Take a look at this.' The voice belonged to a stocky veteran with a short white beard. Pulling up the right sleeve of his tunic, he revealed a purple welt that ran up to his shoulder and beyond. 'Should have lost the arm, I should.'

His companions nodded and muttered in agreement.

A green-eyed man with a broad grin jerked a thumb over the table, at a slight figure with almost black hair, longer than was usual for a soldier. 'To think you served nearly twenty years and only suffered one little scar, Lucius.'

'I was lucky the first few years,' said Lucius. 'Then I broke a leg and spent months on crutches. I was no use to my centurion, so he sent me down the hospital – they were short-handed at the time, see. By the time my leg had healed, one of the surgeons had decided I'd be better use as a stretcher-bearer and orderly. That's how I saw out my time.'

'How did you come by any scar at all then, if you weren't fighting?'

Tullus stared; White Beard was pointing at a scar on the inside of Lucius' right arm, near his wrist.

'Cautery iron slip or something?' asked White Beard.

Lucius looked embarrassed. 'No.'

'What was it – tell us, you dog!' demanded the green-eyed man.

'I burned myself with hot fat, frying meat when I was drunk,' muttered Lucius.

Tullus smiled at the roars of amusement this revelation produced. Lucius wouldn't hear the end of that for some time, he thought.

Sirona was watching him from behind the bar. 'Someone was asking for you.'

In itself, this wasn't unusual – Tullus' old comrades and men who'd served under him often came to share a cup of wine – but there was a difference to Sirona's usual tone. Tullus set the package of cheese on the counter. 'Did he give a name?'

'No, but he said it was urgent. He'll come back later, or so he said.' Sirona shrugged.

'Did he look . . . unfriendly? Do I need . . .' Tullus' right hand moved to the spot on the counter under which his sword and dagger were stashed.

Sirona shook her head. 'He looks like an old soldier. Said he knew you.'

'Half the men in the fort know me. Can you not describe him better?'

She punched him in the arm, hard. 'He looked the same as most men who come in here. Tanned. Tough-looking. Short hair. A few scars. Oh – he had a short white beard.'

Curiosity piqued, Tullus couldn't think of who it might be. 'Did you—'

But Sirona had moved down the bar to attend to a waiting customer.

Beards were common among Germans and Gauls, but not Romans. Racking his brains, Tullus retrieved the cheese and carried it through to the cooking area. The four slaves, three women, one man – all German – nodded and muttered greetings. Tullus dipped a finger in a stew, pronouncing it delicious but in need of some salt. Rejoicing inside, for the stew was better than what Sirona could cook, he checked that the baking bread wasn't burning – much to the indignation of the slave in charge of the oven – and quietly sliced himself a hunk of cheese before he left the slaves to it, and headed for the back room that served as Sirona's (and now his) office.

He had barely put his feet up on the desk before the sound of crashing furniture reached him. Men were shouting. Sirona's authoritative voice restored order for a few heartbeats, and then he heard the distinctive sound of something heavy hitting the floor. Tullus made haste for the main room.

Sirona and the barmaids were safe behind the bar, watching two men grapple. A table lay on its side; beside were the remains of a stool. A loose circle of customers had already surrounded the pair, cheering one or the other, placing bets on who would win the fight. No one was trying to intervene. They rarely did, thought Tullus in frustration – that was how soldiers were. 'Where are your boys?' he asked Sirona.

A scowl. 'Helping a carter change a wheel down the street. I've sent a slave to fetch them.'

'These pricks will have half the place destroyed by then,' said Tullus, reaching under the counter. Armed with his vitis, ignoring Sirona's warning look, he strode from behind the bar. 'Out of my way,' he roared, wielding the stick to left and right. Angry soldiers turned, but their expressions changed when they saw who it was that had struck them. A path cleared.

Tullus wasted no time trying to reason with the brawlers, who were rolling about on the wine-soaked floor. Uncaring of where his blows landed, he laid into the pair of entwined figures. Up and down his vitis went half a dozen, eight times. Smiling grimly at the yelps this produced, and leering at the pained faces of the now-separated brawlers, Tullus delivered a hefty kick to each.

'Enough!' He used his full parade-ground voice. 'On your feet!'

Sullen-faced, the two obeyed. One, fair-skinned as a Briton, was unknown to Tullus, but the second was Lucius, the soldier whose drunken burn had been the source of his comrades' jokes. He made to speak, but Tullus' vitis shot up and stopped just under his nose.

'Silence, maggot.'

Lucius subsided.

Tullus' attention returned to the fair-skinned man, an auxiliary by his dress. Furious, showing no sign of knowing who Tullus was, he was bunching his fists and clearly spoiling for a fight. Tullus drove the vitis into his belly without hesitation. Winded, the man dropped like a stone down a well.

Tullus cast his eyes about. 'There's one broken stool, Sirona. The table looks to be undamaged. Anything else?'

'Not that I can see.'

Dividing the cost of a stool in two, and adding a fine to the figure, Tullus turned back to the brawlers. Too late, he saw a fist coming in from the side. It connected like a hammer blow, exploding a ball of agony in his skull. Even as Tullus' knees buckled, experience made him take a faltering step to the side, away from his attacker. He brought up the vitis as a defence, but hadn't the strength to strike the burly figure closing on him. I'm in real trouble, he thought.

Another figure swept in, from his left. A curse. A punch, then another. Tullus' attacker reeled back, now occupied with the man who had interrupted *his* assault. Tullus' eyes slowly came back into focus. To his astonishment, Lucius had come to his aid, leaping on the man who'd punched him. Although only half the size of his opponent – another fair-skinned auxiliary – he was more than holding his own. A mighty knee to the groin helped, and as the groaning auxiliary bent double, Lucius used his knee once again, this time to the face.

Broken nose, thought Tullus with satisfaction. As the auxiliary came upright, one hand on his balls and the other on his pulped nose, Tullus hit him with the vitis. A mighty clout on the side of the head, practised a hundred times, it rolled the auxiliary's eyes in his head. Unconscious before he hit the floor, he landed at Tullus' feet in a sprawl of limbs.

'I didn't need that,' protested Lucius. Catching Tullus' granite-hard stare, he added, 'Sir.'

'It's not about help, maggot, but finishing a fight. Did your centurion not teach you that?' Tullus held up his hand, silencing Lucius. 'My thanks for stepping in.'

'Sir.'

'What were you fighting about?' demanded Tullus.

'The prick started laughing at my scar, sir.' Lucius raised his arm, revealing the burn. 'Said I was no kind of legionary to have that and nothing more.'

I would have hit him too, thought Tullus, but he said nothing of the kind. 'You'll pay for half the cost of the broken chair – six asses.'

'Aye, sir,' said Lucius.

'There's a fine of a denarius too, for fighting inside the inn.'

'Yes, sir.' Lucius was rummaging in the leather purse that hung round his neck. He shoved forward his hand. 'It's all there, sir.'

Under normal circumstances, Tullus would also have barred Lucius from the premises for a month, but the fact that he'd saved *him* from a beating counted for something. He took the coins without counting them. 'Piss off back to your mates. And keep yourself to yourself, eh?'

'Yes, sir.' Lucius sidled back to his comrades, who were smirking at the tirade he'd had to endure from Tullus.

Sirona's sons appeared a moment later. They hauled the two semi-conscious auxiliaries to the door, rifled through their purses for the fine, and threw them onto the street with a warning not to come back. With customers watching, Tullus pretended to be amused by their late arrival, that he hadn't needed their muscle; in reality, he was annoyed that they hadn't been there. If it hadn't been for Lucius, the incident might have had an entirely different ending.

There was no denying it, thought Tullus. He was no longer getting old. He *was* old. The hateful realisation sent him spiralling into a black mood. He went behind the bar and filled a jug with the finest wine in the house, a full-bodied Alban. Sirona watched, stony-faced, as he stamped his way to the office and closed the door behind him.

There would be trouble with her in the morning, thought Tullus, filling the cup to the brim. He didn't care. 'Bottoms up,' he said to no one, and downed the contents. He filled the cup again. 'Fenestela, where are you?' he muttered.

No one replied.

Tullus threw back another cup. 'Screw you, Fenestela.'

There was no answer.

A black cloud settled on Tullus' shoulders, and he poured himself another generous measure.

PART II

Tullus awoke with a pounding head. The inside of his mouth felt furry and disgusting, as if some vile creature had taken up residence there while he was asleep. Wiping a line of dribble from the side of his mouth, he sat up.

An oath escaped him.

He was on the floor of the office. Judging by the light creeping in through the shutters, he'd been there overnight. Tullus' bleary eyes took in the jug, lying on its side a hand's reach away. He let out another curse, first because it had been a long time since he'd drunk himself to oblivion, second because it was empty. The hair of the dog that bit you is always the best cure, he thought. He considered going to the bar for a refill, but decided against it. Sirona was likely to be in a mood; there was no point antagonising her further.

He clambered to his feet. A wave of nausea swamped him; a cold sweat sprang out on his forehead. Tullus decided it was a good thing that the jug was empty. He took a few moments, then padded to the door and opened it a crack to peer out. Reach the well in the inn's yard unseen by Sirona, and he could make himself some way presentable. He stepped out into the corridor, cursing the creaking hinges, and headed for the back door.

'Did you sleep well?' Sirona's voice – neutral in tone – from behind him.

Tullus half turned. Sirona was framed in the entrance to the bar. 'Not really,' he said, attempting to smile.

'You look like shit.'

'I feel like it too.'

'Aye, well, best get yourself cleaned up. That man – the one I told you about – came back last night. He said he'd return early this morning.'

'What time is it?'

'An hour after dawn.'

Tullus opened the back door, wincing as bright sunlight seared his eyes.

'When you're ready, there's fresh bread for you. Cheese too.'

Tullus muttered his thanks, deciding that Sirona's caring attitude was almost harder to take than her disapproval.

Stables formed two sides of the yard, storage sheds the others. An archway opposite the inn's back door gave onto a muddy lane which communicated with a side street that led to the main thoroughfare. The yard slave, a simpleton bought by Sirona, watched as Tullus tossed the wooden bucket into the well. His mouth opened as Tullus, heaving it first up to the well's brick parapet, emptied the contents over his head.

'Master?' the slave ventured.

'It's a good way to wake yourself up.'

The slave looked none the wiser.

Feeling a fraction more human, Tullus went in search of a clean, dry tunic.

A short time later, Tullus was perched on a stool by the bar. A plate of bread, cheese and hard-boiled eggs sat before him; a jug of water – half empty already – was by his elbow. He'd wanted wine, but had decided against hair of the dog. The identity of the man wanting to see him remained a mystery, but it looked better to be hungover and *sober* rather than hungover and drinking in the morning.

A pressure on his right knee made him look down. Scylax had come searching for scraps. Tullus slipped him a rind of cheese, then the crust from his bread. 'Good boy. That's enough now,' he said.

Scylax remained where he was, tail moving faintly.

Tullus was considering whether to give him more, but was interrupted by a loud rap on the door. The barmaids, one of whom was sweeping the floor and the other stacking clean cups behind the bar, paid no attention. Eager customers always tried their luck in the mornings; the best policy was to not answer their summons. They went away eventually, and as Sirona was fond of saying, came back later if they were thirsty.

Another bang on the door.

The barmaids exchanged a look, and went back to their tasks.

'Tullus! Are you in there?'

It's him – the one who's been looking for me – thought Tullus, not quite recognising the voice. 'See who it is,' he ordered the nearest barmaid, easing off his stool and behind the counter where he could reach his sword. He had no reason to think the visitor wished him ill, but not knowing who or why he was being sought out made him feel a little uneasy.

'You're a hard man to track down,' said the man who entered.

Tullus squinted to see better, and laughed. 'Vinicius, you dog!' He came out from behind the bar at once. 'It's been too long, my friend.'

Egg-headed, almost bald, short and stumpy-legged, Vinicius had not been a natural officer candidate, but his sheer determination had seen him turn into a better soldier than most men twice his size. By the time Vinicius had retired from the Fifth – a year before Tullus – he'd been an optio in the same cohort. The two had got along well.

They shook hands, and then, laughing, embraced.

Tullus took a step back and appraised Vinicius. 'You're perhaps a bit thicker around the middle, but apart from that and the beard, the same man.'

'You seem no different, sir,' said Vinicius, but his lips were twitching.

'Aye, I know. I look like I spent the night carousing.'

'It wouldn't be for me to say, sir.'

'Diplomatic as ever, Vinicius.' Tullus' resolve not to drink had vanished. 'Some wine?'

'I wouldn't say no, sir.'

Cups filled, they drank a toast to their fallen comrades.

'Fenestela all right, sir?'

'Last I saw him, aye,' said Tullus. He wasn't going to mention the argument he'd had with his old optio. They'd both been drunk, and the next day, *he* had been too proud to go and make amends. It seemed Fenestela felt the same way, for Tullus hadn't seen him in the month since. Wanting to change the subject, he pinned Vinicius with a stare. 'What brings you to my door?'

'I have a business proposition, sir.'

Tullus thought of the slippery wine merchant and obsequious builder with whom he'd trusted his coin and shook his head. 'You've come to the wrong man.' Vinicius looked confused, and he explained a little.

Vinicius smiled. 'Ah, not that type of business, sir. I'm talking about our line of work.' He mimed a sword thrust with his right fist.

Tullus felt a tiny thrill. 'Is that so?'

Vinicius grinned. 'Civilian life isn't for me, sir.'

'Not sure it is for me either,' said Tullus ruefully. If he didn't start avoiding confrontation, fights like the one he'd had the day before would begin to have unhappy endings. 'You didn't say what you've been doing since I saw you last.'

'Like so many after their discharge, sir, I drank myself stupid for a month, and spent too much money on whores. Truth be told, I was at a loss. I'm no farmer or craftsman. Haven't got a wife to tell me what to do either.' Vinicius looked embarrassed. 'Not saying yours does, sir. When the chance to serve as a guard for a merchant came my way, I thought it was worth a try.'

'You've been going over the river and back?' Good numbers of veterans did the same, providing security to traders who ventured into Germania in search of furs, amber, and slaves.

'Much further than that, sir. The lands near the Rhenus are too close, you see. Every man who's ever held a sword or spear seeks employment as a guard, so the pay's not that good. If I was going to risk my skin, I decided, I needed to be suitably recompensed.' Vinicius lowered his voice. 'I've been sailing to the land of the Venedi, sir. Know where that is?'

'They live to the north or north-east of the German tribes we fought, beyond the River Albis, don't they?' It was a great deal further than Tullus had ever been.

'Aye, that's right, sir. It's close to where electrum can be found.' Electrum was the name given to amber.

'Meaning it is cheap.' In a fit of extravagance, Tullus had once bought Sirona an amber necklace that had cost the equivalent of three months' pay. In Rome, the piece would have fetched many times what he'd paid.

'Exactly, sir.' Eyes gleaming, Vinicius laid a lump of blood-red amber the size of a man's fist on the counter. 'I can sell that for a fortune. The furs that can be bought there are of finer quality too, and you can sometimes find ones from the giant snow bears that live far to the north.'

Tullus examined the amber with interest. 'The voyage must be dangerous, or else everyone would do it.'

'I won't lie to you, sir. It is – but I've done it twice now, and lived to tell the tale. Made a tidy sum.' A wink. 'You could do the same as me, and buy your own amber to carry back.'

'I have no need of coin.'

Vinicius looked a little abashed, but he said quickly, 'What about the comradeship, sir? I'd wager you miss *that*.'

Tullus didn't answer but Vinicius had hit the nail on the head. Unwilling to agree to something so fast, however, he eyed the former optio, noticing the not-quite-healed scab on his left cheek. Tullus put two and two together, and said, 'You suffered a lot of casualties on the last trip. That's the reason you're here.'

Vinicius held up his hands. 'Aye, sir. I need quite a few replacements. It goes without saying that I want good men, and they don't come much better than you.'

Tullus waved a dismissive hand, but he was pleased by the praise, nonetheless. He took a sup of wine, and catching Sirona's curious eye from down the bar, gave her a smile. Gods, but she won't be happy, he thought.

It didn't change his mind.

He turned back to Vinicius, and asked, 'How many men exactly?'

In the event, Sirona didn't lose her temper, nor even evict him from their bed. Instead her eyes filled with tears and she whispered, 'I knew this day would come.' When Tullus, guilty that he'd upset her, took her hand, she managed a smile and said, 'You must go. Serving wine and heaving drunks out the door is not in your nature.'

'And the risks?' asked Tullus softly.

A tear rolled down her cheek, but her voice was firm as she said, 'They are what they are. Go, Tullus, with my blessing.'

This was why he loved her, thought Tullus, wrapping Sirona in his arms. She was content to let him be himself, no matter the consequences.

Artio was less understanding.

'What do you mean, you've got to go?' Delivered in a scream, it turned every head in the inn.

'Shhh,' said Tullus, wishing he'd broached the subject in the family's quarters rather than in the bar.

Artio gave no sign of having heard. 'Why do you have to go?' she cried. 'Why? It's not for the money. You have enough, and so does

Mother – you've said so.' She glared at him, her chin wobbling.

'You're right, it's not about coin. It's difficult to explain.' Tullus struggled for the words. He looked at her face, full of outrage and hurt, and thought: tell her the truth. 'I miss it,' he said.

Her brow wrinkled. 'Miss what?'

'I miss army life, and the comradeship.' The combat too, he thought.

'What about us? We're your family.'

Tullus took her hand. 'You are, you and Mother, and I love you both. It's not the same, though.'

Her chin shot out. 'We're not good enough, is it?'

'No,' said Tullus, squeezing her hand. 'No. It's different.'

'How? I don't understand.'

At a loss how to explain it better, Tullus said, 'You will when you're older.'

'I hate you!' Ripping free her hand, Artio fled. Her feet pounded the stairs to the first floor; a moment later, her door slammed.

Tullus sighed.

Sirona had been watching. 'You'd better come back, or she'll be cursing your shade for the rest of her life.'

Tullus pulled a smile, but he was thinking of what Vinicius had told him. Between dangerous tides and uncertain weather, barely navigable waterways and islands populated by hostile tribes, the voyage alone would be as dangerous as any march he'd ever made. The Venedi trading settlements sounded little better – wild, lawless places where scores of eyes watched every amber transaction. There would be no legion behind him either – the ship owned by Vinicius' employer held fifty men, of whom thirty-four were German crew. Although they would fight if needs be, they were no legionaries. It'll be sixteen of us, thought Tullus grimly, against all the savages of the east.

'You will return?' Sirona's question was part plea, part threat.

'For you, my love, I would walk across Hades,' said Tullus, thinking, *that* might be the easier task. And yet, despite the terrible danger he was about to put himself in, he felt a growing excitement – a joy, even, that he hadn't felt in years.

Vinicius had rounded up seven men who'd served in his century, making eight, and leaving Tullus to find the same number. Fenestela was top of his list, naturally, which meant that their quarrel had to be laid to rest. Armed with a small amphora of the good Alban he'd got pissed on the night of the brawl, he made his way through the settlement the next morning. His destination was the little house Fenestela had lived in since leaving the Fifth. A ramshackle structure on a quiet street, it screamed 'unmarried veteran'. It was years since the walls had seen any limewash, and the thatch was in bad need of repair. The front door hung askew, and from the reek, Fenestela was in the habit of emptying his chamber pot right outside.

Taking care where he placed his boots, Tullus stepped up to the door.

'Read your future, sir?' The voice came from behind him.

Tullus half turned, and found a portly soothsayer regarding him from the house opposite. Recognisable thanks to his blunt-peaked hat, he was a better-fed specimen than many of his type, but his piggy eyes were as sharp as every single haruspex Tullus had ever come across.

'Six asses, and I'll kill a hen, read its entrails for you. Men round here swear by my readings.'

'No.' Tullus turned his back. He had no love for soothsayers, who were liars and charlatans, every last one of them. Remembering the mad-eyed figure who had foretold Arminius' ambush fifteen years before it took place, he corrected himself. Not all were tricksters. He had no wish to discover which category this one fell into. If something bad was going to happen on the voyage, he didn't want to know. And, he decided, rapping on the door with his knuckles, if his optio was with him, nothing would go wrong. Fenestela had been with him through thick and thin.

He tried again. 'Are you in there?'

A long silence.

'Four asses,' called the soothsayer, 'just because you're a friend of my neighbour.'

Tullus ignored him. 'Fenestela?'

'I'm not here. Piss off.'

Smiling, Tullus pulled wide the door and stepped inside. He coughed, the acrid smell of sweat, animals and wood fire clawing the back of his throat. As his eyes adjusted to the gloom, he made out Fenestela sitting on a stool by the hearth, three dogs by his feet.

'There you are.'

'Here I am.' Fenestela didn't turn his head. 'The soothsayer trying to con you?'

'Trying,' said Tullus. He hesitated, unsure how to break the ice further.

'Come to apologise, have you?'

Startled and a little annoyed, Tullus bit back the word 'sir', or an even sharper response. He took a breath, then said, 'Aye, I have.'

Fenestela twisted around, a disbelieving look creasing his ugly features. 'By all the gods, I never thought I'd see the day.'

The last of Tullus' bad temper vanished. 'It was a stupid argument – Hades, I can't even remember how it began – and I'm sorry. You're my oldest friend, Fenestela. What say we end this stupidity?' He held out the amphora. 'A peace offering.'

Fenestela got up with a scowl; he smiled his crooked smile. 'To be truthful, I've been of a mind to seek you out and say the same. You're a bigger man to have come first.' He stepped forward and thrust out his hand. 'Friends.'

'Friends.' Tullus' throat had a tightness to it that hadn't been there a heartbeat before.

True to form, Fenestela rowed in with him the instant Vinicius' voyage was mentioned. 'Just try and leave me behind,' he'd threatened.

Tullus' next instinct would have been to take the handful of men from his original century in the Eighteenth, reliable characters such as Metilius and the jovial Dulcius. More than a decade younger than he and Fenestela, however, they were all still serving. There was no question of leave, for the journey would take upwards of two months. They therefore needed veterans, men who were still able-bodied, and who could handle themselves in a tight corner. Sad to say, men like these were harder to find than one might have thought in a settlement inhabited by those who'd spent a lifetime in the legions. Many men never fully emerged from the initial drinking binge mentioned by Vinicius. A good proportion of the regulars at the Ox and Plough drank and talked about army life, and did little else.

Tullus and Fenestela bandied a few names about without success.

'D'you know a stretcher-bearer by the name of Lucius?' Tullus asked, remembering the man who'd saved him from the auxiliary. Not only was he able to handle himself – he had medical training, which might prove invaluable.

Fenestela shook his head.

'We'll ask him first,' said Tullus.

Lucius jumped at Tullus' offer. He also vouched for his friend, the green-eyed, amiable veteran who went by the nickname of Smiler. That was easier to remember than his name of Vibius Manlius Mus, Tullus declared, and Smiler hadn't argued. A third comrade Lucius swore by was Eurysaces, the stocky, white-bearded man who'd been at the table when the uproar over Lucius' burn had begun. A scion of a famous baking family from Rome, as he explained, he'd joined the legions to escape the boredom of standing by hot ovens for the rest of his life. Born left-handed, he had been forced by his centurion to learn to use a sword with his right. 'Been regretting my decision for a quarter of a century, sir,' he quipped. 'No one minds how a baker holds his paddle.'

His companions groaned that if they'd heard this once, they had heard it a thousand times and Tullus thought: Eurysaces and Smiler are the jokers. They'll keep spirits up if needs be. The last of their group was a strongly built, brown-eyed veteran by the name of Magnus, whom Tullus thought he had met before. A long cicatrice on his right forearm was matched by a jagged scar over his left eye. The latter had not been sustained in a battle, Eurysaces was quick to reveal, but in a tavern brawl. 'Amazing how deep a piece of broken pottery can cut, sir,' he'd chortled as Magnus eyed Tullus, wary of his reaction. He'd grinned with delight at Tullus' declaration that as long as he never started a fight in the Ox and Plough, he was welcome to join their venture.

Tullus found two more men in the restaurant that served his favourite lamb stew. Calling in with Fenestela after their meeting with Lucius and his comrades, he recognised the pair who'd been making fun of one another the day he'd walked by. Never one for prevaricating, Tullus left Fenestela to order the food, and walked along the counter towards them.

Cato, the man with the unusual arm tattoo, was a couple of inches taller than Tullus, and more heavily muscled. Despite being shorter, his friend the bear-catcher was also in good physical shape. Both capable men, Tullus decided, who had not gone to seed after their discharge. He coughed to get their attention.

Cato ignored him. Bear looked around. 'Can I help you, friend?'

'You're both veterans?'

'Aye. Like you, clearly.' Bear showed no sign of knowing who Tullus was. If Cato did, he wasn't letting on either.

'I was a centurion in the Fifth.' Tullus wasn't a man to sing his own praises; he said nothing more about his past. 'The stew is good here,' he said, indicating the bowls in front of the pair.

'That why you came in?' asked Bear. A heartbeat later, he added, 'Sir.'

The delay had made Cato's lips twitch, and Tullus felt a flicker of irritation. Calm, he told himself. We're none of us in the legion any longer, and they don't know me from a steaming pile of horse shit. 'Aye. It's the best stew in the settlement.'

'You didn't seek us out to talk about food,' said Cato. There was no 'sir'.

'I didn't,' said Tullus. 'You're a plain-talking man. I like that.'

'I don't care what you like or don't like. Say your piece and piss off.' Cato jerked his head at the door.

If it came to a fight, Tullus wondered who would come out on top. He'd have his work cut out toppling Cato, who reminded him of an oak tree. Still, he thought, a quick sideways stamp would break the big man's knee before he had a chance to step away from the counter. If that didn't work, well, he'd have to hope that Fenestela bettered Bear and came to his aid. 'Very well.' He jingled his purse. 'Are either of you looking for work?'

'Depends,' said Bear. 'What kind?'

'The dangerous kind,' said Tullus.

'It's well paid.' Fenestela appeared by his side.

'Let me guess. You were his optio,' Cato growled.

Tullus chuckled as Fenestela muttered, 'Is it that obvious?'

The pair listened as Tullus quietly explained the details of the voyage.

'If we sign up, do we have to call you "sir"?' Cato's eyes glittered.

Seize the bull by the horns now, thought Tullus, or he would never have any authority. 'I'll be in charge, so yes, you do.'

Cato and Bear exchanged a look.

'I'm not sure,' began Cato.

'D'you pricks not know who this man is?' hissed Fenestela. 'He dragged fifteen of his men, me included, out of the hell that was the Saltus Teutobergiensis.'

Bear's eyes widened. 'You're *the* Tullus? From the Eighteenth?'
Tullus nodded.

Bear stuck out his hand. 'I'm Lamia, sir. It's an honour to meet you.'
They shook, then Tullus glanced at Cato.

'Shake his hand, Cato, you big ox,' said Bear.

'Few men could have done what you did,' said Cato, shoving forward a great paw. 'Sir.'

Dark memories scourged Tullus as he took the grip. 'I looked after my boys, same as anyone would have done. Do your bit, obey orders, and I'll take care of you on this trip too. We should all come back rich men.'

'Shall we drink to that?' Fenestela clicked his fingers to gain the attention of the proprietor, a rotund German who looked as if he ate as much food as he sold.

'Aye,' said Tullus. 'And this afternoon, we'll have a session on the training ground.' He felt Cato's and Bear's eyes on him, and added with a shrug, 'Only a fool doesn't ride a horse before he buys it. I want to see if you and the rest can still handle a sword and shield.'

PART III

At the mouth of the Flevo Lacus

Three days later, Tullus was standing at the prow of a lean, low-in-the-water ship; he was peering at the open sea. Complete cloud cover had rendered the junction between sky and water into a blurred, grey-blue line. A light wind issued from the west. Waves lapped off the hull; every dozen heartbeats, the oars struck the water behind him. Tullus was glad no one could see his face; try as he might to appear otherwise, he wasn't happy about leaving the protection of the Flevo Lacus behind.

Their voyage thus far, down the fast-flowing Rhenus, had been swift and easy, but once the vessel entered the German Sea, it would be at the mercy of the weather. That was controlled by the gods, fickle at the best of times. During Germanicus' campaigns, hundreds of legionaries sent to Germania by ship had drowned; Tullus counted himself fortunate to have marched to meet the enemy. But now *it's my turn*, he thought, rubbing his phallus amulet and throwing up a prayer to his old nemesis, Fortuna, the goddess of luck. *Be good to me on this voyage*, he prayed, *and I'll be good to you*. He asked the same of Neptunus, god of the sea.

Dressed in one of his old tunics, he was wearing his metalled belt, sword and dagger again. Wrapped in an oiled cloth, safe from the salty air, his mail shirt lay amongst the other gear at the base of the mast: the stacked, leather-covered shields, helmets, pots, pans and blankets.

'We need to pick up speed; the open water is close. Put your backs into it, curse you,' shouted the captain. 'Row!'

Tullus watched as the German crewmen – along with six of his men – responded, digging their oars deep. The ship wasn't big – with twenty oars a side, it was less than half the size of a trireme. The rowers on their benches took up most of the space. A narrow space down

409

the centre of the vessel had been covered in planking; this served as a walkway from prow to stern.

'Belly all right?' Fenestela had come to join him.

'So far, aye, but I'm not so sure how I'll fare once we get out there. What about you?'

Fenestela gave a resigned shrug. 'I'll be spewing soon enough.'

'And the men?'

'Most listened to your advice, and ate little. Not Bear. He insists nothing can upset his stomach. Eurysaces is taking bets that he'll be puking same as everyone else.'

Tullus chuckled.

'Making sure the sea is clear of danger?' The high-pitched nasal voice belonged to Azmelqart, the oily-mannered Phoenician merchant in whose pay Tullus now found himself.

'No. I was talking about who'll be vomiting and who won't when we leave the Flevo Lacus.'

Tullus had disliked Azmelqart from the first moment he'd set eyes on the conical-hat-wearing, slope-shouldered, money-grabbing wretch. In the three days since they had first met, his opinion hadn't changed. 'I wouldn't trust him as far as I could throw him,' he'd said to Vinicius, who'd laughed and said that every Phoenician was the same. Azmelqart was all right, he declared, as long as you let him know where things stood from the start. Tullus stared at the merchant. 'There won't be any pirates round here – our patrol vessels see to that. It's one or two days' sail from here that the danger begins. You know that as well as I do.'

'I was just making conversation, being friendly.' Azmelqart's teeth were yellow and pointed, like a rat's. 'If the gods are kind, our voyage will be peaceful. I have known it to be so.'

Not on the last trip, Tullus wanted to say, thinking of Vinicius' tales of how his men had been lost. There was no point in tempting Fortuna, however, so he said, 'Well, if it's not, me and my boys will be ready.'

'They can fight?' asked Azmelqart, smoothing down his long, straight woollen singlet. He didn't appear to carry a weapon, although Vinicius said there was a dagger secreted in one leg of his knee-length breeches.

'Aye,' said Tullus. 'Be sure of that.' The training session he had organised on the parade ground – permission granted after he'd had a word with an old centurion friend in the Fifth – had been most rewarding. The men he had chosen, Lucius, Eurysaces, Smiler, Bear, Cato and Magnus were good fighters. He judged the last four to be very dangerous, the kind of soldiers Tullus wanted at his back if needs be. As it turned out, he had met Magnus and also Smiler more than a decade before, during the war of the Batos in Illyricum. They had proved themselves during the brutal siege of Raetinum. Vinicius' veterans seemed of similar quality: old comrades, some a little long in the tooth, but hard as the hobs on the soles of their sandals.

'Good,' said Azmelqart. 'That's good.'

He no more thinks we'll have a trouble-free voyage than he does I'm a dancing girl, thought Tullus. There was nothing more to be said, however. Everyone aboard knew what he'd signed up for.

Like as not, some would not be returning to Vetera.

Hidden in among the sand dunes, a hundred paces from the beached ship, Tullus pulled his cloak tighter round his shoulders, and inched the toes of his boots a little nearer to the small fire. A blackened pot hung low over the flames from an iron tripod. Fenestela was squatting on his haunches, the better to stir the broth simmering in the pot. He noticed what Tullus was doing, and said, 'Spring comes late to these parts.'

'Aye. It wouldn't surprise me if there's a frost.'

Fenestela's eyes followed Tullus' round the little group of tents. 'It's good you insisted on the military ones,' he said.

'He's a typical Phoenician, isn't he, trying to have us buy on the cheap.' Azmelqart had balked at the price for the eight-man goatskin tents – those used by every legionary in the empire – but Tullus had been having none of it. 'Soldiers have to be cared for,' he'd said. Spotting the disbelieving look in Azmelqart's eyes, he had added cynically, 'Think of them as beasts of burden. Would you deny a stable to a horse in bad weather?'

Azmelqart had given in with bad grace. Perhaps because he could see more direct use from their purchase, he had not argued over the list of weapons and equipment that Tullus had also presented him with before their departure. Every veteran had his own kit, but naturally enough, most had needed a few bits and pieces. The German crewmen had been badly armed with a selection of old spears and a few axes;

Vinicius related how he'd tried several times to have Azmelqart pay for better equipment, but to no avail.

Tullus had immediately seen the entire crew supplied with decent shields, helmets and spears. To his surprise, the Phoenician hadn't protested, but questioned why he hadn't armed them like his legionaries. Because it would have been a waste of time and money, Tullus had explained. German tribesmen fought like Roman scouts. Lightly armed, wearing no armour, they were fast-moving, deadly troops – 'And I should know,' he'd added.

Azmelqart knew enough about his past not to probe further.

Tullus' belly rumbled, and he eyed the pot. 'Is it nearly ready?'

'Almost.'

'I'll go and check on the sentries.'

Fenestela saluted him with his spoon.

Tullus didn't just want to patrol the camp's perimeter. He'd seen Azmelqart emerge from his tent, and head in their direction. The less time he had to spend with the man, he decided, the better. Spotting Vinicius returning from the latrine trench, he waved him over. 'Walk with me.'

'Happy, sir?' asked Vinicius.

'As I can be.' It wasn't far to the freshly built rampart, little more than sand piled the height of a man, tamped down with sandals and shovels. Beyond it lay a ditch, the spoil from which had provided the wherewithal for the rampart. Tiny in comparison to even a cohort-sized marching camp, it nonetheless provided the same protection to its fifty inhabitants. He cast a sideways look at Vinicius, and asked, 'Have your lot stopped grumbling?'

'Oh aye, sir. Realising that you'd ordered the Germans to dig as well silenced most of the whingers. The rest had shut up by the time they saw the wisdom in sleeping behind a wall that sentries are patrolling.'

'Funny how a few years of civilian life makes a man forget what's good for him.' Tullus had had much the same experience with his veterans; Cato had been the unhappiest, muttering under his breath and only kept in line by Bear.

Vinicius snorted, and tugged at his mail shirt. 'It's not the only thing a man forgets. This bastard weighs twice as much as it used to, I swear.'

'I'm with you there,' said Tullus, smiling. 'That won't stop me from sleeping in mine.' He clambered onto the rampart, then gave Vinicius a hand up.

A sentry stood at each corner, and another pair walked around the entire perimeter, checking on the others. Every hour or so, the two patrollers would change places with men on the corners. It was early yet, so Tullus didn't expect to find anyone dozing – that would come later. Like as not, it would be one of the Germans – men who didn't have the memory of comrades being beaten to death for such an offence. He didn't much care who it was; they would get the hiding of their lives.

The first sentry was Smiler, who grinned and reported he'd heard and seen nothing. The next was Eurysaces, who said he was bored and asked if he could start singing. 'Joke, sir,' he said as Tullus glared and told him no, he couldn't. Magnus was the most alert, barely taking his eyes off the murk over the rampart when Tullus greeted him. He had nothing to report, however.

A couple of Germans were next. Dour, bearded men in patterned trousers, they seemed alert enough. The men patrolling the rampart were Bear and Cato. Bear had passed them once already, and soon emerged again from the gloom. There was no sign of Cato, and when Tullus asked, Bear shrugged and said he was on the side facing away from the sea – the last one Tullus and Vinicius would reach.

'Cato's a troublemaker, sir, or I've never seen one,' said Vinicius as Bear walked off.

'The man's headstrong, that's certain, but I think he's a good soldier. He just needs to know who's in charge.' Ten years before, even five, Tullus would have engineered a confrontation with Cato, and beaten the shit out of him. The recent brawl at the inn had rammed home the unpleasant truth that he could no longer be certain of winning, which meant he had first to intimidate Cato – so he didn't cause trouble – and then win his respect another way.

The initial part of the solution was simple. Sending Vinicius off to approach the big veteran from the other side, Tullus slid forward on cat-soft feet. He had closed with Cato before the other had time to react. With Tullus' right foot behind both of his, and a strong arm sweeping backward, he could do nothing but tumble backwards into the camp. It wasn't a big fall; cursing, he was half up by the time Tullus had leaped down to join him, and tugging on his sword.

'I wouldn't do that.' From nowhere, the tip of Vinicius' sword appeared under Cato's chin.

Cato's furious eyes darted from Tullus to Vinicius and back again, but he had the sense not to move. 'What was that for, *sir*?' Anger dripped from the last word.

'You're the one who wasn't following orders,' said Tullus, a hand on his dagger. 'You were supposed to be patrolling the entire walkway.'

'Fucking waste of time,' muttered Cato.

Tullus shoved his face into the big man's. 'Sir.'

Cato frowned.

'Feel that?' said Tullus with a quick movement of his left hand. 'That's my dagger at your balls. You will call me "sir" from now on, or I'll geld you right here and now.'

'You wouldn't dare.'

'Try me.' Tullus pushed, so that the tip pressed into Cato's groin. 'I've done it before, to bigger men.'

'Sir.' Cato spoke from between clenched teeth.

'That's better,' said Tullus. 'Now, get up on that rampart and do what you were told earlier, or me and Vinicius here will have to beat the shit out of you as well.'

'Yes, sir.'

'You've made an enemy,' said Vinicius as Cato vanished into the darkness.

'It had to be done. You know what it's like when a man won't do what he's told. Indiscipline spreads, like rot in a barrel of apples.'

'True,' said Vinicius. 'We'll need to keep an eye on Cato, though, until you can win him over, and that might be easier said than done.'

Tullus gave him a clout. 'Gods, this is like the old days!'

The next morning was crisp and cold. A rime of frost coated the tents; men's breath plumed in front of their faces, and the short grass crunched underfoot. Tullus had slept with an unsheathed dagger under the rolled cloak that served as his pillow; noticing the black glances Cato was throwing in his direction, he judged it to have been a wise move. Perhaps Vinicius had been right, he thought. The last thing he needed was to have a dangerous man who might do him harm. Fortuna, he prayed, give me a chance to make the bastard see sense.

The early chill was a presage of things to come. Thick banks of fog covered the coastline. With the danger of running aground very real, the captain was forced to have the oarsmen row at snail speed. Perched in the prow with a weighted line, he spent the voyage checking the water's depth and peering into the murk. Concerned that disaster would strike despite his best attempts, he persuaded Azmelqart to call a halt after only a few hours. Beaching the ship on a stone-shingled beach, they set up camp on a flattish area close to the edge of a scrubby forest. There was fallen timber aplenty, but even the best of it was damp, which meant no fires. The men's mood was subdued, Germans and Romans both, and plenty of resentful looks were thrown Tullus' way as he supervised the construction of a fresh temporary camp. They didn't affect him – decades in the legion had given him a thick skin – but he became aware of something else, a tickle between his shoulder blades. It felt as if he were being watched. He told himself it was nothing.

Advising Vinicius to see to his men, Tullus went to do the same with his. Morale was vital. During the carnage of Arminius' ambush, he had somehow kept his soldiers' spirits from falling into the abyss. They weren't in that kind of situation now, and he had no reason to think things would get that bad, but it didn't hurt to ensure that they were as happy as the situation would allow.

Picking up a shovel, he helped finish off the section of ditch and rampart his men were working on. Cato scowled at him, but the rest gave him welcoming, surprised grins or nods. It didn't take long – they'd left the legions, but none had forgotten the routine. Tamping part of the top of the 'wall', formed by the spoil from the ditch, Tullus pronounced, 'Fine work, boys.'

'In fairness, it's been a few years since I could have been called a boy, sir,' said Eurysaces.

'And me,' said Magnus, rubbing his bald head.

There was a general rumble of amusement.

'I'm in the same boat as you lot,' admitted Tullus with a rueful grin. 'But you've done a good job, all of you. There'll be an extra issue of wine with the evening meal.'

Satisfied by their pleased faces, he walked the camp perimeter, staring into the enveloping wall of fog, wishing he could see further. He went to check on the ship, some hundred and fifty paces away, and the four sentries he'd left to guard it. They had nothing to report, but that didn't stop Tullus taking up a position by the vessel, listening. Water lapped quietly off the planking; from somewhere out on the water came the lonely call of a sea bird. Giving the sentries a confident smile, he left them to it.

The uncomfortable feeling between his shoulder blades returned as he walked back to the camp. He could have led out a patrol but with such poor visibility, he had little chance of finding anyone who might be spying on them. It was far more likely that he would get lost or even lose a couple of men. No, he decided, it was better to sit tight and stay alert. The morning would bring clear skies, gods willing, and they would resume their voyage.

Not-completely-stale bread, cheese and cured ham formed a decent enough meal with Fenestela and Vinicius a short time later. They drank watered-down wine – cautious to the last, Tullus had diluted it more than usual – and discussed their situation. The other two made no mention of feeling uneasy, and he again told himself not to be concerned. Although Vinicius had made the voyage before, he didn't know the inlet they had found themselves in. That they were in Frisii territory, or perhaps that of the Chauci, was the extent of his knowledge.

'Which would be worse?' asked Fenestela sourly. Both the Frisii and Chauci had been allied to Rome up to and during Germanicus' campaigns. Now, with Roman influence east of the Rhenus limited to patrols from the western bank, there was no reason for either tribe to keep faith.

He and Tullus looked at Vinicius.

'Hard to say. Most contact we've had with them has been civil enough, in the main because we've been well-armed. If there was a war band keen for plunder, however, I wouldn't put it past them to attack us.' Vinicius' shoulders went up and down in a 'There's nothing we can do about that' shrug.

Fenestela spat.

'It's no different to how it was ten years ago, really,' said Tullus cynically. 'Those German bastards can't be trusted one bit.'

'We'd better come back rich men, you whoreson.' It was hard to tell whether Fenestela was joking or threatening.

'Of course we will,' said Vinicius, but he didn't sound as confident as he had in Vetera.

The hairs on the back of Tullus' neck prickled, and he stared around the camp. It was quieter than usual – he told himself that the poor visibility made men talk in low voices. The fog was still heavy: he couldn't even see the just-built wall. Closer to hand, the tents were large black shapes. Wraiths – legionaries and German crewmen – materialised now and again out of the gloom, going about their business.

Despite the mist, everything was as it should be, Tullus decided.

The hours dragged by, but eventually the daylight, such as it was, began to ebb. The sun was falling. Night, and after it, a new day, couldn't come too soon for Tullus. He'd had to stop tramping the camp perimeter, because, as Fenestela said quietly, the men would sense his unease. In the end, he had done something that would have been unthinkable in the legions, and taken a nap. It was not a pleasant one. For the first time in many months, he relived the horror that had been the Saltus Teutobergiensis. Mud, endless mud. Low clouds, heavy rain. Unearthly chanting from the trees – the German barritus, or war chant. Spears scudding in from nowhere, felling his legionaries, leaching their courage. Limb-sucking, mule-drowning mud. A tree blocking the track. Naked berserkers, killing his men.

A hand grabbed his shoulder, and Tullus came awake with a cry. Grabbing for his dagger, he realised Fenestela was crouched over him, not a German tribesman. 'What is it?' demanded Tullus, more sharply than he intended.

'You were shouting.' Fenestela's expression was understanding.

Tullus rubbed a hand across his eyes, grateful that he didn't feel judged, or need to explain. Like as not, Fenestela suffered nightmares too. He heaved himself to a sitting position. 'Is all well?'

'Aye. It's full dark now, maybe even getting on for midnight.'

He'd been out for hours, thought Tullus. There'd be no getting back to sleep now. 'Anything to report?'

'The fog seems to be lifting a little.' Fenestela unclipped his scabbard from his baldric and sat down on his blanket. 'I've just been around the sentries, who are all alert.'

'Even Cato?'

An amused snort. 'Aye, even him.'

Tullus moved from one foot to the other, trying to get warm. His cloak covered his torso; its ends could also wrap around his arms, but his legs were exposed from the knee down. He'd been constantly on the move around the rampart, but a chill had still settled in his leg bones. A fire would have chased it away, but there wasn't one to be had this night. The only thing to be done was to shift about as he was, and wait for dawn.

He was standing close to Smiler and Magnus, who were from the same part of Italy. They had passed an enjoyable hour reminiscing, and chuckling at how neither had been back to their village since joining the legions.

'I always thought I'd head straight home once my time was up,' said Smiler. 'But once I'd done the decent thing and married my woman, there didn't seem much point. My children are Roman, there's no question of that – two are in the Fifth – but they're not Italian.'

'Aye, and mine,' said Magnus. 'You got any family, sir?'

'A daughter,' said Tullus, thinking of Artio with a pang. 'She'll never want to live in Italy, though. As for my parents, they're long dead, and I haven't seen my sisters for more than twenty years. Never met their husbands or children either. Gods, they could be dead for all I know.' The thought was sobering. He would write a letter to his eldest sister upon his return, Tullus decided. Even if they were never reunited, it would be good to re-establish contact.

'The ship, sir.' Smiler pointed.

Tullus stared out over the rampart. Moved by a slight breeze, the fog had thinned considerably. Tendrils of it clung to the branches of the nearby oaks, and threads yet coated the ground, but, for the first time since their arrival, he could make out the ship. One, two, three sentries, Tullus counted. He searched the shadows around the hull, and along the shingle to either side, but could not see the fourth man. He's gone for a piss in the trees, thought Tullus. He didn't like it.

'Hades, sir, look.'

Noting the tremor in Smiler's voice, Tullus forgot about the missing sentry and turned his gaze to the right.

'What's that, sir?' Magnus pointed.

There was something hanging from a thick bough on an old beech. Tullus squinted, realised, and his gorge rose. 'It's a man.' The sentry, his inner voice cried, but he didn't let himself panic. The chances of the sentry having been slain and hung from the tree – a Germanic religious ritual – in a few short hours was tiny. Tullus studied the clearing in which the gruesome offering was hanging and made out two more rope-swinging corpses. A great flat stone lay in the centre. His skin crawled. 'That's where the local tribe sacrifice to their gods,' he whispered.

'And we've camped beside it.' Smiler swore.

Magnus muttered a prayer.

Tullus wasn't happy either; a better way to anger the local tribe's gods he couldn't think of.

'What shall we do, sir?' From nowhere, Bear had materialised beside him; he had also seen the grim evidence.

'Not much we can do except wait for the morning, and hope we're not seen,' said Tullus. Setting to sea in the dark would be madness – the mud flats and narrow passages were hard enough to see in the daylight.

'D'you want me and Cato to take a look over there, sir, and make sure one of their cursed priests isn't lurking about? We'll take off our mail shirts, and move like mice.' Bear's teeth showed white in his beard. He didn't seem remotely worried about wandering into a clearing full of dangling corpses and only the gods knew what else.

Worried about losing more men, Tullus almost refused, but the idea was sound. 'Aye, go on. Take Lucius and Eurysaces too. See if you can find the fourth sentry, and be sure to blacken your faces and arms with mud.'

'Let me go as well, sir,' said Magnus. 'I'm a keen hunter.'

Tullus wavered, but Magnus looked well capable of handling himself. He nodded. 'All right.'

Before long, led by Magnus, the five veterans had emerged from the nearest entrance in the defences. Soon they disappeared among the trees. An owl hooted, perhaps annoyed by their intrusion. The crack from a trodden-on twig carried, seeming as loud as a thunderclap in the virtual silence. Then, nothing. Tullus' guts were tying themselves in knots; he hadn't felt so nervous for years. Running alongside his nerves, however, was the old, familiar thrill that a fight was possible. If that happened, quite how they would get everyone out of the camp and into the ship without being overwhelmed was unclear. So was the other possibility, how the camp might be defended, while simultaneously protecting the ship from being holed or set on fire. Despite these concerns, a long-forgotten part of Tullus had come alive again.

In the event, the five returned unharmed, reporting that they had seen and heard no one. The corpses were days old, backing their assertion that the clearing had not been visited in some time. Relieved, Tullus was also unprepared to take chances. Everyone in the camp was quietly woken, and ordered to strike their tents. When Azmelqart came blustering up to the rampart to complain at being turned out of his blankets, Tullus' inclination was to lay into him with his vitis. This was the man who held the purse strings, however, so he explained his reasoning. Unconvinced, the Phoenician had raised his voice. Angered, Tullus had told him in no uncertain terms that *he*, and he alone, was responsible for the group's safety. 'You pay for the ship and the men's wages, and do what you want with the amber. But if I say we strike camp here and leave at dawn, that's what we'll do,' he'd hissed. 'Do you understand?'

Azmelqart had nodded, but his eyes had been venomous.

'You're doing well,' said Fenestela as the Phoenician stamped off in a temper. 'Two enemies you've made now.'

'Cato's coming around,' said Tullus under his breath. 'Did you not see how pleased he was to be picked to go with Bear?'

With his unease about the corpse-clearing reduced somewhat, his thoughts returned to the fourth sentry. Before he could order a search of the area around the ship, he saw a veteran running towards the camp. His belly tightened.

Spying Tullus, the man cupped a hand to his mouth. 'One of our boys is gone, sir. Vanished!'

Cursing that others had heard, for already unhappy murmurs were spreading between those standing on the defences, Tullus waved the veteran to the closest part of the ditch. 'What's going on?' he called down.

Chest heaving, the man – one of Vinicius' – came to a halt and saluted.

Old habits died hard, thought Tullus wryly.

'He went for a shit, sir. Said he'd be a while. We waited a reasonable time, and then called his name, but there was no answer. We've searched around the ship. Nothing.'

'He's dead,' said Tullus.

'Anywhere else, and I might have disagreed, but beside that hellish grove, I think you're right.' Fenestela glanced over his shoulder.

'Everyone's ready. We should take a quick look for him, and then piss off out of here.'

Tullus nodded, unhappy with the idea of leaving a man behind, but alive to the potential danger. If a priest came to the grove, and saw their camp, slipping away unseen, they'd soon be overwhelmed by a tide of screaming, spear-hurling warriors.

He had lived through that hell enough times never to want to repeat it.

PART IV

They left without finding the sentry. Against his better judgement, Tullus had been considering sending out patrols to look for him, but unexpectedly hearing boys' voices – excited, playing-chase voices – from deep among the trees, had decided the risk was too great. The boys could easily come to the shoreline, and their presence meant a village was nearby. Even a small settlement would have more spears than he had men. Fenestela and Vinicius had not argued with his decision; clearly scared, neither had Azmelqart.

Another man died before they reached the open sea. Leaning out too far when pulling in the anchor, he'd fallen overboard head first. The water wasn't deep – no more than four men's height – but weighed down by his mail, he had sunk like a stone. Lucius, a good swimmer, had shed his own mail shirt and dived in after the unfortunate man, but hampered by the murky waters, had been unable to find him. A sombre air descended at this second loss. Vinicius' veterans, who had now lost another comrade, muttered unhappily to one another. There was none of the usual singing from the German crewmen. Even Azmelqart was affected; sour-faced still from Tullus' dressing down, he had the wit to hold his tongue.

Eager to get away from the ill-fortuned beach, the rowers soon had the ship half a mile out from the coast, a safe distance from the dreaded sand banks and shoals. With the prow to the east and the sail billowing, they bent their backs to the task, letting hard physical labour take their minds from the night's dark events. The fog had disappeared, but the low cloud remained. It was the kind of weather Tullus hated, when a man didn't know where land or sea ended and sky began. There was a backing wind from the west, however, and that meant they could make some distance at last. Wanting to forget the poor bastard who was lying somewhere with a slit throat, or hanging by his neck in the grove, he took a turn on the benches himself.

His presence did not go unnoticed; Smiler it was who cracked the first joke at his expense, something about things being bad when old men had to row. Wise to the importance of a bond between himself and the men, Tullus laughed with the rest. Taking his turn, he jibed at Smiler, who took it in good humour. Not to be outdone, Eurysaces poked fun at Tullus next. He gave back as good as he got. His willingness to take part in the soldiers' banter caught on; soon there were ribald insults being thrown back and forth across the rowing benches. After a time, knowing that someone might grow overconfident and overstep the mark, and also because he was feeling his age, Tullus relinquished his oar to the German he'd taken it from and rejoined Fenestela and Vinicius at the prow. Pleasingly, Azmelqart was at the stern, and as far as Tullus was concerned, there he could stay.

Eurysaces it was who started singing, launching into a rendition of an old familiar marching song. Surprised by his deep, melodic voice, and relishing the tune – he'd heard it hundreds of times over the years, but not that often since leaving the army – Tullus found himself singing along. Encouraged by the veterans' enthusiastic joining in, Eurysaces sang another favourite, and another. The mood lifted, and even the German crewmen looked happier.

Later that day, they passed an isle Vinicius said was Fabaria, 'Bean Island', named by Drusus' legionaries more than a quarter of a century before. Byrchanis to its inhabitants – part of the Frisii tribe – it had seen bitter fighting. Drusus' troops had been victorious, but those glory days were long gone. Alone on the sea, without a fleet of Roman vessels around him, Tullus was grateful to pass the island without seeing any boats.

Fabaria was located a little to the west of the mouth of the River Amisia, which marked the easternmost landing points of Germanicus' ships during his war against Arminius. Rowing past the river's opening, clearly visible on the port side, was a turning point in the voyage for the Romans on board. Only Vinicius had been further east. Asked by Tullus to relate the next part of the journey as he had done before their departure, he explained that the coastline was much the same as that which they had rowed past from the Flevo Lacus.

Flat and featureless, apart from a line of islands – of which Fabaria was one – it had plentiful places to beach a ship. The natives were not to be trusted, Vinicius said. Night attacks on sentries weren't unknown, for example, but nor would they generally attack in daylight if presented with a good show of force. Azmelqart was as shrewd as many of his type, carrying goods to trade with the peoples of this coast. Roman pottery and wine were highly desirable items; so too were the small items of glass- and silverware he'd brought to trade or make a gift of to chieftains.

After several days' voyage, the land turned sharply to the north. A long, narrow peninsula, it would take them to the Pillars of Hercules. Here Vinicius rubbed his phallus amulet to avert evil, and said that they had the same name as the narrowing of the Mare Nostrum between Hispania and Africa, but formed a different opening into a cold sea that led far to the east. Vinicius had never done anything but turned southward, rowing with the same peninsula on his port side; Azmelqart had not travelled east on the cold, wind-prone sea either, but he knew Phoenicians who had. 'Who knows if it's true,' said Vinicius, 'but they say there are lands out there so cold that men wear furs all winter long.'

Tullus shuddered. 'Why would you go to a place like that?'

Vinicius rubbed his right thumb and forefinger together. 'The same reason that men do anything.'

'Coin.' Fenestela made the word sound like poison. 'I didn't join the legions for coin. I didn't fight or bleed for it either.'

'We're here now for coin,' said Tullus, chuckling.

Fenestela scowled. 'Maybe so, but if it comes to fighting, we won't be doing that for the money.'

'It'll be for one another, same as it always was,' agreed Tullus. He glanced at Vinicius. 'Would it not be faster to march across the base of this peninsula and find a ship on the other side? You'd need mules, and a guide and so on, but it could be done.'

'Azmelqart tried it once. A disaster, by all accounts,' said Vinicius. 'They were attacked in the middle of nowhere, and had to turn around well before they'd crossed the cursed thing. It takes far longer to sail around the peninsula, but it's easier overall.' Again, he rubbed his amulet. 'Unless we are hit by a storm or the like.'

'I'm beginning to understand why amber is so expensive,' said Tullus ruefully. 'We're going to be in the shit, one way or another.'

'Might as well stop whingeing and make the best of it,' said Fenestela, finishing the old military saying.

'True enough,' said Tullus, winking at Vinicius, who was also smiling.

Half a month later, and Tullus' good humour had long gone. Although they had rounded the tip of the peninsula without difficulty, they had then weathered not one, but two storms in close succession. The first had torn their not-quickly-enough-reefed sail into flitters, and then tossed them about like a twig for a day and a night. Three men had gone overboard, two German crewmen and a veteran; it had been good fortune that five times that number hadn't been lost. The second storm had not been as severe, but it had swept them out to sea, east, towards the ice-bound wilderness that Vinicius had spoken of. When the winds and waves had finally abated, it had taken several days of rowing to bring the coastline into sight again.

Morale had been low; there had been unhappy mutterings aplenty on the rowing benches. Fights between the veterans and crewmen threatened at every turn. Tullus had managed the situation with a combination of his old tricks, threatening and cajoling the veterans by turn, and making sure they had an issue of wine three times a day. The captain had done the same with the crewmen, and together they had maintained an uneasy peace.

The weather and ill-feeling had not been their only tribulations. A hidden sandbank at the entrance to a bay had seen the ship run aground one afternoon. Luckily, the turning tide at dawn the next morning had brought the water level down to waist height. With every man on board pushing – Azmelqart included – they had managed to free the ship. It had come not a moment too soon. Like wolves who scent an injured deer, the local tribesmen come paddling out from the beach in a score of small craft. Ill-feelings and tensions forgotten, the veterans and German crewmen had rowed like heroes to take the ship beyond the locals' reach.

Low on supplies because of losses overboard and food that had been spoiled with saltwater, they had come ashore a day's voyage to the south of the bay with the sandbank. A spring had seen their water replenished, but the hunting parties sent out returned with little more than a few birds. Bellies rumbling, resentful, they were forced to set to sea again by the arrival on the beach of a pair of youths with fishing nets. Taking to their heels at the sight of the ship, they would like as not have returned with warriors, Tullus had told Azmelqart. To his credit, the Phoenician had not argued.

Reaching a coastal village the next day known to the captain, they had traded some pottery and glassware for a couple of sheep, which were swiftly slaughtered and set to cook over fires. Everyone's spirits had risen to have their hunger addressed, and thirst set right with extra wine. It was obvious to a blind man that a plentiful supply – as Tullus had insisted on before leaving Vetera – was vital at times like this, but that hadn't stopped Azmelqart from having a face like a dried prune as the wine was ladled out for a second and third time. Only Vinicius' intervention had prevented Tullus from punching the Phoenician when he'd come to protest.

'Those men are drinking too much. Remember who's paying you,' Azmelqart had threatened, flashing his rat-point teeth at Tullus like a rodent caught in a corner. 'Me.'

'Why don't *you* think about who will soon prevent you from having your throat slit for the silver in your purse,' Tullus had growled in reply.

Azmelqart's look had been poisonous; he had glared at Vinicius, who, unwilling to go against Tullus, had shrugged. The merchant had then gone to the German crewmen, seeking support, but, happy with their wine and recognising Tullus' leadership – and like as not, his men's handiness with weapons – they had refused to act.

An unpleasant tension existed between Tullus and Azmelqart. It was, thought Tullus, similar to the smell in a latrine block when a sewer blocked up with turds. There would be no flushing the pipes through with a score of buckets of water, though, no clearing of the air. Azmelqart had to be tolerated until they reached their destination – thank the gods, only a day's voyage away – and he did his business. Only then could the ship return to Vetera. Tullus had already decided that he would spend the entire time at the prow, no matter the weather. Azmelqart kept to the shelter of the half-timbered cabin at the stern, and there he could stay.

If avoiding the Phoenician was all he had to worry about between now and seeing Sirona and Artio again, Tullus decided, it was a small price to pay.

*

426

They arrived the following day, rowing in on a calm sea with everyone in a good mood, even Azmelqart. Not a large town by Roman standards, the settlement was nonetheless the largest they had seen since leaving Vetera. It sprawled along the shoreline, a tangle of low buildings surrounded by a palisade. Smoke trickled skyward from a hundred fires; the smell of rotten fish and human waste filled the clammy air. Two rough jetties had been built a short distance apart on the stony beach; at least a score of vessels was tied up along their lengths. More bobbed about in the shallows to either side. The majority seemed to be trading ships, with the rest being small craft used by the locals for fishing. Children played up and down the shore; beside a little stream that issued into the sea, women washed and beat clothes on stones. A greybeard crouched over a fishing net, repairing holes.

'Doesn't look like much,' said Tullus.

'It doesn't.' Somehow Azmelqart had materialised beside him. The Phoenician's eyes were bright. 'Yet the amber and furs here are the best that can be found.'

'How long will you need?' asked Tullus, keeping his tone civil.

'That depends on the amber and furs,' said Azmelqart without rancour.

'And if you were to guess?' Tullus was imagining the difficulties of remaining. Between German crewmen disappearing into the taverns and thieves trying to sneak onto the ship, he would have little rest once they docked.

'Two days, perhaps three.' Azmelqart gave him a hard look. 'We stay until I am happy.'

Tullus returned the stare. 'Or until I am concerned enough to leave.'

'We are not at war. The dangers come from cutpurses and back-alley thieves, not armies,' said Azmelqart with a sneer. He didn't wait for Tullus to answer, instead drawing the captain into a discussion about how much space there was at the stern and between the rowing benches for furs.

Irritated that he had let the merchant get the better of the exchange, Tullus busied himself ensuring that all the veterans knew to don their armour and weapons once the ship was moored. 'I want you ready at all times,' he told them. 'Everyone is to live in his mail shirt until I say so.'

No one argued, not even Cato.

Directed by a squint-eyed man who rowed out to meet the ship – the port's harbour master, he claimed – they tied up at the end of the westernmost jetty. The position pleased Tullus; it would allow a quick departure, should that be necessary.

Azmelqart had clambered onto the rough-hewn planking before the last rope had even been tied. Tullus was ready. 'Cato. Eurysaces. Smiler. Lucius. Bear. Magnus. Fenestela. Onto the dock.'

'Tullus—' Vinicius began.

'What do you think you're doing?' Azmelqart's expression was pained.

'Giving you a decent escort,' said Tullus.

'This is a trading settlement, not an enemy position. If I walk in there with eight men at my back, every lowlife for miles will know about it by nightfall. The assumption will be that I am carrying a vast fortune in silver. If the ship isn't ransacked here, we'll be attacked the first opportunity they have once we set out for home.' Contempt dripped from Azmelqart's voice. He smiled at Tullus, but there was no kindness in it. 'Two men will suffice. You and one other.'

Tullus jerked his chin in stiff acknowledgement; delighted, Azmelqart almost preened himself.

'You weren't to know, sir,' muttered Vinicius. 'I should have told you.'

'Yes, you should,' said Tullus, furious at being made to look the fool in front of the entire crew.

'Who d'you want?' Fenestela asked eagerly.

'You are staying, old friend,' said Tullus. 'I want eyes at the end of the jetty, and enough men on watch in the ship so that nothing gets missed. Not a fisherman setting sail, a woman washing clothes. I even want to know about the fish jumping. Set a duty rota as well. Get in fresh food – meat, if you can, and beer, or whatever piss they have instead of wine. You and Vinicius are in charge until I get back. Clear?'

Fenestela hid his disappointment well. 'Yes, sir.'

'Take me, sir,' said Eurysaces. Several others muttered their desire to go.

'You'll have your turn,' said Tullus, with an approving look. His gaze moved. 'Cato. You're coming with me.'

The big man lumbered over, grinning. 'Expecting trouble, sir?'

'I always expect trouble,' said Tullus so Azmelqart couldn't hear.

'And I'd wager you're a good man to have by my side. Am I right?'

'Aye, sir,' rumbled Cato.

Tullus clapped him on the shoulder, and thought, I'm halfway to winning his loyalty.

Standing behind Azmelqart as he haggled over pieces of rare blue amber, Tullus moved from foot to foot. He'd only had the mail shirt on for an hour, and already his lower back was complaining. How in all the gods' names did I wear it for days on end? he thought. The shame of admitting his discomfort meant that he would rather die than let it be known, so he cast his eyes about, searching for trouble, making sure that no one was paying too much attention to his employer.

The place was a shithole, he concluded. That had been his initial impression at the dock, and it hadn't changed. The unpaved streets were ankle deep in glutinous mud that stank of everything vile under the sun. Worse was to be found in the alleys between the one-storeyed thatched houses: on their journey thus far, he'd spied two dead dogs and what looked very like a human corpse. Busy keeping an eye on Azmelqart, he hadn't had the opportunity to look into any shops, but what he had seen hadn't impressed. Even Vetera, a dump in its early days, had been better than this godsforsaken place.

That the traders of amber weren't from here was clear. Without premises of their own, they squatted on their haunches in every available open space, fur-clad, bearded, uniformly sharp-eyed. Rolled-out blankets were their display cases, handfuls of scattered straw their shop floors. Men with clubs and spears stood behind them as security.

'It's beautiful stuff,' said Cato quietly. 'Look at that piece.'

The seller had heard. With an unerring sense of what possible customers wanted, he held up the irregular piece, which was filled with thousands of tiny bubbles. He said a word in the local language.

Tullus asked him what it was in German, and was gratified to get a response. 'Bony amber,' he said to Cato.

'Aye, sir. I speak German. My mother was Marsi.'

Tullus made a mental note to ask Cato about that when the chance arose. Catching Azmelqart's irritated expression, he waved a hand, no, thank you, at the seller, and gestured that he should continue dealing with the Phoenician.

Collected by hand, on secret beaches far to the east, or fished from the sea, amber was quite an extraordinary substance, thought Tullus. Yellow, orange or brown-coloured for the most part, there were also rare blue varieties, such as the pieces being haggled over by Azmelqart, and dark, almost black types. The 'bony' type had endless variations, but what interested Tullus most were the lumps with insects trapped within. He'd set his heart on buying Artio a piece with a bee in it; one such had been on sale a little way along the street. With luck, an opportunity would arise at some stage to slip away and purchase it. Tullus' heart squeezed; he and Artio had not left on good terms. She would not forgive him for leaving; on the morning of his departure, all he'd got from her hunched form under the blankets was, 'Go away. I hate you.'

He looked down. Azmelqart had finished haggling. The seller set aside five pieces of blue amber, and barked a figure in the local dialect. He held out a calloused hand; into it, Azmelqart carefully counted forty denarii.

'I wonder what he'll sell them for, sir,' said Cato.

'You should do the same with your money,' advised Tullus.

'I wouldn't know what to look for, quality-wise, sir.'

'Ask Vinicius. He's got an eye for the stuff.'

Cato grinned. 'I will, sir.'

'On to the next.' Azmelqart had swept his purchases into his leather bag and stood up.

A loud protest rose from the man he'd just paid. Snarling with rage, he bit into one of the denarii, and shoved it at Azmelqart, screaming words in both German and the local tongue. His heavies laid hands to their weapons. Tullus caught the words 'bad', and 'silver', and intuited what had happened. 'Did you slip him any counterfeits?' he whispered in Azmelqart's ear. The greasy smile he received told him everything. Tullus gave the amber-seller an apologetic smile, and said in German, 'Mistake. A mistake. How many coins are bad?'

'Eight,' came the outraged reply.

Azmelqart was muttering under his breath about walking away. Tullus was having none of it. Taking the Phoenician's shoulder in a grip of iron, he twisted so that Azmelqart had to face the amber-seller. 'Apologise, and give him a dozen denarii,' said Tullus.

'He said eight!' Azmelqart's voice was an outraged cry.

'I know, and you'll give him a dozen so that he doesn't tell everyone not to trust you.' Tullus tightened his hold, and Azmelqart squawked.

'All right, all right.' With bad grace, he handed over eight denarii, and then with a pathetic attempt to seem apologetic, another four.

There was no thanks from the amber-seller, and the sweetener made no difference. Tullus and his companions were still within earshot when he began telling the men to either side what had happened.

Azmelqart seemed oblivious. 'How dare you?' he hissed. 'Eight would have sufficed.'

'If you're going to use debased or forged coins, have the wit only to use a couple. A fifth of the sum you owed?' Tullus snorted. 'A man would have to be blind not to notice that many.'

'I've got away with it before,' said Azmelqart. 'They're good copies.'

Tullus wanted to wring the Phoenician by his neck. Through gritted teeth, he said, 'My advice is to avoid that trick for the rest of our time here.'

Azmelqart appeared unconvinced, but the wary attitude of the next two amber-sellers – word had spread faster than they had walked, Tullus warned – made him change his mind. The Phoenician tried no more trickery in the hours that followed, and in the end pronounced himself ready to return to the ship.

Bored to tears, angered by Azmelqart's dishonesty, Tullus was only too glad to obey. Fenestela or Vinicius could take his place on the next outing, he decided, and fuck what Azmelqart wanted.

A voice shouted something in German, and was answered by another. Tullus' ears pricked. The only German he'd heard here was the locals' mispronounced mangling. They came alongside a stall selling mead, and his gaze roved over the gathered men before it. Astonishment rocked Tullus; there, plain as day, was a Cherusci warrior he recognised. Older, black hair and beard streaked with grey, but there was no mistaking him as one of Arminius' chosen men. He and Tullus had briefly come up against each other in the forest the day the Eighteenth's eagle had been recovered.

The Cherusci had at least half a dozen companions; this was trouble they did not need, thought Tullus. He twisted his head, looking away, and gave Azmelqart a hefty nudge. 'Get a move on,' said Tullus. 'Don't ask why.'

Azmelqart gave him a venomous glance, but obeyed.

As soon as they were a safe distance away, Tullus explained the situation. 'We shall have to keep a low profile from this point on,' he said. Cato scowled, and said it would be better to go and bloody their blades, while Azmelqart threatened and blustered that it was unacceptable to have to curtail his business opportunities because of a few savages. He made such a fuss that in the end Tullus, sighing, told him that he would find out how many Cherusci there were. If there weren't many, as Azmelqart seemed to think, they would have nothing to worry about. Tullus didn't vocalise his concern that the warriors might be part of a larger group.

If that turned out to be the case, they were in grave danger.

PART V

An uneasy afternoon dragged by. As the daylight leached from the sky, a thick fog rolled in, shrouding the ship, the jetty and everything beyond. Despite the cover this offered, Tullus was on edge; a few coins in the hand of the mead-seller had revealed that the Cherusci were here in strength. Upwards of four score warriors were camped on the western edge of the town, here to sell furs and buy amber. In such a small place, it wouldn't be long before the Cherusci heard of the Romans' presence. The safest thing to do was leave. Tullus hadn't yet gone to Azmelqart because the merchant was still in a foul humour about the counterfeit coins. He didn't panic. Reason dictated nothing would happen overnight.

A discontented air hung over the ship. Vinicius had turned an ankle on the slippery jetty, and was hobbling about, cursing anything and everything. Fenestela reported that the only meat to be had was gristly or on the turn; this was borne out by the uniformly unhappy reaction to the stew produced for the evening meal. After consulting with Fenestela and Vinicius, he had ordered the veterans to remain on the ship that evening. There had been far less opposition than he'd expected; told of the Cherusci presence, with Lucius and Smiler nodding agreement, they had cursed and spat, but agreed his was the sensible option. Insisting that the German crewmen do the same had been a harder battle. Tullus had only got his way by promising that barrels of beer could be brought on board that night.

If he could have had his way, they would have departed the moment the fog lifted, but on this Azmelqart had refused to budge. He was here to trade, he ranted, and trade he would. Even if Tullus could have persuaded the captain to take the ship to sea, Azmelqart held the purse strings. No one would be paid until they reached Vetera, at the time of his choosing, and so they stayed.

433

Powerless, Tullus reduced the risks the next day by staying on the boat himself (for fear of recognition) and directing the veterans who went with the Phoenician not to wear their mail shirts. It was a risky move – injury or death to those men was far more likely in the event of a fight – but the only one he could think of. Other than wearing a centurion's transverse-crested helmet, there were few better ways to announce oneself as Roman.

His hopes that Azmelqart would have bought enough amber by that evening were dashed by the Phoenician's announcement that he'd heard of a ship loaded with furs that was expected in port. 'One or two days longer, that's all,' said Azmelqart airily. Tullus' protests that the Phoenician had already bought goodly quantities of furs were in vain.

Another evening arrived, and in the face of mounting resentment from the German crew, Tullus had had to agree to their going ashore. Soon more than half had vanished, doing what sailors in ports do. Again, Tullus prevented the veterans from leaving the ship. Setting double sentries, he made sure that either he, Fenestela or Vinicius was also on duty throughout.

Dawn arrived on the third day. Nothing untoward had happened overnight, but Tullus wasn't happy. Irritable, itchy-eyed from lack of sleep, and hungry for fresh bread, he decided to stretch his legs. There was a bakery close to the end of the jetty; if the wind blew from the south, a man could smell it. Belly rumbling, pleased to be off the confined space that was the ship, Tullus' guard slipped. He fell to thinking about the amber-trapped bee – bought at his request by the ship's captain – and how delighted Artio would be with it. Sirona would be pleased with his decision not to voyage away from home again. It wasn't the danger, thought Tullus, but having to receive orders from a prick like Azmelqart that was so hard to take.

Pondering his latest idea – setting up a business to provide the security for merchants' warehouses in Vetera – and deciding that it had distinct possibilities, he wasn't paying attention to his surroundings. Coming off the end of the jetty, he was at the baker's within fifty strides. To his horror, there, right in front of him, was the Cherusci warrior he'd seen on the first day. This was no accidental meeting, for beside him was the amber-seller whom Azmelqart had tried to cheat. The three stared at each other. Recognition dawned in the warrior's eyes, and Tullus swore.

He and the warrior reached for their daggers at the same time. His job done, the amber-seller retreated. Any hope Tullus had for a quick fight vanished as the warrior was joined by three companions, all of whom had spears. He took to his heels. Shouts rang out behind him. The timbers of the jetty creaked and pounded beneath his passage. A startled gull took off from under his feet; a snaggle-toothed fisherman looked up in surprise from his boat. Tullus shot a glance over his shoulder; his guts squeezed. The warrior was close behind, no more than a dozen paces. His comrades were right behind. Younger, fitter, they would catch up with him long before the ship. One, overtaking the rest, looked to do it within the next few heartbeats.

It was ironic, thought Tullus, that he should have survived so many horrific battles and ambushes only to lose his life on a fish-scale-spattered, rickety jetty in the middle of nowhere. He would take at least one warrior with him, he decided, screeching to a halt. There was fight in this old dog yet.

He dropped to a knee, dodging the spear thrust that would have taken him in the chest, and skewered the leading warrior – who, horrified, was unable to stop him – in the belly. Coming up off his other leg, blade still in place, Tullus drove his screaming victim backwards. A temporary shield against his companions' weapons, and already a deadweight, it took little for Tullus to heave him off the dagger. The dying warrior collided with the bearded man, and they fell in a tangle of arms and legs. In the heartbeat's pause that followed, Tullus managed to sweep up his victim's spear and threaten the two remaining warriors. Both armed as he, they at once moved to the edges of the jetty in a flanking attempt. Tullus stayed close to the men who were down, a quick stab into the bearded one's throat ensuring that he had nothing to fear from the ground. The bodies, one still living, then formed an obstacle that the other warriors had to cross to reach him.

'Come on, you goat-fuckers,' Tullus taunted in German, loving the red battle mist that had cloaked him for the first time in years. 'Scared of dying?'

One warrior hawked and spat, and said something under his breath to the other. A brief conversation followed, and then, facing Tullus, they walked backwards along the jetty.

Tullus' pleasure at their retreat was brief. Cold reality sank in before the pair had even been lost to sight. They would be back soon. Very soon – and in force. Dispassionately, he finished off the first man, and keeping an eye behind him, made his way to the ship. He'd not gone far before Fenestela came loping towards him, with four men close behind. They had their shields – ready for real trouble, thought Tullus proudly.

'Problem?' Fenestela peered over Tullus' shoulder.

'Aye. We need to leave. Now.' Tullus explained, and Fenestela's brow furrowed.

'Azmelqart won't be happy.'

'He's partly to blame,' said Tullus. 'Leave him to me.'

'Let's slit his throat and toss him overboard, sir,' suggested one of the veterans. 'His amber should be enough—'

'No,' said Tullus sharply. 'He's a whoreson, but he doesn't deserve murdering. You three. Go to the end of the jetty and keep watch. You, stand on the halfway point. If they shout to tell you there's trouble, come running to the ship.' He glanced at Fenestela. 'Where are Cato, Bear and the others?'

'I was coming to that.' Fenestela's expression was grim. 'Lucius, Smiler and Magnus are on the boat, but . . .'

Tullus rapped the spear butt off the planking with rage. 'Cato, Bear and Eurysaces slipped off the ship last night.'

'Aye. Someone must have noticed, but no one will say anything.'

'Men don't rat on their comrades.' It had always been the same, thought Tullus, his mind racing.

'We don't have long, do we?'

'As long as it takes to get to their camp, rouse every warrior and return here.' Tullus met Fenestela's gaze, was relieved to see the same grim resolve he felt. 'We can't leave them.'

'No.'

Back at the ship, neither was surprised by Azmelqart's reaction. 'We must set to sea at once,' he cried, looking to the captain for support.

The situation would unravel fast. The captain and his crew didn't care if a few veterans were left behind. Tullus swept out his sword and placed the tip at the captain's throat. 'The ship stays on the dock until I say so.'

Eyes flickering from the enraged but powerless Azmelqart to Tullus, the captain muttered, 'As you say.'

Frustration clawed at Tullus. The captain could not be left alone, and his crewmen looked almost as unhappy as he. He would have to divide his remaining forces – ten men, including himself – in three. 'Vinicius.'

'Aye, sir.' Vinicius came close.

'Can you hold the ship? I'm taking two men, and I want four on the end of the jetty.'

'In that case, I only need two, sir.' Vinicius' smile was all teeth.

'I don't need to explain how important—'

'The ship will be here until you get back, sir.' Vinicius saluted as if he were on parade.

Heartened, Tullus laid out the situation to Lucius, Smiler, Magnus and the men who'd been on sentry duty. Shamefaced, they revealed that Cato and the two others had been intent on visiting the settlement's largest inn. 'The beer is good, apparently, sir,' said Magnus by way of a lame excuse.

'Smiler, Magnus.' Tullus beckoned. 'Almost a hundred Cherusci warriors will shortly arrive, and your idiot friends are out there somewhere, sleeping off a bender. We are going to fetch them. I don't know if we'll find them in time, nor if we will get back here before the cursed Cherusci. Even if we do, there's no certainty of fighting free, and getting to sea. You with me?'

Fierce mutters. 'Aye, sir!'

'I want to come too, sir,' protested Lucius.

'You're needed here,' said Tullus. 'Stay with Fenestela.'

Lucius didn't look happy, but he nodded.

Stripping the cover from his shield, donning his helmet – a plain legionary's one – Tullus led the way onto the dock. Fenestela, Lucius and two others came as far as the jetty's end. 'I'll hold the position, sir,' said Fenestela, calm as if he'd announced that it was about to rain. 'You find Cato, Bear and Eurysaces.'

Gods, thought Tullus as he began to run. What had he been thinking to come on this voyage?

Despite his fears, a tiny part of him was exultant. He hadn't felt so alive in years.

Thanks to the early hour, they made good progress through the settlement. Shops were beginning to open, but there were few people about. Their passage didn't go unnoticed, however: three heavily armed men carrying shields and naked swords meant trouble. A woman dropped the chamber pot she'd been emptying, and fled back inside her house. Shopkeepers closed the shutters they'd just opened. Two builders erecting scaffolding on the side of a house retreated down an alley. A small boy followed them for a short distance, his eyes the size of plates.

'That's the place, sir,' said Magnus from behind Tullus. 'The building with the barrels outside.'

Tullus had seen the inn before, but never been inside. Reaching the door, which was shut, he rapped on it with his sword hilt. 'Open up!' he roared in German, hoping whoever was inside understood. 'Cato! Bear! Eurysaces!' he added in Latin. 'Wake up, you useless maggots!'

After a short time, footsteps echoed within. Tullus renewed his hammering, demanding in German and Latin to be let in. A quavering voice asked a question – Tullus didn't understand – and then repeated itself.

Tullus banged so hard that the door rattled on its hinges, and shouted in German, 'Open this fucking door or I'll smash it in!'

His intent came across; a bolt rasped back, then another. The door opened, revealing a fearful-looking man in late middle age, wearing a stained tunic and trousers. He quailed at the sight of Tullus, who shoved past without a word. His men followed.

The tavern's interior was gloomy, lit only by a few oil lamps and the glow from a fire in the centre of the room. Straw covered the floor; rough tables and benches filled most of the open space. Sleeping figures lay sprawled everywhere. Directing his men to start on the left, Tullus began his search on the right. To his immense relief, he soon found Cato and Bear. They were sleeping like babes beside one another, empty jugs all around. Eurysaces lay close by, his arm around a woman. Tullus picked up a half-full jug and carefully poured its contents first on Cato, then Bear and last of all, Eurysaces. They woke, spluttering and cursing, and he told them in his loudest parade voice that they were worthless pieces of shit who didn't deserve to have been in the legions. 'Up!' he roared. 'Up!'

Their resentment died away as he explained the danger they were in.

'Weapons?' he demanded, eyes sweeping up and down each man.

'Daggers only, sir,' said Eurysaces, looking ashamed.

'The same for me and Cato, sir,' said Bear.

Tullus unslung the extra baldric and scabbard he'd grabbed before leaving the ship. Smiler and Magnus did the same. 'You're in luck, you stupid bastards,' said Tullus as the grinning miscreants took the swords. 'Now, follow me.'

'Have we time for a drink, sir?' asked Eurysaces. 'Hair of the dog and all that.'

Denied the revelry that the three others had had, Smiler's and Magnus' eyes lit up.

'Not a fucking chance,' said Tullus, glowering.

Eurysaces shrugged. 'It's always worth asking, sir.'

In the past, Tullus would have marked Eurysaces down for a punishment detail later; now he just rolled his eyes. Striding past the still shocked-looking innkeeper, he paused at the door. Carefully, he glanced onto the street. Not a sign of the Cherusci. Fortuna, be good to me, Tullus asked. Let me get to the jetty first, and I'll make it worth your while.

Somewhere above, the goddess laughed.

They had gone perhaps a hundred paces before a band of Cherusci headed by the bearded warrior appeared further down the main street. Whether they'd been told about Cato and the others sleeping in the tavern, Tullus never found out. The ten Cherusci spread out, blocking their path.

Tullus slowed his pace. Forming his five men into a diamond with the shieldless men in the middle, he walked towards the warriors, who were about to lob their first spears. Let them throw early, thought Tullus, and miss. A barked order from the bearded warrior thwarted his hope. The warriors didn't loose until Tullus and his men were within fifty paces. Eurysaces was the only one hit, a leg wound that bled profusely but which he swore would not stop him from running when the time came. Tullus took him at his word – he was busy wrenching at the spear which had stuck in his shield – and told his men that they were to punch through and keep moving, no matter what.

Luckily, German spears didn't have barbed heads like Roman javelins. Tullus tugged out the weapon and handed it back to Cato, who hurled it at the warriors. He hit one in the arm. A lucky shot, Bear told him. The pair started arguing even as Tullus advanced again. 'Give me a spear, and I'll show you how to throw,' said Bear as Cato laughed.

'Shut your mouths! Stay close,' ordered Tullus, glad to have Smiler on one side and Magnus on the other, but acutely aware that they were six men, not a century, and that half had no shields. 'Swords ready, shields high.'

The bearded warrior was no fool. Just before Tullus reached him, he shouted. The Cherusci split apart, leaving a clear passage through their midst. Arms cocked back, ready to stab with their spears, they would attack the sides of Tullus' little group.

Stop, and he risked being surrounded, thought Tullus. Split his formation, and he would expose the shieldless men. Retreat, and the Cherusci would be on them like a pack of wolves. Press on, and the same would happen. He had one choice only.

'On my word, change direction,' he said, praying the warriors spoke no Latin. His gaze raked from right to left. An alley to the left seemed to beckon. Punch that way, and they could take refuge in the alley, which led he had no idea where.

Ten paces separated them from the Cherusci. A spear thrown by an overeager warrior shot past, a handspan over Tullus' head and the men behind. Eight paces. Six.

'To the left,' Tullus bellowed, turning fifteen degrees and charging. He slammed his shield boss into the nearest warrior's face. A dull crunch, a scream, which became a mewl as Tullus' sword followed, sliding into the warrior's guts. Impacts to either side told him Smiler and Magnus were with him; shouts and cries proof that men were being hurt. He hoped they were Cherusci. Tullus stepped over the smashed-nosed warrior and battered his shield at the next man, who stabbed back with his spear even as he retreated. They traded shadow blows, *one-two*, *one-two*, Tullus unable to reach the warrior, the warrior unable to get past his shield.

'Into the alley,' he cried, hoping no one had fallen. He thrust again at the warrior, who danced out of range, and pushed to stand beside the alley's entrance, with his back to the wall of the building on one corner. 'In,' he ordered Smiler, who was with him. 'Magnus, where are you?'

There was no answer, but Cato and Bear were there next. Urged by Tullus, they entered the alley. Tullus and Cato followed, turning to face the street. There were seven warriors left standing; one was badly wounded. Bodies lay behind them; at least one was in a mail shirt.

'Magnus?' asked Tullus again.

'He fell, sir. I don't think he even saw the warrior who did for him,' said Cato. 'I managed to pick up his shield.'

An uncomfortable silence.

'And Eurysaces?' asked Tullus.

'He was lagging a little, sir,' said Smiler. 'I think he took a spear in the back.'

This was not supposed to happen, thought Tullus, holding in his rage and anguish. Eurysaces' leg wound had been worse than he'd said, but the poor bastard hadn't wanted to admit it. And Magnus, well, it had been his time.

There was no opportunity to grieve the fallen men further. Four warriors advanced on the alley; the injured man sank down, moaning; the other two loped off down the street.

Curse you, Fortuna, thought Tullus. They're gone for reinforcements, or to flank us. 'Back,' he said. 'Whoever's behind me, face about so you can see where we're going. Move!'

The alley was no different to any in a Roman town. Broken pottery crunched underfoot; there were liquid patches too, which stank of human ordure. Tullus didn't care; shit-covered boots were the least of his worries.

'Does anyone know where this leads?' he asked.

A grim chorus of 'No, sir.'

Perhaps a hundred paces in, with the warriors still following, they came to a crossroads, where another alley crossed theirs at an oblique angle. Tullus trusted to his sense of direction, and directed Smiler and Bear to turn right.

His choice proved correct; the alley emerged onto the street that led straight to the dock area. There was no sign of the warriors who'd run; Tullus concluded that they had gone to find the main party of their brethren. Judging by the sounds of fighting, *they* had already arrived at the jetty.

If there was to be any chance of breaking through the Cherusci, he and his men needed the element of surprise – an impossibility given the warriors dogging their footsteps. Quickly, Tullus explained his thinking. 'We've got to lay those four in the mud, and fast.'

'How, sir?' asked Smiler.

Tullus didn't know. He felt old and tired.

'Let them close with us, sir, and then just charge them,' said Bear. 'Cato and I can do it.' He grinned as Cato muttered his approval, and continued, 'Drive into them at full pelt, do the old *one-two*. That will kill two, I'm sure of it, and gods willing, we'll get the other two before they can run.'

'Aye,' said Tullus. 'Simple plans are often the best. Cato and I will do it, though.'

Bear looked disappointed, but he saw Tullus' determination, and nodded. 'Aye, sir.'

'You follow close behind, Bear. Smiler, keep a watch on the end of the alley.'

Tullus' heart hammered as the warriors drew near. There was a good chance he'd die in the clash – this close, the German spears were lethal. Rather than fear, he felt an odd acceptance. This type of situation held no surprises, and he was with good men. Men who would die for him, as he would for them.

'Ready, brothers?' he called, and charged.

The fight was short, sharp and brutal. Tullus and Cato hit the front warriors blind, ducking their heads below their shield rims as they struck. Two, three steps they drove the warriors back. Without raising his head to look, Tullus thrust with his sword. The blade scraped off wood, and ran into something much softer. A man screamed; then there was an odd choking noise from behind him. Tugging free his sword, he risked a glance over the top of his shield. Both his opponent and Cato's were injured, and staggering backwards. The men behind were ready to fight still; the spear tip of one was bloody.

'Forward!' cried Tullus, bringing the bottom rim of his shield down. *Crack* went the iron on his wounded opponent's helmetless head. Vacant-eyed, he slumped against the building to Tullus' left. Cato finished his warrior, and together they tramped over the bodies, keeping their shields up against the probing spears of the two remaining Cherusci.

'They're about to turn and run, sir,' muttered Cato.

Tullus peered, saw that the big veteran was right. The warriors were decades younger than both of he and Cato; with a head start, there would be no catching them once they ran. 'We'd best charge then, eh?'

A few moments later, it was all over. One of the pair had slipped as he turned, and stumbled into his comrade. Tullus and Cato made short work of them. They exchanged a satisfied glance, then turned round. Bear wasn't with them.

Tullus cursed.

'Hades,' said Cato.

It was Bear whose blood had been on the warrior's spear. He lay on his back, very still. Bloody fluid leaked from the ruin of his left eye.

'Cherusci cunts,' said Cato, his voice throbbing with anger.

Tullus felt the same way, but he stayed focused. A cool head was needed, or they would all end up the same way. He led the way onto the street.

Staying close to the buildings on one side, they crept towards the jetties, which lay around a slight bend in the shoreline. Not a local was to be seen, but scared faces looked out from windows and part-open doors as they passed.

Tullus' hunch was that the two warriors who'd run from the clash outside the inn had been correct. As they neared the last building that shielded them from the jetties, amid the shouts and clash of weapons, he heard pounding feet. A glance, and he was bundling his three men into the closest house. Smiler shut the door gently, and placed an eye against a crack in the timbers. With fierce gestures and a finger on his lips, Tullus indicated to the terrified boy and his mother – the only people within – that they should remain silent.

'How many?' he whispered to Smiler.

'Ten, twelve. Fifteen, sir.'

Thank you, great Mars, thought Tullus. 'We'll wait a little longer, until they're well gone, and then we move.'

The wait dragged, but it must have seemed like an eternity to the unfortunate woman and child, who no doubt assumed they were about to be murdered. When Tullus judged it was time, he left a handful of silver on the table as thanks.

A mass of Cherusci – about fifty, if the numbers he'd been told were correct – swarmed about at the end of one jetty. They hadn't fought their way onto it yet, thought Tullus, fiercely proud of Fenestela, but their overwhelming numbers would be telling with every moment that passed.

Half a hundred paces remained between their position and the jetty – a long way to make it without being seen or heard. Tullus cast about in vain for an alley that might take them behind the nearest buildings and bring them out closer. 'Nothing for it but to walk, brothers. Quiet as mice, eh?'

Faces set with determination, Cato and Smiler muttered, 'Aye, sir.'

'Stay close. We'll hit them at the waterline.'

Placing his hobs with care, grateful for the lack of paving, Tullus took the first step into the open. The Cherusci at the rear were roaring encouragement at their comrades who were fighting Fenestela's men. Five paces Tullus went, then ten and fifteen. Still every warrior had his back to him.

Twenty-five paces, Tullus counted. Halfway there. His mouth was dry, but he could feel sweat trickling down his back. Thirty. Thirty-five paces.

A warrior turned. Saw. Roared the alarm.

Breaking into a run, Tullus aimed for the water's edge. The men there had heard their comrade's shout, but were still unprepared for him to arrive like a battering ram. Knocked backwards by Tullus' shield, the first went down on his arse into the shallows. The next took Tullus' blade in the mouth. The third managed a spear thrust, which missed, and then retreated before Tullus' savage *one-two* combinations with his sword and shield.

Behind him, Cato and Smiler were roaring, 'ROMA! ROMA!'

Confused, not entirely sure what was going on, the nearest warriors edged away from the water. Tullus drove on, into open space. He wasn't alone, but he didn't know if it was one man or two. There was the jetty, side on to him. Fenestela and several others were fighting for their lives. Tullus didn't hesitate. 'With me!' he roared, and made for the end of the jetty.

Something made Fenestela turn and see them. He timed his attack to perfection, driving at the warriors facing him just as Tullus struck from the side. Four Cherusci went down; several others were wounded, and then the entire mass of warriors was pulling back.

Tullus and Fenestela stared at each other, both blood-spattered, sweating, grinning like fools.

'I thought you were never coming,' said Fenestela.

'It felt like we'd never make it at times.' Tullus twisted, saw only Cato. His heart sank. 'Where's Smiler?'

'Back there somewhere, sir,' said Cato grimly.

Fortuna, you old bitch, thought Tullus. Will you leave me none of my men?

Fenestela had it almost as bad, having lost two of his three men. Tragically, one was Lucius. He'd slain a number of Cherusci before

444

being isolated from the rest and cut down. Ten German crewmen had joined Fenestela, which was how, as he explained to Tullus, he was still alive. Of those crewmen, five had already fallen, but with Tullus back again, the entire group withdrew down the jetty, keeping the warriors at bay with a shield wall.

The captain saw them coming; by the time they arrived, every rope had been untied, leaving the ship resting against the jetty. The moment Tullus was aware of this, he, Cato and Fenestela held off the Cherusci while the rest jumped aboard. Seeing this, the warriors redoubled their attack, spears stabbing back and forth in concert. Shit, thought Tullus. Whoever went last risked being butchered.

'You next,' he ordered Cato.

'No, sir. You go.'

'Do as you're told, curse you.' Busy shielding himself from a determined attack by a warrior with long braids, Tullus could not even look at the big man.

'We're not in the legion now, sir. Jump!' Cato shoved forward with his shield, and quick as lightning, thrust his sword deep into a warrior. Almost at once, another man replaced him.

Tullus stabbed the warrior with braids, and tried another tack. 'Fenestela, get on the ship.'

'Only when you go, sir.' Fenestela ducked; a spear shot over the top of his shield, taking one of his feathers with it.

'You're a pair of stubborn bastards!' cried Tullus, but the fighting was so desperate that he could do nothing more.

A huge warrior elbowed his way forward. Clad in a mail shirt, he was even bigger than Cato. Encouraged, his comrades advanced a step.

'We're all going to die if you don't go, sir.' Cato's voice was calm.

'He's right, sir,' said Fenestela.

Tullus didn't want to admit it, but he couldn't fight for much longer. Age had caught up with him. He couldn't force Cato to jump into the boat either. He swore savagely, and muttered, 'You're a brave man, Cato.'

Cato didn't answer. Instead he threw himself at the big warrior with an angry bellow.

Tullus half turned and jumped; Fenestela thumped down beside him a heartbeat later. Tullus looked up, a cry to Cato forming on his lips, but the big man was almost surrounded. A warrior went down under his blade, and he shouted in triumph, but another enemy filled the gap, and the hungry spears came stabbing in from every side.

Tullus was about to throw himself back up on the jetty, but Fenestela seized his arm. 'You'll fall in the fucking sea!'

Tullus' eyes came into focus. Pushed out by the crewmen's poles, the ship was already a man's height out from the jetty, with the distance increasing every heartbeat.

'We left him to die,' said Tullus, shame lashing him.

'No. He chose his death,' Fenestela replied. 'A glorious one too.'

Tullus looked back at the jetty. Cato had killed another warrior, and was still fending off the big man and the others. With blood pouring from every part of him not covered by helmet or mail, he was spitting curses and laughing as he fought. A spear went into the back of one thigh, and he staggered, managing to gut-wound another warrior before he went down on one knee.

Tullus couldn't bear it, but to honour Cato's sacrifice, he had to watch. He fixed his gaze on the fight as the crewmen heaved on their oars, taking the ship into safer, deeper water. Two more warriors died beneath Cato's blade. At last the Cherusci giant landed a blow. His spear drove into Cato's neck, a mortal wound if Tullus had ever seen one. Cato dropped his shield and sword, but even now he was not done. With the last of his strength, he lashed out, wrapping an arm around the huge warrior's lower legs. Unbalanced, the warrior toppled like a falling tree, and Cato took him off the jetty. A mighty splash. Water fountained into the air as the pair, entwined unto death, hit the sea together.

No one came to the surface.

Tullus leaned against the mast, utterly drained. Once, *he* would have been able to stand where Cato had, that his men might escape. He might even had made it onto the ship. Not now. 'He was right to disobey me.'

'Aye. I couldn't have done what he did either. He saved us.' Fenestela's voice was full of respect.

'He would have fitted right into the century.' This was the ultimate accolade for Tullus, to set a man alongside the men who'd served under him in the Eighteenth, and since, in the Fifth.

'So would all of them,' said Fenestela.

Tullus had a lump in his throat. 'Aye,' he said. 'Aye.'

EPILOGUE

Near Vetera

Catching sight of the dock that lay close to the bridge over the Rhenus, Tullus felt a wave of relief. Not as great as the time he'd come marching back from the wreck of Aliso, and the massacre in the forest, but sizeable all the same. The return voyage had not been easy. There had been one bad storm, and a near escape from marauding warriors on Fabaria Island. But they were almost home, he thought with a fierce joy. 'Glad to be back?' he asked Fenestela.

'Aye. My dogs will have forgotten me.' Fenestela had left them in the care of his slave, an old Gaul almost as taciturn as himself.

'Dogs? You need a wife,' said Tullus, relishing the thought of seeing Sirona again. Artio would have forgiven him by now, he hoped. If not, the piece of amber with the trapped bee would soon sweeten her.

A snort. 'Who'd put up with me? It's easier on my own. The dogs don't criticise me for drinking before midday. They don't complain at my farts either.'

'What about your slave?'

'His farts are as bad as mine.'

They both laughed.

Vinicius, who'd been talking with Azmelqart, joined them.

'He still unhappy?' asked Tullus. At his insistence, the Phoenician had paid everyone several days previously. 'Why?' Tullus had replied to Azmelqart's whine of protest. 'Because I don't fucking trust you, that's why.' He had next demanded and received the coin that would have been paid to every veteran who'd died. 'It's bad enough that they died, but every one of them has a wife back in Vetera. A family,' Tullus had grated, nose-to-nose with the Phoenician. Eyes simmering with hate, Azmelqart had subsided. The two hadn't spoken since.

'Oh aye, sir. He's still bitching about you.'

Tullus spat on the deck.

'The whoreson's lucky we didn't heave him over the side,' said Fenestela.

'That would have given me a great deal of pleasure,' said Tullus, 'but if we were to murder everyone who was stupid or dishonest, there'd be precious few people left.' As Fenestela and Vinicius chuckled, he went on, 'Azmelqart wasn't to know the man he tried to dupe would fall into conversation with the Cherusci, and then lead them to our ship. That was Fortuna, playing one of her little games.'

For all the goddess' capriciousness, Tullus still planned to offer her a couple of fine sheep in gratitude for his having survived. He would also ensure that every one of his men had a fitting funeral. Cato's would be the grandest. Sadly, there were no bodies, but it was still important to remember. Having talked it through with Fenestela, Tullus had decided to have the six veterans' tombstones erected beside that of Piso, one of his men from the Eighteenth. They would rub along well, he thought with wry amusement, and Piso could teach them to play dice.

'Someone's waiting for you.' Fenestela was pointing. The dock was no more than two hundred paces away.

Tullus stared.

Amid the fishermen and sailors, he picked out a familiar figure, and beside it, a dog.

'As I live and breathe.' There was moisture in the corners of Tullus' eyes.

'That's Artio and Scylax, or I'm no judge,' said Fenestela, grinning despite himself.

'Aye,' said Tullus, his voice hoarse with emotion. 'It is.'

AUTHOR'S NOTE

In case you were wondering, Denmark was the peninsula Tullus sailed around, and the amber trading settlement was in Poland. Why Poland? You may have heard of the Roman military fittings that have been found there in the last couple of years. Excited by the news in 2018, I posted about it on Facebook, neglecting to mention that I *knew* that the legions had never invaded that part of Europe. 'Experts' were quick to weigh in, pointing out in no uncertain terms that Rome had not conquered Poland. I know that, thanks! It's entirely possible, however, that some veterans might have worked as 'security' for an amber-buying merchant. Domitian is recorded as having sent a unit of cavalry east for this purpose. If these ex-legionaries were killed while in the east, their kit could have ended up being used or sold on by locals. Prove me wrong! (I'm very grateful to Dr Bartosz Kontny for his help with details of the Roman finds in Poland.)

Six of you lovely readers feature in this story. It's been great fun talking to you by email, working out names and so on. I really hope you like my portrayals – apologies that you died! I've got to do that, in case I write more stories about Tullus in the future.

Importantly, Tullus thought well of each and every one of you; being buried close to Piso is a mark of the highest respect. Watch your purses, mind! Clive May, to whom this story is dedicated, stars as Cato. Thank you, Clive, for your sterling support of this story. Beers next time I'm in Chester! Thank you hugely for your support as well, Andrew Cartlidge (Smiler), Sean Sickler (Bear), Mike Maloney (Eurysaces), Rick van Strien (Lucius) and Randy Higgins (Magnus) – one day I hope to raise a glass with all of you. Thanks also to Stephen McIntyre, and his son Ruaridh, both keen readers of my books, and the legion of wonderful readers who backed the Kickstarter campaign that helped see this story come to light.

In alphabetical order, you are: David Albanis, Collette Allen, Neal Aplin, Steve Anstey, Tony Baker, Sergio Bannino, James Barham, Gary Bentley, Bill Bright, Martyn Blake, Steve Blake, James Brittain, Dominic Bronk, Robin Brown, Davy Buchan, Andy Canty, Josh Catlin, Vincent Cenni, Luke Challen, Ksenia Chabarova, Carl Chapman, Phill Clegg, Darren Collins, Paul Conlon, Frances Cripps, Bill Cushley, Tom D'Arcy, Wim DC, Mark Downing, Ollie Drake, Richard Emery, Tommy Evans, R.B. J. Farries, Lothar Fischer, Garry Fitzgerald, Malcolm Frener, Martin Gander, Steve Glüning, Christopher Godfrey, Adam Gontar, Daniel Grave, Karen Griffiths, Gary Guilford, Nick Harpin, Stephen Harman, James Harrison, Krystal Holmgren, Iain (from Scotland), Taff James, Jan Jetmar, Lesley Jolley, Daniel Kelly, Steven John Kelly, Darryl and Vicky Kidney, Patrick Krippendorf, Alan Laws, Pat Leighton, Nick Lewin, Ellis Lewis, Mark Lewis, Daniel Loose, Jonathan Lowe, Isabelle Magin, Alejandro Hinojosa Martinez, Wullie McMartin, Jay Mead, B. Yurko Mikels, Devon James Mitchell, Cliff Moon, Derek Moss, Kevin Murphy, Jarno Mustakallio, Eliot Nichols, Will Norman, Marie A. Parsons, Barry Patton, Donald Peterssen, Ben Pickersgill, Micheal John Polanski, David Priest, Brent Quigley, Jonathan Redman, Charlene Robertson, Phil Robinson, Edna Russell, Cris Samways, Mark Schuurman, John Sibley, Joseph Silvoso, Dave Sinclair, Graham Sizmur, Kirk Smith, Maureen Smith, Vic Smith, Bryan Spencer, Lennard Steur, Alan Swankie, Joseph Tartaglia, Alex Thornhill, Mary Travis, Christopher Turner, Adrian Tyte, Maurits van der Vegt, Daniel Vaupel, Sara Waddington, Mark Ward, Jay Warden, Chris Watkins, Samantha Wilkinson, Anne Willis, Milca and Andy Wilson, Jason, and Guest 1686203822 (from Glasgow), Guest 2002,691563, Guest 71686538, Guest 771949, Guest 1800405777, Guest 1171483479 and Guest 1573386522 – could not get any more info/got no responses to my messages from Kickstarter.

CREDITS

Orion Fiction would like to thank everyone at Orion who worked on the publication of *Sands of the Arena and Other Stories* in the UK. And so would Ben!

Editorial
Francesca Pathak
Lucy Frederick

Copy editor
Steve O'Gorman

Proof reader
Becca Allen

Contracts
Anne Goddard
Jake Alderson

Design
Rabab Adams
Tomas Almeida
Joanna Ridley
Nick May

Editorial Management
Charlie Panayiotou
Jane Hughes
Alice Davis

Production
Ruth Sharvell

Rights
Susan Howe
Krystyna Kujawinska
Jessica Purdue
Louise Henderson

Finance
Jasdip Nandra
Afeera Ahmed
Elizabeth Beaumont
Sue Baker

Audio
Paul Stark
Amber Bates

Publicity
Virginia Woolstencroft

Marketing
Cait Davies
Lucy Cameron

Sales
Jen Wilson
Esther Waters
Victoria Laws
Rachael Hum
Ellie Kyrke-Smith
Frances Doyle
Georgina Cutler

Operations
Jo Jacobs
Sharon Willis
Lisa Pryde
Lucy Brem

THE
CLASH OF EMPIRES
SERIES

A thrilling series about the Roman invasion of Greece.

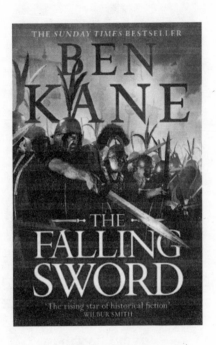

Can Greece resist the might of Rome?
The final showdown between two great civilisations begins . . .

'A triumph!'
Harry Sidebottom

'Fans of battle-heavy historical fiction will, justly, adore Clash of Empires'
The Times

THE
LIONHEART
SERIES

A rip-roaring epic series about of one of history's greatest warriors . . .

REBEL. LEADER.
BROTHER. KING.

KING. POLITICIAN.
WARRIOR. CONQUEROR.

And coming 2022, the third and final instalment:

KING

'A rip-roaring epic, filled with arrows and spattered with blood.
Gird yourself with mail when you start'
Paul Finch